KING ARTHUR
AND HIS KNIGHTS

Here begynneth the fyrst boke of the noble kyng . Kyng Arthur . somtyme kynge of Englonde and of his noble actes and feates of armes of chyualrye & his noble knyghtes & table rounde. and is deuyded in to .xxi. bookes.

¶ How Vtherpendragon sent for the duke of Cornewayll and Igrayne his wyf / and of theyr departynge sodaynly agayne. Capl'm primu.

IT befell in the dayes of Vtherpendragon / whan he was kyng of all Englonde / and so regned that there was a myghty duke in Cornewayll that helde warre ayenst hym longe tyme . And the duke was called the duke of Tyntagyll / & so by meanes kynge Vther sende for this duke / chargynge hym to brynge his wyfe with hym / for she was called a fayre lady / & a passynge wyse / and hyr name was called Igrayne . So whan the duke & his wyf were comen vnto the kyng by meanes of grete lordes they were accorded both / the kyng lyked & loued this lady well / & he made them grete chere out of mesure / & desyred to; aue lyen

a i

The first page of Wynkyn de Worde's First Edition (1498) of *Morte d'Arthur* from the unique copy in *The John Rylands University Library of Manchester.*

KING ARTHUR AND HIS KNIGHTS

Selected Tales
by
Sir Thomas Malory

Edited with an Introduction by Eugène Vinaver

Oxford University Press
London   Oxford   New York

OXFORD UNIVERSITY PRESS
Oxford   London   Glasgow
New York   Toronto   Melbourne   Wellington
Nairobi   Dar es Salaam   Cape Town
Kuala Lumpur   Singapore   Jakarta   Hong Kong   Tokyo
Delhi   Bombay   Calcutta   Madras   Karachi

978-0-19-501905-6

printing, last digit: 39 38 37 36

CONTENTS

INTRODUCTION

by Eugène Vinaver

Mr. Lionel Hale once described in the following terms his impressions of a broadcast of Malory's *Quest of the Holy Grail:*

"But this is going to pall, this is going to start becoming tedious!" I said to myself at about 9.30 p.m. on Tuesday, after ten minutes of the *Quest of the Holy Grail* adapted by Mr. Douglas Cleverdon from Malory. Yet 11 p.m. found me still listening, and indeed coming back to the surroundings of a drawing-room with a start of surprise. Such knights, such ladies in distress, such single combats, such ships in samite, such fiends, such vows — the chivalry went briskly by, with their own beauty and their own simplicity of bravura, and never even relapsed into a dog-trot.

My groundless fears were of the method — the use of spoken narration, with short interspersed dramatic dialogue. Surely, I thought, the narrator must begin to sound intrusive: surely not even Mr. Deryck Guyler as Gawayne or Mr. Robert Harris as Lancelot can make anything of such fleeting and fugitive appearances. Wrong: one settled easily into the formula. Much was due, I thought, to the tact and variety with which that impeccable air-voice of Mr. Norman Shelley read the narration. But really the triumph was Malory's. What tales, and what a teller!

Very little is known of the author of these tales. A knight, an adventurer and a soldier, he was born in the early years of the fifteenth century and died on 14 March 1471, having spent much of the last twenty years of his life in prison. It was there that he wrote most, if not all, of his works, completing the last one in 1469 or early in 1470. Fifteen years later, on 31 July 1485, William Caxton published the entire collection in one volume entitled *Le Morte Darthur* which has since become the fountainhead of English Arthurian fiction. With the possible exception of *The Canterbury Tales*, no English book bequeathed to us by the Middle Ages has to the same degree caught the imagination of modern readers. And yet, when one asks oneself how this came about, how the obscure fifteenth-century 'knight-prisoner' achieved his lasting triumph, the answer is not easy to find. What he did was to 'reduce into English,' as Caxton puts it, certain French prose romances of the thirteenth century. Outwardly, apart from the 'reduction,' his work did not differ much from its French prototypes. But while the modern reprints of Malory's Arthurian tales rival in number those of the great English classics, while English listeners to-day find delight in his 'knights, ladies in distress, single combats and ships in samite,' Malory's 'French books' as he calls them have long since lost their appeal and not a single trace of their once powerful influence remains in modern French poetry and fiction. They have not even been condemned, as great literature often is, in the name of newly fashioned doctrines, but simply forgotten as though they had never existed. English criticism may occasionally have been severe to Malory. Even such a devout Malory scholar as E. K. Chambers felt obliged to make some reservations. He was perturbed by the 'overgrowth of chivalric adventures,' by Malory's failure to maintain certain characters 'on the same plane throughout,' by his apparent inability to tell completely 'two of the world's dozen great love stories' — that of Tristan and Iseult and that of Lancelot and Guinevere. 'Through much of it,' he wrote, 'we walk perplexedly.' But fortunately such perplexities never hinder the suspension of disbelief except in the critic's own mind; and much as Malory's readers may have been puzzled by his incoherences, they have never on that account ceased to experience the fascination of his narrative.

Wherein this fascination lies is for each reader to determine for himself: all 'definiteness' in this field, as Valéry reminded us not long ago, 'remains subjective.' But one aspect of the problem might perhaps be clarified without detriment to individual judgment, namely Malory's method of dealing with the peculiarities of early French fiction. It is customary to say that any medieval French romance of chivalry is — the phrase is George Saintsbury's — 'a vast assemblage of stories,' a collection of heterogeneous tales put together without any sequence or logic, incoherent, often absurd, and calculated to confuse even the most careful reader. More than three centuries ago one of Don Quixote's friends expressed surprise that 'more people did not go mad when they read such books'; for they were composed, he thought, 'in such a way that no reader could find his way about them.' And because it is as difficult for us to-day as it was for the late sixteenth-century readers to discern any design or method behind the complex texture of these vast and unwieldy volumes, we conclude that they are devoid of such things altogether and should be written off as an unfortunate accident in the literary history of Europe. Recent research has shown, however, how rash this condemnation is, and how important the aesthetic principle underlying the structure of the works which Malory used as his models. One of his main sources was the French Arthurian Prose Cycle — the 'Vulgate' Cycle as it is usually called nowadays — composed in the first half of the thirteenth century, probably between 1225 and 1230. It contained, in addition to the chivalric stories dealing with Lancelot's adventurous life, the chronicle stories concerned with the history of Arthur's kingdom, and the Grail stories which introduced into the realm of romance the mystical aspirations of the knights engaged in a holy quest. The central portion of the cycle was the romance of Lancelot, the longest of all; on either side of it were two other branches: a Grail branch and a chronicle at one end — the *History of the Grail* and the *Merlin* — and a Grail branch and a chronicle at the other — the *Quest of the Holy Grail* and the *Death of Arthur*. The cycle as a whole was certainly vast, so vast that no complete critical edition of it has yet been attempted, but it did not grow up by dint of a mere accumulation of narrative material. In most cases, when a 'branch' or an incident was added, the purpose of the addition was to elucidate or to anticipate stories which were already in existence. Thus, the *History of the Grail,* which was the last of the branches to be produced, was placed first in the final arrangement because its purpose was to prepare the ground for an earlier branch, the *Quest of the Holy Grail.* This 'backward' growth of the narrative implies a method still clearly distinguishable in the work of Rabelais, who began with the adventures of Pantagruel and then went on to the life story of Pantagruel's father, Gargantua: a modern novelist would probably have written his *Gargantua* first. The same process can be observed in such early forms of imaginative narrative as the French epic poems of the twelfth century, many of which were written to commemorate the early life or the lives of the parents and ancestors of a hero whose deeds were already on record.

It stands to reason that if a story or a set of stories is to be added as a preliminary to an already existing sequence of

episodes, and each of these sequences lengthened simulta-
neously with the others, the result can only be a very complex
pattern of themes alternating one with another like the strands
of a woven fabric. There can be no steady progression of a
single theme from the beginning to the middle and from the
middle to the end, such as we are accustomed to find in a work
of fiction composed in accordance with our modern idea of
coherence. The beginning is no longer, according to Aristotle's
definition, 'that before which there is nothing' or the end that
which calls for no continuation. On the wide and constantly
expanding canvas of a cycle of romances there is always room
for a further lengthening of any one of the carefully interwoven threads. Nothing is more alien to our idea of 'structure'
than this remarkable structural achievement. It represents in
the field of fiction a sense of shape which is the very opposite
of our cherished notion of 'beginning, middle, and end,' the
negation of our well-established formal values; and the impact
of the romances of chivalry on Don Quixote's mind is perhaps
nothing more than the extreme form of the bewilderment
experienced by any modern reader in face of these strange
compositions.

Had Malory lived a hundred years later his reaction might
have been similar to Don Quixote's; but he was sufficiently close
to the tradition of early French romances to understand their
elusive mechanism, and yet sufficiently independent of that
tradition to be able to discover the means by which they could
be adapted to a new conception of narrative. Mere condensa-
tion, such as many adaptors have practised before and since,
was clearly not enough. The entire fabric of the text had to be
unravelled and each thread, as far as possible, separated from
the others. This involved the use of two different techniques.
Certain stories, reproduced with minor modifications, could be
made self-contained by being simply detached from their context. *Lancelot and Elaine* and *The Knight of the Cart* are examples of this relatively easy process. In the manuscript of the
French prose *Tristan* which Malory used for his *Lancelot and
Elaine* the story served as an introduction to an expanded version of the Grail quest, the 'third book' of the *Tristan*. Malory's
story has no such sequel; it stands all by itself and, Malory tells
us, there is 'no rehearsal of the third book.' The incidents
which form the basis of Malory's *Knight of the Cart* originally
occurred half-way through the prose *Lancelot*, long before the

Grail adventures began; they were part of a complex sequence of themes and their place in the sequence was essential to their meaning and purpose. Yet such is Malory's indifference to this delicate arrangement that he inserts his *Knight of the Cart* among the incidents supposed to have taken place some time after the completion of the Grail quest. The other method is more elaborate. It consists in building a continuous narrative upon the frail structure of fragments scattered over wide stretches of the French cycle. One of Malory's early works, *The Noble Tale of Sir Lancelot*, consists of three such fragments. By carefully selecting them and bringing them together he gives his *Tale* perfect continuity and, by modern standards, a degree of coherence which its component elements never possessed. In his later writings such as *The Poisoned Apple* and *The Fair Maid of Astolat* his use of this technique shows still greater subtlety and skill. In the French romance — the *Mort Artu* — from which he borrowed both these stories, they occurred in the form of episodes interwoven with each other and interspersed with digressions in such a way that one series of episodes — *The Poisoned Apple* — was split into four fragments and the other into eight. Malory straightens out the pattern and tells each story from beginning to end without a single interruption, occasionally adding short connecting passages so as to avoid a break between sections which in his original stood apart. The result is a narrative well suited to modern taste — a short story about Guinevere's rescue by Lancelot and another about the tragic love of the Maid of Astolat, both composed with a transparent simplicity closely approximating that of a modern work of fiction.

Needless to say, such results are rare; it is one thing to have a preference for a certain type of writing, and quite another to be conscious of the aesthetic issue involved and apply the method consistently. Hence the 'perplexities' of E. K. Chambers and others who, failing to realize that throughout Malory's work two conflicting conceptions of structure are pulling violently against each other, imagine that he has 'bungled his structural problem.' Had this been so his work would not have lived. It was his solution of the problem, partial though it was, that secured the survival of his writings. How significant this solution was, two further examples will suffice to show. The story of *Balin or The Knight with the Two Swords* and *The Tale of the Death of King Arthur* were originally conceived as a prelude and as a sequel to the quest for the Grail. Challenged by King Pellam, Balin engages in a long and arduous combat in the course of which his sword is broken. Rushing into a room in the castle to find another weapon, he comes upon a sacred lance kept in the Grail sanctuary, and with it strikes the 'Dolorous Stroke' which lays waste two kingdoms. His punishment comes when he unwittingly slays his brother Balan, but the main purpose of the story is to explain through Balin's violation of the sanctuary and the Dolorous Stroke the themes of the Blighted Land and the Maimed King as presented in the *Queste del Saint Graal* — a branch of the Cycle written long before the Balin episode. In Malory the sequence is broken. The Dolorous Stroke is not an anticipation of the Grail mysteries, but a sequel to the adventure with which the story of Balin begins: in a moment of anger Balin kills the messenger who is sent by the Lady of the Lake to ask for his head, and henceforth a curse is laid upon him and all his deeds . The dénouement is reached in the encounter with a knight whose horse is 'trapped all red, and himself in the same colour,' and in whom Balin fails to recognize his brother. And so the work as a whole is not a prelude to another work, but a tale complete in itself and marked at each end by a sharp break. Once divorced from its context it assumes both a new shape and a new meaning, as if the form were productive of substance. As we read the simple account of Balin's last battle, we do not look for any sequel that might resolve the tragic issue: the very principle of 'singleness' removes from our minds any thought of resolution or escape. Relieved of any reference to a wider scheme of things and centred upon a single human destiny, the story acquires a sense of the irretrievable, of the end 'beyond which there is nothing,' and so becomes endowed with the one unmistakable characteristic of a modern tragedy.

This is equally true of Malory's last work, *The Tale of the Death of King Arthur*, or *The Morte Arthur Saunz Guerdon*, the only one which is reproduced here in full. Even in a collection of extracts this work has to be left unabridged; a shortening would inevitably make it both less attractive and less intelligible: every single part of this romance is of importance for the understanding of the whole, and no summary can replace the striking cadence of Malory's prose, through which the tragedy of Arthur is made into a human reality. Here Malory seems to transform everything he touches, even the heavy-footed lines of his English source, the stanzaic *Le Morte Arthur*.

> Certes, sir, he said, no thing
> But waters deep and wawes wan

becomes: 'Sir, he said, I saw nothing but waters wap and waves wan.' But as one compares Malory's text with the voluminous 'French book' which he used at the same time, one becomes aware of yet another kind of transformation — of a change of tempo and structure brought about by the English prose writer and reflecting a deeply rooted sense of shape and outline, a striving, perhaps unconscious, towards a compactness and a simplicity of the narrative pattern unknown to any earlier Arthurian writer. It is here that Malory's feeling for organic unity and coherent composition shows itself most effectively. And as a result of the general re-shaping of the matter of the story — of the transition from what was a branch of a cycle to a self-contained work — the very substance of the narrative undergoes a radical change: the action, made to revolve around a new-found centre, finds in it a sufficiency of power and interest. The story is turned in upon itself and its liberation from the cyclic context goes hand in hand with the characters' liberation from external fate. It is not the advent of the Grail that henceforth accounts for the downfall of Arthur's kingdom, but the interplay of emotions, which reveals with increasing intensity and clarity the harmony that might have been and the irrepressible forces bent upon its destruction. The action springs from the clash of the two most noble forms of love and loyalty — the blind devotion of the knight-lover to his lady and the heroic devotion of man to man. The task of the novelist is to show that there is no conceivable choice between them and so make us understand the magnitude of the drama enacted by the now familiar characters — Lancelot, Gawain, Guinevere and Arthur — all cast for the first time in profoundly tragic parts.

*
*   *

The arrangement of Malory's tales in the following pages will, it is hoped, be found in the main consistent with his own technique and design as a story-teller. Except for the story of Merlin or the 'coming of Arthur' — too famous to be omitted from any representative selection — and *The Holy Grail*, these tales were all conceived as independent compositions, and it seems proper, therefore, to present them as such. What we have here is not the whole of Malory, but the best of Malory, including his one great novel, *The Tale of the Death of King Arthur*. We see him first as a short-story writer who is already master of his medium, but who prefers to work on a relatively small scale: a writer, moreover, who, fascinated as he is by the mere progress of adventure and dialogue, does not as yet seek to raise the issue of conflicting loyalties upon which the fortunes of Arthur's kingdom break in his last romance. Knight-errantry as Malory understood it then was the happy and heroic life 'in Arthur's days,' a life 'hung about,' as one critic said, 'with outdoor sights and sounds.' Knights 'ride into a little leafy wood' to watch a tournament, 'hold them still,' and then enter the lists and fight with such dint of strokes that the noise rings 'by the water and the wood.' Vistas of the English country-side are superimposed upon the conventional setting of the French romance, the brevities of racy speech upon the rhetorical refinements of French dialogue, and simple human relationships upon the subtleties of courtly love.

Pelleas and Ettard and *The Knight of the Cart* are examples of this last peculiarity of Malory's treatment of his material. The French originals of these tales contained in a modified but recognizable form an expression of the medieval doctrine of *courtoisie*. The story of Pelleas was the story of love requited after many disappointments. Gawain betrays the friend on whose behalf he has set out to win a lady's love; he wins it for himself, but when Pelleas discovers the betrayal he refrains from vengeance and, leaving a naked sword by the lover's bed as a token of forgiveness, goes home resolved to die. He asks that his heart be sent after his death to his lady on a silver plate which he once received from her as a reward for his feats of bravery at a tournament. The lovers find the sword and realize that the man whom they have so cruelly betrayed has forgiven them. Conscience-stricken, they decide to make restitution to Pelleas; Gawain begs him to accept the lady's love, and Pelleas returns to the lady and marries her. From the French prose writers' point of view, Pelleas's conduct is an example of how a courtly lover should behave. Scorned by his lady, he allows himself to be ill-treated merely to obey her. In the opening episode of the story she sends out ten knights to attack him and orders him by the faith he owes her to stand still and refrain from any resistance. He obeys, and the knights bring him back to her having first tied him to his horse's tail. When she asks him whether he still has it in his heart to love her, he replies that he loves her more than ever because he knows that the suffering she has inflicted upon him will not have been borne in vain. And when finally he finds himself betrayed both by her and by Gawain he puts aside all thoughts of vengeance and is ready to die, wishing his lady more happiness than he has ever been allowed to have.

Malory's reaction to the doctrine underlying this story was that of a man bred up in arms who valued the dignity of knighthood above all else. Most of his knights are men of brief speech and unsophisticated behaviour. They engage in extraordinary adventures, but their motives admit of no sentimental refinement: they are first and foremost men of action. And so when Malory's Pelleas lets himself be tied to his horse's tail the reason is not, as in the French, that he wishes to obey his lady's capricious command, but that he hopes to gain access to her castle. The sword which he leaves with the sleeping lovers 'overthwart both their throats' is a token not of forgiveness, but of vengeance; and naturally enough, the lady does not escape punishment: Ninive, the Lady of the Lake, casts a spell on Pelleas so as to make him hate the woman he once loved, a similar spell causing her to fall in love with Pelleas. 'So this lady Ettard died for sorrow, and the Damsel of the Lake rejoiced Sir Pelleas, and loved together during their life.' In a world where vice is punished and injured men redress with their own hands the wrongs done to their honour, no other ending is possible.

On one occasion, however, in the opening passage of *The Knight of the Cart*, Malory attempts an exposition of what he thinks true love should be. He begins by saying that 'in many persons there is no stability': 'like as trees and herbs burgeoneth and flourisheth in May, in like wise every lusty heart that is any manner of lover springeth, burgeoneth, buddeth and flourisheth in lusty deeds.' Human feelings are apt to change like the seasons of the year: 'for a little blast of winter's rasure, anon we shall deface and lay apart true love.' A wise man should let his heart flourish in this world, 'first unto God, and next unto the joy of them that he promised his faith unto. . . . Such love I call virtuous love.' Love as it is today can be likened to summer and winter: 'soon hot, soon cold'; real love, 'the old love,' was the love that could endure, 'for men and women could love together seven years, and no lecherous lusts betwixt them, and then was love truth and faithfulness.' Virtue, he seems to suggest, lies in moderation, in the subordination of love to a higher purpose, not in a blind submission to its commands.

What, then, is to become of Lancelot, the hero of the story to which this disquisition serves as a preface? When he first appeared in Arthurian romance — in Chrétien de Troyes' *Conte de la Charrette* written between 1171 and 1173 — the cart which gave this work its title was the symbol of ignominy to which he was prepared to stoop for the sake of his lady: for, having lost his horse, he had allowed himself to be driven in a cart like one condemned, rather than fail in the rescue of Guinevere. To the Lancelot of Chrétien de Troyes any humiliation he was called upon to bear for his love was welcome; and there was no end to his humiliation: as a punishment for having hesitated for 'two steps' before getting into the cart he found himself rebuked by his lady in spite of all the trials he had faced for her sake. The story never reached Malory in this form, and the book to which he refers as *Le Chevalier de Chariot* was a prose work of the thirteenth century in which Guinevere's behaviour had been made somewhat less unnatural. She still rebuked Lancelot, but for a different reason: not because she thought that by weighing for one moment his knightly honour against his duties as a lover he had transgressed the code of courtly love, but because she knew that he had parted with her ring to Morgan le Fay. The ignominious cart was, however, still there, driven by a mysterious dwarf who promised to take Lancelot to a place where he would see the queen, and Lancelot's behaviour was still prompted by the same motives as in Chrétien de Troyes. It is only in Malory that a radical change occurs. The dwarf's cart becomes a woodman's cart driven by two men who go to fetch wood for their master, Mellyagaunce, and who offer Lancelot no help. It is he who takes the initiative, stops the cart, savagely attacks and kills one of the men and forces the other to take him to Mellyagaunce's castle, not from a sense of duty towards Guinevere, but because his armour is too heavy and uncomfortable to walk in. And just as the cart loses all symbolic value, the distant and jealously guarded land where Guinevere is held captive, the *terre foraine* from which no traveller returns, becomes part of a familiar landscape — a castle situated within a few miles of Lambeth.

Lancelot reaches it in less than two hours. The journey is un-eventful and he is spared many trials, among them the sword bridge which, according to all French versions, he crossed on his knees, oblivious of the pain he was inflicting upon himself and ever ready to bear any sacrifice or hardship in the service of love. 'Love in King Arthur's days,' as Malory imagined it, chivalry as he understood it, required no such trials: it implied a reasonable rule of life, a sense of loyalty without sophistica-tion and a hierarchy of values which deprived the courtly lady of her supremacy and the theme of courtly love of its unique position in romance.

The treatment of sentiment inevitably affects the whole character of romantic imagination, and it is no accident that in medieval romance courtly idealism is associated with poetic fantasy: its natural setting is a world ruled by supernatural forces. Nothing is more characteristic of Malory's attitude to the French tradition than his frequent refusal to explain un-usual occurrences in purely supernatural terms. His caution and moderation are as noticeable here as in his thoughts about 'true love.' In one of his French books there was the story of the Lady of the Lake walking to the centre of a lake upon an invisible bridge and returning with a sword for King Arthur. This Malory could not accept; and so in his account the Lady of the Lake simply tells Arthur and Merlin to take a boat and row across the lake until they come to the sword 'that the hand held.' The presence of the hand coming out of the water and holding the sword shows, if not a belief, at least some degree of acquiescence in the supernatural, which goes hand in hand with the desire to restrict the operation of supernatural forces. The invisible bridge vanishes, but the hand remains. And so it often is when Malory has to deal with magic: the marvels are not abolished, but reduced in number, and there is more realistic detail. Yet in the end the feeling of the marvellous is not less-ened, but intensified. This is especially true of the story of Balin. At every stage of Balin's journey towards the en-chanted castle the sense of approaching doom is enhanced by the compression of the narrative. Balin sees a cross with the in-scription: 'It is not for no knight alone to ride toward this castle.' He meets an old grey-bearded man coming towards him who says, 'Thou passest thy bounds to come this way, therefore turn, and it will avail thee.' The man vanishes and Balin hears 'a horn blow as it had been the death of a beast.' 'That blast,' he says, 'is blown for me, for I am the prize and yet I am not dead.' It matters little if after this Malory suppresses the mysterious details of Balin's reception at the castle where over a hundred maidens greet him with alluring voices to announce new enchantments. The essential magic of the tale is retained and its poetic meaning brought home to us the more clearly because it is relieved of some of its fairy-tale trappings. Malory may have 'thinned the romantic forest' and transferred what was left of it from the regions of fancy to the banks of the Thames; he has not in fact lessened its appeal. For his is a method of creative adaptation which takes traditional matter for granted and by the mere process of re-shaping and remodelling draws new values from the old.

By the same token, as we leave the smiling landscape of romance, we come to discover, in *The Tale of the Death of King Arthur*, the dark and unhappy world of human antagonisms, the 'anger and unhap that stinted not till the flower of all the world was destroyed and slain': not, despite all appearances, the world of the chronicles, with its record of past and present misfortunes that have befallen the land of King Arthur. The great king's defeat could never be to Malory what it was to Geoffrey of Monmouth — a story of military disaster for which an accident of warfare was alone to blame. Much as the great chronicler liked indulging his fancy in composing his *Historia Regum Britanniae*, he never asked himself the question that since his time has been uppermost in the minds of romance writers and novelists concerned with the 'matter of Britain': why was Arthur defeated and his kingdom lost? He stated the fact, described the ferocious battle between Arthur and Mordred and left it at that. The change from chronicle to romance is the change from a factual attitude of mind to the inquiring one, and the history of Arthurian romance in late medieval times is but a history of the various attempts to explain the significance of the events which constitute the story of Arthur's kingdom. Malory stands at the end of a long line of writers who have a share in this great endeavour — in the effort of three centuries which he brought firmly to its noble close.

*

*   *

In a preface to Boulenger's adaptation of Arthurian romances Bédier wrote: 'What is the mysterious power of taste, of a sound language, of good style? Malory was but a translator, an

Arthur's fight with Mordred. Ms. 6, *St. Alban's Chronicle*, fol. 66v. *Lambeth Palace Library, London.*

Figure of Arthur, glass, St. Mary's
Hall, Coventry, c. 1450. *Victoria and
Albert Museum, London.*

adaptor: and yet without him, in the England of to-day, neither poetry, nor thought, nor art would have been exactly what they are.' The miracle can safely be left unexpounded except for one detail. Andrew Lang thought that Malory's style was 'based on the fresh and simple manner' of his French sources. This is far from being the case. The manner of Malory's French sources was neither fresh nor simple; it was laborious and sophisticated. Like the literary English of Malory's time, it was intended to please the intelligence, not to stir the imagination. Its texture was not unlike that of a thirteenth-century cycle of romances: clauses were interwoven with one another and interspersed with digressions referring to earlier or subsequent statements. But strangely enough, there is the same contrast between this pattern and Malory's way of writing as between his method of telling a story and the older medieval method. One can observe in his prose the emergence of a rhythm which raises his language to a new level of expressiveness. For the complex symmetry of a carefully planned period Malory substitutes as a rule a succession of abruptly divided clauses, some of them strikingly brief and compact, and all modelled on the natural cadence of living speech:

> 'Certes,' said Sir Lancelot, 'all that ye have said is true, and from henceforward I cast me, by thy grace of God, never to be so wicked as I have been but as to sue knighthood and do feats of arms.'

Each pause is clearly marked, not for its rhetorical value, but to give a rest to the voice in a speech charged with feeling. The corresponding French sentence is scarcely different in meaning; but instead of 'all that ye have said is true' it has a recapitulation, introduced by the words 'because you have told me' (*por ce que m'avez dit*), of what the hermit had said to Lancelot, and there is naturally no break such as 'and from henceforward.' A no less striking effect is achieved in the following words spoken by Galahad:

> 'Lord, I thank Thee, for now I see that that hath been my desire many a day. Now, my Blessed Lord, I would not live in this wretched world no longer if it might please Thee, Lord.'

Every one of these words is gleaned from a much longer passage. By a careful process of selection the essential threads of the original texture are unravelled so as to bring out the deeper sense of the speech, accelerate its rhythm and restore the natural emphasis of the spoken word. The 'gentle yet hardy' prose of Malory, so different from its amorphous prototype, is often the result of some such re-phrasing. Not that the spacious pages of Malory's books are always free from the dead wood of traditional rhetorical syntax or the monotony of set descriptive phrases; but once his voice is heard in its own unmistakable register it bears the narrative on with a natural rise and fall through all the vicissitudes of 'life in Arthur's days,' through the sudden changes of scenery and the complexities of romantic sentiment, as if the grace and glory of that half-forgotten world had never been and never could be lost.

*

*　　　*

The present edition differs from the first in that it contains *The Tale of the Death of King Arthur*, which is reproduced here in full. The other eight tales appear in much the same form as before. In this as in the first edition I have taken few liberties with the text. A passage has been omitted from *Balin or The Knight with the Two Swords* and another from *Lancelot and Elaine;* both passages represent digressions highly characteristic of the French romances but not of Malory's own work. The omission, indicated in each case by suspension marks, avoids a break in the narrative in a way which Malory himself would no doubt have thought appropriate. The most important innovation in both editions is the modernization of the spelling. Of the innumerable previous printings of Malory's works in modern orthography not a single one preserves the text as written by him; in all without exception obsolete words are removed or replaced by their modern equivalents in spite of the claim of some editors to have taken 'the most anxious care' to produce a text modernized 'as to its spelling only.' True, the distinction between modernizing the spelling and bringing the vocabulary up to date is not always easy to make, and it may legitimately be held, for instance, that to transcribe the pronoun *hir* as *their* is to substitute one form of the possessive plural for another. But as long as the form adopted exists in Malory side by side with the other and is in fact predominant, there is no great harm in preferring it and thus earning the gratitude of the lay reader. For any detailed study of Malory's language the specialist will naturally go to editions in the original spelling; all one can hope to achieve in a work such as this is the preservation of all those peculiarities of the original which are consistent with a normalized modern transcription. This applies equally to proper names. All variations in their treatment have been eliminated.

The text itself, apart from the spelling, is the same as that of my revised three-volume edition of *The Works of Sir Thomas Malory* (Oxford, 1967). It is based upon a collation of the manuscript discovered in 1934 in the Fellows' Library of Winchester College with Caxton's *Le Morte Darthur* and with Malory's sources. The manuscript having lost a gathering of eight leaves at each end and a few leaves in the middle, Caxton is our only authority for certain sections of the text including the first of the tales published here and part of the second.

The footnotes, revised and supplemented, are intended to facilitate the reading of the text by means of such renderings and comments as would otherwise have required the addition of a glossary. A certain degree of familiarity with obsolete words and constructions is, of course, assumed; and some simple words and phrases, such as those in the following list, are left unexplained: *an* (if), *anon* (immediately), *brast* (burst), *brent* (burnt), *dole* (sorrow), *essay* (try), *I will well* (I readily agree), *on life* (alive), *or* (before), *other* (or), *passing* (extremely), *salew* (greet, salute), *swough* (swoon), *syn, sith*[*en*] (since), *that* (in the sense of 'so that'), *wit* (know). An attempt is made, however, to give the meaning of most of the unusual or polyvalent words and to elucidate all the less intelligible passages. The only abbreviations I have used are *M* for Malory, *O* for the 1967 edition of his works, and *F* for the French texts which represent his sources. To conform to the general pattern of the series I have dispensed with the Index of proper names. Anyone unduly puzzled by these and tempted to turn to the end of the volume should recall the warning contained in the preface to a famous translation of Plutarch: 'As for the strange names, stick not in them, for who that can take no fruit in it without he know clearly every tale that is here touched, I would he should not read this book.'

My grateful thanks are due to Mr. Gordon N. Ray who first suggested an edition of extracts from Malory in modern spelling, to Mr. John W. Wright of the Oxford University Press for his constant encouragement and to Mr. Barry J. Gaines for his invaluable help in the preparation of this work.

KING ARTHUR
AND HIS KNIGHTS

Merlin

It befell in the days of Uther Pendragon, when he was king of all England and so reigned, that there was a mighty duke in Cornwall that held war against him long time, and the duke was called the duke of Tintagel. And so by means[1] King Uther sent for this duke, charging him to bring his wife with him, for she was called a fair lady and a passing wise, and her name was called Igraine.

So when the duke and his wife were come unto the king, by the means of great lords they were accorded[2] both. The king liked and loved this lady well, and he made them great cheer out of measure, and desired to have lain by her. But she was a passing good woman and would not assent unto the king. And then she told the duke her husband, and said,

'I suppose that we were sent for that I should be dishonoured. Wherefore, husband, I counsel you that we depart from hence suddenly, that we may ride all night unto our own castle.'

And in like wise as she said so they departed, that neither the king nor none of his council were ware of their departing. Also[3] soon as King Uther knew of their departing so suddenly, he was wonderly wroth; then he called to him his privy council and told them of the sudden departing of the duke and his wife. Then they advised the king to send for the duke and his wife by a great charge[4]:

'And if he will not come at your summons, then may ye do your best; then have ye cause to make mighty war upon him.'

So that was done, and the messengers had their answers; and that was this, shortly, that neither he nor his wife would not come at him. Then was the king wonderly wroth; and then the king sent him plain word again and bade him be

[1] intermediaries
[2] reconciled
[3] As
[4] solemn command

3

ready and stuff him and garnish him,[5] for within forty days he would fetch him out of the biggest castle that he hath.

When the duke had this warning, anon he went and furnished and garnished two strong castles of his, of the which the one hight Tintagel, and the other castle hight Terrabil. So his wife Dame Igraine he put in the castle of Tintagel, and himself he put in the castle of Terrabil, the which had many issues and posterns out. Then in all haste came Uther with a great host and laid a siege about the castle of Terrabil, and there he pight[6] many pavilions. And there was great war made on both parties and much people slain.

Then for pure anger and for great love of fair Igraine the king Uther fell sick. So came to the King Uther Sir Ulfius, a noble knight, and asked the king why he was sick.

'I shall tell thee,' said the king, 'I am sick for anger and for love of fair Igraine, that I may not be whole.'

'Well, my lord,' said Sir Ulfius, 'I shall seek Merlin and he shall do you remedy, that your heart shall be pleased.'

So Ulfius departed and by adventure he met Merlin in a beggar's array, and there Merlin asked Ulfius whom he sought, and he said he had little ado[7] to tell him.

'Well,' said Merlin, 'I know whom thou seekest, for thou seekest Merlin; therefore seek no farther, for I am he. And if King Uther will well reward me and be sworn unto me to fulfil my desire, that shall be his honour and profit more than mine, for I shall cause him to have all his desire.'

'All this will I undertake,' said Ulfius, 'that there shall be nothing reasonable but thou shalt have thy desire.'

'Well,' said Merlin, 'he shall have his intent and desire. And therefore,' said Merlin, 'ride on your way, for I will not be long behind.'

Then Ulfius was glad and rode on more than a pace[8] till that he came to King Uther Pendragon and told him he had met with Merlin.

'Where is he?' said the king.

'Sir,' said Ulfius, 'he will not dwell long.'

Therewithal Ulfius was ware where Merlin stood at the porch of the pavilion's door, and then Merlin was bound[9] to

---

[5] furnish himself with men and stores
[6] set up
[7] reason
[8] rode at a good speed
[9] ready

come to the king. When King Uther saw him he said he was welcome.

'Sir,' said Merlin, 'I know all your heart every deal.[10] So[11] ye will be sworn unto me, as ye be a true king anointed, to fulfil my desire, ye shall have your desire.'

Then the king was sworn upon the four Evangelists.

'Sir,' said Merlin, 'this is my desire: the first night that ye shall lie by Igraine ye shall get a child on her; and when that is born, that it shall be delivered to me for to nourish thereas[12] I will have it; for it shall be your worship and the child's avail[13] as mickle as the child is worth.'

'I will well,' said the king, 'as thou wilt have it.'

'Now make you ready,' said Merlin. 'This night ye shall lie with Igraine in the castle of Tintagel. And ye shall be like the duke her husband, Ulfius shall be like Sir Brastias, a knight of the duke's, and I will be like a knight that hight Sir Jordanus, a knight of the duke's. But wait[14] ye make not many questions with her nor her men, but say ye are diseased,[15] and so hie you to bed and rise not on the morn till I come to you, for the castle of Tintagel is but ten mile hence.'

So this was done as they devised. But the duke of Tintagel espied how the king rode from the siege of Terrabil. And therefore that night he issued out of the castle at a postern for to have distressed[16] the king's host, and so through his own issue[17] the duke himself was slain or ever the king came at the castle of Tintagel. So after the death of the duke King Uther lay with Igraine, more than three hours after his death, and begat on her that night Arthur; and or day came, Merlin came to the king and bade him make him ready, and so he kissed the lady Igraine and departed in all haste. But when the lady heard tell of the duke her husband, and by all record he was dead or ever King Uther came to her, then she marvelled who that might be that lay with her in likeness of her lord. So she mourned privily[18] and held her peace.

Then all the barons by one assent prayed the king of accord[19]

[10] all that is in your heart
[11] provided that
[12] where
[13] to your honour and the child's advantage
[14] take care
[15] indisposed
[16] in order to attack
[17] sally
[18] secret(ly)
[19] for reconciliation

betwixt the lady Igraine and him. The king gave them leave,[20] for fain would he have been accorded[1] with her; so the king put all the trust in Ulfius to entreat[2] between them. So by the entreaty at the last the king and she met together.

'Now will we do well,'[3] said Ulfius. 'Our king is a lusty knight and wifeless, and my lady Igraine is a passing fair lady; it were great joy unto us all an it might please the king to make her his queen.'

Unto that they all well accorded[4] and moved it to the king. And anon, like a lusty knight, he assented thereto with good will, and so in all haste they were married in a morning with great mirth and joy.

And King Lot of Lothian and of Orkney then wedded Margawse that was Gawain's mother, and King Nentres of the land of Garlot wedded Elaine. All this was done at the request of King Uther. And the third sister, Morgan le Fay, was put to school in a nunnery, and there she learned so much that she was a great clerk of necromancy. And after she was wedded to King Uriens of the land of Gore, that was Sir Ywain le Blanchemain's father.

Then Queen Igraine waxed daily greater and greater. So it befell after within half a year, as King Uther lay by his queen, he asked her, by the faith she owed to him, whose was the child within her body. Then was she sore abashed to give answer.

'Dismay you not,' said the king, 'but tell me the truth, and I shall love you the better, by the faith of my body!'[5]

'Sir,' said she, 'I shall tell you the truth. The same night that my lord was dead, the hour of his death, as his knights record, there came into my castle of Tintagel a man like my lord in speech and in countenance, and two knights with him in likeness of his two knights Brastias and Jordanus, and so I went unto bed with him as I ought to do with my lord; and the same night, as I shall answer unto God, this child was begotten upon me.'

'That is truth,' said the king, 'as ye say, for it was I myself that came in the likeness. And therefore dismay you not, for I am father of the child'; and there he told her all the cause[6]

---

20 granted their request   4 agreed
 1 reconciled   5 my faith
 2 negotiate   6 the whole matter
 3 do the right thing

how it was by Merlin's counsel. Then the queen made great joy when she knew who was the father of her child.

Soon came Merlin unto the king and said,

'Sir, ye must purvey you[7] for the nourishing of your child.'

'As thou wilt,' said the king, 'be it.'

'Well,' said Merlin, 'I know a lord of yours in this land that is a passing true man and a faithful, and he shall have the nourishing of your child; and his name is Sir Ector, and he is a lord of fair livelihood[8] in many parts in England and Wales. And this lord, Sir Ector, let him be sent for for to come and speak with you, and desire him yourself, as he loveth you, that he will put his own child to nourishing to another woman and that his wife nourish yours. And when the child is born let it be delivered to me at yonder privy postern unchristened.'

So like as Merlin devised it was done. And when Sir Ector was come he made fiaunce to[9] the king for to nourish the child like as the king desired; and there the king granted Sir Ector great rewards. Then when the lady was delivered the king commanded two knights and two ladies to take the child bound in a cloth of gold, 'and that ye deliver him to what poor man ye meet at the postern gate of the castle.' So the child was delivered unto Merlin, and so he bare it forth unto Sir Ector, and made an holy man to christen him, and named him Arthur. And so Sir Ector's wife nourished him with her own pap.

Then within two years King Uther fell sick of a great malady. And in the meanwhile his enemies usurped upon him[10] and did a great battle upon his men and slew many of his people.

'Sir,' said Merlin, 'ye may not lie so as ye do, for ye must to the field, though ye ride on an horse-litter. For ye shall never have the better of your enemies but if your person be there, and then shall ye have the victory.'

So it was done as Merlin had devised, and they carried the king forth in an horse-litter with a great host towards his enemies, and at St. Albans there met with the king a great host of the North.[11] And that day Sir Ulfius and Sir Brastias

[7] arrange
[8] possessions
[9] promised
[10] encroached upon his land
[11] *Probably a reminiscence of the* first battle of St. Albans (22 May 1455) when another sick king, Henry VI, was carried forth at the head of his troops to meet a rebel army.

did great deeds of arms, and King Uther's men overcame the Northern battle[12] and slew many people and put the remnant to flight; and then the king returned unto London and made great joy of his victory.

And then he fell passing sore sick, so that three days and three nights he was speechless; wherefore all the barons made great sorrow and asked Merlin what counsel were best.

'There is none other remedy,' said Merlin, 'but God will have His will. But look ye all barons be before King Uther to-morn, and God and I shall make him to speak.'

So on the morn all the barons with Merlin came tofore the king. Then Merlin said aloud unto King Uther,

'Sir, shall your son Arthur be king after your days of this realm with all the appurtenance?'[13]

Then Uther Pendragon turned him and said in hearing of them all,

'I give him God's blessing and mine, and bid him pray for my soul, and righteously and worshipfully that he claim the crown upon forfeiture of my blessing;' and therewith he yielded up the ghost. And then was he interred as longed to[14] a king, wherefore the queen, fair Igraine, made great sorrow, and all the barons.

Then stood the realm in great jeopardy long while, for every lord that was mighty of men made him strong, and many weened to have been[15] king. Then Merlin went to the Archbishop of Canterbury and counselled him for to send for all the lords of the realm and all the gentlemen of arms, that they should to London come by Christmas upon pain of cursing, and for this cause, that Jesu, that was born on that night, that He would of His great mercy show some miracle, as He was come to be King of mankind, for to show some miracle who should be rightwise king of this realm. So the Archbishop, by the advice of Merlin, sent for all the lords and gentlemen of arms that they should come by Christmas even unto London; and many of them made them clean of their life, that their prayer might be the more acceptable unto God.

So in the greatest church of London, whether it were Paul's or not the French book maketh no mention, all the estates

---

[12] army
[13] privileges belonging to the crown
[14] buried as befits
[15] expected to be made

were long or day[16] in the church for to pray. And when matins and the first mass was done there was seen in the churchyard, against the high altar, a great stone four square, like unto a marble stone, and in midst thereof was like an anvil of steel a foot on high, and therein stuck a fair sword naked by the point, and letters there were written in gold about the sword that said thus: 'WHOSO PULLETH OUT THIS SWORD OF THIS STONE AND ANVIL IS RIGHTWISE KING BORN OF ALL ENGLAND.' Then the people marvelled and told it to the Archbishop.

'I command,' said the Archbishop, 'that ye keep you within your church and pray unto God still; that no man touch the sword till the high mass be all done.'

So when all masses were done all the lords went to behold the stone and the sword. And when they saw the scripture some essayed, such as would have been king, but none might stir the sword nor move it.

'He is not here,' said the Archbishop, 'that shall achieve the sword, but doubt not God will make him known. But this is my counsel,' said the Archbishop, 'that we let purvey[17] ten knights, men of good fame, and they to keep this sword.'

So it was ordained, and then there was made a cry that every man should essay that would for to win the sword. And upon New Year's Day the barons let make a jousts and a tournament, that all knights that would joust or tourney there might play. And all this was ordained for to keep the lords together and the commons, for the Archbishop trusted that God would make him known that should win the sword.

So upon New Year's Day, when the service was done, the barons rode unto the field, some to joust and some to tourney. And so it happed that Sir Ector, that had great livelihood[18] about London, rode unto the jousts, and with him rode Sir Kay, his son, and young Arthur that was his nourished brother; and Sir Kay was made knight at All Hallowmass afore. So as they rode to the jousts-ward Sir Kay had lost[19] his sword, for he had left it at his father's lodging, and so he prayed young Arthur for to ride for his sword.

'I will well,' said Arthur, and rode fast after the sword.

And when he came home the lady and all were out to see the jousting. Then was Arthur wroth, and said to himself,

---

[16] long before dawn
[17] appoint
[18] estates
[19] Sir Kay missed

'I will ride to the churchyard and take the sword with me that sticketh in the stone, for my brother Sir Kay shall not be without a sword this day.' So when he came to the church-yard Sir Arthur alight and tied his horse to the stile, and so he went to the tent and found no knights there, for they were at the jousting. And so he handled the sword by the handles, and lightly and fiercely[20] pulled it out of the stone, and took his horse and rode his way until he came to his brother Sir Kay and delivered him the sword.

And as soon as Sir Kay saw the sword he wist well it was the sword of the stone, and so he rode to his father Sir Ector and said,

'Sir, lo here is the sword of the stone, wherefore I must be king of this land.'

When Sir Ector beheld the sword he returned again[1] and came to the church, and there they alight all three and went into the church, and anon he made Sir Kay to swear upon a book how he came to that sword.

'Sir,' said Sir Kay, 'by my brother Arthur, for he brought it to me.'

'How gat ye this sword?' said Sir Ector to Arthur.

'Sir, I will tell you. When I came home for my brother's sword I found nobody at home to deliver me his sword, and so I thought my brother Sir Kay should not be swordless, and so I came hither eagerly[2] and pulled it out of the stone without any pain.'[3]

'Found ye any knights about this sword?' said Sir Ector.

'Nay,' said Arthur.

'Now,' said Sir Ector to Arthur, 'I understand ye must be king of this land.'

'Wherefore I?' said Arthur, 'and for what cause?'

'Sir,' said Ector, 'for God will have it so, for there should never man have drawn out this sword but he that shall be rightwise king of this land. Now let me see whether ye can put the sword thereas[4] it was and pull it out again.'

'That is no mastery,'[5] said Arthur, and so he put it in the stone. Therewithal Sir Ector essayed to pull out the sword and failed.

---

[20] quickly and vigorously
[1] went back
[2] quickly
[3] difficulty
[4] where
[5] deed of prowess

'Now essay,' said Sir Ector unto Sir Kay. And anon he pulled at the sword with all his might, but it would not be.

'Now shall ye essay,' said Sir Ector to Arthur.

'I will well,' said Arthur, and pulled it out easily.

And therewithal Sir Ector kneeled down to the earth and Sir Kay.

'Alas!' said Arthur, 'my own dear father and brother, why kneel ye to me?'

'Nay, nay, my lord Arthur, it is not so. I was never your father nor of your blood, but I wot well ye are of an higher blood than I weened ye were,' and then Sir Ector told him all, how he was betaken[6] him for to nourish him and by whose commandment, and by Merlin's deliverance.[7]

Then Arthur made great dole when he understood that Sir Ector was not his father.

'Sir,' said Ector unto Arthur, 'will ye be my good and gracious lord when ye are king?'

'Else were I to blame,' said Arthur, 'for ye are the man in the world that I am most beholding to, and my good lady and mother your wife that as well as her own hath fostered me and kept. And if ever it be God's will that I be king as ye say, ye shall desire of me what I may do, and I shall not fail you. God forbid I should fail you.'

'Sir,' said Sir Ector, 'I will ask no more of you but that ye will make my son, your foster brother Sir Kay, seneschal[8] of all your lands.'

'That shall be done,' said Arthur, 'and more, by the faith of my body,[9] that never man shall have that office but he while he and I live.'

Therewithal they went unto the Archbishop and told him how the sword was achieved and by whom. And on Twelfth-day all the barons came thither and to essay to take the sword who that would essay, but there afore them all there might none take it out but Arthur. Wherefore there were many lords wroth, and said it was great shame unto them all and the realm to be overgoverned with a boy of no high blood born. And so they fell out at that time, that[10] it was put off till Candlemas, and then all the barons should meet there again;

---

[6] entrusted to
[7] and how he was handed over to Sir Ector by Merlin
[8] steward
[9] my faith
[10] with the result that

but always the ten knights were ordained to watch the sword day and night, and so they set a pavilion over the stone and the sword, and five always watched.

So at Candlemas many more great lords came hither for to have won the sword, but there might none prevail. And right as Arthur did at Christmas he did at Candlemas, and pulled out the sword easily, whereof the barons were sore aggrieved and put it off in delay till the high feast of Easter. And as Arthur sped[11] afore so did he at Easter. Yet there were some of the great lords had indignation that Arthur should be king, and put it off in a delay till the feast of Pentecost. Then the Archbishop of Canterbury, by Merlin's providence,[12] let purvey[13] then of the best knights that they might get, and such knights as Uther Pendragon loved best and most trusted in his days, and such knights were put about Arthur as Sir Baudwin of Britain, Sir Kaynes, Sir Ulfius, Sir Brastias; all these with many other were always about Arthur day and night till the feast of Pentecost.

And at the feast of Pentecost all manner of men essayed to pull at the sword that would essay, but none might prevail but Arthur, and he pulled it out afore all the lords and commons that were there. Wherefore all the commons cried at once,

'We will have Arthur unto our king! We will put him no more in delay, for we all see that it is God's will that he shall be our king, and who that holdeth against it we will slay him!'

And therewithal they kneeled at once, both rich and poor, and cried Arthur mercy because they had delayed him so long. And Arthur forgave them, and took the sword between both his hands and offered it upon the altar where the Archbishop was, and so was he made knight of the best man that was there.

And so anon was the coronation made, and there was he sworn unto his lords and the commons for to be a true king, to stand with true justice from thenceforth the days of this life. Also then he made all lords that held of the crown to come in and to do service as they ought to. And many complaints were made unto Sir Arthur of great wrongs that were done since the death of King Uther, of many lands that were bereaved lords, knights, ladies, and gentlemen; where-

[11] succeeded   [13] appointed
[12] contriving

fore King Arthur made the lands to be given again unto them that ought them.[14]

When this was done, that the king had stablished[15] all the countries about London, then he let make Sir Kay seneschal of England; and Sir Baudwin of Britain was made constable, and Sir Ulfius was made chamberlain, and Sir Brastias was made warden to wait upon the North from Trent forwards, for it was that time the most party the king's enemies. But within few years after Arthur won all the North, Scotland and all that were under their obeissance, also Wales. A part of it held against Arthur, but he overcame them all as he did the remnant, through the noble prowess of himself and his knights of the Round Table.[16]

[14] to whom they rightfully belonged

[15] restored order to

[16] *According to the French romance, the Round Table was at that time the property of King Leodegan, who had received it as a present from King Uther. When Arthur married Guinevere, King Leodegan's daughter, she brought the Round Table with her as part of her dowry.*

Of a damoysell whiche came gyrde with a swerde for to fynde a
man of suche vertue to drawe it out of the scauberde. *Morte
d'Arthur*, edition of Wynkyn de Worde, 1498. *The John Rylands
University Library of Manchester.*

Balin

or The Knight with the Two Swords

After the death of Uther reigned Arthur, his son, which had great war in his days for to get all England into his hand; for there were many kings within the realm of England and of Scotland, Wales and Cornwall.

So it befell on a time when King Arthur was at London, there came a knight and told the king tidings how the King Rions of North Wales had reared[1] a great number of people, and were entered in the land and brent and slew the king's true liege people.

'If this be true,' said Arthur, 'it were great shame unto mine estate[2] but that he were mightily withstood.'

'It is truth,' said the knight, 'for I saw the host myself.'

'Well,' said the king, 'I shall ordain to withstand his malice.'[3]

Then the king let make a cry that all the lords, knights and gentlemen of arms should draw unto the castle called Camelot in those days, and there the king would let make a council-general and a great jousts. So when the king was come thither with all his baronage and lodged as they seemed best, also there was come a damsel the which was sent from the great Lady Lyle of Avalon.[4] And when she came before King Arthur she told from whence she came, and how she was sent on message unto him for these causes. Then she let her mantle fall that was richly furred, and then was she girt with a noble sword, whereof the king had marvel and said,

'Damsel, for what cause are ye girt with that sword? It beseemeth you nought.'[5]

'Now shall I tell you,' said the damsel. 'This sword that I

---

[1] raised
[2] insult to my dignity
[3] evil design
[4] F: *Dame de l'Isle Avalon*
[5] it does not become you

am girt withal doth me great sorrow and cumbrance, for I
may not be delivered of this sword but by a knight, and he
must be a passing good man of his hands and of his deeds, and
without villainy other treachery,[6] and without treason. And
if I may find such a knight that hath all these virtues, he may
draw out this sword out of the sheath. For I have been at
King Rions, for it was told me there were passing good
knights; and he and all his knights hath essayed and none can
speed.'[7]

'This is a great marvel,' said Arthur. 'If this be sooth I will
essay myself to draw out the sword, not presuming myself
that I am the best knight; but I will begin to draw your sword
in giving an example to all the barons, that they shall essay
everych one after other when I have essayed.'

Then Arthur took the sword by the sheath and girdle and
pulled at it eagerly, but the sword would not out.

'Sir,' said the damsel, 'ye need not for to pull half so sore,[8]
for he that shall pull it out shall do it with little might.'

'Ye say well,' said Arthur. 'Now essay ye all, my barons.'

'But beware ye be not defiled with shame, treachery, neither
guile, for then it will not avail,' said the damsel, 'for he must
be a clean knight without villainy and of gentle strain of father
side and of mother side.'

The most part of all the barons of the Round Table that
were there at that time essayed all by row,[9] but there might
none speed.[7] Wherefore the damsel made great sorrow out of
measure and said,

'Alas! I weened in this court had been the best knights of
the world without treachery other treason.'

'By my faith,' said Arthur, 'here are good knights, as I deem,
as any be in the world, but their grace is not[10] to help you,
wherefore I am sore displeased.'

Then it befell so that time there was a poor knight with
King Arthur that had been prisoner with him half a year for
slaying of a knight which was cousin unto King Arthur. And
the name of this knight was called Balin, and by good means
of the barons he was delivered out of prison, for he was a
good man named of his body,[11] and he was born in Northum-

---

[6] deceit (Old Fr.: *tricherie*)
[7] succeed
[8] hard
[9] in turn (M: *rew*)

[10] they have not had the good
fortune
[11] reputed as a good man

berland. And so he went privily[12] into the court and saw this adventure whereof it raised his heart, and would essay[13] as other knights did. But for he was poor and poorly arrayed, he put himself not far in press.[14] But in his heart he was fully assured to do as well, if his grace happed him,[15] as any knight that there was. And as the damsel took her leave of Arthur and of all the barons, so departing, this knight Balin called unto her and said,

'Damsel, I pray you of your courtesy suffer me as well to essay as these other lords. Though that I be poorly arrayed yet in my heart meseemeth I am fully assured[16] as some of these other, and meseemeth in mine heart to speed[7] right well.'

This damsel then beheld this poor knight and saw he was a likely[17] man; but for his poor arrayment she thought he should not be of no worship[18] without villainy or treachery. And then she said unto that knight,

'Sir, it needeth not you to put me to no more pain,[19] for it seemeth[20] not you to speed[7] thereas[1] all these other knights have failed.'

'Ah, fair damsel,' said Balin, 'worthiness and good tatches[2] and also good deeds is not only in arrayment, but manhood and worship[3] is hid within a man's person; and many a worshipful[4] knight is not known unto all people. And therefore worship and hardiness[5] is not in arrayment.'

'By God,' said the damsel, 'ye say sooth, therefore ye shall essay to do what ye may.'

Then Balin took the sword by the girdle and sheath and drew it out easily; and when he looked on the sword it pleased him much. Then had the king and all the barons great marvel that Balin had done that adventure; many knights had great despite[6] at him.

'Certes,' said the damsel, 'this is a passing good knight and the best that ever I found, and most of worship without treason, treachery, or felony. And many marvels shall he do. Now, gentle and courteous knight, give me the sword again.'

[12] secretly
[13] wished to try it
[14] forward
[15] if fortune favoured him
[16] confident
[17] handsome
[18] could not be a person of quality
[19] any further trouble
[20] becomes
[1] where
[2] qualities
[3] honour
[4] honourable
[5] nobility and valour
[6] anger

'Nay,' said Balin, 'for this sword will I keep but it be taken from me with force.'

'Well,' said the damsel, 'ye are not wise to keep the sword from me, for ye shall slay with that sword the best friend that ye have and the man that ye most love in the world, and that sword shall be your destruction.'

'I shall take the adventure,' said Balin, 'that God will ordain for me. But the sword ye shall not have at this time, by the faith of my body!'

'Ye shall repent it within short time,' said the damsel, 'for I would have the sword more for your advantage than for mine; for I am passing heavy[7] for your sake, for an ye will not leave that sword it shall be your destruction, and that is great pity.'

So with that departed the damsel and great sorrow she made. And anon after Balin sent for his horse and armour, and so would depart from the court, and took his leave of King Arthur.

'Nay,' said the king, 'I suppose ye will not[8] depart so lightly from this fellowship. I suppose that ye are displeased that I have showed you unkindness. But blame me the less, for I was misinformed against you: but I weened ye had not been such a knight as ye are of worship and prowess. And if ye will abide in this court among my fellowship, I shall so advance you as ye shall be pleased.'

'God thank your Highness,' said Balin. 'Your bounty may no man praise half unto the value, but at this time I must needs depart, beseeching you always of your good grace.'

'Truly,' said the king, 'I am right wroth of your departing. But I pray you, fair knight, that ye tarry not long from me, and ye shall be right welcome unto me and to my barons, and I shall amend all miss that[9] I have done against you.'

'God thank your good grace,' said Balin, and therewith made him ready to depart. Then the most party of the knights of the Round Table said that Balin did not this adventure all only by might but by witchcraft.

So the meanwhile that this knight was making him ready to depart there came into the court the Lady of the Lake, and she came on horseback richly beseen,[10] and salewed King Arthur and there asked him a gift that he promised her when she gave him the sword.

---

[7] very sad   [9] such wrong as
[8] I do not expect you to   [10] dressed

'That is sooth,' said Arthur, 'a gift I promised you, but I have forgotten the name of my sword[11] that ye gave me.'

'The name of it,' said the lady, 'is Excalibur, that is as much to say as Cut Steel.'

'Ye say well,' said the king. 'Ask what ye will and ye shall have it an it lie in my power to give it.'

'Well,' said this lady, 'then I ask the head of this knight that hath won this sword, other else the damsel's head that brought it. I take no force though[12] I have both their heads: for he slew my brother, a good knight and a true; and that gentlewoman was causer of my father's death.'

'Truly,' said King Arthur, 'I may not grant you neither of their heads with my worship;[13] therefore ask what ye will else, and I shall fulfil your desire.'

'I will ask none other thing,' said the lady.

So when Balin was ready to depart, he saw the Lady of the Lake which by her means had slain his mother; and he had sought her three year before. And when it was told him how she had asked his head of King Arthur, he went to her straight and said,

'Evil be ye found:[14] ye would have mine head, and therefore ye shall lose yours!'

And with his sword lightly[15] he smote off her head before King Arthur.

'Alas, for shame!' said the king. 'Why have ye do so? Ye have shamed me and all my court, for this lady was a lady that I was much beholding to, and hither she came under my safe-conduct. Therefore I shall never forgive you that trespass.'[16]

'Sir,' said Balin, 'me forthinketh of[17] your displeasure, for this same lady was the untruest lady living, and by enchantment and by sorcery she hath been the destroyer of many good knights, and she was causer that my mother was brent through her falsehood and treachery.'

'For what cause soever[18] ye had,' said Arthur, 'ye should have forborne in my presence. Therefore think not the con-

---

[11] *A misreading of the French 'je vos obliai a demander' ('I forgot to ask you')*

[12] I do not care if

[13] honour forbids me to grant you either

[14] may you be cursed

[15] quickly

[16] offence

[17] I grieve at

[18] whatever reason

trary; ye shall repent it, for such another despite[19] had I never in my court. Therefore withdraw you out of my court in all haste that ye may!'

Then Balin took up the head of the lady and bore it with him to his ostry,[20] and there met with his squire that was sorry he had displeased King Arthur, and so they rode forth out of town.

'Now,' said Balin, 'we must depart; therefore take thou this head and bear it to my friends and tell them how I have sped,[1] and tell them in Northumberland how my most foe is dead. Also tell them how I am out of prison, and what adventure befell me at the getting of this sword.'

'Alas!' said the squire, 'ye are greatly to blame for to displease King Arthur.'

'As for that,' said Balin, 'I will hie me in all the haste that I may to meet with King Rions and destroy him, other else to die therefore.[2] And if it may hap me[3] to win him, then will King Arthur be my good friend.'

'Sir, where shall I meet with you?' said his squire.

'In King Arthur's court,' said Balin.

So his squire and he departed at that time. Then King Arthur and all the court made great dole and had great shame of the Lady of the Lake. Then the king buried her richly.

So at that time there was a knight the which was the king's son of Ireland, and his name was Lanceor, the which was an orgulous[4] knight and accounted himself one of the best of the court. And he had great despite[5] at Balin for the achieving of the sword, that any should be accounted more hardy[6] or more of prowess, and he asked King Arthur license to ride after Balin and to revenge the despite[7] that he had done.

'Do your best,' said Arthur. 'I am right wroth with Balin. I would he were quit of the despite[8] that he hath done unto me and my court.'

Then this Lanceor went to his ostry[9] to make him ready. So in the meanwhile came Merlin unto the court of King Arthur, and anon was told him the adventure of the sword and the death of the Lady of the Lake.

---

[19] insult
[20] lodging
[1] succeeded
[2] or die in the attempt
[3] if I should have the good fortune
[4] proud, boastful

[5] resentment
[6] brave
[7] avenge the wrong
[8] I wish he would redeem the wrong
[9] lodging

'Now shall I say you,' said Merlin; 'this same damsel that here standeth,[10] that brought the sword unto your court, I shall tell you the cause of her coming. She is the falsest damsel that liveth — she shall not say nay! For she hath a brother, a passing good knight of prowess and a full true man, and this damsel loved another knight that held her as paramour. And this good knight, her brother, met with the knight that held her to paramour, and slew him by force of his hands. And when this false damsel understood this she went to the Lady Lyle of Avalon and took her his sword and besought her of help to be revenged on her own brother.

'And so this Lady Lyle of Avalon took her this sword that she brought with her, and told there should no man pull it out of the sheath but if he be one of the best knights of this realm, and he should be hardy[6] and full of prowess; and with that sword he should slay his brother. This was the cause, damsel, that ye came into this court. I know it as well as ye. God would ye had not come here; but ye came never in fellowship of worshipful folk for to do good, but always great harm. And that knight that hath achieved the sword shall be destroyed through the sword; for which will be great damage,[11] for there liveth not a knight of more prowess than he is. And he shall do unto you, my lord Arthur, great honour and kindness; and it is great pity he shall not endure but a while, for of his strength and hardiness[12] I know him not living his match.'

So this knight of Ireland armed him at all points and dressed his shield on his shoulder and mounted upon horseback and took his glaive[13] in his hand, and rode after a great pace as much as his horse might drive.[14] And within a little space, on a mountain, he had a sight of Balin, and with a loud voice he cried,

'Abide, knight! for else ye shall abide whether ye will either no! And the shield that is tofore you shall not help you,' said this Irish knight, 'therefore come I after you.'

'Peradventure,'[15] said Balin, 'ye had been better to have hold you at home. For many a man weeneth to put his enemy to a rebuke,[16] and oft it falleth on himself. Out of what court be ye come from?' said Balin.

---

[10] *The French romance says that the damsel had in the meantime returned to court*

[11] pity

[12] bravery

[13] lance

[14] as fast as his horse could go

[15] perchance

[16] expects to defeat his opponent

'I am come from the court of King Arthur,' said the knight of Ireland, 'that am come hither to revenge the despite[17] ye did this day unto King Arthur and to his court.'

'Well,' said Balin, 'I see well I must have ado with you; that me forthinketh[18] that I have grieved King Arthur or any of his court. And your quarrel is full simple,' said Balin, 'unto me;[19] for the lady that is dead did to me great damage, and else I would have been loath as any knight that liveth for to slay a lady.'

'Make you ready, said the knight Lanceor, 'and dress you unto me,[20] for that one[1] shall abide in the field.'

Then they feautred[2] their spears in their rests and came togethei as much as their horses might drive. And the Irish knight smote Balin on the shield that all went to shivers[3] off his spear. And Balin smote him again through the shield, and the hauberk perished,[4] and so bore him through the body and over the horse crupper; and anon turned his horse fiercely and drew out his sword, and wist not that he had slain him.

Then[5] he saw him lie as a dead corpse, he looked about him and was ware of a damsel that came riding full fast as the horse might drive, on a fair palfrey. And when she espied that Lanceor was slain she made sorrow out of measure and said,

'Ah! Balin, two bodies thou hast slain in one heart, and two hearts in one body, and two souls thou hast lost.'

And therewith she took the sword from her love that lay dead, and fell to the ground in a swough. And when she arose she made great dole out of measure, which sorrow grieved Balin passingly sore. And he went unto her for to have taken the sword out of her hand; but she held it so fast he might not take it out of her hand but if he should have hurt her. And suddenly she set the pommel to the ground, and rove[6] herself throughout the body.

When Balin espied her deeds he was passing heavy in his heart and ashamed that so fair a damsel had destroyed herself for the love of[7] his death. 'Alas!' said Balin, 'me repenteth sore the death of this knight for the love of[7] this damsel, for

---

[17] avenge the wrong
[18] much as it distresses me
[19] you have little reason to pick a quarrel with me
[20] prepare to fight with me
[1] one of us

[2] fixed
[3] pieces
[4] coat of mail was destroyed
[5] when
[6] stabbed
[7] because of

there was much true love betwixt them.' And so for sorrow he might no longer behold them, but turned his horse and looked toward a fair forest.

And then was he ware by his arms that there came riding his brother Balan. And when they were met they put off their helms and kissed together and wept for joy and pity. Then Balan said,

'Brother, I little weened to have met with you at this sudden adventure, but I am right glad of your deliverance of your dolorous prisonment: for a man told me in the Castle of Four Stones that ye were delivered, and that man had seen you in the court of King Arthur. And therefore I came hither into this country, for here I supposed to find you.'

And anon Balin told his brother of his adventure of the sword and the death of the Lady of the Lake, and how King Arthur was displeased with him.

'Wherefore he sent this knight after me that lieth here dead. And the death of this damsel grieveth me sore.'

'So doth it me,' said Balan, 'but ye must take the adventure that God will ordain you.'

'Truly,' said Balan, 'I am right heavy that my lord Arthur is displeased with me, for he is the most worshipfullest king that reigneth now in earth; and his love I will get other else I will put my life in adventure.[8] For King Rions lieth at the siege of the Castle Terrabil, and thither will we draw in all goodly haste to prove our worship and prowess upon him.'

'I will well,' said Balan, 'that ye do so; and I will ride with you and put my body in adventure[8] with you, as a brother ought to do.'

'Now go we hence,' said Balin, 'and well we be met.'

The meanwhile as they talked there came a dwarf from the city of Camelot on horseback as much as he might,[9] and found the dead bodies; wherefore he made great dole, and pulled his hair for sorrow, and said,

'Which of two knights have done this deed?'

'Whereby asketh thou?' said Balan.

'For I would wit,' said the dwarf.

'It was I,' said Balin, 'that slew this knight in my defendant;[10] for hither he came to chase me, and either I must slay him either he me. And this damsel slew herself for his love,

---

[8] risk my life   [10] in self-defence
[9] as fast as he could

which repenteth me. And for her sake I shall owe all women
the better will and service all the days of my life.'

'Alas!' said the dwarf, 'thou hast done great damage unto
thyself. For this knight that is here dead was one of the most
valiant men that lived. And trust well, Balin, the kin of this
knight will chase you through the world till they have slain
you.'

'As for that,' said Balin, 'them I fear not greatly; but I am
right heavy that I should displease my lord, King Arthur, for
the death of this knight.'

So as they talked together there came a king of Cornwall
riding, which hight King Mark. And when he saw these two
bodies dead, and understood how they were dead by the two
knights above-said, then made the king great sorrow for the
true love that was betwixt them, and said, 'I will not depart
till I have on this earth made a tomb.' And there he pight[11]
his pavilions and sought all the country to find a tomb, and
in a church they found one was fair and rich. And then the
king let put them both in the earth, and laid the tomb upon
them, and wrote the names of them both on the tomb, how
'here lieth Lanceor, the king's son of Ireland, that at his own
request was slain by the hands of Balin,' and how 'this lady
Columbe and paramour to him slew herself with his sword for
dole and sorrow.'

The meanwhile as this was a-doing in came Merlin to King
Mark and saw all this doing.

'Here shall be,' said Merlin, 'in this same place the greatest
battle betwixt two knights that ever was or ever shall be, and
the truest lovers; and yet none of them shall slay the other.'

And there Merlin wrote their names upon the tomb with
letters of gold, that shall fight in that place: which names was
Lancelot du Lake and Tristram.

'Thou art a marvellous man,' said King Mark unto Merlin,
'that speakest of such marvels. Thou art a boisterous man and
an unlikely[12] to tell of such deeds. What is thy name?' said
King Mark.

'At this time,' said Merlin, 'I will not tell you. But at that
time Sir Tristram is taken with his sovereign lady, then shall
ye hear and know my name; and at that time ye shall hear
tidings that shall not please you. Ah, Balin!' said Merlin,
'thou hast done thyself great hurt that thou saved not this

[11] pitched, set up   [12] unseemly

lady that slew herself; for thou mightest have saved her an thou hadst would.'

'By the faith of my body,'[13] said Balin, 'I might not save her, for she slew herself suddenly.'

'Me repenteth it,'[14] said Merlin; 'because of the death of that lady thou shalt strike a stroke most dolorous that ever man struck, except the stroke of Our Lord Jesus Christ. For thou shalt hurt the truest knight and the man of most worship that now liveth; and through that stroke three kingdoms shall be brought into great poverty, misery and wretchedness twelve year. And the knight shall not be whole[15] of that wound many years.' Then Merlin took his leave.

'Nay,' said Balin, 'not so; for an I wist thou said sooth, I would do so perilous a deed that I would slay myself to make thee a liar.'

Therewith Merlin vanished away suddenly, and then Balin and his brother took their leave of King Mark.

'But first,' said the king, 'tell me your name.'

'Sir,' said Balan, 'ye may see he beareth two swords, and thereby ye may call him the Knight with the Two Swords.'

And so departed King Mark unto Camelot to King Arthur.

And Balin took the way to King Rions, and as they rode together they met with Merlin disguised so that they knew him nought.

'But whitherward ride ye?' said Merlin.

'We had little ado[16] to tell you,' said these two knights.

'But what is thy name?' said Balin.

'At this time,' said Merlin, 'I will not tell.'

'It is an evil sign,' said the knights, 'that thou art a true man, that[17] thou wilt not tell thy name.'

'As for that,' said Merlin, 'be as it be may. But I can tell you wherefore ye ride this way: for to meet with King Rions. But it will not avail you without ye have my counsel.'

'Ah,' said Balin, 'ye are Merlin! We will be ruled by your counsel!'

'Come on,' said Merlin, 'and ye shall have great worship. And look that ye do knightly, for ye shall have need.'

'As for that,' said Balin, 'dread you not, for we will do what we may.'

---

[13] my faith
[14] this distresses me
[15] healed

[16] no reason
[17] it is a sign that you are not an honest man if

Then there lodged Merlin and these two knights in a wood among the leaves beside the highway, and took off the bridles of their horses and put them to grass, and laid them[18] down to rest till it was nigh midnight. Then Merlin bade them rise and make them ready: 'for here cometh the king nighhand, that was[19] stolen away from his host with a three score horses of his best knights, and twenty of them rode tofore the lord to warn the Lady de Vaunce that the king was coming.' For that night King Rions should have lain with her.

'Which is the king?' said Balin.

'Abide,' said Merlin, 'for here in a strait way ye shall meet with him.' And therewith he showed Balin and his brother the king.

And anon they met with him, and smote him down and wounded him freshly,[20] and laid him to the ground. And there they slew on the right hand and on the left hand more than forty of his men; and the remnant fled. Then went they again unto King Rions and would have slain him, had he not yielded him unto their grace. Then said he thus:

'Knights full of prowess, slay me not! For by my life ye may win, and by my death little.'

'Ye say sooth,' said the knights, and so laid him on a horse-litter.

So with that Merlin vanished, and came to King Arthur aforehand[1] and told him how his most enemy was taken and discomfit.[2]

'By whom?' said King Arthur.

'By two knights,' said Merlin, 'that would fain have your lordship. And to-morrow ye shall know what knights they are.'

So anon after came the Knight with the Two Swords and his brother, and brought with them King Rions of North Wales, and there delivered him to the porters, and charged them with him.[3]

And so they two returned again[4] in the dawning of the day.

Then King Arthur came to King Rions and said,

'Sir king, ye are welcome. By what adventure came ye hither?'

---

[18] themselves
[19] had
[20] grievously

[1] in advance
[2] vanquished
[3] entrusted him to them
[4] went back

'Sir,' said King Rions, 'I came hither by a hard adventure.'
'Who won you?' said King Arthur.

'Sir,' said he, 'the Knight with the Two Swords and his brother, which are two marvellous knights of prowess.'

'I know them not,' said Arthur, 'but much am I beholding unto them.'

'Ah, sir,' said Merlin, 'I shall tell you. It is Balin that achieved the sword and his brother Balan, a good knight: there liveth not a better of prowess, nother of worthiness. And it shall be the greatest dole of him that ever I knew of knight; for he shall not long endure.'

'Alas,' said King Arthur, 'that is great pity; for I am much beholding unto him, and I have evil deserved it again for his kindness.'[5]

'Nay, nay,' said Merlin, 'he shall do much more for you, and that shall ye know in haste.'

. . . So within a day or two[6] King Arthur was somewhat sick, and he let pitch his pavilion in a meadow, and there he laid him down on a pallet to sleep; but he might have no rest. Right so he heard a great noise of a horse, and therewith the king looked out at the porch door of the pavilion and saw a knight coming even[7] by him making great dole.

'Abide, fair sir,' said Arthur, 'and tell me wherefore thou makest this sorrow.'

'Ye may little amend[8] me,' said the knight, and so passed forth to the castle of Meliot.

And anon after that came Balin. And when he saw King Arthur he alight of his horse and came to the king on foot and salewed him. 'By my head,' said Arthur, 'ye be welcome. Sir, right now came riding this way a knight making great mourn, and for what cause I cannot tell. Wherefore I would desire of you of your courtesy and of your gentleness to fetch again that knight either by force either by his good will.'

'I shall do more for your lordship than that,' said Balin, 'other else I will grieve him.'[9]

---

[5] I have not deserved that he should return kindness

[6] *Here M describes in some detail (O pp. 75–9) Arthur's attack on Nero, King Rions's brother. Arthur's brother-in-law, King Lot of Orkney, fights on Nero's side and is killed in battle.*

[7] close

[8] help

[9] and hurt him if need be

So Balin rode more than a pace and found the knight with a damsel under a forest and said,

'Sir knight, ye must come with me unto King Arthur for to tell him of your sorrow.'

'That will I not,' said the knight, 'for it will harm me greatly and do you none avail.'[10]

'Sir,' said Balin, 'I pray you make you ready, for ye must go with me other else I must fight with you and bring you by force. And that were me loath to do.'

'Will ye be my warrant,'[11] said the knight, 'an I go with you?'

'Yea,' said Balin, 'other else, by the faith of my body,[12] I will die therefore.'

And so he made him ready to go with Balin and left the damsel still.[13] And as they were even before[14] Arthur's pavilion, there came one invisible and smote the knight that went with Balin throughout the body with a spear.

'Alas!' said the knight, 'I am slain under your conduit[15] with a knight called Garlon. Therefore take my horse that is better than yours, and ride to the damsel and follow the quest that I was in as she will lead you, and revenge my death when ye may.'

'That shall I do,' said Balin, 'and that[16] I make a vow to God and knighthood.'

And so he departed from King Arthur with great sorrow.

So King Arthur let bury this knight richly, and made mention on his tomb how here was slain Berbeus and by whom the treachery was done, of[17] the knight Garlon. But ever the damsel bore the truncheon[18] of the spear with her that Sir Harleus le Berbeus was slain withal.

So Balin and the damsel rode into the forest and there met with a knight that had been a-hunting. And that knight asked Balin for what cause he made so great sorrow.

'Me list not[19] to tell,' said Balin.

'Now,' said the knight, 'an I were armed as ye be, I would fight with you but if ye told me.'

---

[10] no good	[15] protection
[11] protect me	[16] to do this
[12] my faith	[17] by
[13] where she was	[18] shaft
[14] close to	[19] I do not wish

'That should little need,' said Balin, 'I am not afeard to tell you,' and so told him all the case[20] how it was.

'Ah,' said the knight, 'is this all? Here I ensure you by the faith of my body never to depart from you while my life lasteth.'

And so they went to their ostry[1] and armed them and so rode forth with Balin. And as they came by an hermitage even[2] by a churchyard, there came Garlon invisible and smote this knight, Perin de Mount Beliard, throughout the body with a glaive.[3]

'Alas!' said the knight, 'I am slain by this traitor knight that rideth invisible.'

'Alas,' said Balin, 'this is not the first despite[4] that he hath done me!'

And there the hermit and Balin buried the knight under a rich[5] stone and a tomb royal. And on the morn they found letters of gold written how that Sir Gawain shall revenge his father's death, King Lot, on King Pellinor.

And anon after this Balin and the damsel rode forth till they came to a castle. And anon Balin alight and went in. And as soon as Balin came within the castle's gate the portcullis were let down at his back, and there fell many men about the damsel[6] and would have slain her. When Balin saw that, he was sore grieved for he might not help her. But then he went up into a tower and leapt over the walls into the ditch and hurt not himself. And anon he pulled out his sword and would have fought with them. And they all said nay, they would not fight with him, for they did nothing but the old custom of this castle, and told him that their lady was sick and had lain many years, and she might not be whole but if she had blood in a silver dish full, of a clean maid and a king's daughter. 'And therefore the custom of this castle is that there shall no damsel pass this way but she shall bleed of her blood a silver dish full.'

'Well,' said Balin, 'she shall bleed as much as she may bleed, but I will not lose the life of her while my life lasteth.'

And so Balin made her to bleed by her good will, but her

---

[20] circumstances
[1] lodgings
[2] close
[3] spear
[4] wrong
[5] beautiful
[6] many men surrounded the damsel

blood helped not the lady. And so she and he rested there all
that night and had good cheer, and in the morning they passed
on their ways. And as it telleth after in the *Sankgreall*, that
Sir Perceval his[7] sister helped that lady with her blood, whereof
she was dead.

Then they rode three or four days and never met with
adventure. And so by fortune they were lodged with a gentleman that was a rich man and well at ease. And as they sat
at supper Balin heard one complain grievously by him in a
chamber.

'What is this noise?' said Balin.

'Forsooth,' said his host, 'I will tell you. I was but late at
a jousting and there I jousted with a knight that is brother
unto King Pellam, and twice I smote him down. And then
he promised to quit me on[8] my best friend. And so he wounded
thus my son that cannot be whole[9] till I have of that knight's
blood. And he rideth all invisible, but[10] I know not his name.'

'Ah,' said Balin, 'I know that knight's name, which is Garlon,
and he hath slain two knights of mine in the same manner.
Therefore I had liefer meet with that knight than all the gold
in this realm, for the despite[11] he hath done me.'

'Well,' said his host, 'I shall tell you how. King Pellam of
Listenoise hath made do cry in all the country a great feast
that shall be within these twenty days, and no knight may
come there but he bring his wife with him other his paramour. And that your enemy and mine ye shall see that day.'

'Then I promise you,' said Balin, 'part of his blood to heal
your son withal.'

'Then we will be forward[12] to-morn,' said he.

So on the morn they rode all three toward King Pellam,
and they had fifteen days' journey or they came thither. And
that same day began the great feast. And so they alight and
stabled their horses and went into the castle, but Balin's host
might not be let in because he had no lady. But Balin was well
received and brought unto a chamber and unarmed him. And
there was brought him robes to his pleasure, and would have
had Balin[13] leave his sword behind him.

'Nay,' said Balin, 'that will I not, for it is the custom of my

7 Perceval's
8 take his revenge upon
9 healed
10 and

11 wrong
12 set off
13 they wished Balin to

country a knight[14] always to keep his weapon with him. Other else,' said he, 'I will depart as I came.'

Then they gave him leave with his sword,[15] and so he went into the castle and was among knights of worship, and his lady afore him. So after this Balin asked a knight and said,

'Is there not a knight in this court which his[16] name is Garlon?'

'Yes, sir, yonder he goeth, the knight with the black face, for he is the marvellest knight that is now living. And he destroyeth many good knights, for he goeth invisible.'

'Well,' said Balin, 'is that he?' Then Balin advised him[17] long, and thought: 'If I slay him here, I shall not escape. And if I leave him now, peradventure[18] I shall never meet with him again at such a steven,[19] and much harm he will do an he live.'

And therewith this Garlon espied that Balin visaged[20] him, so he came and slapped him on the face with the back of his hand and said,

'Knight, why beholdest thou me so? For shame, eat thy meat and do that[1] thou come for.'

'Thou sayest sooth,' said Balin, 'this is not the first spite[2] that thou hast done me, and therefore I will do that I come for.' And rose him up fiercely and clave his head to the shoulders.

'Now give me the truncheon,'[3] said Balin to his lady, 'that he slew your knight with.'

And anon she gave it him, for always she bore the truncheon with her. And therewith Balin smote him through the body and said openly,

'With that truncheon thou slewest a good knight, and now it sticketh in thy body.' Then Balin called unto his host and said, 'Now may ye fetch blood enough to heal your son withal.'

So anon all the knights rose from the table for to set on Balin. And King Pellam himself arose up fiercely and said,

'Knight, why hast thou slain my brother? Thou shalt die therefore or thou depart.'

'Well,' said Balin, 'do it yourself.'

---

[14] for a knight	[19] occasion
[15] to keep his sword	[20] stared at
[16] whose	[1] what
[17] reflected	[2] wrong
[18] perhaps	[3] shaft

'Yes,' said King Pellam, 'there shall be no man have ado with thee but I myself, for the love of my brother.'

Then King Pellam caught in his hand a grim[4] weapon and smote eagerly[5] at Balin, but he[6] put his sword betwixt his head and the stroke, and therewith his sword brast in sunder.[7] And when Balin was weaponless[8] he ran into a chamber for to seek a weapon, and from chamber to chamber, and no weapon could he find. And always King Pellam followed after him. And at last he entered into a chamber which was marvellously dight[9] and rich, and a bed arrayed[10] with cloth of gold, the richest that might be, and one lying therein. And thereby stood a table of clean gold with four pillars of silver that bore up the table, and upon the table stood a marvellous spear strangely[11] wrought.

So when Balin saw the spear he got it in his hand and turned to King Pellam and felled him and smote him passingly sore with that spear, that[12] King Pellam fell down in a swough. And therewith the castle broke, roof and walls, and fell down to the earth. And Balin fell down and might not stir hand nor foot, and for the most party of[13] that castle was dead through the Dolorous Stroke.

Right so lay King Pellam and Balin three days.

Then Merlin came thither, and took up Balin and gat him a good horse, for his was dead, and bade him void out of[14] that country.

'Sir, I would have my damsel,' said Balin.

'Lo,' said Merlin, 'where she lieth dead.'

And King Pellam lay so many years sore wounded, and might never be whole[15] till that Galahad the Haut Prince healed him in the quest of the Sankgreall. For in that place was part of the blood of Our Lord Jesu Christ, which Joseph of Arimathea brought into this land. And there himself lay

---

[4] formidable. *According to* F, *the 'grim weapon' was a great log of wood.*

[5] fiercely

[6] = Balin

[7] broke in two

[8] *Balin still had his other sword with him, the one with which he was to kill 'the man he loved most in the world.' The fact was deliberately overlooked both in* F *and in* M *because any reference to it would have spoilt the motivation of the Dolorous Stroke.*

[9] furnished

[10] covered

[11] wonderfully

[12] so that

[13] most of the people in

[14] leave

[15] healed

in that rich bed. And that was the spear which Longius smote Our Lord with to the heart. And King Pellam was nigh of Joseph his kin,[16] and that was the most worshipfullest man on life in those days, and great pity it was of his hurt, for through that stroke it turned to great dole, tray and teen.[17]

Then departed Balin from Merlin, 'for,'[18] he said, 'never in this world we part neither meet no more.' So he rode forth through the fair countries and cities and found the people dead and slain on every side, and all that ever were on live cried and said,

'Ah, Balin! Thou has done and caused great damage in these countries! For the Dolorous Stroke thou gave unto King Pellam these three countries are destroyed. And doubt not but the vengeance will fall on thee at the last!'

But when Balin was past those countries he was passing fain,[19] and so he rode eight days or he met with many adventure.[20] And at the last he came into a fair forest in a valley, and was ware of a tower. And there beside he met with a great horse tied to a tree, and beside there sat a fair knight on the ground and made great mourning, and he was a likely[1] man and a well made. Balin said,

'God you save! Why be ye so heavy?[2] Tell me, and I will amend, an I may, to my power.'[3]

'Sir knight,' he said, 'thou dost me great grief, for I was in merry thoughts and thou puttest me to more pain.'

Then Balin went a little from him and looked on his horse; then heard Balin him say thus:

'Ah, fair lady! Why have ye broken my promise? For ye promised me to meet me here by noon. And I may curse you that ever ye gave me that sword, for with this sword I will slay myself,' and pulled it out.

And therewith came Balin and stert[4] unto him and took him by the hand.

'Let go my hand,' said the knight, 'or else I shall slay thee!'

'That shall not need,' said Balin, 'for I shall promise you my help to get you your lady an ye will tell me where she is.'

'What is your name?' said the knight.

---

[16] close kin to Joseph

[17] suffering and sorrow

[18] and

[19] eager

[20] adventures

[1] handsome

[2] sad

[3] as far as I am able

[4] rushed

'Sir, my name is Balin le Savage.'

'Ah, sir, I know you well enough: ye are the Knight with the Two Swords, and the man of most prowess of your hands living.'

'What is your name?' said Balin.

'My name is Garnish of the Mount, a poor man's son, and by[5] my prowess and hardiness[6] a duke made me knight and gave me lands. His name is Duke Harmel, and his daughter is she that I love, and she me, as I deemed.'

'How far is she hence?' said Balin.

'But six mile,' said the knight.

'Now ride we hence,' said these two knights.

So they rode more than a pace[7] till that they came to a fair castle well walled and ditched.

'I will into the castle,' said Balin, 'and look if she be there.'

So he went in and searched from chamber to chamber, and found her bed, but she was not there. Then Balin looked into a fair little garden, and under a laurel tree he saw her lie upon a quilt of green samite,[8] and a knight in her arms, fast halsing either other.[9] and under their heads grass and herbs. When Balin saw her lie so with the foulest knight that ever he saw, and she a fair lady, then Balin went through all the chambers again, and told the knight how he found her as she had slept fast, and so brought him in the place where she lay fast sleeping.

And when Garnish beheld her so lying, for pure sorrow his mouth and nose burst out on-bleeding, and with his sword he smote off both their heads, and then he made sorrow out of measure, and said,

'O Balin! much sorrow hast thou brought unto me, for hadst thou not showed me that sight I should have passed[10] my sorrow.'

'Forsooth,' said Balin, 'I did it to this intent that it should better thy courage,[11] and that ye might see and know her falsehood, and to cause you to leave love of such a lady. God knoweth I did none other but as I would ye did to me.'

'Alas!' said Garnish, 'now is my sorrow double that I may not[12] endure, now have I slain that I most loved in all my life!'

And therewith suddenly[13] he rove himself on[14] his own sword unto the hilts.

---

5 for
6 courage
7 at a good speed
8 rich silk
9 embracing each other

10 I should have been spared
11 strengthen your resolution
12 and too great for me to
13 swiftly
14 ran upon

When Balin saw that, he dressed him[15] thenceward, lest folk would say he had slain them; and so he rode forth, and within three days, he came by a cross, and thereon were letters of gold written, that said: IT IS NOT FOR NO KNIGHT ALONE TO RIDE TOWARD THIS CASTLE. Then saw he an old hoar gentleman coming toward him, that said,

'Balin le Savage, thou passest thy bounds to come this way, therefore turn again[16] and it will avail thee.' And he vanished away anon.

And so he heard an horn blow as it had been the death of a beast. 'That blast,' said Balin, 'is blown for me, for I am the prize and yet am I not dead.' Anon withal he saw an hundred ladies and many knights that welcomed him with fair semblaunt,[17] and made him passing good cheer unto his sight,[18] and led him into the castle, and there was dancing and minstrelry and all manner of joy. Then the chief lady of the castle said,

'Knight with the Two Swords, ye must have ado and joust with a knight hereby that keepeth an island, for there may no man pass this way but he must joust or he pass.'

'That is an unhappy custom,' said Balin, 'that a knight may not pass this way but if he joust.'

'Ye shall not have ado but with one knight,' said the lady.

'Well,' said Balin, 'syn I shall, thereto I am ready; but travelling men are oft weary and their horses too, but though my horse be weary my heart is not weary. I would be fain there my death should be.'[19]

'Sir,' said a knight to Balin, 'methinketh your shield is not good, I will lend you a bigger, thereof I pray you.'

And so he took the shield that was unknown and left his own, and so rode unto the island, and put him and his horse in a great boat. And when he came on the other side he met with a damsel, and she said,

'O knight Balin, why have ye left your own shield? Alas! ye have put yourself in great danger, for by your shield ye should have been known. It is great pity of you as ever was of knight, for of[20] thy prowess and hardiness[1] thou hast no fellow living.'

'Me repenteth,' said Balin, 'that ever I came within this

---

[15] went
[16] back
[17] received him with pleasant looks
[18] showed him great welcome
[19] even though I should find death
[20] as to
[1] bravery

country, but I may not turn now again[2] for shame, and what adventure shall fall to me, be it life or death, I will take the adventure that shall come to me.'

And then he looked on his armour and understood he was well armed, and therewith blessed him[3] and mounted upon his horse. Then afore him he saw come riding out of a castle a knight, and his horse trapped all red,[4] and himself in the same colour. When this knight in the red beheld Balin, him thought it should be his brother Balin because of his two swords,[5] but because he knew not his shield he deemed it was not he.

And so they aventred[6] their spears and came marvellously fast together, and they smote other[7] in the shields, but their spears and their course[8] were so big[9] that it bare down horse and man, that they lay both in a swoon; but Balin was bruised sore with the fall of the horse, for he was weary of travel. And Balan was the first that rose on foot and drew his sword, and went toward Balin, and he arose and went against him; but Balan smote Balin first, and he put up his shield and smote him through the shield and tamed[10] his helm. Then Balin smote him again[2] with that unhappy sword, and well-nigh had felled his brother Balan, and so they fought there together till their breaths failed.

Then Balin looked up to the castle and saw the towers stand full of ladies. So they went unto battle again, and wounded everych other dolefully, and then they breathed ofttimes, and so went unto battle that all the place thereas[11] they fought was blood red. And at that time there was none of them both but they had either smitten other seven great wounds, so that the least of them might have been the death of the mightiest giant in this world.

Then they went to battle again so marvellously that doubt[12] it was to hear of that battle for the great blood-shedding, and their hauberks unnailed,[13] that naked they were on every side.

---

[2] back
[3] crossed himself
[4] in red trappings
[5] *Balin had only one sword left. 'Because of his two swords' is a misreading of 'chelui a deus espees' ('quant il voit chelui a deus espees') used in F as a proper name.*

[6] levelled. *Possibly a corruption of* afeautryd, *'set.'*
[7] each other
[8] coming together
[9] strong
[10] split
[11] where
[12] a fearful thing
[13] their coats of mail fell apart

At the last Balan, the younger brother, withdrew him a little and laid him down. Then said Balin le Savage,

'What knight art thou? For or now I[14] found never no knight that matched me.'

'My name is,' said he, 'Balan, brother unto the good knight Balin.'

'Alas,' said Balin, 'that ever I should see this day!' and therewith he fell backward in a swoon.

Then Balan yode[15] on all four, feet and hands, and put off the helm of his brother, and might not know him by the visage, it was so full hewn and bled; but when he awoke he said,

'O Balan, my brother! Thou hast slain me and I thee, wherefore all the wide world shall speak of us both.'

'Alas,' said Balin, 'that ever I saw this day, that through mishap[16] I might not know you! For I espied well your two swords,[17] but because ye had another shield I deemed ye had been another knight.'

'Alas,' said Balin, 'all that made an unhappy knight[18] in the castle, for he caused me to leave mine own shield to our both's destruction. And if I might live I would destroy that castle for ill customs.'

'That were[19] well done,' said Balan, 'for I had never grace[20] to depart from them syn that I came hither, for here it happed me to slay a knight that kept this island, and syn might I never depart. And no more should ye, brother, and ye might have slain me as ye have and escaped yourself with the life.'

Right so came the lady of the tower with four knights and six ladies and six yeomen unto them, and there she heard how they made their moan either to other and said, 'We came both out of one womb, that is to say one mother's belly, and so shall we lie both in one pit.' So Balan prayed the lady of her gentleness for his true service that she would bury them both in that same place there the battle was done, and she granted them, with weeping, it should be done richly in the best manner.

'Now, will ye send for a priest, that we may receive our sacrament, and receive the blessed body of Our Lord Jesu Christ?'

---

[14] until now I have
[15] went
[16] ill fortune
[17] *See above, note 5.*

[18] all this was done by an unlucky knight
[19] would have been
[20] the good fortune

'Yea,' said the lady, 'it shall be done;' and so she sent for a priest and gave[1] them their rites.

'Now,' said Balin, 'when we are buried in one tomb, and the mention made over us how two brethren slew each other, there will never good knight nor good man see our tomb but they will pray for our souls.' And so all the ladies and gentlewomen wept for pity.

Then anon Balan died, but Balin died not till the midnight after. And so were they buried both, and the lady let make a mention of Balan how he was there slain by his brother's hands, but she knew not Balin's name.

In the morn came Merlin and let write Balin's name on the tomb with letters of gold, that HERE LIETH BALIN LE SAVAGE THAT WAS THE KNIGHT WITH THE TWO SWORDS, AND HE THAT SMOTE THE DOLOROUS STROKE. Also Merlin let make there a bed, that there should never man lie therein but he went out of his wit. Yet Lancelot du Lake forbid[2] that bed through his noblesse.[3]

And anon after Balin was dead Merlin took his[4] sword and took off the pommel and set on another pommel. So Merlin bade a knight that stood before him to handle that sword, and he essayed it and might not handle it. Then Merlin laughed.

'Why laugh ye?' said the knight.

'This is the cause,' said Merlin: 'there shall never man handle this sword but the best knight of the world, and that shall be Sir Lancelot other else Galahad, his son. And Lancelot with this sword shall slay the man that in the world he loveth best, that shall be Sir Gawain.'

And all this he let write in the pommel of the sword.

Then Merlin let make a bridge of iron and steel into that island, and it was but half a foot broad, 'and there shall never man pass that bridge, nother have hardiness[5] to go over it but if he were a passing good man and a good knight without treachery or villainy.' Also the scabbard of Balin's sword Merlin left it on this side the island, that Galahad should find it. Also Merlin let make by his subtlety[6] that Balin's sword was put in a marble stone standing upright as great as a millstone, and hoved[7] always above the water, and did many years.

---

[1] he gave
[2] destroyed. *The spell was to be broken by Lancelot's ring.*
[3] valour
[4] = Balin's
[5] courage
[6] cunning
[7] rose

And so by adventure it swam down the stream to the City of Camelot, that is in English called Winchester.[8] And the same day Galahad the Haute Prince came with King Arthur, and so Galahad brought with him the scabbard and achieved the sword that was in the marble stone hoving[9] upon the water. And on Whitsunday he achieved the sword, as it is rehearsed[10] in *The Book of the Sankgreall*.

Soon after this was done Merlin came to King Arthur and told him of the Dolorous Stroke that Balin gave King Pellam, and how Balin and Balan fought together the most marvellous[11] battle that ever was heard of, and how they were buried both in one tomb.

'Alas!' said King Arthur, 'this is the greatest pity that ever I heard tell of two knights, for in this world I knew never such two knights.'

THUS ENDETH THE TALE OF BALIN AND OF BALAN, TWO BRETHREN THAT WERE BORN IN NORTHUMBERLAND, THAT WERE TWO PASSING GOOD KNIGHTS AS EVER WERE IN THOSE DAYS.

[8] *See below,* The Fair Maid of Astolat, *note 2.*
[9] floating
[10] narrated
[11] hardest

Pelleas and Ettard

Three knights, Gawain, Ywain, and Marhalt, each accompanied by a damsel of his choice, go in search of adventures. Ywain 'takes the way that lies west,' Marhalt goes south and Gawain north (cf. note 12).

Now will we begin at Sir Gawain that held that way till that he came to a fair manor where dwelled an old knight and a good householder. And there Sir Gawain asked the knight if he knew of any adventures.

'I shall show you to-morn,' said the knight, 'marvellous adventures.'

So on the morn they rode all in same[1] to the Forest of Adventures till they came to a laund,[2] and thereby they found a cross. And as they stood and hoved,[3] there came by them the fairest knight and the seemliest[4] man that ever they saw, but he made the greatest dole that ever man made. And then he was ware of Sir Gawain and salewed him, and prayed to God to send him much worship.[5]

'As for that,' said Sir Gawain, 'gramercy. Also I pray to God send you honour and worship.'

'Ah,' said the knight, 'I may lay that on side,[6] for sorrow and shame cometh unto me after worship.'

And therewith he passed unto that one side of the laund,[2] and on the other side saw Sir Gawain ten knights that hoved[3] and made them ready with their shields and with their spears against that one knight that came by Sir Gawain. Then this one knight feautred[7] a great spear, and one of the knights encountered with him. But this woeful knight smote him so hard that he fell over his horse[8] tail. So this dolorous knight served[9] them all, that at the leastway[10] he smote down horse

---

[1] together
[2] glade
[3] waited
[4] handsomest
[5] honour

[6] I can dispense with that
[7] fixed in its rest
[8] horse's
[9] treated
[10] leastways

41

and man, and all he did with one spear. And so when
they were all ten on foot they went to the one knight, and
he stood stone-still and suffered them to pull him down off his
horse, and bound him hand and foot, and tied him under the
horse[8] belly, and so led him with them.

'Ah, Jesu,' said Sir Gawain, 'this is a doleful sight to see the
yonder knight so to be entreated! And it seemeth by the
knight that he suffereth them to bind him so, for he maketh
no resistance.'

'No,' said the host, 'that is truth, for, an he would, they
all were[11] too weak for him.'

'Sir,' said the damsel[12] unto Sir Gawain, 'meseemeth it were
your worship[5] to help that dolorous knight, for methinketh
he is one of the best knights that ever I saw.'

'I would do for him,'[13] said Sir Gawain, 'but it seemeth he
would have no help.'

'No,' said the damsel, 'methinketh ye have no list[14] to help
him.'

Thus as they taked they saw a knight on the other side of
the laund,[2] all armed save the head. And on the other side
there came a dwarf on horseback, all armed save the head, with
a great mouth and a short nose. And when the dwarf came
nigh he said,

'Where is this lady should meet us here?'

And therewithal she came forth out of the wood. And then
they began to strive for the lady, for the knight said he would
have her, and the dwarf said he would have her.

'Will we do well?'[15] said the dwarf. 'Yonder is a knight at
the cross. Let it be put upon him[16], and as he deemeth it, so
shall it be.'

'I will well,' said the knight.

And so they went all three unto Sir Gawain and told him
wherefore they strove.

'Well, sirs, will ye put the matter in mine hand?'

'Yea, sir,' they said both.

'Now, damsel,' said Sir Gawain, 'ye shall stand betwixt
them both, and whither[17] ye list better[18] to go to he shall have
you.'

---

[11] would be

[12] *Gawain, Ywain, and Marhalt
met the three damsels while wait-
ing for 'any of the errant knights
to teach them unto strange adventures'* (O, *pp. 162–3*).

[13] would willingly help him

[14] desire

[15] shall we do the right thing?

[16] entrusted to

[17] to whichever one

[18] prefer

And when she was set between them both she left the knight and went to the dwarf. And then the dwarf took her up and went his way singing, and the knight went his way with great mourning.

Then came there two knights all armed and cried on hight, 'Sir Gawain, knight of the court of King Arthur! Make thee ready in haste and joust with me!'

So they ran together, that either[19] fell down. And then on foot they drew their swords and did full actually.[20] The meanwhile the other knight went to the damsel[1] and asked her why she abode with that knight, and said,

'If ye would abide with me I would be your faithful knight.'

'And with you will I be,' said the damsel, 'for I may not find in my heart to be with him, for right now here was one knight that scomfited[2] ten knights, and at the last he was cowardly led away. And therefore let us two go[3] while they fight.'

And Sir Gawain fought with that other knight long, but at the last they accorded both.[4] And then the knight prayed Sir Gawain to lodge with him that night. So as Sir Gawain went with this knight he said,

'What knight is he in this country that smote down the ten knights? For[5] when he had done so manfully he suffered them to bind him hand and foot, and so led[6] him away.'

'Ah,' said the knight, 'that is the best knight, I trow, in the world, and the most man of prowess. And it is the greatest pity of him as of any knight living, for he hath been served[7] so as he was at this time more than ten times. And his name hight Sir Pelleas; and he loveth a great lady in this country, and her name is Ettard. And so when he loved her there was[8] cried in this country a great jousts three days,[9] and all these knights of this country were there and gentlewomen. And who that proved him the best knight should have a passing good sword and a circlet of gold, and that circlet the knight should give it to the fairest lady that was at that jousts.

---

[19] with such force that both
[20] fought vigorously
[1] *i.e. the one who accompanied Gawain*
[2] defeated
[3] *The damsel considers Gawain unworthy of her company because he has allowed the knight to be ill-treated in his presence.*
[4] were reconciled
[5] And
[6] they led
[7] treated
[8] and so he loved her; and then was
[9] a great tournament which was to last three days

'And this knight Sir Pelleas was far the best of any that was there, and there were five hundred knights, but there was never man that ever Sir Pelleas met but he struck him down, other else from his horse,[10] and every day of three days he struck down twenty knights. And therefore they gave him the prize. And forthwithal he went thereas[11] the lady Ettard was and gave her the circlet and said openly she was the fairest lady that there was, and that would he prove upon any knight that would say nay.

'And so he chose her for his sovereign lady, and never to love other but her. But she was so proud that she had scorn of him and said she would never love him though he would die for her; wherefore all ladies and gentlewomen had scorn of her that[12] she was so proud, for there were fairer than she, and there was none that was there but an Sir Pelleas would have proffered them love they would have showed him the same for his noble prowess. And so this knight promised Ettard to follow her into this country and never to leave her till she loved him, and thus he is here the most party[13] nigh her and lodged by a priory.

'And every week she sendeth knights to fight with him, and when he hath put them to the worse, then will he suffer them wilfully[14] to take him prisoner because he would have a sight of this lady. And always she doth him great despite,[15] for sometimes she maketh his knights to tie him to his horse[16] tail, and sometime bind him under the horse[16] belly. Thus in the most shamefullest wise that she can think he is brought to her, and all she doth it for to[17] cause him to leave this country and to leave his loving. But all this cannot make him to leave, for an he would have fought on foot he might have had the better of the ten knights as well on foot as on horseback.'

'Alas,' said Sir Gawain, 'it is great pity of him, and after this night I will seek him to-morrow in this forest to do him all the help I can.'

So on the morrow Sir Gawain took his leave of his host, Sir Carados, and rode into the forest. And at the last he met with Sir Peleas making great moan out of measure; so each of them salewed other, and asked[18] him why he made such sorrow. And as it above rehearseth[19] Sir Pelleas told Sir Gawain:

[10] or unhorsed him	[15] she scorns him
[11] where	[16] horse's
[12] because	[17] all this she does in order to
[13] for the most part	[18] Gawain asked
[14] voluntarily	[19] is narrated

'But always I suffer her knights to fare so with me as ye saw yesterday, in trust at the last to win her love; for she knoweth well all her knights should not lightly win me an me list[20] to fight with them to the uttermost. Wherefore an I loved her not so sore I had liefer[1] die an hundred times, an I might die so oft, rather than I would suffer that despite,[2] but I trust she will have pity upon me at the last; for love causeth many a good knight to suffer to have his intent,[3] but alas, I am unfortunate!' And therewith he made so great dole that unnethe[4] he might hold him on his horse[16] back.

'Now,' said Sir Gawain, 'leave your mourning, and I shall promise you by the faith of my body to do all that lieth in my power to get you the love of your lady, and thereto I will plight you my troth.'

'Ah,' said Sir Pelleas, 'of what court are ye?'

'Sir, I am of the court of King Arthur, and his sister[5] son, and King Lot of Orkney was my father, and my name is Sir Gawain.'

'And my name is Sir Pelleas, born in the Isles, and of many Isles I am lord. And never loved I lady nother damsel till now. And, sir knight, since ye are so nigh cousin unto King Arthur and are a king's son, therefore betray me not, but help me, for I may never come by her but by some good knight. For she is in a strong castle here fast by, within this four mile, and over all this country she is lady of.

'And so I may never come to her presence but as[6] I suffer her knights to take me, and but if I did so that I might have a sight of her, I had been dead long or this time.[7] And yet fair word had I never none of her. But when I am brought tofore her she rebuketh me in the foulest manner; and then they take me my horse and harness and putteth me out of the gates, and she will not suffer me to eat nother drink. And always I offer me to be her prisoner, but that will she not suffer me; for I would desire no more, what pains that ever I had, so that I might have a sight of her daily.'

'Well,' said Sir Gawain, 'all this shall I amend, and ye will do as I shall devise. I will have your armour, and so will I ride unto her castle and tell her that I have slain you, and so shall I

20 if I wished
1 rather
2 scorn
3 the object of his desire
4 hardly

5 sister's
6 unless
7 and had I not done this so that I might have sight of her I should have died long since

come within her to cause her to cherish me.[8] And then shall I do my true part,[9] that ye shall not fail to have the love of her.'

And there, when Sir Gawain plight his troth unto Sir Pelleas to be true and faithful unto him, so each one plight their troth to other, and so they changed horse and harness. And Sir Gawain departed and came to the castle where stood her pavilions without the gate. And as soon as Ettard had espied Sir Gawain she fled toward the castle. But Sir Gawain spake on hight[10] and bade her abide, for he was not Sir Pelleas:

'I am another knight that have slain Sir Pelleas.'

'Then do off your helm,' said the lady Ettard, 'that I may see your visage.'[11]

So when she saw that it was not Sir Pelleas she made him alight and led him into her castle and asked him faithfully whether he had slain Sir Pelleas, and he said yea. Then he told her his name was Sir Gawain, of the court of King Arthur, and his sister's son, and how he had slain Sir Pelleas.

'Truly,' said she, 'that is great pity for he was a passing good knight of his body.[12] But of all men on live I hated him most, for I could never be quit[13] of him. And for ye have slain him I shall be your woman and to do anything that may please you.'

So she made Sir Gawain good cheer. Then Sir Gawain said that he loved a lady and by no mean she would love him.

'She is to blame,' said Ettard, 'an she will not love you, for ye that be so well-born a man and such a man of prowess, there is no lady in this world too good for you.'

'Will ye,' said Sir Gawain, 'promise me to do what that ye may do, by the faith of your body,[14] to get me the love of my lady?'

'Yea, sir, and that I promise you by my faith.'

'Now,' said Sir Gawain, 'it is yourself that I love so well, therefore hold your promise.'

'I may not choose,' said the lady Ettard, 'but if[15] I should be forsworn.'

And so she granted him to fulfil all his desire.

So it was in the month of May that she and Sir Gawain went out of the castle and supped in a pavilion, and there was

[8] go into the place where she lives and earn her esteem
[9] duty
[10] loudly
[11] face

[12] a good and strong knight
[13] rid
[14] your (his) faith
[15] or else

made a bed, and there Sir Gawain and Ettard went to bed together. And in another pavilion she laid her damsels, and in the third pavilion she laid part of her knights, for then she had no dread of Sir Pelleas. And there Sir Gawain lay with her in the pavilion two days and two nights.

And on the third day on the morn early Sir Pelleas armed him, for he had never slept since Sir Gawain departed from him, for Sir Gawain promised him by the faith of his body[14] to come to him unto his pavilion by the priory within the space of a day and a night. Then Sir Pelleas mounted upon horseback and came to the pavilions that stood without the castle, and found in the first pavilion three knights in three beds, and three squires lying at their feet. Then went he to the second pavilion and found four gentlewomen lying in four beds. And then he yode[16] to the third pavilion and found Sir Gawain lying in the bed with his lady Ettard and either clipping[17] other in arms. And when he saw that, his heart well-nigh brast for sorrow, and said, 'Alas, that ever a knight should be found so false!'

And then he took his horse and might not abide no longer for pure sorrow, and when he had ridden nigh half a mile he turned again and thought for to slay them both. And when he saw them lie so both sleeping fast that unnethe he might[18] hold him on horseback for sorrow, and said thus to himself: 'Though this knight be never[19] so false, I will never slay him sleeping, for I will never destroy the high Order of Knighthood,' and therewith he departed again. And or[20] he had ridden half a mile he returned again and thought then to slay them both, making the greatest sorrow that ever man made. And when he came to the pavilions he tied his horse to a tree and pulled his sword naked in his hand and went to them thereas[1] they lay. And yet he thought shame to slay them, and laid the naked sword overthwart[2] both their throats, and so took his horse and rode his way.

And when Sir Pelleas came to his pavilions he told his knights and his squires how he had sped,[3] and said thus unto them:

'For your good and true service ye have done me I shall

<hr>

[16] went

[17] embracing

[18] he could hardly

[19] ever

[20] But before

[1] where

[2] across

[3] succeeded

give you all my goods, for I will go unto my bed and never arise till I be dead. And when that I am dead, I charge[4] you that ye take the heart out of my body and bear it her betwixt two silver dishes and tell her how I saw her lie with that false knight Sir Gawain.'

Right so Sir Pelleas unarmed himself and went unto his bed making marvellous[5] dole and sorrow.

Then Sir Gawain and Ettard awoke of their sleep and found the naked sword overthwart[2] their throats. Then she knew it was the sword of Sir Pelleas.

'Alas!' she said, 'Sir Gawain, ye have betrayed Sir Pelleas and me, for you told me you had slain him, and now I know well it is not so: he is on live. But had he been so uncourteous unto you as ye have been to him, ye had been a dead knight. But ye have deceived me that[6] all ladies and damsels may beware by you and me.'

And therewith Sir Gawain made him ready and went into the forest.

So it happed the Damsel of the Lake, Nineve, met with a knight of Sir Pelleas that went on his foot[7] in this forest making great dole, and she asked him the cause; and so the woeful knight told her all how his master and lord was betrayed through a knight and a lady, and how he will never arise out of his bed till he be dead.

'Bring me to him,' said she anon, 'and I will warrant[8] his life. He shall not die for love, and she that hath caused him so to love she shall be in as evil plight as he is or it be long to,[9] for it is no joy of such a proud lady that will not have no mercy of such a valiant knight.'

Anon that knight brought her unto him, and when she saw him lie on his bed she thought she saw never so likely[10] a knight. And therewith she threw an enchantment upon him, and he fell on sleep. And then she rode unto the lady Ettard, and charged[4] that no man should awake him till she came again.[11] So within two hours she brought the lady Ettard thither, and both the ladies found him on sleep.

'Lo,' said the Damsel of the Lake, 'ye ought to be ashamed for to murder such a knight,' and therewith she threw such an

---

4 command (ed)
5 great
6 in such a way that
7 on foot

8 save
9 before long
10 handsome
11 back

enchantment upon her that she loved him so sore that well-nigh she was near out of her mind.

'Ah, Lord Jesu,' said this lady Ettard, 'how is it befallen unto me that I love now that[12] I have hated most of any man on life?'

'That is the righteous judgment of God,' said the damsel.

And then anon Sir Pelleas awaked and looked upon Ettard, and when he saw her he knew her, and then he hated her more than any woman on live, and said,

'Away, traitress, and come never in my sight!'

And when she heard him say so she wept and made great sorrow out of mind.[13]

'Sir knight Pelleas,' said the Damsel of the Lake, 'take your horse and come forth without of this country, and ye shall love a lady that will love you.'

'I will well,' said Sir Pelleas, 'for this lady Ettard hath done me great despite[14] and shame;' and there he told her the beginning and ending, and how he had never purposed to have risen again till he had been dead. 'And now such grace God hath sent me that I hate her as much as I have loved her.'

'Thank me therefor,' said the Lady of the Lake.

Anon Sir Pelleas armed him and took his horse and commanded his men to bring after[15] his pavilions and his stuff where the Lady of the Lake would assign them. So this lady Ettard died for sorrow, and the Damsel of the Lake rejoiced Sir Pelleas, and loved together during their life.

[12] him whom
[13] beyond measure (F: *raison*)
[14] wrong
[15] follow him with

The Knight of the Cart

And thus it passed on from Candlemas until after Easter, that[1] the month of May was come, when every lusty[2] heart beginneth to blossom and to burgeon. For, like as trees and herbs burgeoneth and flourisheth in May, in like wise every lusty[2] heart that is any manner of lover springeth,[3] burgeoneth, buddeth and flourisheth in lusty[2] deeds. For it giveth unto all lovers courage,[4] that lusty[2] month of May, in some thing[5] to constrain him to[6] some manner of thing, more than in any other month, for diverse causes: for then all herbs and trees reneweth a man and woman, and in like wise lovers calleth to their mind old gentleness[7] and old service, and many kind deeds that was forgotten by negligence.

For like as winter rasure[8] doth alway erase[9] and deface green summer, so fareth it by unstable love in man and woman, for in many persons there is no stability: for we may see all[10] day, for a little blast of winter's rasure,[8] anon we shall deface and lay apart[11] true love, for little or nought, that cost much thing.[12] This is no wisdom nother no stability, but it is feebleness of nature and great disworship,[13] whosomever useth this.

Therefore, like as May month flowereth and flourisheth in every man's garden, so in like wise let every man of worship[14] flourish his heart in this word; first unto God, and next unto the joy of them that he promised his faith unto; for there was never worshipful[14] man nor worshipful woman but they loved one better than another; and worship in arms may never be foiled.[15] But first reserve the honour to God, and secondly

[1] so that
[2] merry
[3] breaks forth
[4] desire
[5] for certain things
[6] to exert oneself in
[7] courtesy
[8] biting wind

[9] demolish
[10] every
[11] discard
[12] that is so precious
[13] disgrace
[14] honour(able)
[15] cast down

51

thy quarrel must come of[16] thy lady. And such love I call virtuous love.

But nowadays men cannot love seven night but they must have all their desires. That love may not endure by reason, for where they be soon accorded and hasty,[17] heat soon cooleth. And right so fareth the love nowadays, soon hot, soon cold. This is no stability. But the old love was not so; for men and women could love together seven years, and no lecherous lusts[18] was betwixt them, and then was love truth and faithfulness. And so in like wise was used such love in King Arthur's days.

Wherefore I liken love nowadays unto summer and winter: for, like as the one is cold and the other is hot, so fareth love nowadays. And therefore all ye that be lovers, call unto your remembrance the month of May, like as did Queen Guinevere, for whom I make here a little mention, that[19] while she lived she was a true lover, and therefore she had a good end.

So it befell in the month of May, Queen Guinevere called unto her ten knights of the Table Round, and she gave them warning that early upon the morn she would ride on-maying into woods and fields besides Westminster:

'And I warn you that there be none of you but he be well horsed, and that ye all be clothed all in green, either in silk other in cloth. And I shall bring with me ten ladies, and every knight shall have a lady by him. And every knight shall have a squire and two yeomen; and I will that all be well horsed.'

So they made them ready in the freshest[20] manner, and these were the names of the knights: Sir Kay le Seneschal, Sir Agravain, Sir Braundiles, Sir Sagramore le Desirous, Sir Dodinas le Savage, Sir Ozanna le Cure Hardy, Sir Ladinas of the Forest Savage, Sir Persaunt of Inde, Sir Ironside, that was called the Knight of the Red Launds, and Sir Pelleas the Lover. And these ten knights made them ready in the freshest[20] manner to ride with the queen.

An so upon the morn or it were day, in a May morning, they took their horses with the queen, and rode on-maying in woods and meadows as it pleased them, in great joy and delights. For the queen had cast[1] to have been again with King

---

[16] must be for the sake of
[17] when such desires are quickly and hastily fulfilled
[18] pleasures

[19] because
[20] gayest
[1] intended

Lancelot and Guinivere. Ms. Fr. 118. *Bibliothèque Nationale, Paris.*

Arthur at the furthest by ten of the clock, and so[2] was that time her purpose.

Then there was a knight which hight Sir Mellyagaunce, and he was son unto King Bagdemagus, and this knight had that time a castle of the gift of King Arthur within seven mile of Westminster. And this knight Sir Mellyagaunce loved passingly well Queen Guinevere, and so had he done long and many years. And the book saith he had lain in await[3] for to steal away the queen, but evermore he forbare for because of Sir Lancelot; for in no wise he would meddle with the queen an Sir Lancelot were in her company other else an he were near-hand.

And that time was such a custom that the queen rode never without a great fellowship of men of arms about her. And they were many good knights, and the most party[4] were young men that would have worship[5] and they were called the Queen's Knights. And never in no battle, tournament nother jousts they bare none of them no manner of knowledging of their own arms but[6] plain white shields, and thereby they were called the Queen's Knights. And when it happed any of them to be of great worship by his noble deeds, then at the next feast of Pentecost, if there were any slain or dead (as there was none year that there failed but there were some dead), then was there chosen in his stead that was dead the most men of worship that were called the Queen's Knights. And thus they came up first, or they were renowned men of worship, both Sir Lancelot and all the remnant of them.

But this knight Sir Mellyagaunce had espied the queen well and her purpose, and how Sir Lancelot was not with her, and how she had no men of arms with her but the ten noble knights all rayed[7] in green for maying. Then he purveyed him[8] a twenty men of arms and an hundred archers for to distress the queen and her knights; for he thought that time was best season to take the queen.

So as the queen was out on-maying with all her knights, which were bedashed[9] with herbs, mosses and flowers in the freshest[10] manner, right so there came out of a wood Sir

---

2 such
3 ambush
4 most of them
5 wished to distinguish themselves

6 bore no arms by which they could be recognized, but only
7 dressed
8 chose
9 adorned
10 gayest

Mellyagaunce with an eight score men, all harnessed as they should fight in a battle of arrest,[11] and bade the queen and her knights abide, for maugre their heads[12] they should abide.

'Traitor knight,' said Queen Guinevere, 'what cast[13] thou to do? Wilt thou shame thyself? Bethink thee how thou art a king's son, and a knight of the Table Round, and thou thus to be about to dishonour the noble king that made thee knight! Thou shamest all knighthood and thyself and me. And I let thee wit thou shalt never shame me, for I had liefer[14] cut mine own throat in twain rather than thou should dishonour me!'

'As for all this language,' said Sir Mellyagaunce, 'be as it be may. For wit you well, madam, I have loved you many a year, and never or now could I get you at such avail.[15] And therefore I will take you as I find you.'

Then spake all the ten noble knights at once and said,

'Sir Mellyagaunce, wit thou well thou art about to jeopardy thy worship to dishonour,[16] and also ye cast[13] to jeopardy your persons. Howbeit we be unarmed and ye have us at a great advantage, for it seemeth by you that ye have laid watch upon us, but rather than ye should put the queen to a shame and us all, we had as lief to depart from our lives, for an we otherways did we were shamed forever.'

Then said Sir Mellyagaunce:

'Dress[17] you as well ye can, and keep the queen!'

Then the ten knights of the Round Table drew their swords and these other let run at them with their spears. And the ten knights manly abode[18] them, and smote away their spears, that no spear did them no harm. Then they lashed together with swords, and anon Sir Kay, Sir Sagramore, Sir Agravain, Sir Dodinas, Sir Ladinas, and Sir Ozanna were smitten to the earth with grimly wounds. Then Sir Braundiles and Sir Persaunt, Sir Ironside, and Sir Pelleas fought long, and they were sore wounded, for these ten knights, or ever they were laid to the ground, slew forty men of the boldest and the best of them.

So when the queen saw her knights thus dolefully wounded and needs must be slain at the last, then for very pity and sorrow she cried and said,

'Sir Mellyagaunce, slay not my noble knights, and I will go

---

[11] fight for capture	[15] advantage
[12] whether they wished it or not	[16] put your honour in jeopardy
[13] intend (est)	[17] prepare
[14] rather	[18] withstood

with thee upon this covenant: that thou save them and suffer them no more to be hurt, with this[19] that they be led with me wheresomever thou leadest me. For I will rather slay myself than I will go with thee, unless that these noble knights may be in my presence.'

'Madam,' said Sir Mellyagaunce, 'for your sake they shall be led with you into mine own castle, with that[20] ye will be ruled[1] and ride with me.'

Then the queen prayed the four knights to leave their fighting, and[2] she and they would not depart.[3]

'Madam,' said Sir Pelleas, 'we will do as ye do, for as for me I take no force of my life nor death.'[4]

For, as the French book saith, Sir Pelleas gave such buffets there that none armour might hold[5] him.

Then by the queen's commandment they left battle and dressed[6] the wounded knights on horseback, some sitting and some overthwart their horses, that it was pity to behold. And then Sir Mellyagaunce charged the queen and all her knights that none of all her fellowship should depart from her, for full sore he dread Sir Lancelot du Lake, lest he should have any knowledging.[7] And all this espied the queen, and privily[8] she called unto her a childe[9] of her chamber which was swiftly horsed of a great advantage.[10]

'Now go thou,' said she, 'when thou seest thy time, and bear this ring unto Sir Lancelot du Lake, and pray him as he loveth me that he will see me and rescue me, if ever he will have joy of me. And spare not thy horse,' said the queen, 'nother for water nother for land.'

So the childe[9] espied his time, and lightly[11] he took his horse with spurs and departed as fast he might. And when Sir Mellyagaunce saw him so flee, he understood that it was by the queen's commandment for to warn Sir Lancelot. Then they that were best horsed chased him and shot at him, but from them all the childe[9] went deliverly.[12]

And then Sir Mellyagaunce said unto the queen,

---

[19] on this condition
[20] provided that
[1] submit
[2] and [said that]
[3] part
[4] it matters not whether I live or die
[5] withstand

[6] lifted
[7] lest this should come to his knowledge
[8] secretly
[9] young nobleman
[10] mounted on a good horse
[11] swiftly
[12] cunningly escaped

'Madam, ye are about to betray me, but I shall ordain for Sir Lancelot that he shall not come lightly[11] at you.'

And then he rode with her and all the fellowship in all the haste that they might. And so by the way Sir Mellyagaunce laid in bushment[13] of the best archers that he might get in his country, to the number of a thirty, to await upon Sir Lancelot, charging[14] them that if they saw such a manner a knight come by the way upon a white horse, 'that in any wise ye slay his horse, but in no manner have ye ado with him bodily, for he is overhardy[15] to be overcome.' So this was done, and they were come to his castle; but in no wise the queen would never let none of the ten knights and her ladies out of her sight, but always they were in her presence. For the book saith Sir Mellyagaunce durst make no masteries,[16] for dread of Sir Lancelot, insomuch he deemed that he had warning.

So when the childe[9] was departed from the fellowship of Sir Mellyagaunce, within a while he came to Westminster, and anon he found Sir Lancelot. And when he had told his message and delivered him the queen's ring,

'Alas!' said Sir Lancelot, 'now am I shamed for ever, unless that I may rescue that noble lady from dishonour.'

Then eagerly he asked his arms. And ever[17] the childe[9] told Sir Lancelot how the ten knights fought marvellously, and how Sir Pelleas, and Sir Ironside, Sir Braundiles, and Sir Persaunt of Inde fought strongly, but namely Sir Pelleas, there might none harness hold[18] him; and how they all fought till they were laid to the earth, and how the queen made appointment[19] for to save their lives and to go with Sir Mellyagaunce.

'Alas,' said Sir Lancelot, 'that most noble lady, that she should be so destroyed! I had liefer,'[20] said Sir Lancelot, 'than all France that I had been there well armed.'

So when Sir Lancelot was armed and upon his horse, he prayed the childe[9] of the queen's chamber to warn Sir Lavain[1] how suddenly he was departed, and for what cause. 'And pray him as he loveth me, that he will hie him after me, and that he stint[2] not until he come to the castle where Sir Mellyagaunce

---

[13] ambush
[14] ordering
[15] too strong
[16] advances
[17] again
[18] withstand
[19] contrived

[20] rather
[1] *Gawain, according to* F. *Lavain, brother of Elaine, is a character in* The Fair Maid of Astolat *which in* F *comes after* The Knight of the Cart.
[2] cease

abideth. For there,' said Sir Lancelot, 'he shall hear of me an I be a man living, and then shall I rescue the queen and the ten knights the which he[3] traitorly hath taken, and that shall I prove upon his head, and all of them that hold with him.[4]

Then Sir Lancelot rode as fast as he might, and the book saith he took the water[5] at Westminster Bridge, and made his horse swim over the Thames unto Lambeth. And so within a while he came to that same place thereas[6] the ten noble knights fought with Sir Mellyagaunce. And then Sir Lancelot followed the track until that he came to a wood, and there was a strait way, and there the thirty archers bade Sir Lancelot turn again, 'and follow no longer that track.'

'What commandment have ye,' said Sir Lancelot, 'to cause me, that am a knight of the Round Table, to leave my right way?'

'These ways shalt thou leave, other else thou shalt go it on thy foot, for wit thou well thy horse shall be slain.'

'That is little mastery,'[7] said Sir Lancelot, 'to slay mine horse! But as for myself, when my horse is slain I give right nought of you,[8] not an ye were five hundred more!'

So then they shot Sir Lancelot's horse and smote him with many arrows. And then Sir Lancelot avoided[9] his horse and went on foot, but there were so many ditches and hedges betwixt them and him that he might not meddle with none[10] of them.

'Alas, for shame!' said Sir Lancelot, 'that ever one knight should betray another knight! But it is an old said saw, "A good man is never in danger but when he is in the danger[11] of a coward." '

Then Sir Lancelot walked on a while, and was sore acumbered of[12] his armour, his shield, and his spear. Wit you well he was full sore annoyed! And full loath he was for to leave anything that longed unto[13] him, for he dread sore the treason of Sir Mellyagaunce.

Then by fortune there came by him a chariot[14] that came thither to fetch wood.

3 = Mellyagaunce
4 fight on his side
5 crossed the river
6 where
7 no deed of prowess
8 I do not fear you
9 dismounted from

10 could not fight with any
11 at the mercy. *In the phrase 'never in danger' the word is used in the modern sense.*
12 heavily burdened with
13 belonged to
14 cart

'Say me, carter,' said Sir Lancelot, 'what shall I give thee to suffer me to leap into thy chariot, and that thou will bring me unto a castle within this two mile?'

'Thou shalt not enter this chariot,' said the carter, 'for I am sent for to fetch wood.'

'Unto whom?' said Sir Lancelot.

'Unto my lord, Sir Mellyagaunce,' said the carter.

'And with him would I speak,' said Sir Lancelot.

'Thou shalt not go with me!' said the carter.

When Sir Lancelot leapt to him and gave him backward with his gauntlet a rearmain[15] that he fell to the earth stark dead, then the other carter, his fellow, was afeard, and weened to have gone[16] the same way. And then he said,

'Fair lord, save my life, and I shall bring you where ye will.'

'Then I charge thee,' said Sir Lancelot, 'that thou drive me and this chariot unto Sir Mellyagaunce[17] gate.'

'Then leap ye up into the chariot,' said the carter, 'and ye shall be there anon.'

So the carter drove on a great wallop,[18] and Sir Lancelot's horse followed the chariot, with more than forty arrows in him.

And more than an hour and an half Queen Guinevere was awaiting in a bay window. Then one of her ladies espied an armed knight standing in a chariot.

'Ah, see, madam,' said the lady, 'where rideth in a chariot a goodly armed knight, and we suppose he rideth unto hanging.'[19]

'Where?' said the queen.

Then she espied by his shield that it was Sir Lancelot, and then she was ware where came his horse after the chariot, and ever he trod his guts and his paunch under his feet.

'Alas,' said the queen, 'now I may prove and see that well is that creature that hath a trusty friend. A ha!' said Queen Guinevere, 'I see well that ye were hard bestead when[20] ye ride in a chariot.' And then she rebuked that lady that likened Sir Lancelot to ride in a chariot to hanging: 'Forsooth, it was foul-mouthed,' said the queen, 'and evil-likened, so for to liken the most noble knight of the world unto such a shameful

---

[15] back-handed stroke
[16] thought he would fare
[17] Mellyagaunce's
[18] at full speed

[19] *A cart was used in those days to convey criminals to the gallows* (F).
[20] hard-pressed if

Lancelot in the Cart. *Morte d'Arthur*, edition of Wynkyn de Worde 1498. *The John Rylands University Library of Manchester.*

death. Ah! Jesu defend him and keep him,' said the queen, 'from all mischievous[1] end!'

So by this was Sir Lancelot comen to the gates of that castle, and there he descended down and cried, that all the castle might ring:

'Where art thou, thou false traitor, Sir Mellyagaunce, and knight of the Table Round? Come forth, thou traitor knight, thou and all thy fellowship with thee, for here I am, Sir Lancelot du Lake, that shall fight with you all!'

And therewithal he bare[2] the gate wide open upon the porter, and smote him under the ear with his gauntlet, that his neck brast in two pieces. When Sir Mellyagaunce heard that Sir Lancelot was comen he ran unto the queen and fell upon his knee and said:

'Mercy, madam, for now I put me wholly in your good grace.'

'What aileth you now?' said Queen Guinevere. 'Perdy,[3] I might well wit that some good knight would revenge me, though my lord King Arthur knew not of this your work.'

'Ah, madam,' said Sir Mellyagaunce, 'all this that is amiss on my party[4] shall be amended right as yourself will devise, and wholly I put me in your grace.'

'What would ye that I did?' said the queen.

'Madam, I would no more,' said Sir Mellyagaunce, 'but that ye would take all in your own hands, and that ye will rule my lord Sir Lancelot.[5] And such cheer as may be made him in this poor castle, ye and he shall have until to-morn, and then may ye and all they return again unto Westminster. And my body and all that I have I shall put in your rule.'

'Ye say well,' said the queen, 'and better is peace than evermore war, and the less noise[6] the more is my worship.'[7]

Then the queen and her ladies went down unto Sir Lancelot that stood wood wroth out of measure[8] in the inner court to abide battle, and ever[9] he said: 'Thou traitor knight, come forth!' Then the queen came unto him and said,

'Sir Lancelot, why be ye so amoved?'[10]

'Ah, madam,' said Sir Lancelot, 'why ask ye me that ques-

---

[1] shameful	[6] scandal
[2] forced	[7] honour
[3] by God (*par Dieu*)	[8] violently angry
[4] all the wrong I have done	[9] repeatedly
[5] and let my lord Sir Lancelot obey you	[10] angry

tion? For meseemeth ye ought to be more wrother than I am, for ye have the hurt and the dishonour. For wit you well, madam, my hurt is but little in regard for the slaying of a mare's son, but the despite[11] grieveth me much more than all my hurt.'

'Truly,' said the queen, 'ye say truth, but[12] heartily I thank you,' said the queen. 'But ye must come in with me peaceably, for all thing is put in mine hand, and all that is amiss shall be amended, for the knight full sore repenteth him of this misadventure that is befallen him.'

'Madam,' said Sir Lancelot, 'sith it is so that ye be accorded[13] with him, as for me I may not againsay it, howbeit Sir Mellyagaunce hath done full shamefully to me and cowardly. And, madam,' said Sir Lancelot, 'an I had wist ye would have been so lightly[14] accorded[13] with him I would not a made such haste unto you.'

'Why say ye so?' said the queen. 'Do ye forthink yourself of[15] your good deeds? Wit you well,' said the queen, 'I accorded never with him for no favour nor love that I had unto him, but of every shameful noise of wisdom to lay adown.'[16]

'Madam,' said Sir Lancelot, 'ye understand full well I was never willing nor glad of shameful slander nor noise.[6] And there is nother king, queen, ne knight that beareth the life, except my lord King Arthur, and you, madam, that should let[17] me but I should make Sir Mellyagaunce[18] heart full cold or ever I departed from hence.'

'That wot I well,' said the queen, 'but what will ye more? Ye shall have all thing ruled as ye list to have it.'

'Madam,' said Sir Lancelot, 'so ye be pleased,[19] as for my part ye shall soon please me.'

Right so the queen took Sir Lancelot by the bare hand, for he had put off his gauntlet, and so she went with him till her chamber; and then she commanded him to be unarmed.

And then Sir Lancelot asked the queen where were her ten knights that were wounded with her. Then she showed them unto him, and there they made great joy of the coming of Sir Lancelot, and he made great sorrow of their hurts. And

---

11 insult
12 and
13 reconciled
14 quickly
15 regret

16 wisely to prevent any scandal
17 prevent
18 Mellyagaunce's
19 if it pleases you

there Sir Lancelot told them how cowardly and traitorly he[20] set archers to slay his horse, and how he[1] was fain to put himself in a chariot. And thus they complained everych to other, and full fain they would have been revenged, but they kept the peace because of the queen.

Then, as the French book saith, Sir Lancelot was called many days after 'le Chevalier de Chariot,' and so he did many deeds and great adventures.

AND SO WE LEAVE OFF HERE OF LE CHEVALIER DE CHARIOT, AND TURN WE TO THIS TALE.

So Sir Lancelot had great cheer with the queen. And then he made a promise with the queen that the same night he should come to a window outward toward a garden, and that window was barred with iron, and there Sir Lancelot promised to meet her when all folks were on sleep.

So then came Sir Lavain driving to the gates, saying, 'Where is my lord, Sir Lancelot?' Anon he was sent for, and when Sir Lavain saw Sir Lancelot, he said,

'Ah, my lord, I found how ye were hard bestead,[2] for I have found your horse that was slain with arrows.'

'As for that,' said Sir Lancelot, 'I pray you, Sir Lavain, speak ye of other matters and let this pass, and right it another time an we may.'

Then the knights that were hurt were searched,[3] and soft salves were laid to their wounds, and so it passed on till supper time. And all the cheer that might be made them there was done unto the queen and all her knights. And when season was[4] they went unto their chambers, but in no wise the queen would not suffer her wounded knights to be from her, but that they were laid inwith draughts by[5] her chamber, upon beds and pallets, that she herself might see unto them that they wanted nothing.

So when Sir Lancelot was in his chamber which was assigned unto him, he called unto him Sir Lavain, and told him that night he must speak with his lady, Queen Guinevere.

'Sir,' said Sir Lavain, 'let me go with you an it please you, for I dread me sore of the treason of Sir Mellyagaunce.'

'Nay,' said Sir Lancelot, 'I thank you, but I will have nobody with me.'

---

[20] = Mellyagaunce
[1] = Lancelot
[2] hard-pressed

[3] had their wounds probed
[4] at the proper time
[5] in the recesses of

Then Sir Lancelot took his sword in his hand and privily[6] went to the place where he had spied a ladder toforehand, and that he took under his arm, and bare it through the garden and set it up to the window. And anon the queen was there ready to meet him.

And then they made their complaints[7] to other of many divers things, and then Sir Lancelot wished that he might have comen in to her.

'Wit you well,' said the queen, 'I would as fain as ye that ye might come in to me.'

'Would ye so, madam,' said Sir Lancelot, 'with your heart that I were with you?'

'Yea, truly,' said the queen.

'Then shall I prove my might,' said Sir Lancelot, 'for your love.'

And then he set his hands upon the bars of iron and pulled at them with such a might that he brast[8] them clean out of the stone walls. And therewithal one of the bars of iron cut the brawn[9] of his hands throughout to the bone. And then he leapt into the chamber to the queen.

'Make ye no noise,' said the queen, 'for my wounded knights lie here fast by me.'

So, to pass upon[10] this tale, Sir Lancelot went to bed with the queen, and took no force[11] of his hurt hand, but took his pleasaunce and his liking[12] until it was the dawning of the day; for wit you well he slept not, but watched.[13] And when he saw his time that he might tarry no longer, he took his leave and departed at the window, and put it together as well as he might again, and so departed unto his own chamber. And there he told Sir Lavain how he was hurt. Then Sir Lavain dressed his hand and staunched it,[14] and put upon it a glove, that it should not be espied. And so they lay long abed in the morning till it was nine of the clock.

Then Sir Mellyagaunce went to the queen's chamber and found her ladies there ready clothed.

'Ah, Jesu mercy,' said Sir Mellyagaunce, 'what ails you, madam, that ye sleep this long?'

---

6 secretly
7 lamentations
8 tore
9 flesh
10 continue briefly with
11 notice
12 his pleasure and his joy
13 lay awake
14 stopped the bleeding

And therewithal he opened the curtain for to behold her. And then was he ware where she lay, and the head-sheet, pillow and over-sheet was bebled of[15] the blood of Sir Lancelot and of his hurt hand. When Sir Mellyagaunce espied that blood then he deemed in her that she was[16] false to the king, and that some of the wounded knights had lain by her all that night.

'A ha, madam,' said Sir Mellyagaunce, 'now I have found you a false traitress unto my lord Arthur, for now I prove well[17] it was not for nought that ye laid these wounded knights within the bounds of your chamber. Therefore I call you[18] of treason before my lord King Arthur. And now I have proved you, madam, with[19] a shameful deed; and that they been all false, or some of them, I will make it good,[20] for a wounded knight this night hath lain by you.'

'That is false,' said the queen, 'that I will report me unto them.'[1]

But[2] when the ten knights heard of Sir Mellyagaunce's words, and then they spake all at once, and said,

'Sir Mellyagaunce, thou falsely beliest[3] my lady the queen, and that we will make good[4] upon thee, any of us. Now choose which thou list of us, when we are whole of the wounds thou gavest us.'

'Ye shall not! Away with your proud language! For here ye may all see that a wounded knight this night hath lain by the queen.'

Then they all looked and were sore ashamed[5] when they saw that blood. And wit you well Sir Mellyagaunce was passing glad that he had the queen at such advantage,[6] for he deemed by that to hide his own treason.

And so in this rumour[7] came in Sir Lancelot and found them at a great affray.[8]

'What array is this?'[9] said Sir Lancelot.

Then Sir Mellyagaunce told them what he had found, and so he showed him the queen's bed.

---

[15] covered with
[16] suspected her of being
[17] declare
[18] accuse you
[19] found you guilty, madam, of
[20] prove it
[1] I shall ask them to bear witness
[2] And

[3] slanderest
[4] prove
[5] perturbed
[6] disadvantage
[7] as they were arguing
[8] greatly disturbed
[9] what is the matter?

'Now, truly,' said Sir Lancelot, 'ye did not your part nor
knightly, to touch a queen's bed while it was drawn[10] and
she lying therein. And I dare say,' said Sir Lancelot, 'my lord
King Arthur himself would not have displayed[11] her curtains,
and she being within her bed, unless that it had pleased him
to have lain him down by her. And therefore, Sir Mellyagaunce, ye have done unworshipfully and shamefully to yourself.'

'Sir, I wot not what ye mean,' said Sir Mellyagaunce, 'but
well I am sure there hath one of her hurt knights lain with
her this night. And that will I prove with mine hands, that
she is a traitress unto my lord King Arthur.'

'Beware what ye do,' said Sir Lancelot, 'for an ye say so,
and will prove it, it will be taken at your hands.'[12]

'My lord Sir Lancelot,' said Sir Mellyagaunce, 'I read[13] you
beware what ye do; for though ye are never so good a knight,
as I wot well ye are renowned the best knight of the world,
yet should ye be advised to do[14] battle in a wrong quarrel, for
God will have a stroke in every battle.'

'As for that,' said Sir Lancelot, 'God is to be dread! But
as to that, I say nay plainly, that this night there lay none of
these ten knights wounded with my lady Queen Guinevere,
and that will I prove with mine hands that ye say untruly in
that. Now, what say ye?' said Sir Lancelot.

'Thus I say,' said Sir Mellyagaunce, 'here is my glove, that
she is a traitress unto my lord King Arthur, and that this night
one of the wounded knights lay with her.'

'Well, sir, and I receive your glove,' said Sir Lancelot.

And anon they were sealed[15] with their signets, and delivered
unto the ten knights.

'At what day shall we do battle together?' said Sir Lancelot.

'This day eight days,'[16] said Sir Mellyagaunce, 'in the field
beside Westminster.'

'I am agreed,' said Sir Lancelot.

'But now,' said Sir Mellyagaunce, 'sithen it is so that we
must needs fight together, I pray you, as ye be a noble knight,
await me with no treason[17] nother no villainy the meanwhile,
nother none for you.'[18]

---

10 while the curtains were drawn
11 opened
12 your challenge will be accepted
13 advise
14 you should beware of doing
15 their challenge was sealed
16 eight days from today
17 do not try to betray me
18 and none shall be done to you

'So God me help,' said Sir Lancelot, 'ye shall right well wit I was never of no such conditions.[19] For I report me to[20] all knights that ever have known me, I fared never with no treason, nother I loved never the fellowship of him that fared with treason.'

'Then let us go unto dinner,' said Sir Mellyagaunce, 'and after dinner the queen and ye may ride all unto Westminster.'

'I will well,' said Sir Lancelot.

Then Sir Mellyagaunce said to Sir Lancelot,

'Sir, pleaseth you to see estures[1] of this castle?'

'With a good will,' said Sir Lancelot.

And then they went together from chamber to chamber, for Sir Lancelot dread no perils; for ever a man of worship and of prowess dreads but little of perils, for they ween that every man be as they been. But ever he that fareth with treason putteth often a true man in great danger. And so it befell upon Sir Lancelot that no peril dread: as he went with Sir Mellyagaunce he trod on a trap, and the board rolled, and there Sir Lancelot fell down more than ten fathom into a cave full of straw.

And then Sir Mellyagaunce departed and made no fare,[2] no more than he that wist not where he[3] was. And when Sir Lancelot was thus missed they marvelled where he was becomen,[4] and then the queen and many of them deemed that he was departed, as he was wont to do, suddenly. For Sir Mellyagaunce made suddenly to put on side[5] Sir Lavain's horse, that they might all understand that Sir Lancelot were departed suddenly.

So then it passed on till after dinner, and then Sir Lavain would not stint[6] until he had horse-litters for the wounded knights, that they might be carried in them. And so with the queen both ladies and gentlewomen and other rode unto Westminster, and there the knights told how Sir Mellyagaunce had appealed[7] the queen of high treason, and how Sir Lancelot received the glove of him: 'And this day eight days[8] they shall do battle before you.'

---

[19] I have never been guilty of such a behaviour

[20] I call upon for confirmation

[1] rooms

[2] went away quietly

[3] as if he did not know where Lancelot was

[4] what had become of him

[5] conceal

[6] stop

[7] accused

[8] eight days from today

'By my head,' said King Arthur, 'I am afeard Sir Mellya-gaunce hath charged himself with a great charge.[9] But where is Sir Lancelot?' said the king.

'Sir, we wot not where he is, but we deem he is ridden to some adventure, as he is oftentimes wont to do, for he hath Sir Lavain's horse.'

'Let him be,' said the king, 'for he will be founden but if[10] he be trapped with some treason.'

Thus leave we Sir Lancelot lying within that cave in great pain.[11] And every day there came a lady and brought his meat and his drink, and wooed him every day to have lain by her; and ever Sir Lancelot said her nay. Then said she:

'Sir, ye are not wise, for ye may never out of this prison but if[10] ye have my help. And also your lady, Queen Guin-evere, shall be brent in your default[12] unless that ye be there at the day of battle.'

'God defend,' said Sir Lancelot, 'that she should be brent in my default! And if it be so,' said Sir Lancelot, 'that I may not be there, it shall be well understood, both at[13] the king and the queen and with[13] all men of worship,[14] that I am dead-sick other[15] in prison. For all men that know me will say for me that I am in some evil case[16] an I be not that day there. And thus well I understand that there is some good knight, other of my blood other some other that loves me, that will take my quarrel in hand. And therefore,' said Sir Lancelot, 'wit you well, ye shall not fear[17] me, and if there were no more women in all this land but ye, yet shall not I have ado with you.'

'Then are ye shamed,' said the lady, 'and destroyed for ever.'

'As for world's shame, now Jesu defend me! And as for my distress, it is welcome, whatsomever it be that God sends me.'

So she came to him again the same day that the battle should be and said,

'Sir Lancelot, bethink you, for ye are too hard-hearted. And therefore an ye would but once kiss me I should deliver you and your armour, and the best horse that was within Sir Mellyagaunce[18] stable.'

[9] taken upon himself a heavy task
[10] unless
[11] distress
[12] burnt through your failure to appear
[13] by
[14] honour
[15] gravely ill or
[16] plight
[17] frighten
[18] Mellyagaunce's

'As for to kiss you,' said Sir Lancelot, 'I may do that and lose no worship.[14] And wit you well an I understood there were any disworship[19] for to kiss you, I would not do it.'

And then he kissed her, and anon she gat him up until[20] his armour. And when he was armed she brought him till[20] a stable where stood twelve good coursers, and bade him to choose the best. Then Sir Lancelot looked upon a white courser and that liked[1] him best, and anon he commanded him to be saddled with the best saddle of war, and so it was done. Then he gat his own spear in his hand and his sword by his side, and then he commended the lady unto God, and said,

'Lady, for this day's deed I shall do you service if ever it lie in my power.'

Now leave we here Sir Lancelot, all that ever he might wallop,[2] and speak we of Queen Guinevere that was brought till a fire to be brent; for Sir Mellyagaunce was sure, him thought, that Sir Lancelot should not be at that battle, and therefore he ever cried upon Sir Arthur to do[3] him justice other else bring forth Sir Lancelot. Then was the king and all the court full sore abashed and shamed that the queen should have be brent in the default of Sir Lancelot.[4]

'My lord, King Arthur,' said Sir Lavain, 'ye may understand that it is not well with my lord Sir Lancelot, for an he were on live, so he be not sick other in prison, wit you well he would have been here. For never heard ye that ever he failed yet his part for whom he should do battle for. And therefore,' said Sir Lavain, 'my lord, King Arthur, I beseech you that ye will give me license to do battle here this day for my lord and master, and for to save my lady the queen.'

'Gramercy, gentle Sir Lavain,' said King Arthur, 'for I dare say all that Sir Mellyagaunce putteth upon my lady the queen is wrong. For I have spoken with all the ten wounded knights, and there is not one of them, an he were whole and able to do battle, but he would prove upon Sir Mellyagaunce[5] body that it is false that he putteth upon[6] my lady.'

---

[19] dishonour
[20] brought him (in)to
[1] pleased
[2] gallop
[3] kept calling upon Sir Arthur to give

[4] because of Sir Lancelot's failure to take up the challenge
[5] Mellyagaunce's
[6] accuses

'And so shall I,' said Sir Lavain, 'in the defence of my lord, Sir Lancelot, and ye will give me leave.'

'And I give you leave,' said King Arthur, 'and do your best, for I dare well say there is some treason done to Sir Lancelot.'

Then was Sir Lavain armed and horsed, and deliverly[7] at the lists' end he rode to perform his battle. And right as the heralds should cry: *Laissez-les aller!*[8] right so came Sir Lancelot driving with all the might of his horse. And then King Arthur cried 'Wo!' and 'Abide!'

And then Sir Lancelot called[9] tofore King Arthur and there he told openly tofore the king all how that Sir Mellyagaunce had served him first and last. And when the king and queen and all the lords knew of the treason of Sir Mellyagaunce, they were all ashamed on his behalf. Then was the queen sent for and set by the king in the great trust of her champion.

And then Sir Lancelot and Sir Mellyagaunce dressed them together[10] with spears as thunder, and there Sir Lancelot bare him quit[11] over his horse's croup.[12] And then Sir Lancelot alight and dressed[13] his shield on his shoulder, and took his sword in his hand, and so they dressed to each other[10] and smote many great strokes together. And at the last Sir Lancelot smote him such a buffet upon the helmet that he fell on the one side to the earth. And then he cried upon him[14] loud and said,

'Most noble knight, Sir Lancelot, save my life! For I yield me unto you, and I require you, as ye be a knight and fellow of the Table Round, slay me not, for I yield me as overcomen; and whether I shall live or die I put me in the king's hand and yours.'

Then Sir Lancelot wist not what to do, for he had liefer than all the good in the world he might be revenged upon him. So Sir Lancelot looked upon the queen, if he might espy by any sign or countenance what she would have done. And anon the queen wagged her head upon[15] Sir Lancelot, as who saith,[16] 'Slay him!' And full well knew Sir Lancelot by her

---

[7] quickly
[8] 'Let them go!'
[9] brought a charge
[10] came together
[11] threw him off
[12] hind-quarters
[13] positioned
[14] begged him
[15] nodded to
[16] as if to say (Old Fr.: *comme celle qui dit*)

signs that she would have him dead. Then Sir Lancelot bade him,

'Arise for shame, and perform this battle with me to the utterance.'

'Nay,' said Sir Mellyagaunce, 'I will never arise until that ye take me as yolden and recreant.'[17]

'Well, I shall proffer you a large proffer,'[18] said Sir Lancelot, 'that is for to say I shall unarm my head and my left quarter of my body, all that may be unarmed as for that quarter, and I will let bind my left hand behind me there[19] it shall not help me, and right so I shall do battle with you.'

Then Sir Mellyagaunce start up and said on hight,

'Take heed, my lord Arthur, of this proffer,[20] for I will take it. And let him be disarmed and bounden according to his proffer.'

'What say ye?' said King Arthur unto Sir Lancelot. 'Will ye abide by your proffer?'

'Yea, my lord,' said Sir Lancelot, 'for I will never go from that I have once said.'

Then the knights' partners of the field[1] disarmed Sir Lancelot, first his head and then his left arm and his left side, and they bound his left arm to his left side fast behind his back, without shield or anything. And anon they yode[2] together.

Wit you well there was many a lady and many a knight marvelled of Sir Lancelot that would jeopardy himself in such wise.

Then Sir Mellyagaunce came with sword all on hight,[3] and Sir Lancelot showed him openly his bare head and the bare left side. And when he weened to have smitten him upon the bare head, then lightly[4] he devoided[5] to the left leg and the left side, and put his hand and his sword to[6] that stroke, and so put it on side with great sleight.[7] And then with great force Sir Lancelot smote him on the helmet with such a buffet that the stroke carved the head in two parties.[8]

Then there was no more to do, but he was drawn out of the field, and at the great instance of the knights of the Table

[17] as one who has yielded and surrendered
[18] make you a generous offer
[19] where
[20] offer
[1] stewards
[2] went

[3] holding his sword high
[4] quickly
[5] withdrew
[6] against
[7] skill
[8] halves

Round the king suffered him to be interred,[9] and the mention made upon him who slew him and for what cause he was slain.

And then the king and the queen made more of Sir Lancelot, and more he was cherished than ever he was aforehand.

. . . And so I leave here of this tale and overleap great books of Sir Lancelot, what great adventures he did when he was called Le Chevalier de Chariot.[10] For, as the French book saith, because of despite that knights and ladies[11] called him 'the knight that rode in the chariot,' like as[12] he were judged to the gibbet,[13] therefore, in the despite of all them that[14] named him so, he was carried in a chariot a twelvemonth; for but little after that[15] he had slain Sir Mellyagaunce in the queen's quarrel he never of a twelvemonth come on horseback. And as the French book saith, he did that twelvemonth more than forty battles.

[9] buried
[10] 'The Knight of the Cart'
[11] because he had been insulted by knights and ladies who
[12] as if
[13] gallows
[14] out of contempt for all those who
[15] soon after

Lancelot and Elaine

NOW . . . SPEAK WE OF SIR LANCELOT DU LAKE AND OF SIR
GALAHAD, SIR LANCELOT'S SON, HOW HE WAS BEGOTTEN AND IN
WHAT MANNER.

As the book of French maketh mention, afore the time that
Sir Galahad was begotten or born, there came in an hermit
unto King Arthur upon Whitsunday, as the knights sat at
the Table Round. And when the hermit saw the Siege Perilous he asked the king and all the knights why that siege[1] was
void.

Then King Arthur for all the knights answered and said,

'There shall never none sit in that siege[1] but one, but if he
be[2] destroyed.'

Then said the hermit, 'Sir, wot ye what he is?'

'Nay,' said King Arthur and all the knights, 'we know not
who he is yet that shall sit there.'

'Then wot I,' said the hermit. 'For he that shall sit there
is yet unborn and unbegotten, and this same year he shall be
begotten that sall sit in that Siege Perilous, and he shall win
the Sankgreall.' When this hermit had made this mention he
departed from the court of King Arthur.

And so after this feast Sir Lancelot rode on his adventure
till on a time by adventure he passed over the Pont de Corbin.
And there he saw the fairest tower that ever he saw, and there-
under was a fair little town full of people. And all the people,
men and women, cried at once.

'Welcome, Sir Lancelot, the flower of knighthood! For by
thee all we shall be holpen out of danger.'[3]

'What mean ye,' said Sir Lancelot, 'that ye cry thus upon
me?'

'Ah, fair knight,' said they all, 'here is within this tower a

---

[1] seat   [3] delivered
[2] without being

71

dolorous[4] lady that hath been there in pains[5] many winters and days, for ever she boileth in scalding water. And but late,' said all the people, 'Sir Gawain was here and he might not help her, and so he left her in pain[5] still.'

'Peradventure[6] so may I,' said Sir Lancelot, 'leave her in pain as well as Sir Gawain.'

'Nay,' said the people, 'we know well that it is ye, Sir Lancelot, that shall deliver her.'

'Well,' said Sir Lancelot, 'then tell me what I shall[7] do.'

And so anon they brought Sir Lancelot into the tower. And when he came to the chamber thereas[8] this lady was, the doors of iron unlocked and unbolted, and so Sir Lancelot went into the chamber that was as hot as any stew.[9] And there Sir Lancelot took the fairest lady by the hand that ever he saw, and she was as naked as a needle. And by enchantment Queen Morgan le Fay and the Queen of North Wales had put her there in that pains,[5] because she was called the fairest lady of that country; and there she had been five year, and never might she be delivered out of her pains[5] unto the time the best knight of the world had taken her by the hand.

Then the people brought her clothes, and when she was arrayed Sir Lancelot thought she was the fairest lady that ever he saw but if it were Queen Guinevere. Then this lady said to Sir Lancelot,

'Sir, if it please you, will ye go with me hereby into a chapel, that we may give loving[10] to God?'

'Madam,' said Sir Lancelot, 'cometh on with me and I will go with you.'

So when they came there they gave thankings to God, all the people both learned and lewd,[11] and said,

'Sir knight, syn ye have delivered this lady ye must deliver us also from a serpent which is here in a tomb.'

Then Sir Lancelot took his shield and said,

'Sirs, bring me thither, and what that I may do to the pleasure of God and of you I shall do.'

So when Sir Lancelot came thither he saw written upon the tomb with letters of gold that said thus:

'HERE SHALL COME A LEOPARD OF KING'S BLOOD AND HE SHALL

---

[4] unfortunate	[8] where
[5] distress	[9] stove
[6] perhaps	[10] praise
[7] must	[11] ignorant

SLAY THIS SERPENT. AND THIS LEOPARD SHALL ENGENDER A LION
IN THIS FOREIGN COUNTRY WHICH LION SHALL PASS ALL OTHER
KNIGHTS.'

So when Sir Lancelot had lift up the tomb there came out
an horrible and a fiendly dragon spitting wild fire out of his
mouth. Then Sir Lancelot drew his sword and fought with
that dragon long, and at the last with great pain Sir Lancelot
slew that dragon.

And therewithal come King Pelles, the good and noble king,
and salewed Sir Lancelot and he him again.

'Now, fair knight,' said the king, 'what is your name? I
require you of your knighthood tell ye me.'

'Sir,' said Sir Lancelot, 'wit you well my name is Sir Lancelot du Lake.'

'And my name is King Pelles, king of the foreign country
and cousin nigh unto Joseph of Arimathea.'

And then either of them made much of other, and so they
went into the castle to take their repast. And anon there
came in a dove at a window, and in her mouth there seemed
a little censer of gold, and therewithal there was such a savour[12] as all the spicery[13] of the world had been there. And
forthwithal there was upon the table all manner of meats and
drinks that they could think upon.

So there came in a damsel passing fair and young, and she
bare a vessel of gold betwixt her hands; and thereto the king
kneeled devoutly and said his prayers, and so did all that were
there.

'Ah, Jesu,' said Sir Lancelot, 'what may this mean?'

'Sir,' said the king, 'this is the richest thing that any man
hath living, and when this thing goeth abroad the Round
Table shall be broken for a season.[14] And wit you well,' said
the king, 'this is the Holy Sankgreall that ye have here seen.'

So the king and Sir Lancelot led their life the most party
of that day[15] together. And fain would King Pelles have found
the mean that[16] Sir Lancelot should have lain by his daughter,
fair Elaine, and for this intent: the king knew well that Sir
Lancelot should get a pusell[17] upon his daughter, which should
be called Sir Galahad, the good knight by whom all the foreign

---

12 scent
13 spices
14 for a time

15 that day spent most of their
time
16 how to contrive that
17 chaste youth

country should be brought out of danger;[18] and by him the Holy Grail should be achieved.

Then came forth a lady that hight Dame Brusen, and she said unto the king,

'Sir, wit you well Sir Lancelot loveth no lady in the world but all only[19] Queen Guinevere. And therefore work ye by my counsel, and I shall make him to lie with your daughter, and he shall not wit[20] but that he lieth by Queen Guinevere.'

'Ah, fair lady,' said the king, 'hope ye that ye may bring this matter about?'

'Sir,' said she, 'upon pain of my life, let me deal.'[1]

For this Dame Brusen was one of the greatest enchanters that was that time in the world.

And so anon by Dame Brusen's wit she made one to come to Sir Lancelot that he knew well, and this man brought a ring from Queen Guinevere like as it had come from her, and such one as she was wont for the most part[2] to wear. And when Sir Lancelot saw that token, wit you well he was never so fain.

'Where is my lady?' said Sir Lancelot.

'In the castle of Case,' said the messenger, 'but five mile hence.'

Then thought Sir Lancelot to be there the same night. And then this Dame Brusen, by the commandment of King Pelles, she let send Elaine to this castle with five-and-twenty knights, unto the castle of Case.

Then Sir Lancelot against[3] night rode unto the castle, and there anon he was received worshipfully with such people, to his seeming,[4] as were about Queen Guinevere secret.[5] So when Sir Lancelot was alight he asked where the queen was. So Dame Brusen said she was in her bed.

And then people were avoided,[6] and Sir Lancelot was led into her chamber. And then Dame Brusen brought Sir Lancelot a cup of wine, and anon as he had drunken that wine he was so assotted[7] and mad that he might make no delay, but without any let[8] he went to bed. And so he weened that maiden Elaine had been Queen Guinevere. And wit you well

[18] delivered (from the powers of evil)
[19] except
[20] so that he shall not think otherwise
[1] contrive it
[2] usually
[3] shortly before
[4] as it seemed to him
[5] in Queen Guinevere's confidence
[6] sent away
[7] infatuated
[8] unhindered

that Sir Lancelot was glad, and so was lady Elaine that she had gotten Sir Lancelot in her arms, for well she knew that that same night should be begotten Sir Galahad upon her, that should prove the best knight of the world.

And so they lay together until undern of the morn;[9] and all the windows and holes[10] of that chamber were stopped, that no manner of day[11] might be seen. And anon Sir Lancelot remembered him and arose up and went to the window, and anon as he had unshut the window the enchantment was past. Then he knew himself that he had done amiss.

'Alas!' he said, 'that I have lived so long, for now am I shamed.'

And anon he gat his sword in his hand and said,

'Thou traitress! What are thou that I have lain by all this night? Thou shalt die right here of[12] mine hands!'

Then this fair lady Elaine skipped out of her bed all naked and said,

'Fair courteous knight, Sir Lancelot,' kneeling before him, 'ye are come of king's blood, and therefore I require you have mercy upon me! And as thou art renowned the most noble knight of the world, slay me not, for I have in my womb begotten of thee that shall be the most noblest knight of the world.'

'Ah, false traitress! Why hast thou betrayed me? Tell me, anon,' said Sir Lancelot, 'what thou art.'

'Sir,' she said, 'I am Elaine, the daughter of King Pelles.'

'Well,' said Sir Lancelot, 'I will forgive you.'

And therewith he took her up in his arms and kissed her, for she was a fair lady, and thereto lusty[13] and young, and wise as any was that time living.

'So God me help,' said Sir Lancelot, 'I may not wite this to you,[14] but her that made this enchantment upon me and between you and me. An I may find her, that same lady Dame Brusen shall lose her head for her witchcrafts, for there was never knight deceived as I am this night.'

And then she said, 'My lord, Sir Lancelot, I beseech you, see me as soon as ye may, for I have obeyed me unto the prophecy that my father told me. And by his commandment, to fulfil this prophecy I have given thee the greatest riches

---

[9] nine o'clock the next morning
[10] embrasures
[11] daylight
[12] by
[13] pleasing
[14] blame you for this

and the fairest flower that ever I had, and that is my maiden-hood that I shall never have again. And therefore, gentle knight, owe me your goodwill.'

And so Sir Lancelot arrayed him and armed him, and took his leave mildly at[15] that young lady Elaine. And so he departed and rode to the castle of Corbin where her father was.

And as fast as her time came she was delivered of a fair child, and they christened him Galahad. And wit you well that child was well kept and well nourished, and he was so named Galahad because Sir Lancelot was so named at the fountain stone (and after that the Lady of the Lake confirmed him Sir Lancelot du Lake).

Then after the lady was delivered and churched[16] there came a knight unto her, his name was Sir Bromell la Pleche, the which was a great lord. And he had loved that lady Elaine long, and he evermore desired to wed her. And so by no mean she could put him off, till on a day she said to Sir Bromell,

'Wit you well, sir knight, I will not love you, for my love is set upon the best knight of the world.'

'Who is that?' said Sir Bromell.

'Sir,' she said, 'it is Sir Lancelot du Lake that I love and none other, and therefore woo ye me no longer.'

'Ye say well,' said Sir Bromell, 'and sithen ye have told me so much, ye shall have little joy of Sir Lancelot, for I shall slay him wheresomever I meet him!'

'Sir,' said this lady Elaine, 'do to him no treason, and God forbid that ye spare[17] him.'

"Well, my lady,' said Sir Bromell, 'and I shall promise you this twelvemonth and a day I shall keep Le Pont Corbin for Sir Lancelot sake, that he shall nother come nother go unto you, but I shall meet with him.'

Then as it fell by fortune and adventure, Sir Bors de Ganis that was nephew unto Sir Lancelot came over that bridge; and there Sir Bromell and Sir Bors jousted, and Sir Bors smote Sir Bromell such a buffet that he bare him over his horse croup.[18]

And then Sir Bromell, as an hardy[19] man, pulled out his sword and dressed[20] his shield to do battle with Sir Bors. And anon Sir Bors alight and voided[1] his horse, and there they

---

15 gently bade farewell to
16 blessed (by a priest)
17 find
18 horse's hind-quarters

19 brave
20 positioned
1 left

dashed together[2] many sad[3] strokes. And long thus they
fought, and at the last Sir Bromell was laid to the earth, and
there Sir Bors began to unlace his helm to slay him. Then Sir
Bromell cried him mercy and yielded him.

'Upon this covenant thou shalt have thy life,' said Sir Bors,
'so thou go unto my lord Sir Lancelot upon Whitsunday next
coming and yield thee unto him as a knight recreant.'[4]

'Sir, I will do it,' said Sir Bromell.

And so he sware upon the cross of the sword, and so he[5]
let him depart. And Sir Bors rode unto King Pelles, that was
within Corbin, and when the king and Elaine, his daughter,
knew that Sir Bors was nephew unto Sir Lancelot they made
him great cheer. Then said Dame Elaine,

'We marvel where Sir Lancelot is, for he came never here
but once that ever I saw.'

'Madam, marvel ye not,' said Sir Bors, 'for this half year
he hath been in prison with Queen Morgan le Fay, King
Arthur's sister.'

'Alas!' said Dame Elaine, 'that me sore repenteth!'

And ever Sir Bors beheld that child in her arms, and ever
him seemed it was passing like Sir Lancelot.

'Truly,' said Dame Elaine, 'wit you well, this child he begat
upon me.'

Then Sir Bors wept for joy, and there he prayed to God
it might prove as good a knight as his father was.

And so there came in a white dove, and she bare a little
censer of gold in her mouth, and there was all manner of meats
and drinks. And a maiden bare that Sankgreall, and she said
there openly,

'Wit you well, Sir Bors, that this child, Sir Galahad, shall
sit in the Siege Perilous and achieve the Sankgreall, and he
shall be much better than ever was his father, Sir Lancelot,
that is his own father.'

And then they kneeled down and made their devotions, and
there was such a savour[6] as all the spicery[7] in the world had
been there. And as the dove had taken her flight the maiden
vanished with the Sankgreall as she came.

'Sir,' said Sir Bors then unto King Pelles, 'this castle may be
named the Castle Adventurous, for here be many strange adventures.'

---

[2] fell upon each other with

[3] heavy

[4] as a knight who has surrendered

[5] = Bors

[6] scent

[7] spices

'That is sooth,' said the king, 'for well may this place be called the adventurous place. For there come but few knights here that goeth away with any worship;[8] be he never[9] so strong, here he may be proved.[10] And but late ago Sir Gawain, the good knight, gat little worship[11] here. For I let you wit,' said King Pelles, 'here shall no knight win worship[11] but if he be of worship[12] himself and of good living,[13] and that loveth God and dreadeth God. And else he getteth no worship[8] here, be he never[9] so hardy[14] a man.'

'That is a wonder thing,' said Sir Bors, 'what ye mean in[15] this country, for ye have many strange adventures. And therefore will I lie in this castle this night.'

'Sir, ye shall not do so,' said King Pelles, 'by my counsel, for it is hard an ye escape without a shame.'[16]

'Sir, I shall take the adventure that will fall,'[17] said Sir Bors.

'Then I counsel you,' said the king, 'to be clean confessed.'

'As for that,' said Sir Bors, 'I will be shriven with a good will.'

So Sir Bors was confessed. And all for women Sir Bors was a virgin save for one, that was the daughter of King Braundegoris, and on her he gat a child which hight Elaine. And save for her Sir Bors was a clean maiden.[18]

And so Sir Bors was led unto bed in a fair large chamber, and many doors were shut about[19] the chamber. When Sir Bors espied all these doors he avoided all the people,[20] for he might have[1] nobody with him. But in no wise Sir Bors would unarm him, but so he laid him down upon the bed.

And right so he saw a light come, that he might[2] well see a spear great and long that came straight upon him pointeling,[3] and Sir Bors seemed[4] that the head of the spear brent like a taper. And anon, or Sir Bors wist, the spear smote him in the shoulder an handbreadth in deepness, and that wound grieved Sir Bors passing sore, and then he laid him down for pain.

---

[8] credit
[9] ever
[10] put to the test
[11] distinction
[12] honourable
[13] righteous
[14] brave
[15] what you say about
[16] for you will not easily avoid being put to shame

[17] befall
[18] chaste man
[19] around
[20] made everybody withdraw
[1] wanted
[2] could
[3] point foremost
[4] it seemed to Sir Bors

And anon therewithal came a knight armed with his shield on his shoulder and his sword in his hand, and he bade Sir Bors,

'Arise, sir knight, and fight with me.'

'I am sore hurt, but yet I shall not fail thee.'

And then Sir Bors start up[5] and dressed[6] his shield, and then they lashed together mightily a great while; and at the last Sir Bors bare[7] him backward till that he came to a chamber door, and there that knight yode[8] into that chamber and rested him a great while. And when he had reposed him he came out fiercely again and began new battle with Sir Bors mightily and strongly. Then Sir Bors thought he[9] should no more go into that chamber to rest him, and so Sir Bors dressed him[10] betwixt the knight and the chamber door. And there Sir Bors smote him down, and then that knight yielded him.

'What is your name?' said Sir Bors.

'Sir, my name is Sir Bedivere of the Strait Marches.'

So Sir Bors made him to swear at Whitsunday next coming to come to the court of King Arthur, 'and yield you there as prisoner and as an overcome knight by the hands of Sir Bors.'

So thus departed Sir Bedivere of the Strait Marches. And then Sir Bors laid him down to rest. And anon he heard much noise in that chamber, and then Sir Bors espied that there came in, he wist not whether at doors or at windows, shot[11] of arrows and of quarrels[12] so thick that he marvelled, and many fell upon him and hurt him in the bare places.

And then Sir Bors was ware where came in an hideous lion. So Sir Bors dressed him to[13] that lion, and anon the lion bereft him his shield, and with his sword Sir Bors smote off the lion's head.

Right so forthwithal he saw a dragon in the court, passing perilous[14] and horrible, and there seemed to him that there were letters of gold written in his forhead, and Sir Bors thought that the letters made a signification of 'King Arthur.' And right so there came an horrible leopard and an old, and there they fought long and did great battle together. And at the last the dragon spit out of his mouth as it had been[15] an

[5] stood up
[6] positioned
[7] forced
[8] stepped
[9] = the knight
[10] stepped forward

[11] a flight
[12] arrowheads, short arrows
[13] advanced towards
[14] frightening
[15] what looked like

hundred dragons; and lightly all the small dragons slew the old dragon and tore him all to pieces.

And anon and forthwithal there came an old man into the hall, and he sat him down in a fair chair, and there seemed to be two adders about his neck. And then the old man had an harp, and there he sang an old lay of Joseph of Arimathea how he came into this land. And when he had sungen, this old man bade Sir Bors go from thence. 'For here shall ye have no more adventures; yet full worshipfully have ye achieved this, and better shall ye do hereafter.'

And then Sir Bors seemed that there came the whitest dove that ever he saw with a little golden censer in her mouth. And anon therewithal the tempest ceased and passed away that afore was marvellous to hear.[16] So was all that court full of good savours.[17]

Then Sir Bors saw four fair children bearing four fair tapers, and an old man in the midst of these children with a censer in his hand, and a spear in his other hand, and that spear was called the Spear of Vengeance.

'Now,' said that old man to Sir Bors, 'go ye to your cousin Sir Lancelot and tell him this adventure had been most convenient[18] for him of all earthly knight, but sin is so foul in him that he may not achieve none such holy deeds; for had not been his sin, he had passed all the knights that ever were in his days. And tell thou Sir Lancelot, of[19] all worldly adventures he passeth in manhood and prowess all other, but in these spiritual matters he shall have many his better.

And then Sir Bors saw four gentlewomen come by him, poorly beseen:[20] and he saw where that they entered into a chamber where[1] was great light as it were a summer's light. And the women kneeled down before an altar of silver with four pillars, as it had been a bishop which kneeled afore the table of silver. And as Sir Bors looked over his head he saw a sword like silver, naked, hoving[2] over his head, and clearness thereof smote in his eyen,[3] that as at that time[4] Sir Bors was blind.

And there he heard a voice which said, 'Go hence, thou

[16] made such noise
[17] scents
[18] fitting
[19] in
[20] dressed

[1] there
[2] suspended
[3] dazzled his eyes
[4] so that for a moment

Sir Bors, for as yet thou are not worthy for to be in this place!' And then he yode backward till[5] his bed till on the morn.

And so on the morn King Pelles made great joy of Sir Bors, and then he departed and rode unto Camelot. And there he found Sir Lancelot, and told him of the adventures that he had seen with King Pelles at Corbin.

And so the noise[6] sprang in King Arthur's court that Sir Lancelot had gotten a child upon Elaine, the daughter of King Pelles, wherefore Queen Guinevere was wroth, and she gave many rebukes to Sir Lancelot and called him false knight. And then Sir Lancelot told the queen all, and how he was made to lie by her 'in the likeness of you, my lady the queen;' and so the queen held Sir Lancelot excused.

And as the book saith, King Arthur had been in France, and had warred upon the mighty King Claudas, and had won much of his lands. And when the king was come again[7] he let cry[8] a great feast, that all lords and ladies of all England should be there but if it were[9] such as were rebellious against him.

And when Dame Elaine, the daughter of King Pelles, heard of this feast she yode[10] to her father and required of him that he would give her leave to ride to that feast. The king answered and said,

'I will that ye go thither. But in any wise as ye love me and will have my blessing, look that ye be well beseen[11] in the most richest wise, and look that ye spare not for no cost.[12] Ask and ye shall have all that needeth unto you.'

Then by the advice of Dame Brusen, her maiden, all thing was apparelled[13] unto the purpose, that there was never no lady richlier beseen.[11] So she rode with twenty knights and ten ladies and gentlewomen, to the number of an hundred horse. And when she came to Camelot King Arthur and Queen Guinevere said with all the knights that Dame Elaine was the fairest and the best beseen[11] lady that ever was seen in that court.

And anon as King Arthur wist that she was come, he met her and salewed her, and so did the most party of all the

---

[5] went back to
[6] rumour
[7] back
[8] proclaimed
[9] except
[10] went
[11] dressed
[12] spare no cost
[13] provided

knights of the Round Table, both Sir Tristram, Sir Bleoberis, and Sir Gawain, and many more that I will not rehearse.[14]

But when Sir Lancelot saw her he was so ashamed, and that because he drew his sword to her on the morn after that he had lain by her, that he would not salew her nother speak with her. And yet Sir Lancelot thought that she was the fairest woman that ever he saw in his life-days.

But when Dame Elaine saw Sir Lancelot would not speak unto her she was so heavy[15] she weened her heart would have to-brast;[16] for wit you well, out of measure she loved him. And then Dame Elaine said unto her woman, Dame Brusen,

'The unkindness of Sir Lancelot slayeth mine heart near!'

'Ah! peace, madam,' said Dame Brusen, 'I shall undertake that this night he shall lie with you, an ye will hold you still.'

'That were me liefer,'[17] said Dame Elaine, 'than all the gold that is aboven earth.'

'Let me deal,'[18] said Dame Brusen.

So when Dame Elaine was brought unto the Queen either made other good cheer as by countenance,[19] but nothing with their hearts. But all men and women spake of the beauty of Dame Elaine.

And then it was ordained that Dame Elaine should sleep in a chamber nigh by the queen, and all under one roof. And so it was done as the king commanded. Then the queen sent for Sir Lancelot and bade him come to her chamber that night, 'other else,' said the queen, 'I am sure that ye will go to your lady's bed, Dame Elaine, by whom ye gat[20] Galahad.'

'Ah, madam!' said Sir Lancelot, 'never say ye so, for that[1] I did was against my will.'

'Then,' said the queen, 'look that ye come to me when I send for you.'

'Madam,' said Sir Lancelot, 'I shall not fail you, but I shall be ready at your commandment.'

So this bargain was soon not so[2] done and made between them but Dame Brusen knew it by her crafts, and told it unto her lady, Dame Elaine.

'Alas!' said she, 'how shall I do?'

'Let me deal,'[18] said Dame Brusen, 'for[3] I shall bring him

---

14 name
15 sad
16 would break
17 I would rather that
18 contrive it

19 in outward appearance
20 begot
1 that which
2 no sooner
3 and

by the hand even to your bed, and he shall ween that I am Queen Guinevere's messenger.'

'Then well were me,' said Dame Elaine, 'for all the world I love not so much as I do Sir Lancelot.'

So when time came that all folks were to bed, Dame Brusen came to Sir Lancelot's bed's side and said,

'Sir Lancelot du Lake, sleep ye? My lady, Queen Guinevere, lieth and awaiteth upon you.'

'Ah, my fair lady!' said Sir Lanselot. 'I am ready to go with you whither ye will have me.'

So Sir Lancelot threw upon him a long gown, and so he took his sword in his hand. And then Dame Brusen took him by the finger and led him to her lady's bed, Dame Elaine, and then she departed and left them there in bed together. And wit you well this lady was glad, and so was Sir Lancelot, for he weened that he had had another in his arms.

Now leave we them kissing and clipping,[4] as was a kindly[5] thing, and now speak we of Queen Guinevere that sent one of her women that she most trusted unto Sir Lancelot's bed. And when she came there she found the bed cold, and he was not therein; and so she came to the queen and told her all.

'Alas,' said the queen, 'where is that false knight become?'

So the queen was nigh out of her wit, and then she writhed and weltered[6] as a mad woman, and might not sleep a four or a five hours.

Then Sir Lancelot had a condition that he used of custom,[7] to clatter[8] in his sleep and to speak often of his lady, Queen Guinevere. So Sir Lancelot had awaked as long as it had pleased him, and so by course of kind[9] he slept and Dame Elaine both. And in his sleep he talked and clattered[8] as a jay of the love that had been betwixt Queen Guinevere and him, and as he talked so loud the queen heard him thereas[10] she lay in her chamber. And when she heard him so clatter she was wroth out of measure, and for anger and pain wist not what to do, and then she coughed so loud that Sir Lancelot awaked. And anon he knew her hemming,[11] and then he knew well that he lay by the Queen Elaine, and therewith he leapt out of his bed as he had been a wood man,[12] in his shirt,

---

[4] embracing
[5] natural
[6] tossed about
[7] had a peculiar habit
[8] chatter (ed)

[9] as was natural
[10] where
[11] coughing
[12] madman

and anon the queen met him in the floor; and thus she said:

'Ah, thou false traitor-knight! Look thou never abide in my court, and lightly[13] that thou avoid my chamber! And not so hardy,[14] thou false traitor-knight, that evermore thou come in my sight!'

'Alas!' said Sir Lancelot.

And therewith he took such an heartly sorrow at her words that he fell down to the floor in a swoon. And therwithal Queen Guinevere departed.

And when Sir Lancelot awoke out of his swough he leapt out at a bay-window into a garden, and there with thorns he was all to-scratched of his visage[15] and his body; and so he ran forth he knew not whither, and was as wild-wood[16] as ever was man. And so he ran two year, and never man had grace to know him.[17]

Now turn we unto Queen Guinevere and to the fair Lady Elaine, that when Dame Elaine heard the queen so rebuke Sir Lancelot, and how also he swooned, and how he leapt out at the bay-window, then she said unto Queen Guinevere,

'Madam, ye are greatly to blame for Sir Lancelot, for now have ye lost him, for I saw and heard by his countenance that he is mad for ever. And therefore, alas! madam, ye have done great sin, and yourself great dishonour, for ye have a lord royal of your own, and therefore it were your part to love him; for there is no queen in this world that hath such another king as ye have. And if ye were not, I might have gotten the love of my lord Sir Lancelot; and great cause I have to love him for he had my maidenhood, and by him I have borne a fair son whose name is Sir Galahad. And he shall be in his time the best knight of the world.'

'Well, Dame Elaine,' said the queen, 'as soon as it is daylight I charge you to avoid[18] my court. And for the love you owe unto Sir Lancelot discover[19] not his counsel,[20] for an ye do, it will be his death.'

'As for that,' said Dame Elaine, 'I dare undertake he is marred for ever, and that have you made. For nother ye nor I are like to rejoice him, for he made the most piteous groans when he leapt out at yonder bay-window that ever I heard

---

13 quickly
14 be not so daring
15 in his face
16 raving mad

17 the good fortune to recognize him
18 order you to leave
19 disclose
20 secret

man make.' 'Alas,' said fair Elaine, and 'alas,' said the queen, 'for now I wot well that we have lost him for ever!'

So on the morn Dame Elaine took her leave to depart and would no longer abide. Then King Arthur brought her on her way with more than an hundred knights throughout a forest. And by the way she told Sir Bors de Ganis all how it betid that same night, and how Sir Lancelot leapt out at a window araged[1] out of his wit.

'Alas!' then said Sir Bors, 'where is my lord Sir Lancelot become?'

'Sir,' said Dame Elaine, 'I wot ne'er.'

'Now, alas,' said Sir Bors, 'betwixt you both ye have destroyed a good knight.'

'As for me, sir,' said Dame Elaine, 'I said never nother did thing that should in any wise displease him. But with the rebuke, sir, that Queen Guinevere gave him I saw him swoon to the earth. And when he awoke he took his sword in his hand, naked save his shirt, and leap out at a window with the grisliest groan that ever I heard man make.'

'Now farewell,' said Sir Bors unto Dame Elaine, 'and hold my lord King Arthur with a tale[2] as long as ye can, for I will turn again[3] unto Queen Guinevere and give her an hete.[4] And I require you, as ever ye will have my service, make good watch and espy if ever it may happen you to see my lord Sir Lancelot.'

'Truly,' said Dame Elaine, 'I shall do all that I may do, for I would as fain know and wit where he is become as you or any of his kin or Queen Guinevere, and great cause enough have I thereto as well as any other. And wit you well,' said fair Elaine to Sir Bors, 'I would lose my life for him rather than he should be hurt.'

'Madam,' said Dame Brusen, 'let Sir Bors depart and hie him as fast as he may to seek Sir Lancelot, for I warn you, he is clean out of his mind; and yet he shall be well holpen an but by miracle.'

Then wept Dame Elaine, and so did Sir Bors de Ganis; and anon they departed. And Sir Bors rode straight unto Queen Guinevere, and when she saw Sir Bors she wept as she were wood.[5]

'Now, fie on your weeping!' said Sir Bors de Ganis. 'For

---

[1] frenzied
[2] false story
[3] return
[4] tell her I disapprove of her behaviour
[5] mad

ye weep never but when there is no boot.[6] Alas!' said Sir
Bors, 'that ever Sir Lancelot or any of his blood ever saw you,
for now have ye lost the best knight of our blood, and he
that was all our leader and our succour. And I dare say and
make it good that all kings christened nother heathen may
not find such a knight, for to speak of his nobleness and
courtesy, with his beauty and his gentleness. Alas!' said Sir
Bors, 'what shall we do that be of his blood?'

'Alas!' said Sir Ector de Maris, and 'Alas!' said Sir Lionel.

And when the queen heard them say so she fell to the earth
in a dead swoon. And then Sir Bors took her up and dawed[7]
her, and when she awaked she kneeled afore those three
knights and held up both her hands and besought them to seek
him: 'And spare not for no goods but that[8] he be founden,
for I wot well that he is out of his mind.'

And Sir Bors, Sir Ector and Sir Lionel departed from the
queen, for they might not abide no longer for sorrow. And
then the queen sent them treasure enough for their expense,
and so they took their horses and their armour and departed.
And then they rode from country to country, in forests and
in wilderness and in wastes, and ever they laid watch both at
forests and at all manner of men[9] as they rode, to hearken
and to spare after[10] him, as he that[11] was a naked man in his
shirt with a sword in his hand.

And thus they rode nigh a quarter of a year, long and
overthwart,[12] and never could hear word of him, and wit you
well these three knights were passing sorry. And so at the
last Sir Bors and his fellows met with a knight that hight
Sir Melion de Tartare.

'Now, fair knight,' said Sir Bors, 'whither be ye away?'
(For they knew either other afortime.)

'Sir,' said Sir Melion, 'I am in the way to the court of King
Arthur.'

'Then we pray you,' said Sir Bors, 'that ye woll tell my
lord Arthur and my lady Queen Guinevere and all the fellowship of the Round Table that we cannot in no[13] wise hear
tell where Sir Lancelot is become.'[14]

Then Sir Melion departed from them and said that he would tell the king and the queen and all the fellowship of the Round Table as they had desired him. And when Sir Melion came to the court he told the king and the queen and all the fellowship as they had desired him, how Sir Bors had said of Sir Lancelot.

Then Sir Gawain, Sir Uwain, Sir Sagramore le Desirous, Sir Aglovale, and Sir Perceval de Galis took upon them by the great desire of the king, and in especial[15] by the queen, to seek all England, Wales and Scotland to find Sir Lancelot. And with them rode eighteen knights more to bear them fellowship,[16] and wit you well they lacked no manner of spending;[17] and so were they three-and-twenty knights.

Now turn we unto Sir Lancelot and speak we of his care and woe, and what pain he there endured; for cold, hunger and thirst he had plenty, and[18] . . . suffered and endured many sharp showers, that ever ran wild-wood[19] from place to place and lived by fruit and such as he might get, and drank water two year; and other clothing had he but little but his shirt and his breek.[20] Thus as Sir Lancelot wandered here and there he came into a fair meadow where he found a pavilion. And thereby upon a tree hung a white shield, and two swords hung thereby, and two spears leaned thereby to a tree. And when Sir Lancelot saw the swords, anon he leapt to the one sword, and clutched that sword in his hand and drew it out. And then he lashed at the shield, that all the meadow rang of the dints, that he gave such a noise as ten knights had fought together.

Then came forth a dwarf, and leap unto Sir Lancelot, and would have had the sword out of his hand. And then Sir Lancelot took him by the both shoulders and threw him unto the ground, that he fell upon his neck and had nigh broken it. And therewithal the dwarf cried help.

Then there came forth a likely[1] knight and well apparelled in scarlet furred with miniver.[2] And anon as he saw Sir Lancelot he deemed that he should be out of his wit, and then he said with fair speech,

---

[15] and even more
[16] keep them company
[17] money to spend
[18] M *reproduces here a lengthy account of Perceval's adventures (O, pp. 809–817), which it seems legitimate to omit since there is* evidence to show (O, p. 1528) that he himself was doubtful as to its relevance.
[19] mad
[20] breeches
[1] handsome
[2] trimmed with ermine

'Good man, lay down that sword! For as meseemeth thou hadst more need of a sleep and of warm clothes than to wield that sword.'

'As for that,' said Sir Lancelot, 'come not too nigh, for an thou do, wit thou well I will slay thee.'

And when the knight of the pavilion saw that, he start backward into his pavilion. And then the dwarf armed him lightly,[3] and so the knight thought by force and might to have taken the sword from Sir Lancelot. And so he came stepping upon him, and when Sir Lancelot saw him come so armed with his sword in his hand, then Sir Lancelot flew to him with such a might and smote him upon the helm such a buffet that the stroke troubled[4] his brain, and therewithal the sword brake in three. And the knight fell to the earth and seemed as he had been dead, the blood brasting out of his mouth, nose, and ears.

And then Sir Lancelot ran into the pavilion, and rushed even[5] into the warm bed. And there was a lady that lay in that bed; and anon she gat her smock and ran out of the pavilion, and when she saw her lord lie at the ground like to be dead, then she cried and wept as she had been mad. And so with her noise[6] the knight awaked out of his swough, and looked up weakly with his eyen.

And then he asked where was that mad man that had given him such a buffet, 'for such a one had I never of man's hand.'

'Sir,' said the dwarf, 'it is not your worship[7] to hurt him, for he is a man out of his wit; and doubt ye not he hath been a man of great worship,[8] and for some heartly[9] sorrow that he hath taken, he is fallen mad. And meseemeth,' said the dwarf, 'that he resembleth much unto Sir Lancelot, for him I saw at the tournament of Lonezep.'

'Jesu defend,' said that knight, 'that ever that noble knight, Sir Lancelot, should be in such a plight! But whatsomever he be,' said the knight, 'harm will I none do him.'

And this knight's name was Sir Blyaunt, the which said unto the dwarf,

'Go thou fast on horseback unto my brother Sir Selivaunt, which is at the Castle Blank, and tell him of mine adventure,

---

[3] swiftly
[4] injured
[5] straight
[6] cries

[7] honourable
[8] repute
[9] grievous

and bid him bring with him an horse-litter. And then will
we bear this knight unto my castle.'

So the dwarf rode fast, and he came again[10] and brought
Sir Selivaunt with him, and six men with an horse-litter. And
so they took up the feather bed with Sir Lancelot, and so
carried all away with them unto the Castle Blank, and he
never awaked till he was within the castle. And then they
bound his hands and his feet, and gave him good meats and
good drinks, and brought him again to his strength and his
fairness.[11] But in his wit they could not bring him, nother to
know himself. And thus was Sir Lancelot there more than a
year and an half, honestly arrayed[12] and fair faren[13] withal.

Then upon a day this lord of that castle, Sir Blyaunt, took
his arms on horseback with a spear to seek adventures. And as
he rode in a forest there met him two knights adventurous, the
one was Sir Breuse Saunce Pity, and his brother, Sir Bartelot.
And these two ran both at once on Sir Blyaunt and brake their
spears upon his body. And then they drew their swords and
made great battle, and fought long together. But at the last
Sir Blyaunt was sore wounded, and felt himself faint, and anon
he fled on horseback toward his castle.

And as they came hurling under the castle there was Sir
Lancelot at a window, and saw how two knights laid upon Sir
Blyaunt with their swords. And when Sir Lancelot saw that,
yet as wood[14] as he was he was sorry for his lord, Sir Blyaunt.
And then in a braid[15] Sir Lancelot brake his chains off his
legs and off his arms, and in the breaking he hurt his hands
sore; and so Sir Lancelot ran out at a postern,[16] and there he
met with those two knights that chased Sir Blyaunt. And
there he pulled down Sir Bartelot with his bare hands from
his horse, and therewithal he wroth out[17] the sword out of
his hand, and so he leap unto Sir Breuse and gave him such a
buffet upon the head that he tumbled backward over his horse
croup.[18]

And when Sir Bartelot saw his brother have such a buffet
he gat a spear in his hand, and would have run Sir Lancelot
through. And that saw Sir Blyaunt, and struck off the hand

10 back
11 good looks
12 decently clad
13 well-treated
14 mad

15 sudden movement
16 side door
17 wrenched
18 horse's hind-quarters

of Sir Bartelot. And then Sir Breuse and Sir Bartelot gat their horses and fled away as fast as they might.

So when Sir Selivaunt came and saw what Sir Lancelot had done for his brother, then he thanked God, and so did his brother, that ever they did him any good. But when Sir Blyaunt saw that Sir Lancelot was hurt with the breaking of his irons, then was he heavy[19] that ever he bound him.

'I pray you, brother, Sir Selivaunt, bind him no more, for he is happy[20] and gracious.'[1]

Then they made great joy of Sir Lancelot, and so he abode thereafter an half year and more.

And so on a morn Sir Lancelot was ware where came a great boar with many hounds after him, but the boar was so big there might no hounds tarry[2] him. And so the hunters came after, blowing their horns, both upon horseback and some upon foot, and then Sir Lancelot was ware where one alight and tied his horse till a tree, and leaned his spear against the tree. So there came Sir Lancelot and found the horse, and a good sword tied to the saddle-bow; and anon Sir Lancelot leap into the saddle and gat that spear in his hand, and then he rode fast after the boar.

And anon he was ware where he sat, and his arse to a rock, fast by an hermitage. And then Sir Lancelot ran at the boar with his spear, and all to-shivered[3] his spear. And therewith the boar turned him lightly,[4] and rove[5] out the lungs and the heart of the horse, that Sir Lancelot fell to the earth; and, or ever he might[6] get from his horse, the boar smote him on the brawn[7] of the thigh up unto the hough bone.[8] And then Sir Lancelot was wroth, and up he gat upon his feet, and took his sword and smote off the boar's head at one stroke.

And therewithal came out the hermit and saw him have such a wound. Anon he meaned him,[9] and would have had him home unto his hermitage. But when Sir Lancelot heard him speak, he was so wroth with his wound that he ran upon the hermit to have slain him. Then the hermit ran away, and when Sir Lancelot might not overget[10] him, he threw his

---

[19] filled with regret
[20] harmless
[1] kind-hearted
[2] hinder
[3] shattered
[4] quickly

[5] ripped
[6] before he could
[7] flesh
[8] back part of the knee-joint
[9] pitied him
[10] overtake

sword after him, for he might no further[11] for bleeding. Then the hermit turned again[12] and asked Sir Lancelot how he was hurt.

'Ah, my fellow,' said Sir Lancelot, 'this boar hath bitten me sore.'

'Then come ye with me,' said the hermit, 'and I shall heal you.'

'Go thy way,' said Sir Lancelot, 'and deal[13] not with me!'

Then the hermit ran his way, and there he met with a goodly knight with many men.

'Sir,' said the hermit, 'here is fast by my place the goodliest man that I ever saw, and he is sore wounded with a boar, and yet he hath slain the boar. But well I wot,' said the good man, 'an he be not holpen, he shall die of that wound, and that were great pity.'

Then that knight at the desire of the hermit gat a cart, and therein he put the boar and Sir Lancelot, for he was so feeble that they might right easily deal with him. And so Sir Lancelot was brought into the hermitage, and there the hermit healed him of his wound. But the hermit might not find[14] him his sustenance, so he impaired[15] and waxed feeble, both of body and of his wit: for default of sustenance he waxed more wooder[16] than he was aforetime.

And then upon a day Sir Lancelot ran his way into the forest; and by the adventure he came to the city of Corbin where Dame Elaine was, that bare Galahad, Sir Lancelot's son. And when he was entered into the town he ran through the town to the castle; and then all the young men of that city ran after Sir Lancelot, and there they threw turves[17] at him and gave him many sad[18] strokes. And even as Sir Lancelot might reach any of them, he threw them so that they would never come in his hands no more, for of some he brake the legs and arms.

And so he fled into the castle, and then came out knights and squires and rescued Sir Lancelot. When they beheld him and looked upon his person, they thought they saw never so goodly[19] a man. And when they saw so many wounds upon

---

[11] could run no more
[12] back
[13] trouble
[14] provide
[15] grew worse

[16] more mad
[17] pieces of turf
[18] heavy
[19] handsome

him, they deemed that he had been a man of worship. And
then they ordained him clothes to his body, and straw and
litter under the gate of the castle to lie in. And so every day
they would throw him meat and set him drink, but there was
but few that would bring him meat to his hands.

So it befell that King Pelles had a nephew whose name was
Castor; and so he desired of the king to be made knight, and
at his own request the king made him knight at the feast of
Candlemas. And when Sir Castor was made knight, that same
day he gave many gowns. And then Sir Castor sent for the
fool, which was Sir Lancelot; and when he came afore Sir
Castor, he gave Sir Lancelot a robe of scarlet and all that
longed unto him.[20] And when Sir Lancelot was so arrayed
like a knight he was the seemliest[1] man in all the court, and
none so well made.

So when he saw his time[2] he went into the garden, and
there he laid him down by a well and slept. And so at after
noon Dame Elaine and her maidens came into the garden to
sport them. And as they roamed up and down one of Dame
Elaine's maidens espied where lay a goodly[19] man by the well
sleeping.

'Peace,' said Dame Elaine, 'and say no word, but show me
that man where he lieth.'

So anon she brought Dame Elaine where he lay. And when
that she beheld him, anon she fell in remembrance of him, and
knew him verily for Sir Lancelot. And therewithal she fell
on-weeping so heartily that she sank even[3] to the earth. And
when she had thus wept a great while, then she arose and
called her maidens and said she was sick. And so she yode[4] out
of the garden as straight to her father as she could, and there
she took him by herself apart; and then she said,

'Ah, my dear father, now I have need of your help, and but
if that ye help me now, farewell my good days forever!'

'What is that, daughter?' said King Pelles.

'In your garden I was to sport me, and there, by the well
I found Sir Lancelot du Lake sleeping.'

'I may not believe it!' said King Pelles.

'Truly, sir, he is there!' she said, 'And meseemeth he should
be yet distract[5] out of his wit.'

---

[20] was fitting for him to wear	[3] fell down
[1] handsomest	[4] went
[2] opportunity	[5] distracted

'Then hold you still,' said the king, 'and let me deal.'[6]

Then the king called unto him such as he most trusted, a four persons, and Dame Elaine, his daughter, and Dame Brusen, her servant. And when they came to the well and beheld Sir Lancelot, anon Dame Brusen said to the king,

'We must be wise how we deal with him, for this knight is out of his mind, and if we awake him rudely, what he will do we all know not. And therefore abide ye a while and I shall throw an enchantment upon him, that he shall not awake of[7] an hour.'

And so she did, and then the king commanded that all people should avoid,[8] that none should be in that way thereas[9] the king would come. And so when this was done these four men and these ladies laid hand on Sir Lancelot, and so they bare him into a tower, and so into a chamber where was the holy vessel of the Sankgreall. And before that holy vessel Sir Lancelot was laid. And there came an holy man and unhilled[10] that vessel, and so by miracle and by virtue of that holy vessel Sir Lancelot was healed and recovered.

And as soon as he was awakened he groaned and sighed, and complained him sore of his woodness[11] and strokes that he had had. And as soon as Sir Lancelot saw King Pelles and Dame Elaine, he waxed ashamed and said thus:

'Ah, Lord Jesu, how came I hither? For God's sake, my fair lord, let me wit how that I came hither!'

'Sir,' said Dame Elaine, 'into this country ye came like a mazed man,[12] clean out of your wit. And here have ye been kept as a fool, and no creature here knew what ye were, until by fortune a maiden of mine brought me unto you whereas[13] ye lay sleeping by a well. And anon as I verily beheld you I knew you. Then I told my father, and so were ye brought afore this holy vessel, and by the virtue of it thus were ye healed.'

'Ah Jesu, mercy!' said Sir Lancelot. 'If this be sooth, how many be there that knoweth of my woodness?'[11]

'So God me help,' said Dame Elaine, 'no more but my father, and I, and Dame Brusen.'

---

[6] deal with it
[7] for
[8] withdraw
[9] where
[10] uncovered
[11] madness
[12] man out of his senses
[13] where

'Now for Christ's love,' said Sir Lancelot, 'keep it counsel,[14] and let no man know it in the world. For I am sore ashamed that I have been misfortuned,[15] for I am banished the country of England.'

And so Sir Lancelot lay more than a fortnight or ever that he might[16] stir for soreness. And then upon a day he said unto Dame Elaine these words,

'Fair Lady Elaine, for your sake I have had much care and anguish, it needeth not to rehearse[17] it, ye know how. Notwithstanding I know well I have done foul to you when that I drew my sword to you to have slain you upon the morn after when that I had lain with you. And all was for the cause that ye and Dame Brusen made me for to lie by you maugre mine head.[18] And as ye say, Sir Galahad, your son, was begotten.'

'That is truth,' said Dame Elaine.

'Then will ye for my sake,' said Sir Lancelot, 'go ye unto your father and get me a place of[19] him wherein I may dwell? For in the court of King Arthur may I never come.'

'Sir,' said Dame Elaine, 'I will live and die with you, only for your sake; and if my life might not avail you and my death might avail you, wit you well I would die for your sake. And I will to my father, and I am right sure there is nothing that I can desire of him but I shall have it. And where ye be, my lord Sir Lancelot, doubt ye not but I will be with you with all the service that I may do.'

So forthwithal she went to her father and said,

'Sir, my lord Sir Lancelot desireth to be here by you in some castle of yours.'

'Well, daughter,' said the king, 'sith it is his desire to abide in these marches[20] he shall be in the Castle of Blyaunt, and there shall ye be with him, and twenty of the fairest young ladies that been in this country; and they shall be all of the greatest blood[1] in this country; and ye shall have twenty knights with you. For, daughter, I will that ye wit we all be honoured by the blood[2] of Sir Lancelot.'

Then went Dame Elaine unto Sir Lancelot, and told him

---

[14] a secret
[15] of my misfortune
[16] before he could
[17] describe
[18] against my will

[19] from
[20] this land
[1] nobility
[2] noble ancestry

all how her father had devised. Then came a knight which was called Sir Castor, that was nephew unto King Pelles, and he came unto Sir Lancelot, and asked him what was his name.

'Sir,' said Sir Lancelot, 'my name is Le Chevalier Ill Mafete,[3] that is to say, "the knight that hath trespassed." '

'Sir,' said Sir Castor, 'it may well be so, but ever meseemeth your name should be Sir Lancelot du Lake, for or now I have seen you.'

'Sir,' said Lancelot, 'ye are not gentle,[4] for I put a case[5] my name were Sir Lancelot, and that it list me not to discover[6] my name, what should it grieve you here to keep my counsel[7] and ye not hurt thereby? But wit you well, an ever it lie in my power, I shall grieve you, an ever I meet with you in my way!'

Then Sir Castor kneeled down and besought Sir Lancelot of mercy: 'for I shall never utter what ye be while that ye are in these parts.'

Then Sir Lancelot pardoned him. And so King Pelles with twenty knights, and Dame Elaine with her twenty ladies, rode unto the Castle of Blyaunt that stood in an island beclosed environ[8] with a fair water deep and large. And when they were there Sir Lancelot let call it The Joyous Isle; and there was he called none otherwise but Le Chevalier Mafete, 'the knight that hath trespassed'.

Then Sir Lancelot let made him a shield all of sable, and a queen crowned in the midst,[9] all silver, and a knight clean[10] armed kneeling afore her. And every day once, for any mirths that all the ladies might make him, he would once every day look toward the realm of Logres, where King Arthur and Queen Guinevere was, and then would he fall upon a-weeping as his heart should to-brast.

So it befall that time Sir Lancelot heard of a jousting fast by, within three leagues. Then he called unto him a dwarf, and he bade him go unto that jousting: 'And or ever[11] the knights depart, look that thou make there a cry,[12] in hearing

[3] F: '*li chevaliers Mesfait.*' It is not clear whether M's '*Ill*' is a rendering of the French prefix '*mes*' or whether the whole phrase is a corruption (perhaps deliberate) of '*li chevaliers qui mesfist.*'
[4] courteous
[5] for supposing
[6] disclose
[7] secret
[8] surrounded on all sides
[9] centre
[10] fully
[11] before
[12] proclamation

of all knights, that there is one knight in Joyous Isle, which is the Castle of Blyaunt, and say his name is Le Chevalier Mafete, that will joust against knights all that will come. And who that putteth that knight to the worse, he shall have a fair maiden and a gerfalcon.'

So when his cry[12] was cried, unto Joyous Isle drew the number of five hundred knights. And wit you well there was never seen in King Arthur's day one knight that did so much deeds of arms as Sir Lancelot did those three days together.[13] For, as the book maketh truly mention, he had the better of all the five hundred knights, and there was not one slain of them. And after that Sir Lancelot made them all a great feast.

And in the meanwhile came Sir Perceval de Galis and Sir Ector de Maris under that castle[14] which was called the Joyous Isle. And as they beheld that gay castle they would have gone to that castle, but they might not for the broad water, and bridge could they find none. Then were they ware on the other side where stood a lady with a sparhawk[15] on her hand, and Sir Perceval called unto her, and asked that lady who was in that castle.

'Fair knights,' she said, 'here within this castle is the fairest lady in this land, and her name is Dame Elaine. Also we have in this castle one of the fairest knights and the mightiest man that is, I dare say, living, and he calleth himself Le Chevalier Mafete.'

'How came he into these marches?'[16] said Sir Perceval.

'Truly,' said the damsel, 'he came into this country like a mad man, with dogs and boys chasing him through the city of Corbin, and by the holy vessel of the Sankgreall he was brought into his wit again. But he will not do battle with no knight but by undern[17] or by noon. And if ye list to come into the castle,' said the lady, 'ye must ride unto the further side of the castle, and there shall ye find a vessel that will bear you and your horse.'

Then they departed and came unto the vessel; and then Sir Perceval alight, and said unto Sir Ector de Maris,

'Ye shall abide me here until I wit what manner a knight he is. For it were shame unto us, inasmuch as he is but one knight, an we should both do battle with him.'

---

13 during those three days
14 to the walls of that castle
15 sparrowhawk

16 this land
17 nine o'clock in the morning

'Do ye as ye list,' said Sir Ector, 'and here I shall abide you until that I hear of you.'

Then passed Sir Perceval the water, and when he came to the castle gate he said unto the porter,

'Go thou to the good knight of this castle and tell him here is come an errant knight to joust with him.'

Then the porter yode[18] in and came again[19] and bade him ride into the common[20] place thereas[1] the jousting shall be, 'where lords and ladies may behold you.'

And so anon as Sir Lancelot had a warning he was soon ready, and there Sir Perceval and Sir Lancelot were come both. They encountered with such a might, and their spears were so rude,[2] that both the horses and the knights fell to the ground. Then they avoided[3] their horses, and flung[4] out their noble swords, and hew away many cantles[5] of their shields, and so hurtled together with their shields like two boars, and either wounded other passing sore. And so at the last Sir Perceval spake first, when they had foughten there long, more than two hours:

'Now fair knight,' said Sir Perceval, 'I require you of[6] your knighthood to tell me your name, for I met never with such another knight.'

'Sir, as for my name,' said Sir Lancelot, 'I will not hide it from you, but my name is Le Chevalier Mafete. Now tell me your name,' said Sir Lancelot, 'I require you.'

'Truly,' said Sir Perceval, 'my name is Sir Perceval de Galis, that was brother unto the good knight Sir Lamorak de Galis, and King Pellinore was our father, and Sir Aglovale is my brother.'

'Alas,' said Sir Lancelot, 'what have I done to fight with you which are a knight of the Table Round! And sometime I was your fellow.'

And therewithal Sir Lancelot kneeled down upon his knees and threw away his shield and his sword from him. When Sir Perceval saw him do so he marvelled what he meaned, and then he said thus:

[18] went
[19] back
[20] open
[1] where
[2] heavy

[3] dismounted from
[4] drew
[5] pieces
[6] by

'Sir knight, whatsomever ye be, I require you upon the high Order of Knighthood to tell me your true name.'

Then he answered and said, 'So God me help, my name is Sir Lancelot du Lake, King Ban's son of Benoy.'

'Alas!' then said Sir Perceval, 'what have I now done? For I was sent by the queen for to seek you, and so I have sought you nigh this two year, and yonder is Sir Ector de Maris, your brother, which abideth me on the yonder side of the water. And therefore, for God's sake,' said Sir Perceval, 'forgive me mine offences that I have here done.'

'Sir, it is soon forgiven,' said Sir Lancelot.

Then Sir Perceval sent for Sir Ector de Maris; and when Sir Lancelot had a sight of him he ran unto him and took him in his arms; and then Sir Ector kneeled down, and either wept upon other, that all men had pity to behold them.

Then came forth Dame Elaine. And she made them great cheer as might be made, and there she told Sir Ector and Sir Perceval how and in what manner Sir Lancelot came into that country and how he was healed. And there it was known how long Sir Lancelot was with Sir Blyaunt and with Sir Selyvaunt, and how he first met with them, and how he departed from them because he was hurt with a boar, and how the hermit healed him of his great wound, and how that he came to the city of Corbin.

. . . So it befell[7] on a day that Sir Ector and Sir Perceval came unto Sir Lancelot and asked of him what he would do, and whether he would go with them unto King Arthur.

'Nay,' said Sir Lancelot, 'that may I not do by no mean,[8] for I was so vengeably defended[9] the court that I cast me[10] never to come there more.'

'Sir,' said Sir Ector, 'I am your brother, and ye are the man in the world that I love most. And if I understood that it were your disworship,[11] ye may understand that I would never counsel you thereto. But King Arthur and all his knights, and in especial[12] Queen Guinevere, maketh such dole and sorrow for you that it is marvel[13] to hear and see. And ye must remember the great worship and renown that ye be

---

[7] *The passage omitted here (O, pp. 830–1) contains a brief account of how Bors found his son Elyne le Blank and brought him to Arthur's court.*

[8] I cannot possibly do so

[9] cruelly forbidden

[10] resolved

[11] it would disgrace you

[12] and even more

[13] dreadful

of, how that ye have been more spoken of than any other knight that is now living; for there is none that beareth the name now but ye and Sir Tristram. And therefore, brother,' said Sir Ector, 'make you ready to ride to the court with us. And I daresay and make it good,' said Sir Ector, 'it hath cost my lady the queen twenty thousand pounds, the seeking of you.'

'Well brother,' said Sir Lancelot, 'I will do after your counsel and ride with you.'

So then they took their horses and made ready, and anon they took their leave at King Pelles and at Dame Elaine. And when Sir Lancelot should depart Dame Elaine made great sorrow.

'My lord, Sir Lancelot,' said Dame Elaine, 'this same feast of Pentecost shall your son and mine, Galahad, be made knight, for he is now fully fifteen winter old.'

'Madam, do as ye list,' said Sir Lancelot, 'and God give him grace to prove a good knight.'

'As for that,' said Dame Elaine, 'I doubt not he shall prove the best man of his kin except one.'

'Then shall he be a good man enough,' said Sir Lancelot.

So anon they departed, and within fifteen days' journey they came unto Camelot, that is in English called Winchester.[14] And when Sir Lancelot was come among them, the king and all the knights made great joy of his homecoming.

And there Sir Perceval and Sir Ector de Maris began and told the whole adventures: how Sir Lancelot had been out of his mind in the time of his absence, and how he called himself Le Chevalier Mafete, 'the knight that had trespassed;' and in three days within Joyous Isle Sir Lancelot smote down five hundred knights. And ever as Sir Ector and Sir Perceval told these tales of Sir Lancelot, Queen Guinevere wept as she should have died. Then the queen made him great cheer.

'Ah, Jesu!' said King Arthur, 'I marvel for what cause ye, Sir Lancelot, went out of your mind. For I and many other deem it was for the love of fair Elaine, the daughter of King Pelles, by whom ye are noised[15] that ye have gotten a child, and his name is Galahad. And men say that he shall do many marvellous things.'

---

[14] *See below*, The Fair Maid of Astolat, *note 2*.   [15] it is said

'My lord,' said Sir Lancelot, 'if I did any folly I have that[16] I sought.'

And therewithal the king spake no more. But all Sir Lancelot's kinsmen knew for whom he went out of his mind. And then there was made great feasts, and great joys was there among them. And all lords and ladies made great joy when they heard that Sir Lancelot was come again unto the court.

[16] what

The knights of King Arthur seek a blessing for the Grail quest.
Ms. Fr. 343, fol. 7. *Bibliothèque Nationale, Paris.*

The Holy Grail

Now saith the tale that Sir Galahad rode many journeys in vain, and at last he came to the abbey where King Mordrains was. And when he heard that, he thought he would abide to see him.

And so upon the morn, when he had heard mass, Sir Galahad came unto King Mordrains. And anon the king saw him, which had lain blind of long time, and then he dressed him against him[1] and said,

'Sir Galahad, the servant of Jesu Christ and very[2] knight, whose coming I have abiden long, now embrace me and let me rest on thy breast, so that I may rest[3] between thine arms! For thou art a clean virgin above all knights, as the flower of the lily in whom virginity is signified. And thou art the rose which is the flower of all good virtue, and in colour of fire. For the fire of the Holy Ghost is taken[4] so in thee that my flesh, which was all dead of oldness, is become again young.'

When Galahad heard these words, then he embraced him and all his body. Then said he,[5]

'Fair Lord Jesu Christ, now I have my will! Now I require Thee, in this point[6] that I am in, that Thou come and visit me.'

And anon Our Lord heard his prayer, and therewith the soul departed from the body. And then Sir Galahad put him in the earth as a king ought to be, and so departed and came into a perilous forest where he found the well which boiled with great waves, as the tale telleth tofore.[7]

And as soon as Sir Galahad set his hand thereto it ceased, so that it brent no more, and anon the heat departed away. And cause why it brent, it was a sign of lechery that was that time

[1] rose to meet him
[2] true
[3] die. Cf. F: 'si que je puisse trespasser entre tes bras.'
[4] burning. Cf. F: 'le feu du Saint Esperit est si en toy espris' (= 'aflame').
[5] = King Mordrains
[6] state
[7] See note 11.

101

much used. But that heat might not abide his pure virginity. And so this was taken in the country for a miracle, and so ever after was it called Galahad's Well.

So by adventure he came unto the country of Gore, and into the abbey where Sir Lancelot had been toforehand and found the tomb of King Bagdemagus; but he was founder[8] thereof.[9] For[10] there was the tomb of Joseph of Arimathea's son and the tomb of Simeon, where Lancelot had failed.[11] Then he looked into a croft[12] under the minster, and there he saw a tomb which brent full marvellously. Then asked he the brethren what it was.

'Sir,' said they, 'a marvellous adventure that may not be brought to an end but by him that passeth of bounty and of knighthood all them of the Round Table.'

'I would,' said Sir Galahad, 'that ye would bring me thereto.'

'Gladly,' said they, and so led him till a cave. And he went down upon greses[13] and came unto the tomb. And so the flaming failed, and the fire staunched[14] which many a day had been great.

Then came there a voice which said,

'Much are ye beholden to thank God which hath given you a good hour,[15] that ye may draw out the souls of earthly pain and to put them into the joys of Paradise. Sir, I am of your kindred, which hath dwelled in this heat this three hundred winter and four-and-fifty to be purged of the sin that I did against Arimathea Joseph.'

Then Sir Galahad took the body in his arms and bare it into the minster. And that night lay Sir Galahad in the abbey; and on the morn he gave him his service and put him in the earth before the high altar.

So departed he from thence, and commended the brethren to God, and so he rode five days till that he came to the Maimed King. And ever followed Perceval the five days[16] asking where he had been, and so one told him how the

---

[8] finder

[9] *The repetition is puzzling and may be due to a fault in the text.*

[10] And

[11] *This is a reference to an episode familiar to readers of the French Prose* Lancelot *(cf. The Vulgate Version of the Arthurian Romances, ed. Sommer, IV, 175–7) but not to readers of M. The same may be said of the reference*

in the previous paragraph to the boiling fountain (cf. ibid., V, 244–8).

[12] crypt

[13] steps

[14] was quenched

[15] good fortune ('*bon eur*' mistaken for '*bonne heure*')

[16] *i.e. Perceval followed Galahad. In F they do not part company for five years.*

adventures of Logres were achieved. So on a day it befell that he came out of a great forest, and there they[17] met at traverse[18] with Sir Bors which rode alone. It is no need to ask if they were glad! And so he salewed them, and they yielded to him[19] honour and good adventure, and everych told other how they had sped.[20] Then said Sir Bors,

'It is more than a year and a half that I ne lay[1] ten times where men dwelled, but in wild forests and in mountains. But God was ever my comfort.'

Then rode they a great while till they came to the castle of Corbenic. And when they were entered within, King Pelles knew them. So there was great joy, for he wist well by their coming that they had fulfilled the Sankgreall.[2]

Then Eliazar, King Pelles' son, brought tofore them the broken sword wherewith Joseph was stricken through the thigh. Then Bors set his hand thereto to essay if he might have sowded[3] it again; but it would not be. Then he took it to Perceval, but he had no more power thereto than he.

'Now have ye it again,' said Sir Perceval unto Sir Galahad, 'for an it be ever achieved by any bodily man, ye must do it.'

And then he took the pieces and set them together, and seemed to them as it had never be broken, and as well as it was first forged. And when they within espied that the adventure of the sword was achieved, then they gave the sword to Sir Bors, for it might no better be set,[4] for he was so good a knight and a worthy man.

And a little before even the sword[5] arose, great and marvellous, and was full of great heat, that many men fell for dread. And anon alight a voice among them and said,

'They that ought not to sit at the table of Our Lord Jesu Christ, avoid[6] hence! For now there shall very[7] knights be fed.'

So they went thence, all save King Pelles and Eliazar, his

---

17 = Perceval and Galahad
18 crossways
19 wished him in return
20 fared
1 have not lain
2 F: 'they knew that the adventures of the castle would come to an end' (fauldroient). M anticipates the completion of the quest by altering both the tense and the meaning of the verb.

3 soldered
4 employed (F: *emploiee*)
5 *This should be 'a wind.'* Cf. F: *'ung vent leva grant et merveilleux.'* M misread 'ung vent' as 'un gleve' — no doubt because the two words were not properly divided.
6 withdraw
7 true

son, which were holy men, and a maid which was his niece.
And so there abode these three knights and these three; else
were no more. And anon they saw knights all armed come in
at the hall door, and did off their helms and their arms, and
said unto Sir Galahad,

'Sir, we have hied right much for to be with you at this
table where the holy meat shall be departed.'[8]

Then said he, 'Ye be welcome! But of whence be ye?'

So three of them said they were of Gaul, and other three
said they were of Ireland, and other three said they were of
Denmark.

And so as they sat thus, there came out a bed of tree[9] of[10]
a chamber, which four gentlewomen brought; and in the bed
lay a good man sick, and had a crown of gold upon his head.
And there, in the midst[11] of the palace, they set him down
and went again. Then he lift up his head and said,

'Sir Galahad, good knight, ye be right welcome, for much
have I desired your coming! For in such pain and in such
anguish as I have no man else[12] might have suffered long.
But now I trust to God the term is come that my pain shall
be allayed, and so I shall pass out of this world, so as it was
promised me long ago.'

And therewith a voice said, 'There be two among you that
be not in the quest of the Sankgreall, and therefore departeth!'

Then King Pelles and his son departed. And therewithal
beseemed them[13] that there came an old man and four angels
from heaven, clothed in likeness of a bishop, and had a cross
in his hand. And these four angels bare him up in a chair and
set him down before the table of silver whereupon the Sankgreall was. And it seemed that he had in midst of[14] his forehead letters which said: 'See ye here Joseph, the first bishop
of Christendom, the same which Our Lord succoured[15] in the
city of Sarras in the spiritual palace.' Then the knights marvelled, for that bishop was dead more than three hundred year
tofore.

'Ah, knights,' said he, 'marvel not, for I was sometime an
earthly man.'

---

[8] distributed (F: *departiz*)

[9] a wooden bed (F: *un lit de fust.*)

[10] from

[11] centre

[12] no other man

[13] it seemed to them

[14] upon

[15] F has 'sacra' ('*consecrated*'). M
is often so attracted by the sound
of French words that he loses sight
of their meaning. Cf. O, pp. LXII
(note 3), 1538, 1555, 1561, and
1562.

So with that they heard the chamber door open, and there they saw angels; and two bare candles of wax, and the third bare a towel,[16] and the fourth a spear which bled marvellously, that the drops fell within a box which he held with his other hand. And anon they set the candles upon the table, and the third the towel upon the vessel, and the fourth the holy spear even[17] upright upon the vessel.

And then the bishop made semblaunt[18] as though he would have gone to the sacring of a mass, and then he took an ubblie[19] which was made in likeness of bread. And at the lifting up there came a figure in likeness of a child, and the visage[20] was as red and as bright as any fire, and smote himself[1] into the bread, that all they saw it that the bread was formed of a fleshly man. And then he put it into the holy vessel again, and then he did that longed[2] to a priest to do mass.

And then he went to Sir Galahad and kissed him, and bade him go and kiss his fellows. And so he did anon.

'Now,' said he, 'the servants of Jesu Christ, ye shall be fed afore this table with sweet meats that never knights yet tasted.'

And when he had said he vanished away. And they set them at the table in great dread and made their prayers. Then looked they and saw a Man come out of the holy vessel that had all the signs of the Passion of Jesu Christ, bleeding all openly, and said,

'My knights and my servants and my true children which be come out of deadly life into the spiritual life, I will no longer cover me from you, but ye shall see now a part of my secrets and of my hid things. Now holdeth and receiveth the high order and meat[3] which ye have so much desired.'

Then took He himself the holy vessel and came to Sir Galahad. And he kneeled down and received his Saviour. And after him so received all his fellows, and they thought it so sweet that it was marvellous to tell. Then said He to Sir Galahad,

'Son, wotest thou what I hold betwixt my hands?'

'Nay,' said he, 'but if ye tell me.'

'This is,' said He, 'the holy dish wherein I ate the lamb on Easter Day, and now hast thou seen that thou most desired to

---

16 F: *une touaille* ('a veil') *de ver-meil samit*
17 straight
18 appeared
19 wafer, Host

20 face
1 impressed its image
2 what was fitting
3 F: *la haute viande* ('the holy food')

see. But yet hast thou not seen it so openly as thou shalt see it in the city of Sarras, in the spiritual palace. Therefore thou must go hence and bear with thee this holy vessel, for this night it shall depart from the realm of Logres, and it shall nevermore be seen here. And knowest thou wherefore? For he[4] is not served nother worshipped to his right[5] by them of this land, for they be turned to evil living, and therefore I shall disinherit[6] them of the honour which I have done them. And therefore go ye three to-morn unto the sea, where ye shall find your ship ready, and with you take the sword[7] with the strange girdles, and no more with you but Sir Perceval and Sir Bors. Also I will that ye take with you of this blood of this spear for to anoint the Maimed King, both his legs and his body, and he shall have his heal.'[8]

'Sir,' said Galahad, 'why shall not these other fellows go with us?'

'For this cause: for right as I depart[9] my apostles one here and another there, so I will that ye depart.[9] And two of you shall die in my service, and one of you shall come again[10] and tell tidings.'

Then gave He them His blessing and vanished away.

And Sir Galahad went anon to the spear which lay upon the table and touched the blood with his fingers, and came after to the maimed knight and anointed his legs and his body. And therewith he[11] clothed him anon, and start upon his feet out of his bed as an whole man, and thanked God that He had healed him. And anon he left the world and yielded himself to a place of religion of white monks, and was a full holy man.

And that same night, about midnight, came a voice among them which said,

'My sons, and not my chief sons,[12] my friends, and not mine enemies, go ye hence where ye hope best to do, and as I bade you do.'

'Ah, thanked be Thou, Lord, that Thou wilt whightsauf[13] to call us Thy sons! Now may we well prove that we have not lost our pains.'

---

[4] = the holy vessel (F: *il*)
[5] as it should be
[6] dispossess
[7] *A misreading of F's 'la nef ou tu preis l'espee' ('the ship from which you took the sword').*
[8] shall be restored
[9] separate

[10] back
[11] = the maimed knight
[12] F: *Mi fil et ne mie mi fillastre* (= stepsons). *There seems to be no satisfactory explanation of the change from 'stepsons' to 'chief* (= eldest?) *sons.'*
[13] be willing, vouchsafe

And anon in all haste they took their harness and departed; but the three knights of Gaul (one of them hight Claudine, King Claudas' son, and the other two were great gentlemen) then prayed Sir Galahad to everych of them, that an they come[14] to King Arthur's court, 'to salew my lord Sir Lancelot, my father and them all of the Round Table'; and prayed them, an they came on that party,[15] not to forget it.

Right so departed Sir Galahad, and Sir Perceval and Sir Bors with him, and so they rode three days. And then they came to a rivage[16] and found the ship whereof the tale speaketh of tofore. And when they came to the board[17] they found in the midst of[18] the bed the table of silver which they had left with the Maimed King, and the Sankgreall which was covered with red samite.[19] Then were they glad to have such things in their fellowship; and so they entered and made great reverence thereto, and Sir Galahad fell on his knees and prayed long time to Our Lord, that at what time he asked he might pass out of this world. And so long he prayed till a voice said,

'Sir Galahad, thou shalt have thy request, and when thou asketh the death of thy body thou shalt have it, and then shalt thou have the life of thy soul.'

Then Sir Perceval heard him a little, and prayed him of[20] fellowship that was between them wherefore he asked such things.

'Sir, that shall I tell you,' said Sir Galahad. 'This other day, when we saw a part of the adventures of the Sankgreall, I was in such a joy of heart that I trow never man was that was earthly. And therefore I wot well, when my body is dead, my soul shall be in great joy to see the Blessed Trinity every day, and the majesty of Our Lord, Jesu Christ.'

And so long were they in the ship that they said to Galahad, 'Sir, in this bed ye ought to lie, for so saith the letters.'[1]

And so he laid him down, and slept a great while. And when he awaked he looked tofore him and saw the city of Sarras. And as they would have landed they saw the ship wherein Sir Perceval had put his sister in.

'Truly,' said Sir Perceval, 'in the name of God, well hath my sister holden us covenant.'

---

[14] Galahad then asked each one of the three knights of Gaul (. . .), if they, *etc.*

[15] to that country

[16] shore

[17] on board

[18] upon

[19] rich silk

[20] for the sake of

[1] writings

Then they took out of the ship the table of silver, and he took it to Sir Perceval and to Sir Bors to go tofore,[2] and Sir Galahad came behind, and right so they went into the city. And at the gate of the city they saw an old man crooked, and anon Sir Galahad called him and bade him help 'to bear this heavy thing.'

'Truly,' said the old man, 'it is ten year ago that I might not go but with crutches.'

'Care thou not,' said Galahad, 'and arise up and show thy good will!'

And so he essayed, and found himself as whole as ever he was. Then ran he to the table and took one part against[3] Galahad.

Anon arose there a great noise in the city that a cripple was made whole by knights marvellous that entered into the city. Then anon after the three knights went to the water[4] and brought up into the palace Sir Perceval's sister, and buried her as richly as them ought[5] a king's daughter.

And when the king of that country knew that and saw that fellowship (whose name was Estorause), he asked them of whence they were, and what thing it was that they had brought upon the table of silver. And they told him the truth of the Sankgreall, and the power which God hath set there.

Then this king was a tyrant, and was come of the line of paynims,[6] and took them and put them in prison in a deep hole. But as soon as they were there Our Lord sent them the Sankgreall, through whose grace they were alway fulfilled[7] while that they were in prison.

So at the year's end it befell that this king lay sick and felt that he should die. Then he sent for the three knights, and they came afore him, and he cried them mercy of that he had done to them, and they forgave it him goodly,[8] and he died anon.

When the king was dead all the city stood dismayed and wist not who might be their king. Right so as they were in council there came a voice among them, and made them choose

---

[2] he took it so that Sir Perceval and Sir Bors should carry the front part (F: *si la prist Boorz et Perceval par devant et Galaad par deriere*)

[3] one side of it next to

[4] sea-shore

[5] as it was fitting that they should bury

[6] pagans

[7] fed (F: *repeu*)

[8] graciously

the youngest knight of three to be their king, 'for he shall well maintain you and all yours.'

So they made Sir Galahad king by all the assent of the whole city, and else they would have slain him. And when he was come to behold his land he let make[9] above the table of silver a chest of gold and of precious stones that covered the holy vessel, and every day early the three knights would come before it and make their prayers.

Now at the year's end, and the self Sunday after that Sir Galahad had borne the crown of gold, he arose up early and his fellows, and came to the palace, and saw tofore them the holy vessel and a man kneeling on his knees in likeness of a bishop that had about him a great fellowship of angels, as it had been Jesu Christ himself. And then he arose and began a mass of Our Lady. And so he came to the sacring, and anon made an end. He called Sir Galahad unto him and said,

'Come forth, the servant of Jesu Christ, and thou shalt see that thou hast much desired to see.'

And then he began to tremble right hard when the deadly flesh began to behold the spiritual things. Then he held up his hands toward heaven and said,

'Lord, I thank Thee, for now I see that that hath been my desire many a day. Now, my Blessed Lord, I would not live in this wretched world no longer, if it might please Thee, Lord.'

And therewith the good man took Our Lord's Body betwixt his hands, proffered it to Sir Galahad, and he received it right gladly and meekly.

'Now wotest thou what I am?' said the good man.

'Nay, Sir,' said Sir Galahad.

'I am Joseph, the son of Joseph of Arimathea, which Our Lord hath sent to thee to bear thee fellowship. And wotest thou wherefore He hath sent me more than any other? For thou hast resembled me in two things: that thou hast seen, that is the marvels of the Sankgreall, and for thou hast been a clean maiden[10] as I have been and am.'

And when he had said these words Sir Galahad went to Sir Perceval and kissed him and commended him to God. And so he went to Sir Bors and kissed him and commended him to God, and said,

'My fair lord, salew me unto[11] my lord Sir Lancelot, my

---

[9] ordered to be made   [11] greet on my behalf
[10] chaste man

father, and as soon as ye see him bid him remember of this world unstable.'

And therewith he kneeled down tofore the table and made his prayers. And so suddenly departed his soul to Jesu Christ, and a great multitude of angels bare it up to heaven, even in the sight of his two fellows.

Also these two knights saw come from heaven an hand, but they saw not the body, and so it came right to the vessel, and took it, and the spear, and so bare it up to heaven. And sithen was there never man so hardy to say that he had seen the Sankgreall.

So when Sir Perceval and Sir Bors saw Sir Galahad dead they made as much sorrow as ever did men. And if they had not been good men they might lightly[12] have fallen in despair. And so people of the country and city, they were right heavy.[13] But so he was buried, and soon as he was buried Sir Perceval yielded him to an hermitage out of the city and took religious clothing. And Sir Bors was alway with him, but he changed never his secular clothing, for that he purposed him to go again into the realm of Logres.

Thus a year and two months lived Sir Perceval in the hermitage a full holy life, and then passed out of the world. Then Sir Bors let bury him by his sister and by Sir Galahad in the spiritualities.[14]

So when Bors saw that he was in so far countries as in the parts of Bablyon,[15] he departed from the city of Sarras and armed him and came to the sea, and entered into a ship. And so it befell him, by good adventure, he came unto the realm of Logres, and so he rode a pace[16] till he came to Camelot where the king was.

And then was there made great joy of him in all the court, for they weened all he had been lost forasmuch as he had been so long out of the country. And when they had eaten, the king made great clerks to come before him, for cause they should chronicle of[17] the high adventures of the good knights. So when Sir Bors had told him of the high adventures of the Sankgreall such as had befallen him and his three fellows,

---

[12] easily
[13] sad
[14] consecrated ground
[15] as remote as the region of Babylon

[16] at a good speed
[17] so that they should place on record

which were Sir Lancelot, Perceval, Sir Galahad and himself, then Sir Lancelot told the adventures of the Sankgreall that he had seen. All this was made[18] in great books and put up in almeries[19] at Salisbury.

And anon Sir Bors said to Sir Lancelot,

'Sir Galahad, your own son, salewed you by me, and after you my lord King Arthur and all the whole court, and so did Sir Perceval. For I buried them with both mine own hands in the city of Sarras. Also, Sir Lancelot, Sir Galahad prayed you to remember of this unsiker[20] world, as ye behight[1] him when ye were together more than half a year.'

'This is true,' said Sir Lancelot; 'now I trust to God his prayer shall avail me.'

Then Sir Lancelot took Sir Bors in his arms and said,

'Cousin, ye are right welcome to me! For all that ever I may do for you and for yours, ye shall find my poor body[2] ready at all times while the spirit is in it, and that I promise you faithfully, and never to fail. And wit ye well, gentle cousin Sir Bors, ye and I shall never depart in sunder[3] while our lives may last.'

'Sir,' said he, 'as ye will, so will I.'

THUS ENDETH THE TALE OF THE SANKGREALL THAT WAS BRIEFLY DRAWN OUT OF FRENCH, WHICH IS A TALE CHRONICLED FOR ONE OF THE TRUEST AND OF THE HOLIEST THAT IS IN THIS WORLD, BY SIR THOMAS MALEORRÉ, KNIGHT.

O BLESSED JESU HELP HIM THROUGH HIS MIGHT! AMEN.

[18] written down
[19] ambries, libraries
[20] unstable, uncertain

[1] promised (*pret. of 'behote'*)
[2] my humble self
[3] never part

The Poisoned Apple

So after the quest of the Sankgreall was fulfilled, and all knights that were left on live were come home again unto the Table Round, as *The Book of the Sankgreall* maketh mention, then was there great joy in the court, and in especial King Arthur and Queen Guinevere made great joy of the remnant that were come home. And passing glad was the king and the queen of Sir Lancelot and of Sir Bors, for they had been passing long away in the quest of the Sankgreall.

Then, as the book saith, Sir Lancelot began to resort unto Queen Guinevere again and forgat the promise and the perfection[1] that he made in the quest; for, as the book saith, had not Sir Lancelot been in his privy[2] thoughts and in his mind so set inwardly to the queen as he was in seeming outward[3] to God, there had no knight passed him in the quest of the Sankgreall. But ever his thoughts privily[2] were on the queen, and so they loved together more hotter than they did toforehand, and had many such privy[2] draughts[4] together that many in the court spake of it, and in especial Sir Agravain, Sir Gawain's brother, for he was ever open-mouthed.[5]

So it befell that Sir Lancelot had many resorts of[6] ladies and damsels which daily resorted unto him, that besought him to be their champion. In all such matters of right Sir Lancelot applied him daily to do for the pleasure of Our Lord Jesu Christ, and ever as much as he might he withdrew him from the company of Queen Guinevere for to eschew the slander and noise.[7] Wherefore the queen waxed wroth with Sir Lancelot.

[1] the promise to achieve perfection
[2] secret(ly)
[3] to outward appearances
[4] meetings
[5] F: *pour ce qu'il beast* (= '*intended*') *le roi a vengier de sa honte. Paying no attention to the object of the verb 'beer' M took it to mean 'to be wide open, to gape.' Cf. Mod. Fr. 'bouche bée.'*
[6] requests from
[7] scandal

So on a day she called him unto her chamber and said thus:

'Sir Lancelot, I see and feel daily that your love beginneth to slake,[8] for ye have no joy to be in my presence, but ever ye are out of this court, and quarrels and matters[9] ye have nowadays for ladies, maidens and gentlewomen, more than ever ye were wont to have beforehand.'

'Ah, madam,' said Sir Lancelot, 'in this ye must hold me excused for divers causes. One is, I was but late in the quest of the Sankgreall, and I thank God of His great mercy, and never of my deserving,[10] that I saw in that my quest as much as ever saw any sinful man living, and so was it told me. And if that I had not had my privy[2] thoughts to return to your love again as I do, I had[11] seen as great mysteries as ever saw my son, Sir Galahad, Perceval, other Sir Bors. And therefore,[12] madam, I was but late in that quest, and wit you well, madam, it may not be yet lightly[13] forgotten, the high service in whom I did my diligent labour.

'Also, madam, wit you well that there be many men speaketh of our love in this court, and have you and me greatly in await,[14] as this Sir Agravain and Sir Mordred. And, madam, wit you well I dread them more for your sake than for any fear I have of them myself, for I may happen to escape and rid myself[15] in a great need where, madam, ye must abide[16] all that will be said unto you. And then, if that ye fall in any distress throughout[17] wilful[18] folly, then is there none other help but by me and my blood.[19]

'And wit you well, madam, the boldness of you and me will bring us to shame and slander; and that were me loath to see you dishonoured. And that is the cause I take upon me more for to do for damsels and maidens than ever I did toforn:[20] that men should understand my joy and my delight is my pleasure to have ado for damsels and maidens.'

All this while the queen stood still and let Sir Lancelot say what he would; and when he had all said she brast out of weeping, and so she sobbed and wept a great while. And when she might speak she said,

[8] abate
[9] preoccupations
[10] though I never deserved it
[11] I should have
[12] And so
[13] easily
[14] keep a close watch on you and me

[15] I may succeed in escaping and freeing myself
[16] face
[17] through
[18] deliberate
[19] kinsmen
[20] hitherto

'Sir Lancelot, now I well understand that thou art a false, recreant[1] knight and a common lecher, and lovest and holdest other ladies, and of me thou hast disdain and scorn. For wit thou well, now I understand thy falsehood I shall never love thee more, and look thou be never so hardy[2] to come in my sight. And right here I discharge[3] thee this court, that thou never come within it, and I forfend thee my fellowship,[4] and upon pain[5] of thy head that thou see me nevermore!'

Right so Sir Lancelot departed with great heaviness[6] that unneth he might sustain himself[7] for great dole-making.

Then he called Sir Bors, Ector de Maris and Sir Lionel, and told them how the queen had forfended him[8] the court, and so he was in will to depart into his own country.

'Fair sir,' said Bors de Ganis, 'ye shall not depart out of this land by mine advice, for ye must remember you what ye are, and renowned the most noblest knight of the world, and many great matters ye have in hand. And women in their hastiness will do oftentimes that after them sore repenteth. And therefore, by mine advice, ye shall take your horse and ride to the good hermit[9] here beside Windsor, that sometime was a good knight; his name is Sir Brastias. And there shall ye abide till that I send you word of better tidings.'

'Brother,' said Sir Lancelot, 'wit you well I am full loath to depart out of this realm, but the queen hath defended me so highly,[10] that meseemeth she will never be my good lady as she hath been.'

'Say ye never so,' said Sir Bors, 'for many times or this time she hath been wroth with you, and after that she was the first that repented it.'

'Ye say well,' said Sir Lancelot, 'for[11] now will I do by your counsel and take mine horse and mine harness and ride to the hermit Sir Brastias, and there will I repose me till I hear some manner of tidings from you. But, fair brother, in that ye can[12] get me the love of my lady, Queen Guinevere.'

'Sir,' said Sir Bors, 'ye need not to move[13] me of such matters, for well ye wot I will do what I may to please you.'

---

[1] cowardly
[2] bold
[3] dismiss
[4] I banish you from my company
[5] at the risk
[6] sorrow
[7] so great that he could hardly endure
[8] banished him from
[9] M: *ermytayge*
[10] sent me away so angrily
[11] and
[12] so far as you are able
[13] persuade

And then Sir Lancelot departed suddenly,[14] and no creature wist where he was become[15] but Sir Bors. So when Sir Lancelot was departed the queen outward made no manner of sorrow in showing to none of his blood[16] nor to none other, but wit ye well, inwardly, as the book saith, she took great thought;[17] but she bare it out with a proud countenance, as though she felt no thought nother danger.[18]

So the queen let make a privy dinner in London unto[19] the knights of the Round Table, and all was for to show outward that she had as great joy in all other knights of the Round Table as she had in Sir Lancelot. So there was all only at that dinner Sir Gawain and his brethren, that is for to say Sir Agravain, Sir Gaheris, Sir Gareth and Sir Mordred, also there was Sir Bors de Ganis, Sir Blamore de Ganis, Sir Bleoberis de Ganis, Sir Galihud, Sir Eliodin, Sir Ector de Maris, Sir Lionel, Sir Palomides, Sir Safir, his brother, Sir La Cote Male Tayle, Sir Persaunt, Sir Ironside, Sir Braundiles, Sir Kay le Seneschal, Sir Mador de la Porte, Sir Patrise, a knight of Ireland, Sir Aliduke, Sir Ascamore, and Sir Pinel le Savage, which was cousin to Sir Lamorak de Galis, the good knight that Sir Gawain and his brethren slew by treason.

And so these four-and-twenty knights should dine with the queen in a privy place by themselves, and there was made a great feast of all manner of dainties. But Sir Gawain had a custom that he used daily at meat and at supper, that[20] he loved well all manner of fruit, and in especial apples and pears. And therefore whosomever dined other feasted Sir Gawain would commonly purvey for[1] good fruit for him. And so did the queen; for to please Sir Gawain she let purvey for[1] him all manner of fruit. For[2] Sir Gawain was a passing hot[3] knight of nature, and this Sir Pinel hated Sir Gawain because of his kinsman Sir Lamorak's death, and therefore, for pure envy[4] and hate, Sir Pinel enpoisoned certain apples for to enpoison Sir Gawain.

So this was well yet unto the end of meat,[5] and so it befell by misfortune a good knight Sir Patrise, which was cousin

[14] quickly
[15] had gone
[16] kin
[17] she was grieved
[18] no sorrow or fear
[19] for
[20] namely

[1] provide(d)
[2] But
[3] hot-tempered
[4] spite
[5] already near the end of the feast

unto Sir Mador de la Porte, took an apple, for he was en-chafed[6] with heat of wine. And it mishapped him to take a poisoned apple. And when he had eaten it he swall sore till he brast,[7] and there Sir Patrise fell down suddenly[8] dead among them.

Then every knight leap from the board ashamed, and araged for[9] wrath out of their wits, for they wist not what to say; considering Queen Guinevere made the feast and dinner they had all suspicion unto her.

'My lady the queen!' said Sir Gawain. 'Madam, wit you that this dinner was made for me and my fellows, for all folks that knoweth my condition understand that I love well fruit. And now I see well I had near been slain. Therefore, madam, I dread me lest ye will be shamed.'

Then the queen stood still and was so sore abashed that she wist not what to say.

'This shall not so be ended,' said Sir Mador de la Porte, 'for here have I lost a full noble knight of my blood,[10] and there-fore upon this shame and despite[11] I will be revenged to the utterance!'

And there openly Sir Mador appealed[12] the queen of the death of his cousin Sir Patrise.

Then stood they all still, that[13] none would speak a word against him, for they all had great suspicion unto the queen because she let make that dinner. And the queen was so abashed that she could none otherways do but wept so heartily that she fell on a swough. So with this noise and cry came to them King Arthur, and when he wist of the trouble he was a passing heavy[14] man. And ever Sir Mador stood still before the king, and appealed[12] the queen of treason. (For the cus-tom was such at that time that all manner of shameful death[15] was called treason.)

'Fair lords,' said King Arthur, 'me repenteth of this trouble, but the case is so I may not have ado[16] in this matter, for I must be a rightful judge. And that repenteth me that I may not do battle for my wife, for, as I deem, this deed came never

---

[6] inflamed
[7] swelled so greatly that he burst
[8] instantly
[9] enraged with
[10] kin
[11] wrong
[12] accused
[13] for
[14] sad
[15] murder
[16] take action

by her.[17] And therefore I suppose she shall not be all disdained[18] but that some good knight shall put his body in jeopardy[19] for my queen rather than she should be brent in a wrong quarrel.[20] And therefore, Sir Mador, be not so hasty; for, perdy,[1] it may happen she shall not be all friendless. And therefore desire thou thy day of battle, and she shall purvey her of[2] some good knight that shall answer you, other else it were to me great shame and to all my court.'

'My gracious lord,' said Sir Mador, 'ye must hold me excused, for though ye be our king, in that degree[3] ye are but a knight as we are, and ye are sworn unto knighthood as well as we be.[4] And therefore I beseech you that ye be not displeased, for there is none of all these four-and-twenty knights that were bidden to this dinner but all they have great suspicion unto the queen. What say ye all, my lords?' said Sir Mador.

Then they answered by and by and said they could not excuse the queen for why she made the dinner, and other it must come by her other by her servants.

'Alas,' said the queen, 'I made this dinner for a good intent[5] and never for none evil, so Almighty Jesu help me in my right,[6] as I was never purposed to do such evil deeds, and that I report me unto God.'[7]

'My lord the king,' said Sir Mador, 'I require you as ye be a righteous king, give me my day that[8] I may have justice.'

'Well,' said the king, 'this day fifteen days look thou be ready armed on horseback in the meadow beside Winchester. And if it so fall[9] that there be any knight to encounter against you, there may you do your best, and God speed the right. And if so befall that there be no knight ready at that day, then must my queen be brent, and there she shall be ready to have her judgment.'

---

[17] was not her doing
[18] utterly dishonoured
[19] risk his life
[20] unjustly
[1] by God (*par Dieu*)
[2] provide herself with
[3] in (your) rank
[4] In F *Mador, in accordance with feudal practice, begins by repudiating his allegiance to Arthur ('se devest de toute la terre que il tenoit du roi'). From the*

point of view of the relationship between king and nobleman as M *sees it there is no need for Mador to do this. The reference to equality of rank is enough to justify his behaviour.*
[5] purpose
[6] in my just cause
[7] I trust that God will prove me right
[8] when
[9] happens

'I am answered,' said Sir Mador.

And every knight yode[10] where him liked.

So when the king and the queen were together the king asked the queen how this case[11] befell. Then the queen said, 'Sir, as Jesu be my help!' She wist not how nother in what manner.

'Where is Sir Lancelot?' said King Arthur. 'An he were here he would not grudge to do battle for you.'

'Sir,' said the queen, 'I wot not where he is, but his brother and his kinsmen deem that he be not within this realm.'

'That me repenteth,' said King Arthur, 'for an he were here he would soon stint[12] this strife. Well, then I will counsel you,' said the king, 'that ye go unto Sir Bors, and pray him for to do battle for you for Sir Lancelot's sake, and upon my life he will not refuse you. For well I see,' said the king, 'that none of the four-and-twenty knights that were at your dinner where Sir Patrise was slain that will[13] do battle for you, nother none of them will say well of you, and that shall be great slander to you in this court.'

'Alas,' said the queen, 'an I may not do withall, but now I miss Sir Lancelot, for an he were here he would soon put me in my heart's ease.'

'What aileth you,' said the king, 'that ye cannot keep Sir Lancelot upon your side? For wit you well,' said the king, 'who hath Sir Lancelot upon his party[14] hath the most man of worship[15] in this world upon his side. Now go your way,' said the king unto the queen, 'and require Sir Bors to do battle for you for Sir Lancelot's sake.'

So the queen departed from the king and sent for Sir Bors into[16] the chamber. And when he came she besought him of succour.

'Madam,' said he, 'what would ye that I did? For I may not with my worship[15] have ado[17] in this matter, because I was at the same dinner, for dread of any of those knights would have you in suspicion. Also Madam,' said Sir Bors, 'now miss ye Sir Lancelot, for he would not a failed you in your right nother in your wrong, for when ye have been in right great

---

<table>
<tr><td>[10] went</td><td>[14] side</td></tr>
<tr><td>[11] misfortune</td><td>[15] honour(ed)</td></tr>
<tr><td>[12] put an end to</td><td>[16] to come into</td></tr>
<tr><td>[13] that will = will</td><td>[17] I cannot honourably take action</td></tr>
</table>

dangers he hath succoured you. And now ye have driven him out of this country, by[18] whom ye and all we were daily worshipped[15] by. Therefore, madam, I marvel how ye dare for shame to[19] require me to do anything for you, insomuch ye have enchased[20] out of your court by whom we were up-borne and honoured.'[1]

'Alas, fair knight,' said the queen, 'I put me wholly in your grace, and all that is amiss I will amend as ye will counsel me.' And therewith she kneeled down upon both her knees, and besought Sir Bors to have mercy upon her, 'other else I shall have a shameful death, and thereto I never offended.'[2]

Right so came King Arthur and found the queen kneeling. And then Sir Bors took her up, and said,

'Madam, ye do me great dishonour.'

'Ah, gentle knight,' said the king, 'have mercy upon my queen, courteous knight, for I am now in certain she is untruly defamed![3] And therefore, courteous knight,' the king said, 'promise her to do battle for her, I require you for the love ye owe unto Sir Lancelot.'

'My lord,' said Sir Bors, 'ye require me the greatest thing that any man may require me. And wit you well, if I grant to do battle for the queen I shall wrath[4] many of my fellowship of the Table Round. But as for that,' said Sir Bors, 'I will grant[5] for my lord Sir Lancelot's sake, and for your sake: I will at that day be the queen's champion unless that there come by adventures a better knight than I am to do battle for her.'

'Will ye promise me this,' said the king, 'by your faith?'

'Yea sir,' said Sir Bors, 'of that I shall not fail you, nother her; but if there come a better knight than I am, then shall he have the battle.'

Then was the king and the queen passing glad, and so departed, and thanked him heartily.

Then Sir Bors departed secretly upon a day, and rode unto Sir Lancelot thereas[6] he was with Sir Brastias, and told him of all this adventure.

'Ah Jesu,' Sir Lancelot said, 'this is come happily as I would have it. And therefore I pray you make you ready to do

---

18 through
19 how you can decently
20 driven
  1 the man by whom we were sustained and who brought us honour

2 and of (all) this I am innocent
3 slandered
4 enrage
5 I will agree to do this
6 to the place where

battle, but look that ye tarry till ye see me come as long as
ye may. For I am sure Sir Mador is an hot[7] knight when he
is enchafed[8] for the more ye suffer[9] him the hastier will he
be to battle.'

'Sir,' said Sir Bors, 'let me deal with him. Doubt ye not ye
shall have all your will.'

So departed Sir Bors from him and came to the court again.
Then it was noised[10] in all the court that Sir Bors should do
battle for the queen, wherefore many knights were displeased
with him that he would take upon him to do battle in the
queen's quarrel; for there were but few knights in all the
court but they deemed the queen was in the wrong and that
she had done that treason. So Sir Bors answered thus to his
fellows of the Table Round.

'Wit you well, my fair lords, it were shame to us all an we
suffered to see[11] the most noble queen of the world to be
shamed openly, considering her lord and our lord is the man
of most worship[12] christened, and he hath ever worshipped[12]
us all in all places.'

Many answered him again:[13] 'As for our most noble King
Arthur, we love him and honour him as well as ye do, but as
for Queen Guinevere we love her not, because she is a destroyer
of good knights.'

'Fair lords,' said Sir Bors, 'meseemeth ye say not as ye
should say, for never yet in my days knew I never ne[14] heard
say that ever she was a destroyer of good knights, but at all
times as far as ever I could know, she was a maintainer[15] of
good knights; and ever she hath been large[16] and free of her
goods to all good knights, and the most bounteous lady of her
gifts and her good grace that ever I saw other heard speak of.
And therefore it were shame to us all and to our most noble
king's wife whom we serve an we suffered her to be shamefully slain. And wit ye well,' said Sir Bors, 'I will not suffer
it, for I dare say so much, for the queen is not guilty of Sir
Patrise's death: for she owed[17] him never none evil will nother
none of the four-and-twenty knights that were at that dinner,

---

[7] hot-tempered
[8] roused
[9] keep your distance from
[10] reported
[11] allowed
[12] honour(ed)

[13] made reply
[14] or
[15] protectress
[16] generous
[17] felt towards

for I dare say for good love she bade us to dinner, and not for no mal engine.[18] And that, I doubt not, shall be proved hereafter, for howsomever the game goeth, there was treason among us.'

Then some said to Bors, 'We may well believe your words.' And so some were well pleased and some were not.

So the day came on fast until the even that[19] the battle should be. Then the queen sent for Sir Bors and asked him how he was disposed.[20]

'Truly, madam,' said he, 'I am disposed[1] in like wise as I promised you, that is to say I shall not fail you unless there by adventure come a better knight than I am to do battle for you. Then, madam, I am of[2] you discharged of[3] my promise.'

'Will ye,' said the queen, 'that I tell my lord the king thus?'

'Do as it pleaseth you, madam.'

Then the queen yode[4] unto the king and told the answer of Sir Bors.

'Well, have ye no doubt,' said the king, 'of Sir Bors, for I call him now that is[5] living one of the noblest knights of the world, and most perfectest man.'

And thus it passed on till the morn, and so the king and the queen and all manner of knights that were there at that time drew them[6] unto the meadow beside Winchester where the battle should be. And so when the king was come with the queen and many knights of the Table Round, so the queen was then put in the constable's award,[7] and a great fire made about an iron stake, that an Sir Mador de le Porte had the better, she should there be brent; for such custom was used in those days: for favour, love, nother affinity there should be none other but righteous judgment, as well upon a king as upon a knight, and as well upon a queen as upon another[8] poor lady.

So this meanwhile came in Sir Mador de la Porte, and took his oath before the king, how that the queen did this treason until[9] his cousin Sir Patrise, 'and unto mine oath I will prove it with my body, hand for hand, who that will say the contrary.'

---

[18] evil intent	[4] went
[19] the evening before	[5] of all that are
[20] what his decision was	[6] went
[1] resolved to act	[7] custody
[2] by	[8] any
[3] released from	[9] towards

Right so came in Sir Bors de Ganis and said that as for Queen Guinevere, 'she is in the right, and that will I make good that she is not culpable of this treason that is put upon her.'

'Then make thee ready,' said Sir Mador, 'and we shall prove whether thou be in the right or I.'

'Sir Mador,' said Sir Bors, 'wit you well, I know you for a good[10] knight. Notforthen[11] I shall not fear you so greatly but I trust to God I shall be able to withstand your malice.[12] But thus much have I promised my lord Arthur and my lady the queen, that I shall do battle for her in this cause to the utterest, unless that there come a better knight than I am and discharge me.'[13]

'Is that all?' said Sir Mador. 'Other come thou off and do battle with me, other else say nay!'

'Take your horse,' said Sir Bors, 'and, as I suppose, I shall not tarry long but ye shall be answered.'

Then either departed to their tents and made them ready to horseback[14] as they thought best. And anon Sir Mador came into the field with his shield on his shoulder and his spear in his hand, and so rode about the place crying unto King Arthur,

'Bid your champion come forth an he dare!'

Then was Sir Bors ashamed, and took his horse and came to the lists' end. And then was he ware where came from a wood there fast by a knight all armed upon a white horse with a strange shield of strange arms, and he came driving all that[15] his horse might run. And so he came to Sir Bors and said thus:

'Fair knight, I pray you be not displeased, for here must a better knight than ye are have this battle. Therefore I pray you withdraw you, for wit you well I have had this day a right great journey and this battle ought to be mine. And so I promised you when I spake with you last, and with all my heart I thank you of your good will.'

Then Sir Bors rode unto King Arthur and told him how there was a knight come that would have the battle to fight for the queen.

'What knight is he?' said the king.

'I wot not,' said Sir Bors, 'but such covenant he made with

---

10 strong
11 nevertheless
12 resist your wickedness

13 release me from my obligation
14 to mount
15 as fast as

me to be here this day. Now, my lord,' said Sir Bors, 'here I am discharged.'[16]

Then the king called to that knight, and asked him if he would fight for the queen. Then he answered and said,

'Sir, therefore come I hither. And therefore, sir king, tarry[17] me no longer, for anon as I have finished this battle I must depart hence, for I have to do many battles elsewhere. For wit you well,' said the knight, 'this is dishonour to you and to all knights of the Round Table to see and know so noble a lady and so courteous as Queen Guinevere is, thus to be rebuked[18] and shamed[19] amongst you.'

Then they all marvelled what knight that might be that so took the battle upon him, for there was not one that knew him but if it were Sir Bors. Then said Sir Mador de la Porte unto the king:

'Now let me wit with whom I shall have ado.'

And then they rode to the lists' end, and there they couched[20] their spears and ran together with all their mights. And anon Sir Mador's spear brake all to pieces, but the other's spear held and bare Sir Mador's horse and all[1] backwards to the earth a[2] great fall. But mightily and deliverly[3] he avoided his horse from him[4] and put his shield before him and drew his sword and bade the other knight alight and do battle with him on foot.

Then that knight descended down from his horse and put his shield before him and drew his sword. And so they came eagerly[5] unto battle, and either gave other many sad[6] strokes, tracing and traversing and foining together[7] with their swords as it were wild boars, thus fighting nigh an hour; for this Sir Mador was a strong knight, and mightily proved in many strong[8] battles. But at the last this knight smote Sir Mador grovelling[9] upon the earth, and the knight stepped near him to have pulled Sir Mador flatling[10] upon the ground; and therewith Sir Mador arose, and in his rising he smote that knight through the thick of the thighs, that the blood brast out fiercely.

[16] released
[17] detain
[18] insulted
[19] put to shame
[20] lowered
[1] and the rider
[2] in a
[3] speedily
[4] freed himself from his horse
[5] fiercely
[6] heavy
[7] moving from side to side and thrusting at each other
[8] arduous
[9] headlong
[10] at full length

And when he felt himself so wounded and saw his blood, he let him arise upon his feet, and then he gave him such a buffet upon the helm that he fell to the earth flatling.[10] And therewith he strode to him to have pulled off his helm off his head. And so Sir Mador prayed that knight to save his life. And so he yielded him as overcome, and released the queen of his quarrel.[11]

'I will not grant thee thy life,' said the knight, 'only that thou freely release[12] the queen forever, and that no mention be made upon Sir Patrise's tomb that ever Queen Guinevere consented to that treason.'

'All this shall be done,' said Sir Mador, 'I clearly discharge my quarrel[13] forever.'

Then the knights parters[14] of the lists took up Sir Mador and led him till his tent. And the other knight went straight to the stairfoot where sat King Arthur. And by that time was the queen came to the king, and either kissed other heartily.

And when the king saw that knight he stooped down to him and thanked him, and in like wise did the queen. And the king prayed him put off his helmet and to repose him and to take a sop of wine.

And then he put off his helm to drink, and then every knight knew him that it was Sir Lancelot. And anon as the king wist that, he took the queen in his hand and yode[15] unto Sir Lancelot and said,

'Sir, gramercy of your great travail[16] that ye have had this day for me and for my queen.'

'My lord,' said Sir Lancelot, 'wit you well I ought of right ever to be in your quarrel, and in my lady the queen's quarrel,[17] to do battle; for ye are the man that gave me the high Order of Knighthood, and that day my lady, your queen, did me worship.[18] And else I had been shamed, for that same day that ye made me knight through my hastiness[19] I lost my sword, and my lady, your queen, found it, and lapped[20] it in her train, and gave me my sword when I had need thereto; and else had I been shamed among all knights. And therefore, my lord Ar-

[11] accusation
[12] fully exonerate
[13] withdraw my accusation
[14] stewards
[15] went
[16] labour
[17] on your side and on my lady the queen's side
[18] honour
[19] haste, rashness
[20] wrapped

thur, I promised her at that day ever to be her knight in right other in wrong.'[1]

'Gramercy,' said the king, 'for this journey. And wit you well,' said the king, 'I shall acquit[2] your goodness.'

And evermore the queen beheld Sir Lancelot and wept so tenderly that she sank almost to the ground for sorrow, that[3] he had done to her so great kindness where she showed him great unkindness. Then the knights of his blood[4] drew unto him, and there either of them made great joy of other. And so came all the knights of the Table Round that were there at that time and welcomed him.

And then Sir Mador was healed of[5] his leechcraft, and Sir Lancelot was healed of his play.[6] And so there was made great joy and many mirths there was made in that court.

And so it befell that the Damsel of the Lake that hight Ninive, which wedded the good knight Sir Pelleas, and so she came to the court, for ever she did great goodness unto King Arthur and to all his knights through her sorcery and enchantments. And so when she heard how the queen was grieved for the death of Sir Patrise, then she told it openly that she was never guilty, and there she disclosed by whom it was done, and named him Sir Pinel, and for what cause he did it. There it was openly known and disclosed, and so the queen was excused.[7] And this knight Sir Pinel fled into his country, and was openly known that he enpoisoned the apples at that feast to that intent to have destroyed Sir Gawain, because Sir Gawain and his breathren destroyed Sir Lamorak de Galis which Sir Pinel was cousin unto.

Then was Sir Patrise buried in the church of Westminster in a tomb, and thereupon was written: 'Here lieth Sir Patrise

---

[1] *This explanation of Lancelot's allegiance to Guinevere occurs in the Prose* Lancelot *(ed. Sommer, III, 127–37), but not in F. As Lancelot was being knighted news was brought of an important adventure, and Arthur forgot to give him his sword. The investiture was completed when Guinevere, on receiving homage from Lancelot's defeated opponent, sent her young champion a beautiful sword 'richement appareillie de fuerre et de renge.'*

[2] reward, repay

[3] because

[4] kin

[5] by

[6] wound (F: *plaie*)

[7] *In F Guinevere is 'excused' solely as a result of Lancelot's victory, and there is no reference to the Damsel of the Lake's disclosures. M must have thought that the evidence of a judicial combat was not enough.*

of Ireland, slain by Sir Pinel le Savage, that enpoisoned apples to have slain Sir Gawain, and by misfortune Sir Patrise ate one of the apples, and then suddenly[8] he brast.' Also there was written upon the tomb that Queen Guinevere was appealed of treason of the death[9] of Sir Patrise by Sir Mador de la Porte, and there was made the mention how Sir Lancelot fought with him for Queen Guinevere and overcame him in plain battle. All this was written upon the tomb of Sir Patrise in excusing of the queen.

And then Sir Mador sued daily and long to have the queen's good grace, and so by the means of Sir Lancelot he[10] caused him to stand in the queen's good grace, and all was forgiven.

[8] instantly
[9] accused of treacherously causing the death

[10] i.e. Lancelot

The Fair Maid of Astolat

Thus it passed until Our Lady Day of the Assumption. Within a fifteen days of that feast the king let cry[1] a great jousts and a tournament that should be at that day at Camelot, otherwise called Winchester.[2] And the king let cry[1] that he and the king of Scots would joust against all the world.

And when this cry was made, thither came many good knights, that is to say the King of North Wales, and King Anguish of Ireland, and the King with the Hundred Knights, and Sir Galahalt the Haut Prince, and the King of Northumberland, and many other noble dukes and earls of other divers countries.

So King Arthur made him ready to depart to his jousts, and would have had the queen with him; but at that time she would not, she said, for she was sick and might not ride.

'That me repenteth,' said the king, 'for this seven year ye saw not such a noble fellowship together except at the Whitsuntide when Sir Galahad departed from the court.'

'Truly,' said the queen, 'ye must hold me excused, I may not be there.'

And many deemed the queen would not be there because of Sir Lancelot, for he would not ride with the king, for he said he was not whole of the play[3] of Sir Mador. Wherefore the king was heavy[4] and passing wroth, and so he departed toward Winchester with his fellowship.

And so by the way the king lodged at a town called Astolat, that is in English Guildford,[5] and there the king lay in the castle. So when the king was departed the queen called Sir Lancelot unto her and said thus:

[1] let it be proclaimed

[2] *No such identification is suggested in F. Caxton in his Preface to Le Morte Darthur describes Camelot as a city in Wales.*

[3] wound (F: *plaie*)

[4] grieved

[5] *A natural halt on the way from London to Winchester. By Malory's time the residential quarters of Guildford castle were in ruins and therefore fit to be associated with Arthur's reign.*

'Sir, ye are greatly to blame thus to hold you[6] behind my lord. What will your enemies and mine say and deem? "See how Sir Lancelot holdeth him ever behind the king, and so the queen doth also, for that they would[7] have their pleasure together." And thus will they say,' said the queen.

'Have ye no doubt, madam,' said Sir Lancelot. 'I allow your wit.[8] It is of late come syn ye were waxen[9] so wise! And therefore, madam, at this time I will be ruled by your counsel, and this night I will take my rest, and to-morrow betime I will take my way toward Winchester. But wit you well,' said Sir Lancelot unto the queen, 'at that jousts I will be against the king and against all his fellowship.'

'Sir, ye may there do as ye list,' said the queen, 'but by my counsel ye shall not be against your king and your fellowship, for there been full many hardy[10] knights of your blood.'[11]

'Madam,' said Sir Lancelot, 'I shall take the adventure that God will give me.'

And so upon the morn early he heard mass and dined, and so he took his leave of the queen and departed. And then he rode so much unto the time[12] he came to Astolat; and there it happened him that in the evening-tide he came to an old baron's place that hight Sir Barnard of Astolat. And as Sir Lancelot entered into his lodging, King Arthur espied him as he did walk in a garden beside the castle: he knew him well enough.

'Well, sirs,' said King Arthur unto his knights that were by him beside the castle, 'I have now espied one knight,' he said, 'that will play his play[13] at the jousts, I undertake.'

'Who is that?' said the knights.

'At this time ye shall not wit for me,' said the king, and smiled, and went to his lodging.

So when Sir Lancelot was in his lodging, and unarmed in his chamber, the old baron, Sir Barnard, came to him and welcomed him in the best manner, but he knew not Sir Lancelot.

'Fair sir,' said Sir Lancelot till[14] his host, 'I would pray you to lend me a shield that were not openly known, for mine is well known.'

'Sir,' said his host, 'ye shall have your desire, for meseemeth

---

6 remain
7 because they wish to
8 I commend your judgment
9 It is not long since you have grown
10 brave
11 kin
12 until
13 perform valiant deeds
14 to

ye be one of the likeliest[15] knights that ever I saw, and therefore, sir, I shall show you friendship.' And said: 'Sir, wit you
well I have two sons that were but late made knights. And
the eldest hight Sir Tirry, and he was hurt that same day
he was made knight, and he may not ride; and his shield ye
shall have, for that is not known, I daresay, but here and in
no place else.' And his younger son hight Sir Lavain. 'And if
it please you, he shall ride with you unto that jousts, for he
is of[16] his age strong and wight.[17] For much my heart giveth
unto[18] you, that[19] ye should be a noble knight. And therefore
I pray you to tell me your name,' said Sir Barnard.

'As for that,' said Sir Lancelot, 'ye must hold me excused
as at this time. And if God give me grace to speed[20] well at
the jousts I shall come again[1] and tell you my name. But I
pray you in any wise let me have your son, Sir Lavain, with me,
and that I may have his brother's shield.'

'Sir, all this shall be done,' said Sir Barnard.

So this old baron had a daughter that was called that time
the Fair Maiden of Astolat, and ever she beheld Sir Lancelot
wonderfully.[2] (And as the book saith, she cast such a love
unto[3] Sir Lancelot that she could never withdraw her love,
wherefore she died. And her name was Elaine le Blanke.)

So thus as she came to and fro she was so hot in love that
she besought Sir Lancelot to wear upon him at the jousts a
token of hers.

'Damsel,' said Sir Lancelot, 'and if I grant you that, ye may
say that I do more for your love[4] than ever I did for lady or
gentlewoman.'

Then he remembered himself that he would go to the jousts
disguised, and because he had never aforn[5] borne no manner
of token of no[6] damsel, he bethought him to bear a token of
hers, that[7] none of his blood[8] thereby might know him.[9] And
then he said,

---

[15] handsomest
[16] for
[17] stalwart
[18] I feel drawn to
[19] because
[20] succeed
[1] return
[2] with admiration
[3] had so great a love for
[4] for your sake
[5] before
[6] for any

[7] so that
[8] kin
[9] *In F the damsel asks Lancelot
a boon in the name of his lady
('par la foi que tu doiz a la riens
el monde que tu mieuz ainmes')
and Lancelot cannot refuse it
without infringing the code of
courtly love ('car trop m'avés
conjuré'). M supplies a simpler
motive.*

'Fair maiden, I will grant you to wear a token of yours upon mine helmet. And therefore what is it? Show ye it me.'

'Sir,' she said, 'it is a red sleeve[10] of mine, of scarlet, well embroidered with great pearls.'

And so she brought it him. So Sir Lancelot received it and said,

'Never did I erst[11] so much for no damsel.'

Then Sir Lancelot betook[12] the fair maiden his shield in keeping, and prayed her to keep it until time that he come again.[13] And so that night he had merry rest and great cheer, for this damsel Elaine was ever about Sir Lancelot all the while she might be suffered.[14]

So upon a day, on the morn, King Arthur and all his knights departed, for there the king had tarried three days to abide his noble knights. And so when the king was ridden, Sir Lancelot and Sir Lavain made them ready to ride, and either of them had white shields, and the red sleeve Sir Lancelot let carry with him.

And so they took their leave at Sir Barnard, the old baron, and at his daughter, the fair maiden, and then they rode so long till they came to Camelot, that time called Winchester. And there was great press[15] of kings, dukes, earls and barons, and many noble knights. But Sir Lancelot was lodged privily[16] by the means of Sir Lavain with a rich burgess, that no man in that town was ware what they were. And so they reposed them there till Our Lady Day of the Assumption, that[17] the great jousts should be.

So when trumpets blew unto the field, and King Arthur was set on high upon a chafflet[18] to behold who did best (but, as the French book saith, the king would not suffer Sir Gawain to go from him, for never had Sir Gawain the better an Sir Lancelot were in the field, and many times was Sir Gawain rebuked so when Sir Lancelot was in the field in any jousts disguised), then some of the kings, as King Anguish of Ireland and the King of Scots, were that time turned[19] to be upon the side of King Arthur. And then the other party was the King of North Wales, and the King with the Hundred

---

[10] i.e. a sash
[11] hitherto
[12] entrusted to
[13] until he returned
[14] allowed

[15] throng
[16] secretly
[17] when
[18] platform
[19] decided

Knights, and the King of Northumberland, and Sir Galahalt the Haut Prince. But these three kings and this duke was passing[20] weak to hold against Arthur's party, for with him[1] were the noblest knights of the world.

So then they withdrew them either party from other and every man made him ready in his best manner to do what he might. Then Sir Lancelot made him ready and put the red sleeve upon his helmet and fastened it fast. And so Sir Lancelot and Sir Lavain departed out of Winchester privily and rode until[2] a little leaved[3] wood behind the party that held against King Arthur party. And there they held them[4] still till the parties smote together. And then came in the King of Scots and the King of Ireland on King Arthur's party, and against them came in the King of Northumberland and the King with the Hundred Knights.

And there began a great medley, and there the King of Scots smote down the King of Northumberland, and the King with the Hundred Knights smote down King Anguish of Ireland. Then Sir Palomides, that was on Arthur's party, he encountered with Sir Galahalt, and either of them smote down other, and either party helped their lords on horseback again. So there began a strong assail[5] on both parties.

And then came in Sir Braundiles, Sir Sagramore le Desirous, Sir Dodinas le Savage, Sir Kay le Seneschal, Sir Grifflet le Fyz de Dieu, Sir Lucan de Butler, Sir Bedivere, Sir Agravain, Sir Gaheris, Sir Mordred, Sir Meliot de Logres, Sir Ozanna le Cure Hardy, Sir Safir, Sir Epinogris, Sir Galleron of Galway. All these fifteen knights, that were knights of the Round Table, so these with more other came in together and beat aback the King of Northumberland and the King of North Wales.

When Sir Lancelot saw this, as he hoved[6] in the little leaved[3] wood, then he said unto Sir Lavain,

'See yonder is a company of good knights, and they hold them[7] together as boars that were chased with dogs.'

'That is truth,' said Sir Lavain.

'Now,' said Sir Lancelot, 'an ye will help a little, ye shall see the yonder fellowship that chaseth now these men on our side, that they shall go as fast backward as they went forward.'

[20] too
[1] = Arthur
[2] to
[3] leafy
[4] remained
[5] attack
[6] stood
[7] keep

'Sir, spare ye not for my part,'[8] said Sir Lavain, 'for I shall do what I may.'

Then Sir Lancelot and Sir Lavain came in at the thickest of the press, and there Sir Lancelot smote down Sir Braundiles, Sir Sigramore, Sir Dodinas, Sir Kay, Sir Grifflet, and all this he did with one spear. And Sir Lavain smote down Sir Lucan de Butler and Sir Bedivere. And then Sir Lancelot gat another great spear, and there he smote down Sir Agravain and Sir Gaheris, Sir Mordred, Sir Meliot de Logres; and Sir Lavain smote down Sir Ozanna le Cure Hardy. And then Sir Lancelot drew his sword, and there he smote on the right hand and on the left hand, and by great force he unhorsed Sir Safir, Sir Epinogris, and Sir Galleron.

And then the knights of the Table Round withdrew them aback, after they had gotten[9] their horses as well as they might.

'Ah, mercy Jesu,' said Sir Gawain. 'What knight is yonder that doth so marvellous deeds in that field?'

'I wot what he is,' said the king, 'but as at this time I will not name him.'

'Sir,' said Sir Gawain, 'I would say it were Sir Lancelot by his riding and his buffets[10] that I see him deal. But ever meseemeth it should not be he, for that he beareth the red sleeve upon his helmet; for I wist him never bear token at no jousts of lady ne gentlewoman.'

'Let him be,' said King Arthur, 'for he will be better known and do more or ever he depart.'

Then the party that was against King Arthur were well comforted, and then they held them[11] together that beforehand were sore rebuked.[12] Then Sir Bors, Sir Ector de Maris, and Sir Lionel, they called unto them the knights of their blood,[13] as Sir Blamore de Ganis, Sir Bleoberis, Sir Aliduke, Sir Galihud, Sir Eliodin, Sir Bellengere le Beuse. So these nine knights of Sir Lancelot's kin thrust in mightily, for they were all noble knights, and they of great hate and despite[14] thought to rebuke[15] Sir Lancelot and Sir Lavain, for they knew them not.

And so they came hurling together and smote down many knights of North Wales and of Northumberland. And when

[8] do not hold back on my account
[9] mounted
[10] blows
[11] pressed the attack
[12] shamefully defeated
[13] kin
[14] angered and resentful
[15] defeat

Sir Lancelot saw them fare so, he gat a great spear in his hand; and there encountered with him all at once, Sir Bors, Sir Ector, and Sir Lionel. And they three smote him at once with their spears, and with force of themself[16] they smote Sir Lancelot's horse revers[17] to the earth. And by misfortune Sir Bors smote Sir Lancelot through the shield into the side, and the spear brake, and the head left still[18] in the side.

When Sir Lavain saw his master lie on the ground he ran to the King of Scots and smote him to the earth; and by great force he took his horse and brought him to Sir Lancelot, and maugre[19] them all he made him to mount upon that horse. And then Sir Lancelot gat a spear in his hand, and there he smote Sir Bors, horse and man, to the earth; and in the same wise he served Sir Ector and Sir Lionel; and Sir Lavain smote down Sir Blamore de Ganis. And then Sir Lancelot drew his sword, for he felt himself so sore hurt that he weened there to have had his death. And then he smote Sir Bleoberis such a buffet on the helmet that he fell down to the earth in a swoon and in the same wise he served Sir Aliduke and Sir Galihud. And Sir Lavain smote down Sir Bellengere that was son to Alisaunder le Orphelin.

And by[20] this was done was Sir Bors horsed again and in came with Sir Ector and Sir Lionel, and all they three smote with their swords upon Sir Lancelot's helmet. And when he felt their buffets, and with that[1] his wound grieved him grievously, then he thought to do what he might while he could endure. And then he gave Sir Bors such a buffet that he made him bow his head passing low; and therewithal he raced off[2] his helm, and might have slain him, but when he saw his visage[3] so pulled him down. And in the same wise he served Sir Ector and Sir Lionel; for, as the book saith, he might have slain them, but when he saw their visages[3] his heart might not serve him thereto,[4] but left them there.

And then afterwards he hurled into the thickest press[5] of them all, and did there the marvelloust[6] deeds of arms that ever man saw, and ever Sir Lavain with him. And there Sir Lancelot with his sword smote down and pulled down, as the

[16] with their combined strength
[17] with back-handed blows
[18] sticking
[19] in spite of
[20] when
[1] And as

[2] tore off
[3] face(s)
[4] had no heart to do it
[5] throng
[6] most wonderful

French book saith, more than thirty knights, and the most party were[7] of the Table Round. And there Sir Lavain did full that day, for he smote down ten knights of the Table Round.

'Mercy, Jesu,' said Sir Gawain unto King Arthur, 'I marvel what knight that he is with the red sleeve.'

'Sir,' said King Arthur, 'he will be known or ever he depart.'

And then the king blew unto lodging,[8] and the prize was given by heralds unto the knight with the white shield that bare the red sleeve. Then came the King of North Wales, and the King of Northumberland, and the King with the Hundred Knights, and Sir Galahalt the Haut Prince, and said unto Sir Lancelot:

'Fair knight, God you bless, for much have ye done for us this day. And therefore we pray you that ye will come with us, that ye may receive the honour and the prize as ye have worshipfully[9] deserved it.'

'Fair lords,' said Sir Lancelot, 'wit ye well, if I have deserved thank I have sore[10] bought it, and that me repenteth it, for I am never like[11] to escape with the life. Therefore, my fair lords, I pray you that ye will suffer me to depart where me liketh, for I am sore hurt. And I take none force of none[12] honour, for I had liefer repose me[13] than to be lord of all the world.'

And therewithal he groaned piteously, and rode a great wallop[14] awayward from them until he came under a wood's eves.[15] And when he saw that he was from the field nigh a mile, that he was sure he might not be seen, then he said with an high voice and with a great groan,

'Ah, gentle knight, Sir Lavain! help me that this truncheon[16] were out of my side, for it sticketh so sore that it nigh slayeth me.'

'Ah, mine own lord,' said Sir Lavain, 'I would fain do that might please you, but I dread me sore, an I pull out the truncheon,[16] that ye shall be in peril of death.'

'I charge[17] you,' said Sir Lancelot, 'as ye love me, draw it out!'

And therewithal he descended from his horse, and right so

---

[7] they were mostly
[8] ordered that the fighting should cease for the night
[9] honourably
[10] dearly
[11] not likely
[12] I do not care for any
[13] I would sooner rest
[14] gallop
[15] the edge of a wood
[16] shaft (of spear)
[17] command

did Sir Lavain; and forthwithal he drew the truncheon[16] out
of his side, and gave a great shriek and a grisly groan that[18]
the blood brast out nigh a pint at once, that at the last[19] he sank
down upon his arse and so swooned down, pale and deadly.

'Alas,' said Sir Lavain, 'what shall I do?'

And then he turned Sir Lancelot into the wind, and so he
lay there nigh half-an-hour as he had been dead. And so at
the last Sir Lancelot cast up his eyen, and said,

'Ah, Sir Lavain, help me that I were on my horse! For here
is fast by, within this two mile, a gentle[20] hermit that sometime was a full noble knight and a great lord of possessions.
And for great goodness he hath taken him to wilful[1] poverty,
and forsaken mighty lands. And his name is Sir Baudwin of
Britain, and he is a full noble surgeon and a good leech. Now
let see and help me up that I were there, for ever my heart
giveth me[2] that I shall never die of my cousin-germain's[3] hands.'

And then with great pain Sir Lavain holp him upon his
horse, and then they rode a great wallop[4] together, and ever
Sir Lancelot bled, that it[5] ran down to the earth. And so by
fortune they came to an hermitage which was under a wood,
and a great cliff on the other side, and a fair water[6] running
under it. And then Sir Lavain beat on the gate with the butt
of his spear and cried fast,[7]

'Let in, for Jesu's sake!'

And anon there came a fair childe[8] to them and asked them
what they would.

'Fair son,' said Sir Lavain, 'go and pray thy lord the hermit
for God's sake to let in here a knight that is full sore wounded.
And this day, tell thy lord, I saw him do more deeds of arms
than ever I heard say that any man did.'

So the childe[8] went in lightly,[9] and then he brought the
hermit which was a passing likely[10] man. When Sir Lavain
saw him he prayed him for God's sake of succour.

'What knight is he?' said the hermit. 'Is he of the house of
King Arthur or not?'

'I wot not,' said Sir Lavain, 'what he is, nother what is his

18 as
19 and presently
20 noble
1 voluntary
2 tells me
3 first cousin's
4 at full speed

5 so that the blood
6 stream
7 loudly
8 handsome young nobleman
9 quickly
10 handsome

name, but well I wot I saw him do marvellously this day as of deeds of arms.'

'On whose party was he?' said the hermit.

'Sir,' said Sir Lavain, 'he was this day against King Arthur, and there he won the prize of all the knights of the Round Table.'

'I have seen the day,' said the hermit, 'I would have loved him the worse because he was against my lord, King Arthur, for sometime I was one of the fellowship, but now I thank God I am otherwise disposed. But where is he? Let me see him.'

Then Sir Lavain brought the hermit to him. And when the hermit beheld him as he sat leaning upon the saddle-bow, ever bleeding spiteously,[11] and ever the knight hermit thought that he should know him; but he could not bring him to knowledge because he was so pale for bleeding.

'What knight are ye,' said the hermit, 'and where were ye born?'

'My fair lord,' said Sir Lancelot, 'I am a stranger and a knight adventurous that laboureth throughout many realms for to win worship.'[12]

Then the hermit advised him better[13] and saw by a wound on his cheek that he was Sir Lancelot.

'Alas,' said the hermit, 'mine own lord! Why lain[14] you your name from me? Perdy,[15] I ought to know you of right, for ye are the most noblest knight of the world. For well I know you for Sir Lancelot.'

'Sir,' said he, 'sith ye know me, help me, an ye may, for God's sake! For I would be out of this pain at once, other to death other to life.'

'Have ye no doubt,' said the hermit, 'for ye shall live and fare right well.'

And so the hermit called to him two of his servants, and so they bare him into the hermitage, and lightly[9] unarmed him, and laid him in his bed. And then anon the hermit staunched his blood and made him to drink good wine, that he was well revigoured and knew himself.[16] For in these days it was not the guise[17] as is nowadays; for there were none hermits in those

---

[11] copiously
[12] honour
[13] thought again
[14] conceal

[15] by God (*par Dieu*)
[16] so that his strength returned and his spirits revived
[17] custom

days but that they had been men of worship[12] and prowess, and those hermits held great households and refreshed[18] people that were in distress.

Now turn we unto King Arthur, and leave Sir Lancelot in the hermitage. So when the kings were together on both parties, and the great feast should be holden, King Arthur asked the King of North Wales and their fellowship where was that knight that bare the red sleeve.

'Let bring him before me, that he may have his laud and honour and the prize,[19] as it is right.'

Then spake Sir Galahalt the Haut Prince and the King with the Hundred Knights, and said,

'We suppose that knight is mischieved[20] so that he is never like to see you nother none of us all. And that is the greatest pity that ever we wist of any knight.'

'Alas,' said King Arthur, 'how may this be? Is he so sore hurt? But what is his name?' said King Arthur.

'Truly,' said they all, 'we know not his name, nother from whence he came, nother whither he would.'

'Alas,' said the king, 'this is the worst tidings that came to me this seven year! For I would not for all the lands I wield to know and wit it were so that that noble knight were slain.'

'Sir, know ye aught of him?' said they all.

'As for that,' said King Arthur, 'whether I know him other none, ye shall not know for me what man he is but[1] Almighty Jesu send me good tidings of him.'

And so said they all.

'By my head,' said Sir Gawain, 'if it so be that the good knight be so sore hurt, it is great damage[2] and pity to all this land, for he is one of the noblest knights that ever I saw in a field handle spear or sword. And if he may be found I shall find him, for I am sure he is not far from this country.'

'Sir, ye bear you well,' said King Arthur, 'and ye may find him, unless he be in such a plight that he may not wield himhelf.'[3]

'Jesu defend!' said Sir Gawain. 'But wit well I shall know what he is an I may find him.'

Right so Sir Gawain took a squire with him upon hackneys[4]

---

[18] succoured
[19] be praised, honoured and rewarded
[20] come to some harm

[1] until
[2] misfortune
[3] has lost consciousness
[4] nags

and rode all about Camelot within six or seven mile, but soon[5] he came again[6] and could hear no word of him. Then within two days King Arthur and all the fellowship returned unto London again. And so as they rode by the way it happened Sir Gawain at Astolat to lodge with Sir Barnard thereas[7] was Sir Lancelot lodged.

And so as Sir Gawain was in his chamber to repose him Sir Barnard, the old baron, came in to him, and his daughter Elaine, to cheer him and to ask him what tidings, and who did best at the tournament of Winchester.

'So God me help,' said Sir Gawain, 'there were two knights that bare white shields, but one of them bare a red sleeve upon his head, and certainly he was the best knight that ever I saw joust in field. For I dare say,' said Sir Gawain, 'that one knight with the red sleeve smote down forty knights of the Round Table, and his fellow did right well and worshipfully.'

'Now blessed be God,' said this fair maiden of Astolat, 'that that knight sped[8] so well! For he is the man in the world that I first loved,[9] and truly he shall be the last ever I shall love.'

'Now, fair maiden,' said Sir Gawain, 'is that good knight your love?'

'Certainly, sir,' said she, 'he is my love.'

'Then know ye his name?' said Sir Gawain.

'Nay truly, sir,' said the damsel. 'I know not his name nother from whence he came, but to say that I love him, I promise God and you I love him.'

'How had ye knowledge of him first?' said Sir Gawain.

Then she told him, as ye have heard before, and how her father betook[10] him her brother to do him service, and how her father lent him her brother's, Sir Tirry's, shield: 'and here with me he left his own shield.'

'For what cause did he so?' said Sir Gawain.

'For this cause,' said the damsel, 'for his shield was full well known among many noble knights.'

'Ah, fair damsel,' said Sir Gawain, 'please it you let me have a sight of that shield?'

'Sir,' she said, 'it is in my chamber, covered with a case, and if ye will come with me ye shall see it.'

'Not so,' said Sir Barnard to his daughter, 'but send ye for that shield.'

---

[5] M: *so*
[6] back
[7] where

[8] succeeded
[9] that was my first love
[10] entrusted to

So when the shield was come,[11] Sir Gawain took off the case, and when he beheld that shield he knew it anon that it was Sir Lancelot's shield and his own arms.

'Ah, Jesu, mercy!' said Sir Gawain, 'now is my heart more heavier than ever it was tofore.'

'Why?' said this maid Elaine.

'For I have a great cause,' said Sir Gawain. 'Is that knight that oweth this shield[12] your love?'

'Yea, truly,' she said, 'my love is he. God would that I were his love.'

'So God me speed,' said Sir Gawain, 'fair damsel, ye have right,[13] for an he be your love ye love the most honourablest knight of the world and the man of most worship.'

'So methought ever,' said the damsel, 'for never or that time no knight that ever I saw loved I never none erst.'[14]

'God grant,' said Sir Gawain, 'that either of you may rejoice other, but that is in a great adventure.[15] But truly,' said Sir Gawain unto the damsel, 'ye may say ye have a fair grace,[16] for why I have known that noble knight this four-and-twenty year, and never or that day I nor none other knight, I dare make good, saw never nother heard say that ever he bare token or sign of no lady, gentlewoman, nor maiden at no jousts nother tournament.[17] And therefore, fair maiden, ye are much beholden to him to give him thank. But I dread me,' said Sir Gawain, 'that ye shall never see him in this world, and that is as great pity as ever was of any earthly man.'

'Alas!' said she, 'how may this be? Is he slain?'

'I say not so,' said Sir Gawain, 'but wit you well he is grievously wounded, by all manner of signs, and by means of sight[18] more likelier to be dead than to be on live. And wit you well he is the noble knight Sir Lancelot, for by this shield I know him.'

'Alas!' said this fair maiden of Astolat, 'how may this be? And what was his hurt?'

'Truly,' said Sir Gawain, 'the man in the world that loved best him hurt him. And I dare say,' said Sir Gawain, 'an that knight that hurt him knew the very certainty[19] that he had hurt

---

11 brought
12 to whom this shield belongs
13 are right
14 for never before did I see any knight that I loved
15 there is little chance of this
16 you are extremely fortunate
17 never before that day did I or any other knight . . . see or hear say that he ever carried a token at a tournament
18 by his looks
19 for certain

Sir Lancelot, it were the most sorrow that ever came to his heart.'

'Now, fair father,' said then Elaine, 'I require you give me leave to ride and seek him, other else I wot well I shall go out of my mind. For I shall never stint[20] till that I find him and my brother, Sir Lavain.'

'Do ye as it liketh you,' said her father, 'for me sore repenteth of the hurt of that noble knight.'

Right so the maid made her ready and departed before Sir Gawain making great dole. Then on the morn Sir Gawain came to King Arthur and told him all how he had found Sir Lancelot's shield in the keeping of the fair maiden of Astolat.

'All that knew I aforehand,' said King Arthur, 'and that caused me I would not suffer[1] you to have ado[2] at the great jousts; for I espied him when he came until[3] his lodging, full late in the evening, into Astolat. But great marvel have I,' said King Arthur, 'that ever he would bear any sign of any damsel, for or now I never heard say nor knew that ever he bare any token of none earthly woman.'

'By my head, sir,' said Sir Gawain, 'the fair maiden of Astolat loveth him marvellously well. What it meaneth I cannot say. And she is ridden after to seek him.'

So the king and all came to London, and there Gawain all openly disclosed it to all the court that it was Sir Lancelot that jousted best. And when Sir Bors heard that, wit you well he was an heavy[4] man, and so were all his kinsmen. But when the queen wist that it was Sir Lancelot that bare the red sleeve of the fair maiden of Astolat, she was nigh out of her mind for wrath. And then she sent for Sir Bors de Ganis in all haste that might be. So when Sir Bors was come before the queen she said,

'Ah, Sir Bors! Have ye not heard say how falsely Sir Lancelot hath betrayed me?'

'Alas, madam,' said Sir Bors, 'I am afeard he hath betrayed himself and us all.'

'No force,'[5] said the queen, 'though he be destroyed, for he is a false traitor-knight.'

'Madam,' said Sir Bors, 'I pray you say ye no more so, for wit you well I may not hear no such language of him.'

---

[20] cease
[1] allow
[2] to fight

[3] to
[4] sorrowful
[5] No matter

'Why so, Sir Bors?' said she. 'Should I not call him traitor when he bare the red sleeve upon his head at Winchester, at the great jousts?'

'Madam,' said Sir Bors, 'that sleeve-bearing repenteth me,[6] but I dare say he did bear it to none[7] evil intent, but for this cause he bare the red sleeve that none of his blood[8] should know him. For or then we nother none of us all never knew that ever he bare token or sign of maiden, lady, nother gentlewoman.'

'Fie on him!' said the queen. 'Yet for all his pride and bobaunce,[9] there ye proved yourself better man than he.'

'Nay, madam, say ye nevermore so, for he beat me and my fellows, and might have slain us an he had would.'

'Fie on him!' said the queen. 'For I heard Sir Gawain say before my lord Arthur that it were marvel to tell the great love that is between the fair maiden of Astolat and him.'

'Madam,' said Sir Bors, 'I may not warn[10] Sir Gawain to say what it pleaseth him, but I daresay, as for my lord Sir Lancelot, that he loveth no lady, gentlewoman, nother maiden, but as he loveth all inlike much.[11] And therefore, madam,' said Sir Bors, 'ye may seek what ye will, but wit you well I will haste me to seek him and find him wheresomever he be, and God send me good tidings of him!'

And so leave we them there, and speak we of Sir Lancelot that lay in great peril. And so as this fair maiden Elaine came to Winchester she sought there all about, and by fortune Sir Lavain, her brother, was ridden to sport him to enchafe[12] his horse. And anon as this maiden Elaine saw him she knew him, and then she cried on-loud till him, and when he heard her he came to her. And anon with that she asked her brother,

'How doth my lord, Sir Lancelot?'

'Who told you, sister, that my lord's name was Sir Lancelot?'

Then she told him how Sir Gawain by his shield knew him.

So they rode together till that they came to the hermitage, and anon she alight. So Sir Lavain brought her in to Sir Lancelot, and when she saw him lie so sick and pale in his bed she might not speak, but suddenly she fell down to the earth in

---

[6] I regret
[7] with no
[8] kin
[9] boasting

[10] prevent
[11] equally
[12] exercise

a swough. And there she lay a great while. And when she was relieved[13] she shrieked and said,

'My lord, Sir Lancelot! Alas, why lie ye in this plight?'

And then she swooned again. And then Sir Lancelot prayed Sir Lavain to take her up, 'and bring her hither to me.'

And when she came to herself Sir Lancelot lift her and said,

'Fair maiden, why fare ye thus? For ye put me to more pain.[14] Wherefore make ye no such cheer, for an ye be come to comfort me ye be right welcome; and of this little hurt that I have I shall be right hastily whole,[15] by the grace of God. But I marvel,' said Sir Lancelot, 'who told you my name?'

And so this maiden told him all how Sir Gawain was lodged with her father.

'And there by your shield he discovered your name.'

'Alas,' said Sir Lancelot, 'that repenteth me[16] that my name is known, for I am sure it will turn until anger.'[17]

And then Sir Lancelot compassed in his mind[18] that Sir Gawain would tell Queen Guinevere how he bare the red sleeve, and for whom, that he wist well would turn unto great anger.[19]

So this maiden Elaine never went from Sir Lancelot, but watched[20] him day and night, and did such attendance to him that the French book saith there was never woman did never more kindlier for man. Then Sir Lancelot prayed Sir Lavain to make espies[1] in Winchester for Sir Bors if he came there, and told him by what tokens he should know him: by a wound in his forehead.

'For I am sure,' said Sir Lancelot, 'that Sir Bors will seek me, for he is the same good knight that hurt me.'

Now turn we unto Sir Bors de Ganis that came until Winchester to seek after his cousin Sir Lancelot. And when he[2] came to Winchester Sir Lavain laid watch for[3] Sir Bors. And anon he had warning of him, and so he found him, and anon he salewed him and told him from whence he came.

'Now, fair knight,' said Sir Bors, 'ye be welcome, and I require you that ye will bring me to my lord Sir Lancelot.'

'Sir,' said Sir Lavain, 'take your horse, and within this hour ye shall see him.'

---

[13] recovered	[19] unhappiness
[14] cause me more distress	[20] sat by
[15] healed	[1] send out searchers
[16] I regret	[2] = Sir Lavain
[17] cause ill-feeling	[3] awaited
[18] realised	

So they departed and came to the hermitage. And when Sir Bors saw Sir Lancelot lie in his bed, dead pale and discoloured, anon Sir Bors lost his countenance, and for kindness and pity he might not speak, but wept tenderly a great while. But then when he might speak he said thus:

'Ah, my lord Sir Lancelot, God you bless, and send you hasty recovering! For full heavy[4] am I of my misfortune and of mine unhappiness. For now I may call myself unhappy,[5] and I dread me that God is greatly displeased with me, that He would suffer me to have such a shame for to hurt you that are all our leader and all our worship;[6] and therefore I call myself unhappy.[5] Alas, that ever such a caitiff[7] knight as I am should have power by unhappiness[8] to hurt the most noblest knight of the world! Where I so shamefully set upon you and overcharged you,[9] and where ye might have slain me, ye saved me; and so did not I, for I and all our blood[10] did to you their utterance.[11] I marvel,' said Sir Bors, 'that my heart or my blood would serve me. Wherefore, my lord Sir Lancelot, I ask you mercy.'

'Fair cousin,' said Sir Lancelot, 'ye be right welcome; and wit you well, overmuch ye say for the pleasure of me which pleaseth me nothing,[12] for why I have the same isought;[13] for I would with pride have overcome you all. And there in my pride I was near slain, and that was in mine own default;[14] for I might have given you warning of my being there, and then had I had[15] no hurt. For it is an old-said saw, "there is hard battle thereas[16] kin and friends doth battle either against other," for there may be no mercy but mortal war. Therefore, fair cousin,' said Sir Lancelot, 'let this language overpass,[17] and all shall be welcome that God sendeth. And let us leave off this matter and speak of some rejoicing, for this that is done may not be undone; and let us find a remedy how soon that I may be whole.'[18]

Then Sir Bors leaned upon his bed's side and told Sir Lance-

---

[4] sorry

[5] unfortunate

[6] leader of us all and the glory of our fellowship

[7] miserable

[8] through mischance

[9] sorely pressed you

[10] kin

[11] their worst

[12] you say all this to please me, but it pleases me not

[13] for my intention was the same as yours

[14] that was my own fault

[15] I should have had

[16] where

[17] do not let us speak thus

[18] that would soon make me healthy

lot how the queen was passing wroth with him, 'because ye wore the red sleeve at the great jousts.' And there Sir Bors told him all how Sir Gawain discovered it, 'by your shield that ye left with the fair maiden of Astolat.'

'Then is the queen wroth?' said Sir Lancelot. 'Therefore am I right heavy,[19] but I deserved no wrath, for all that I did was because I would not be known.'

'Sir, right so excused I you,' said Sir Bors, 'but all was in vain, for she said more largelier[20] to me than I to you say now. But, sir, is this she,' said Sir Bors, 'that is so busy about you, that men call the Fair Maiden of Astolat?'

'Forsooth, she it is,' said Sir Lancelot, 'that by no means I cannot put her from me.'[1]

'Why should ye put her from you?' said Sir Bors. 'For she is a passing fair damsel, and well beseen[2] and well taught.[3] And God would, fair cousin,' said Sir Bors, 'that ye could love her, but as to that I may not nother dare not counsel you. But I see well,' said Sir Bors, 'by her diligence about you that she loveth you entirely.'[4]

'That me repenteth,'[5] said Sir Lancelot.

'Well,' said Sir Bors, 'she is not the first that hath lost her pain[6] upon you, and that is the more pity.'

And so they talked of many more things.

And so within three or four days Sir Lancelot waxed big and light.[7] Then Sir Bors told Sir Lancelot how there was sworn a great tournament betwixt King Arthur and the King of North Wales, that should be upon All Hallowmass Day, besides Winchester.

'Is that truth?' said Sir Lancelot. 'Then shall ye abide with me still a little while until that I be whole,[8] for I feel myself reasonably big and strong.'

'Blessed be God!' said Sir Bors.

Then were they there nigh a month together, and ever this maiden Elaine did ever her diligence and labour night and day unto Sir Lancelot, that[9] there was never child nother wife more meeker till[10] father and husband than was this fair maiden of Astolat; wherefore Sir Bors was greatly pleased with her.

---

[19] it grieves me
[20] spoke more harshly
[1] send her away
[2] comely
[3] well behaved
[4] with all her heart
[5] That is a pity
[6] pains
[7] grew strong and active
[8] healed
[9] for
[10] to

So upon a day, by the assent of Sir Lavain, Sir Bors and Sir Lancelot, they made the hermit to seek in woods for divers herbs, and so Sir Lancelot made fair Elaine to gather herbs for him to make him a bain.[11] So in the meanwhile Sir Lancelot made Sir Lavain to arm him at all pieces,[12] and there he thought to essay himself upon horseback with a spear, whether he might wield his armour and his spear for[13] his hurt or not.

And so when he was upon his horse he stirred him freshly,[14] and the horse was passing lusty and frick[15] because he was not laboured of a month before. And then Sir Lancelot bade Sir Lavain give him that great spear, and so Sir Lancelot couched that spear in the rest. The courser leapt mightily when he felt the spurs, and he that was upon him, which was the noblest horseman of the world, strained him[16] mightily and stably, and kept still the spear in the rest. And therewith Sir Lancelot strained himself so straitly,[17] with so great force, to get the courser forward, that the bottom of his wound brast[18] both within and without, and therewithal the blood came out so fiercely that he felt himself so feeble that he might not sit upon his horse. And then Sir Lancelot cried unto Sir Bors,

'Ah, Sir Bors and Sir Lavain, help! For I am come unto mine end!'

And therewith he fell down on the one side to the earth like a dead corpse. And then Sir Bors and Sir Lavain came unto him with sorrow-making out of measure. And so by fortune this maiden Elaine heard their mourning; and then she came, and when she found Sir Lancelot there armed in that place she cried and wept as she had been wood.[19] And then she kissed him and did what she might to awake him, and then she rebuked her brother and Sir Bors, and called them false traitors, and said,

'Why would ye take him out of his bed? For an he die, I will appeal you of[20] his death.'

And so with that came the hermit, Sir Baudwin of Britain, and when he found Sir Lancelot in that plight he said but little, but wit ye well he was wroth. But[1] he said, 'Let us

---

[11] bath
[12] fully
[13] in spite of
[14] urged him on vigorously
[15] frisky
[16] held him

[17] severely
[18] the deepest part of his wound burst
[19] mad
[20] blame you for
[1] And

have him in,' and anon they bore him into the hermitage and unarmed him, and laid him in his bed; and evermore his wound bled spiteously,[2] but he stirred no limb of him. Then the knight-hermit put a thing in his nose and a little deal of water in his mouth, and then Sir Lancelot waked of his swough. And then the hermit staunched[3] his bleeding, and when Sir Lancelot might speak he[4] asked why he put his life so in jeopardy.

'Sir,' said Sir Lancelot, 'because I weened I had been strong enough, and also Sir Bors told me that there should be at Hallowmass a great jousts betwixt King Arthur and the King of North Wales. And therefore I thought to essay myself, whether I might be there or not.'

'Ah, Sir Lancelot,' said the hermit, 'your heart and your courage will never be done until your last day! But ye shall do now by my counsel: let Sir Bors depart from you, and let him do at that tournament what he may; and, by the grace of God,' said the knight-hermit, 'by that[5] the tournament be done and he comen hither again, sir, ye shall be whole,[6] so[7] that ye will be governed by me.'

Then Sir Bors made him ready to depart from him, and Sir Lancelot said,

'Fair cousin, Sir Bors, recommend me unto all those ye ought recommend me unto, and I pray you, enforce[8] yourself at that jousts that ye may be best, for my love. And here shall I abide you, at the mercy of God, till your again-coming.'[9]

And so Sir Bors departed and came to the court of King Arthur, and told them in what place he left Sir Lancelot.

'That me repenteth,'[10] said the king. 'But syn he shall have his life, we all may thank God.'

And then Sir Bors told the queen what jeopardy Sir Lancelot was in when he would essayed[11] his horse:

'And all that he did was for the love of you, because he would have been at this tournament.'

'Fie on him, recreant knight!' said the queen. 'For wit you well I am right sorry an he shall have his life.'

'Madam, his life shall he have,' said Sir Bors, 'and who that

[2] copiously	[7] provided
[3] stopped	[8] exert
[4] = the hermit	[9] your return
[5] by the time	[10] That is a pity
[6] healed	[11] wished to try

would otherwise, except you, madam, we that be of his blood[12] would help to shorten their lives! But, madam,' said Sir Bors, 'ye have been oftentimes displeased with my lord Sir Lancelot, but at all times at the end ye found him a true knight.'

And so he departed. And then every knight of the Round Table that were there that time present made them ready to that jousts at All Hallowmass. And thither drew many knights of divers countries. And as Hallowmass drew near, thither came the King of North Wales, and the King with the Hundred Knights, and Sir Galahalt the Haut Prince of Surluse. And thither came King Anguish of Ireland, and the King of Northumberland, and the King of Scots. So these three kings came to King Arthur's party.

And so that day Sir Gawain did great deeds of arms, and began first; and the heralds numbered that Sir Gawain smote down twenty knights. Then Sir Bors de Ganis came in the same time, and he was numbered that he[13] smote down twenty knights; and therefore the prize was given betwixt[14] them both, for they began first and longest endured. Also Sir Gareth, as the book saith, did that day great deeds of arms, for he smote down and pulled down thirty knights: but when he had done that deeds he tarried not but so departed, and therefore he lost his prize. And Sir Palomides did great deeds of arms that day, for he smote down twenty knights; but he departed suddenly, and men deemed that he and Sir Gareth rode together to some manner[15] adventures.

So when this tournament was done Sir Bors departed, and rode till he came to Sir Lancelot, his cousin. And then he found him walking on his feet, and there either made great joy of other.

And so he told Sir Lancelot of all the jousts, like as ye have heard.

'I marvel,' said Sir Lancelot, 'that Sir Gareth, when he had done such deeds of arms, that he would not tarry.'

'Sir, thereof we marvelled all,' said Sir Bors, 'for but if it were you, other the noble knight Sir Tristram, other the good knight Sir Lamorak de Galis, I saw never knight bear[16] so many knights and smite down in so little a while as did Sir Gareth. And anon as he was gone we all wist not where he became.'[17]

---

[12] kin
[13] it was reckoned that he
[14] divided between

[15] kind of
[16] strike
[17] went

'By my head,' said Sir Lancelot, 'he is a noble knight, and a mighty man and well-breathed;[18] and if he were well essayed,' said Sir Lancelot, 'I would deem he were good enough for any knight that beareth the life.[19] And he is gentle, courteous and right bounteous, meek and mild, and in him is no manner of mal engine,[20] but plain, faithful, and true.'

So then they made them ready to depart from the hermitage. And so upon a morn they took their horses and this Elaine le Blanke with them. And when they came to Astolat there were they well lodged, and had great cheer of Sir Barnard, the old baron, and of Sir Tirry, his son.

And so upon the morn when Sir Lancelot should depart, fair Elaine brought her father with her, and Sir Lavain and Sir Tirry, and then thus she said:

'My lord, Sir Lancelot, now I see ye will depart from me. Now, fair knight and courteous knight,' said she, 'have mercy upon me, and suffer me not to[1] die for your love.'

'Why, what would you that I did?' said Sir Lancelot.

'Sir, I would have you to my husband,' said Elaine.

'Fair damsel, I thank you heartily,' said Sir Lancelot, 'but truly,' said he, 'I cast me never[2] to be wedded man.'

'Then, fair knight,' said she, 'will ye be my paramour?'

'Jesu defend me!' said Sir Lancelot. 'For then I rewarded your father and your brother full evil for their great goodness.'

'Alas! Then,' said she, 'I must die for your love.'

'Ye shall not so,' said Sir Lancelot, 'for wit you well, fair maiden, I might have been married an I had would,[3] but I never applied me yet to be married. But because, fair damsel, that ye love me as ye say ye do, I will for your good will and kindness show to you some goodness. That is this, that wheresomever ye will beset[4] your heart upon some good knight that will wed you, I shall give you together[5] a thousand pound yearly, to you and to your heirs. This much will I give you, fair maiden, for your kindness, and always while I live to be your own knight.'

'Sir, of all this,' said the maiden, 'I will none, for but if ye will wed me, other to be my paramour at the least, wit you well, Sir Lancelot, my good days are done.'

18 strong-winded
19 any knight that lives
20 guile
1 do not let me

2 I never intend
3 wished
4 bestow
5 both

'Fair damsel,' said Sir Lancelot, 'of these two things ye must pardon[6] me.'

Then she shrieked shrilly and fell down in a swough; and then women bare her into her chamber, and there she made overmuch sorrow. And then Sir Lancelot would[7] depart, and there he asked Sir Lavain what he would do.

'Sir, what should I do,' said Sir Lavain, 'but follow you but if[8] ye drive me from you or command me to go from you?'

Then came Sir Barnard to Sir Lancelot and said to him,

'I cannot see but that my daughter will die for your sake.'

'Sir, I may not do withal,'[9] said Sir Lancelot, 'for that me sore repenteth.[10] For I report me to yourself[11] that my proffer is fair. And me repenteth,'[10] said Sir Lancelot, 'that she loveth me as she doth, for I was never the causer of it; for I report me unto your son, I never early nother late proffered her bounty nother fair behests.[12] And as for me,' said Sir Lancelot, 'I dare do that a knight should do, and say that she is a clean maiden for me, both for deed and will. For I am right heavy of[13] her distress! For she is a full fair maiden, good and gentle, and well itaught.'[14]

'Father,' said Sir Lavain, 'I dare make good she is a clean maiden as for my lord Sir Lancelot; but she doth as I do, for sithen I saw first my lord Sir Lancelot I could never depart from him, nother nought I will, an I may[15] follow him.'

Then Sir Lancelot took his leave, and so they departed, and came to Winchester. And when King Arthur wist that Sir Lancelot was come whole and sound, the king made great joy of him; and so did Sir Gawain and all the knights of the Round Table, except Sir Agravain and Sir Mordred. Also Queen Guinevere was wood wroth[16] with Sir Lancelot, and would by no means speak with him, but estranged herself from him. And Sir Lancelot made all the means that he might[17] for to speak with the queen, but it would not be.

Now speak we of the fair maiden of Astolat that made such

---

[6] excuse
[7] was about to
[8] unless
[9] I cannot help it
[10] I grieve
[11] But you will agree
[12] your son will bear witness that at no time did I show her regard or make her sweet promises
[13] sad about
[14] well behaved
[15] and never shall, if I am allowed to
[16] wildly angry
[17] did all he could

sorrow day and night that she never slept, ate, nother drank, and ever she made her complaint[18] unto Sir Lancelot. So when she had thus endured a ten days, that she feebled so that she must needs pass out of this world, then she shrove her clean and received her Creator. And ever she complained[18] still upon Sir Lancelot. Then her ghostly[19] father bade her leave such thoughts. Then she said,

'Why should I leave such thoughts? Am I not an earthly woman? And all the while the breath is in my body I may complain[18] me, for my belief is that I do none offence, though I love an earthly man, unto God, for He formed me thereto, and all manner of good love cometh of God. And other than good love loved I never Sir Lancelot du Lake. And I take God to record, I loved never none but him, nor never shall, of earthly creature; and a clean maiden I am for him and for all other. And sithen it is the sufferance[20] of God that I shall die for so noble a knight, I beseech Thee, High Father of Heaven, have mercy upon me and my soul, and upon mine innumerable pains that I suffer may be allegeance[1] of part of my sins. For, Sweet Lord Jesu,' said the fair maiden, 'I take God to record, I was never to Thee great offencer nother against Thy laws but that I loved this noble knight, Sir Lancelot, out of measure. And of myself, Good Lord, I had no might to withstand the fervent love, wherefore I have my death.'

And then she called her father, Sir Barnard, and her brother, Sir Tirry, and heartily she prayed her father that her brother might write a letter like as she did indite,[2] and so her father granted her. And when the letter was written word by word like as she devised it, then she prayed her father that she might be watched until she was dead. 'And while my body is hot let this letter be put in my right hand, and my hand bound fast with the letter until that I be cold. And let me be put in a fair bed with all the richest clothes that I have about me, and so let my bed and all my richest clothes be laid with me in a chariot[3] unto the next[4] place where the Thames is; and there let me be put within a barget,[5] and but one man with me, such as ye trust to steer me thither; and that my barget be covered

---

18 lament(ed)   2 as she would dictate
19 spiritual   3 cart
20 will   4 nearest
 1 relief   5 small boat

with black samite[6] over and over. And thus, father, I beseech you let it be done.'

So her father granted it her faithfully all thing should be done like as she had devised. Then her father and her brother made great dole for her. And when this was done anon she died.

And when she was dead the corpse and the bed all was led the next way unto the Thames, and there a man and the corpse and all things as she had devised was put in the Thames. And so the man steered the barget unto Westminster, and there it rubbed and rolled to and fro a great while or any man espied it.

So by fortune King Arthur and Queen Guinevere were talking together at a window, and so as they looked into the Thames they espied that black barget and had marvel what it meant. Then the king called Sir Kay, and showed it him.

'Sir,' said Sir Kay, 'wit you well, there is some new tidings.'

'Therefore go ye thither,' said the king to Sir Kay, 'and take with you Sir Braundiles and Sir Agravain, and bring me ready[7] word what is there.'

Then these three knights departed and came to the barget and went in. There they found the fairest corpse lying in a rich bed that ever ye saw, and a poor man sitting in the barget's end, and no word would he speak. So these three knights returned unto the king again, and told him what they found.

'That fair corpse will I see,' said the king.

And so the king took the queen by the hand and went thither. Then the king made the barget to be held fast, and then the king and the queen went in with certain knights with them, and there he saw the fairest woman lie in a rich bed, covered unto her middle[8] with many rich clothes,[9] and all was of cloth of gold. And she lay as she had smiled.

Then the queen espied the letter in her right hand and told the king. Then the king took it and said,

'Now am I sure this letter will tell us what she was, and why she is come hither.'

So then the king and the queen went out of the barget, and so commanded a certain[10] to wait[11] upon the barget. And so when the king was come to his chamber he called many knights

---

[6] rich silk
[7] speedy
[8] waist

[9] coverings
[10] someone
[11] keep watch

about[12] him, and said that he would wit openly[13] what was written within that letter. Then the king brake it, and made a clerk to read it, and this was the intent[14] of the letter.

'Most noble knight, my lord Sir Lancelot, now hath death made us two at debate[15] for your love. And I was your lover, that men called the Fair Maiden of Astolat. Therefore unto all ladies I make my moan,[16] yet for my soul ye pray and bury me at the least and offer ye my mass-penny:[17] this is my last request. And a clean maiden I died, I take God to witness. And pray for my soul, Sir Lancelot, as thou[18] art peerless.'

This was all the substance in the letter. And when it was read, the king, the queen and all the knights wept for pity of the doleful complaints. Then was Sir Lancelot sent for, and when he was come King Arthur made the letter to be read to him. And when Sir Lancelot heard it word by word, he said,

'My lord Arthur, wit ye well I am right heavy of[19] the death of this fair lady. And God knoweth I was never causer of her death by my willing, and that will I report me unto[20] her own brother that here is, Sir Lavain. I will not say nay,' said Sir Lancelot, 'but that she was both fair and good, and much I was beholden unto her, but she loved me out of measure.'

'Sir,' said the queen, 'ye might have showed her some bounty[1] and gentleness which might have preserved her life.'

'Madam,' said Sir Lancelot, 'she would none otherways be answered but that she would be my wife other else my paramour, and of these two I would not grant her. But I proffered her, for her good love that she showed me, a thousand pound yearly to her and to her heirs, and to wed any manner of knight that she could find best to love, in her heart. For, madam,' said Sir Lancelot, 'I love not to be constrained to love, for love must only arise of the heartself, and not by none constraint.'

'That is truth, sir,' said the king, 'and with many knights, love is free in himself, and never will be bound; for where he is bounden he looseth himself.' Then said the king unto Sir

---

[12] to
[13] wished to hear in their presence
[14] content
[15] divided us
[16] lament

[17] mass-penny: *an offering of money made at mass*
[18] thou who
[19] sorry about
[20] as to that I call to witness
[1] favour

Lancelot, 'Sir, it will be your worship that ye oversee[2] that she be interred worshipfully.'[3]

'Sir,' said Sir Lancelot, 'that shall be done as I can best devise.'

And so many knights yode thither to behold that fair dead maiden, and so upon the morn she was interred richly. And Sir Lancelot offered her mass-penny;[17] and all those knights of the Table Round that were there at that time offered with Sir Lancelot. And then the poor man went again[4] with the barget.

Then the queen sent for Sir Lancelot and prayed him of mercy for why that she had been wroth with him causeless.[5]

'This is not the first time,' said Sir Lancelot, 'that ye have been displeased with me causeless. But, madam, ever I must suffer you,[6] but what sorrow that I endure, ye take no force.'[7]

So this passed on all that winter, with all manner of hunting and hawking, and jousts and tourneys were many betwixt many great lords.[8]

[2] take care
[3] with honour
[4] back
[5] prayed him to forgive her for having been unjustly displeased with him
[6] bear with you
[7] it matters not to you
[8] *The story in* M *is concluded by a reference to Lavain who was 'nobly defamed* (= spoken of) *among many knights of the Table Round.'*

The Death of King Arthur

or The Most Piteous Tale of the Morte Arthur Saunz Guerdon

I

Slander and Strife

In May, when every heart flourisheth and burgeoneth (for as the season is lusty to behold and comfortable,[1] so man and woman rejoiceth and gladdeth[2] of summer coming with his fresh flowers, for winter with his rough winds and blasts causeth lusty[3] men and women to cower and to sit by fires), so this season it befell in the month of May a great anger and unhap[4] that stinted[5] not till the flower of chivalry of all the world was destroyed and slain.

And all was long upon[6] two unhappy[7] knights which were named Sir Agravain and Sir Mordred, that were brethren unto Sir Gawain. For this Sir Agravain and Sir Mordred had ever a privy[8] hate unto the Queen, Dame Guinevere, and to Sir Lancelot; and daily and nightly they ever watched upon Sir Lancelot.

So it misfortuned Sir Gawain and all his brethren were in King Arthur's chamber, and then Sir Agravain said thus openly, and not in no counsel,[9] that many knights might hear:

'I marvel that we all be not ashamed both to see and to know how Sir Lancelot lies daily and nightly by the Queen. And all we know well that it is so, and it is shamefully suffered of us all that we should suffer[10] so noble a king as King Arthur is to be shamed.'

[1] pleasant and refreshing to see
[2] are glad
[3] merry
[4] ill-fortune
[5] ceased
[6] due to
[7] ill-fortuned, *or* those who bring ill-luck to others
[8] secret
[9] not in secret
[10] and it shames us all that we should allow

Then spoke Sir Gawain and said,

'Brother, Sir Agravain, I pray you and charge[11] you, move no such matters no more[12] afore me, for wit you well, I will not be of your counsel.'[13]

'So God me help,' said Sir Gaheris and Sir Gareth, 'we will not be known[14] of your deeds.'

'Then will I!' said Sir Mordred.

'I lieve[15] you well,' said Sir Gawain, 'for ever unto all unhappiness,[16] sir, you will grant.[17] And I would that ye left all this and made you not so busy, for I know,' said Sir Gawain, 'what will fall[18] of it.'

'Fall[18] whatsoever fall[18] may,' said Sir Agravain, 'I will disclose it to the king!'

'Not by my counsel,' said Sir Gawain, 'for, an there arise war and wrake[19] betwixt Sir Lancelot and us, wit you well, brother, there will many kings and great lords hold with Sir Lancelot. Also, brother, Sir Agravain,' said Sir Gawain, 'ye must remember how oftentimes Sir Lancelot has rescued the king and the queen; and the best of us all had been full cold to the heart-root[20] had not Sir Lancelot been better than we, and that has he proved himself full oft. And as for my part,' said Sir Gawain, 'I will never be against Sir Lancelot for one day's deed, and that was when he rescued me from King Carados of the Dolorous Tower and slew him and saved my life. Also, brother Sir Agravain, and Sir Mordred, in like wise Sir Lancelot rescued both you and three score and two from Sir Tarquin. And therefore, brother, methinks such noble deeds and kindness should be remembered.'

'Do you as ye list,' said Sir Agravain, 'for I will lain[1] it no longer.'

So with these words came in Sir Arthur.

'Now, brother,' said Sir Gawain, 'stint[2] your strife.'

'That will I not,' said Sir Agravain and Sir Mordred.

'Well, will ye so?' said Sir Gawain. 'Then God speed you, for I will not bear of your tales, neither be of your counsel.'[3]

---

11 command
12 suggest no such thing any more
13 I will have nothing to do with your plotting
14 we will keep away from
15 believe
16 mischief
17 acquiesce

18 come
19 strife
20 the best among us would long since have been dead
1 conceal
2 cease
3 nor have anything to do with your plotting

'No more will I,' said Sir Gaheris.

'Neither I,' said Sir Gareth, 'for I shall never say evil by that man that made me knight.'

And therewithall they three departed making great dole.

'Alas!' said Sir Gawain and Sir Gareth, 'now is this realm wholly destroyed and mischieved,[4] and the noble fellowship of the Round Table shall be disparbled.'[5]

So they departed, and then King Arthur asked them what noise[6] they made.

'My lord,' said Sir Agravain, 'I shall tell you, for I may keep it no longer. Here is I and my brother Sir Mordred break[7] unto my brother Sir Gawain, Sir Gaheris and to Sir Gareth — for this is all, to make it short — how that we know all that Sir Lancelot holdeth your queen, and hath done long, and we be your sister's sons, we may suffer[8] it no longer. And all we wote[9] that you should be above Sir Lancelot; and ye are the king that made him knight, and therefore we will prove it that he is a traitor to your person.'

'If it be so,' said the king, 'wit you well, he is none other. But I would be loth to begin such a thing but I might have proofs of it, for Sir Lancelot is an hardy knight, and all you know that he is the best knight among us all, and but if[10] he be taken with the deed[11] he will fight with him that bringeth up the noise,[12] and I know no knight that is able to match him. Therefore, an it be sooth as ye say, I would that he were taken with the deed.'[11]

For, as the French book saith, the king was full loath that such a noise[13] should be upon Sir Lancelot and his queen; for the king had a deeming[14] of it, but he would not hear thereof, for Sir Lancelot had done so much for him and for the queen so many times that wit you well the king loved him passingly well.

'My lord,' said Sir Agravain, 'ye shall ride to-morn an-hunting, and doubt ye not, Sir Lancelot will not go with you. And so when it draweth toward night ye may send the queen word that ye will lie out all that night, and so may ye send for your

---

[4] put to shame
[5] dispersed
[6] complaint
[7] disclose
[8] allow
[9] know

[10] unless
[11] in the act
[12] spreads the report
[13] scandal
[14] suspicion

cooks. And then, upon pain of death, that night we shall take him with the queen, and we shall bring him unto you, quick[15] or dead.'

'I will well,'[16] said the king. 'Then I counsel you to take with you sure fellowship.'

'Sir,' said Sir Agravain, 'my brother Sir Mordred and I will take with us twelve knights of the Round Table.'

'Beware,' said King Arthur, 'for I warn you, ye shall find him wight.'[17]

'Let us deal,'[18] said Sir Agravain and Sir Mordred.

So on the morn King Arthur rode an-hunting and sent word to the queen that he would be out all the night. Then Sir Agravain and Sir Mordred got to them twelve knights and hid themselves in a chamber in the castle of Carlisle. And these were their names: Sir Colgrevance, Sir Madore de la Porte, Sir Guingalen, Sir Meliot de Logres, Sir Petipace of Winchelsea, Sir Galeron of Galway, Sir Melion de la Mountayne, Sir Ascomore, Sir Gromorsom Eriore, Sir Cursessalain, Sir Florence, and Sir Lovell. So these twelve knights were with Sir Mordred and Sir Agravain, and all they were of Scotland, other else[19] of Sir Gawain's kin, other well-willers[20] to his brother.

So when the night came Sir Lancelot told Sir Bors how he would go that night and speak with the queen.

'Sir,' said Sir Bors, 'ye shall not go this night by my counsel.'

'Why?' said Sir Lancelot.

'Sir, for I dread me ever of Sir Agravain that waits upon you daily to do you shame and us all. And never gave my heart against no going that ever ye went to the queen so much as now,[1] for I mistrust that the king is out this night from the queen because peradventure he has lain some watch for you and the queen. Therefore I dread me sore of some treason.'

'Have you no dread,' said Sir Lancelot, 'for I shall go and come again and make not tarrying.'

'Sir,' said Sir Bors, 'that me repents,[2] for I dread me sore that your going this night shall wrath[3] us all.'

'Fair nephew,' said Sir Lancelot, 'I marvel me much why you say thus, since the queen has sent for me. And wit you well,

---

15 alive
16 readily agree
17 strong
18 act
19 some others
20 well-wishers

1 never did my heart warn me against your going to the queen as much as it does now. *'Ayenste'* governs here both a verbal noun and a noun clause (*'that ever'* etc.).
2 distresses me
3 harm

I will not be so much a coward, but she shall understand I will see her good grace.'

'God speed you well,' said Sir Bors, 'and send you sound and safe again!'

So Sir Lancelot departed and took his sword under his arm, and so he walked in his mantle, that noble knight, and put himself in great jeopardy. And so he passed on till he came to the queen's chamber, and so lightly[4] he was had into the chamber.

For, as the French book says, the queen and Sir Lancelot were together, and whether they were abed other at other manner of disports[5] me list not thereof make no mention,[6] for love at that time was not as love is nowadays.

But thus as they were together there came Sir Agravain and Sir Mordred with twelve knights with them of the Round Table, and they said with great crying and scaring voice,

'Thou traitor, Sir Lancelot, now art thou taken!' And thus they cried with a loud voice, that all the court might hear it. And these fourteen knights all were armed at all points,[7] as they should fight in a battle.

'Alas!' said Queen Guinevere, 'now are we mischieved both!'[8]

'Madame,' said Sir Lancelot, 'is there here any armour within you that might cover my body withall? And if there be any, give it me and I shall soon stint their malice,[9] by the grace of God!'

'Now, truly,' said the queen, 'I have none armour neither helm, shield, sword, neither spear, wherefore I dread me sore our long love is come to a mischievous[10] end. For I hear by their noise there be many noble knights, and well I wot they be surely armed, and against them ye may make no resistance. Wherefore ye are likely to be slain, and then I shall be brent! For an ye might escape them,' said the queen 'I would not doubt but that ye would rescue me in what danger that I ever stood in.'

'Alas,' said Sir Lancelot, 'in all my life thus was I never bestrad[11] that I should be thus shamefully slain for lack of mine armour.'

But ever Sir Agravain and Sir Mordred cried,

[4] quickly
[5] pleasant pastime
[6] I would not like to say. *Malory's sources make no distinction between 'love at that time' and 'nowadays.' Cf. Le Morte Arthur. 1806.*

[7] completely armed
[8] both brought to ruin!
[9] make them powerless
[10] shameful
[11] beset

'Traitor knight, come out of the queen's chamber! For wit thou well thou art beset so that thou shalt not escape.'

'Ah, Jesu mercy!' said Sir Lancelot, 'this shameful cry and noise[12] I may not suffer, for better were death at once than thus to endure this pain.'

Then he took the queen in his arms and kissed her and said, 'Most noblest Christian queen, I beseech ye, as you have been ever my special good lady, and I at all times your poor[13] knight and true unto my power[14] and as I never failed you in right nor in wrong since the first day King Arthur made me knight, that you will pray for my soul if that I be slain. For well I am assured that Sir Bors, my nephew, and all the remnant[15] of my kin, with Sir Lavain and Sir Urry, that they will not fail you to rescue you from the fire. And therefore, mine own lady, recomfort yourself,[16] whatsoever come of me, that ye go with Sir Bors, my nephew; and Sir Urry, and they all will do you all the pleasure that they may, and you shall live like a queen upon my lands.'

'Nay, Sir Lancelot, nay!' said the queen. 'Wit thou well that I will not live long after thy days. But an you be slain I will take my death as meekly as ever dead martyr take his death for Jesu Christ's sake.'

'Well, madame,' said Sir Lancelot, 'sith it is so that the day is come that our love must depart, wit you well I shall sell my life as dear as I may. And a thousandfold,' said Sir Lancelot, 'I am more heavier[17] for ye than for myself! And now I had liefer[18] than to be lord of all Christendom that I had sure armour upon me, that men might speak of my deeds or ever I were slain.'[19]

'Truly,' said the queen, 'an it might please God, I would that they would take me and slay me and suffer[20] you to escape.'

'That shall never be,' said Sir Lancelot, 'God defend me from such a shame! But, Jesu Christ, be thou my shield and mine armour!'

And therewith Sir Lancelot wrapped his mantle about his arm well and surely; and by then they had gotten a great form[1] out of the hall, and therewith they all rushed at the door.

---

12 scandal
13 humble
14 my utmost
15 rest
16 take courage again

17 distressed
18 rather
19 if I should be slain
20 allow
1 bench

'Now, fair lords,' said Sir Lancelot, 'leave your noise and your rushing,[2] and I shall set open this door, and then may ye do with me what it liketh you.'

'Come off, then,' said they all, 'and do it, for it availeth thee not to strive against us all! And therefore let us into this chamber, and we shall save thy life until thou come to King Arthur.'

Then Sir Lancelot unbarred the door, and with his left hand he held it open a little, that but one man might come in at once. And so there came striding a good knight, a much[3] man and a large, and his name was called Sir Colgrevance of Gore. And he with a sword struck at Sir Lancelot mightily, and so he[4] put aside the stroke, and gave him such a buffet upon the helmet that he fell grovelling[5] dead within the chamber door.

Then Sir Lancelot with great might drew the knight within the chamber door. And then Sir Lancelot, with help of the queen and her ladies, he was lightly[6] armed in Colgrevance[7] armour. And ever stood Sir Agravain and Sir Mordred, crying,

'Traitor knight! Come forth out of the queen's chamber!'

'Sirs, leave your noise,'[2] said Sir Lancelot, 'for wit you well, Sir Agravain, ye shall not prison me this night! And therefore, an ye do by my counsel, go ye all from this chamber door and make you no such crying and such manner of sclander[8] as ye do. For I promise you by my knighthood, an ye will depart and make no more noise, I shall as to-morn appear afore you all and before the king, and then let it be seen which of you all, other else ye all,[9] that will depreve[10] me of treason. And there shall I answer you, as a knight should, that hither I came to the queen of no manner of mal engin,[11] and that will I prove and make it good upon you with my hands.'

'Fie upon thee, traitor,' said Sir Agravain and Sir Mordred, for we will have thee maugre thine head[12] and slay thee, an we list![13] For we let thee wit we have the choice of[14] King Arthur to save thee other slay thee.'

'Ah, sirs,' said Sir Lancelot, 'is there none other grace with you? Then keep[15] yourself!'

2 stop your insults and turmoil
3 big
4 = Lancelot
5 face downward
6 quickly
7 Colgrevance's
8 slander
9 or else all of you
10 accuse
11 evil design
12 notwithstanding all you can do
13 if we desire!
14 by the authority of
15 defend

And then Sir Lancelot set all open the chamber door, and mightily and knightly he strode in among them. And anon at the first stroke he slew Sir Agravain, and anon after twelve of his fellows. Within a while he had laid them down cold to the earth, for there was none of the twelve knights might stand[16] Sir Lancelot one buffet. And also he wounded Sir Mordred, and therewithall he[17] fled with all his might. And then Sir Lancelot returned again unto the queen and said,

'Madame, now wit you well, all our true love is brought to an end, for now will King Arthur ever be my foe. And therefore, madame, an it like you that I may have you with me, I shall save you from all manner adventurous[18] dangers.'

'Sir, that is not best,' said the queen, 'meseems, for now ye have done so much harm it will be best that ye hold you still with this.[19] And if ye see that as to-morn they will put me unto death then may ye rescue me as ye think best.'

'I will well,'[20] said Sir Lancelot, 'for have ye no doubt, while I am a man living I shall rescue you.'

And then he kissed her, and either[1] of them gave other a ring, and so the queen he left there and went until[2] his lodging.

When Sir Bors saw Sir Lancelot he was never so glad of his home-coming.

'Jesu mercy!' said Sir Lancelot, 'why be ye all armed? What meaneth this?'

'Sir,' said Sir Bors, 'after ye were departed from us we all that been of your blood and your well-willers[3] were so ad-retched[4] that some of us leapt out of our beds naked, and some in their dreams caught naked swords in their hands. And therefore,' said Sir Bors, 'we deemed there was some great strife on hand, and so we deemed that we were betrapped with some treason; and therefore we made us thus ready what need that ever ye were in.'[5]

'My fair nephew,' said Sir Lancelot unto Sir Bors, 'now shall ye wit all that this night I was more hard bestad[6] than ever I was days of my life.[7] And thanked be God, I am myself escaped their danger.'[8] And so he told them all how and in what

---

[16] withstand
[17] = Mordred
[18] grave
[19] go no further
[20] readily agree
[1] each
[2] unto

[3] well-wishers
[4] troubled, perturbed
[5] ready to give you whatever help you may need
[6] beset
[7] in all my life
[8] I am no longer at their mercy

manner, as ye have heard toforehand. 'And therefore, my fellows,' said Sir Lancelot, 'I pray ye all that you will be of heart good, and help me in what need that ever I stand, for now is war coming to us all.'

'Sir,' said Sir Bors, 'all is welcome that God sendeth us, and we have taken much weal with you and much worship,[9] we will take the woe with you as we have taken the weal.'

And therefore they said, all the good knights,

'Look you take no discomfort! For there is no bands of knights under heaven but we shall be able to grieve[10] them as much as they may us, and therefore discomfort not yourself by no manner. And we shall gather together all that we love and that loves us, and what that you will have done shall be done. And therefore let us take the woe and the joy together.'

'Grantmercy,'[11] said Sir Lancelot, 'of your good comfort, for in my great distress, fair nephew, ye comfort me greatly. But this, my fair nephew, I would that ye did in all haste that you may or it is far days past:[12] that ye will look in their lodging that been lodged nigh here about the king, which will hold with[13] me and which will not. For now I would know which were my friends from my foes.'

'Sir,' said Sir Bors, 'I shall do my pain,[14] and or it be seven of the clock I shall wit of such as ye have doubt for,[15] who that will hold with[13] you.'

Then Sir Bors called unto him Sir Lionel, Sir Ector de Maris, Sir Blamour de Ganis, Sir Bleoberis de Ganis, Sir Gahalantin, Sir Galyhodin, Sir Galihud, Sir Menaduke, Sir Villiers the Valiant, Sir Hebes le Renown, Sir Lavain, Sir Urry of Hungary, Sir Neroveous, Sir Plenorius (for these two were knights that Sir Lancelot won upon a bridge, and therefore they would never be against him[16]), and Sir Garry le Fitz Lake, and Sir Selises of the Dolorous Tower, Sir Melias de Lisle, and Sir Bellengere le Beuse, that was Sir Alexander le Orphelin's son; because his mother was Alice la Belle Pellerine, and she was kin unto Sir Lancelot, he held with him. So came Sir Palomides and Sir Saphir, his brother; Sir Clegis, Sir Sadok, Sir Dinas and Sir Clarius of Cleremont.

---

[9] praise
[10] to inflict damage upon
[11] many thanks
[12] before very long
[13] remain loyal to

[14] exert myself
[15] those of whose loyalty you are not certain
[16] *A reference to an episode in Malory's* Book of Sir Tristram.

So these two-and-twenty[17] knights drew them together, and by then[18] they were armed and on horseback they promised Sir Lancelot to do what he would. Then there fell to them, what of North Wales and of Cornwall, for Sir Lamorak's sake and for Sir Tristram's sake, to the number of a seven score knights. Then spoke Sir Lancelot:

'Wit you well, I have been ever since I came to this court well-willed[19] unto my lord Arthur and unto my lady Queen Guinevere unto my power.[20] And this night because my lady the queen sent for me to speak with her, I suppose it was made by[1] treason; howbeit I dare largely[2] excuse her person, notwithstanding I was there by a forecast[3] nearhand[4] slain but as[5] Jesu provided for me.'

And then that noble knight Sir Lancelot told them how he was hard bestad[6] in the queen's chamber, and how and in what manner he escaped from them.

'And therefore wit you well, my fair lords, I am sure there is but war unto me and to mine. And for cause I have slain this night Sir Agravain, Sir Gawain's brother, and at the least twelve of his fellows, and for this cause now am I sure of mortal war. For these knights were sent by King Arthur to betray me, and therefore the king will in this heat[7] and malice judge the queen unto brenning, and that may not I suffer[8] that she should be brent for my sake. For an I may be heard and suffered[8] and so taken,[9] I will fight for the queen, that[10] she is a true lady until[11] her lord. But the king in his heat,[7] I dread, will not take[9] me as I ought to be taken.'[9]

'My lord, Sir Lancelot,' said Sir Bors, 'by mine advice, ye shall take the woe with the weal, and take it in patience and thank God of it. And since it is fallen as it is, I counsel you to keep[12] yourself, for an ye will yourself,[13] there is no fellowship of knights christened that shall do you wrong. And also I will counsel you, my lord, that my lady Queen Guinevere, an she be in any distress, insomuch as she is in pain for your sake, that

---

[17] *Possibly a scribal error for 'five-and-twenty'.*
[18] when
[19] well-disposed
[20] as far as it lay in my power
[1] made out to be
[2] wholeheartedly
[3] by design
[4] nearly
[5] had not
[6] beset
[7] anger
[8] allow(ed)
[9] accept(ed) as a champion
[10] because; *or* to prove that
[11] unto
[12] guard, look after
[13] will guard yourself

ye knightly rescue her; for an you did any other wise all the world would speak you shame to the world's end. Insomuch as ye were taken with her, whether you did right other wrong, it is now your part to hold with[14] the queen, that she be not slain and put to a mischievous[15] death. For an she so die, the shame shall be evermore yours.'

'Now Jesu defend me from shame,' said Sir Lancelot, 'and keep[12] and save my lady the queen from villainy and shameful death, and that she never be destroyed in my default.'[16] Wherefore, my fair lords, my kin and my friends,' said Sir Lancelot, 'what will ye do?'

And anon they said all with one voice,

'We will do as ye will do.'

'Than I put this case[17] unto you,' said Sir Lancelot, 'that my lord King Arthur by evil counsel will to-morn in his heat[7] put my lady the queen unto the fire, and there to be brent, then, I pray you, counsel me what is best for me to do.'

Then they said all at once with one voice,

'Sir, us thinks best that ye knightly rescue the queen. Insomuch as she shall be brent, it is for your sake; and it is to suppose, an ye might be handled,[18] ye should have the same death, other else a more shamefuller death. And, sir, we say all that you have rescued her from her death many times for other men's quarrels; therefore us seems it is more your worship[19] that you rescue the queen from this quarrel, insomuch that she has it for your sake.'

Then Sir Lancelot stood still and said,

'My fair lords, wit you well I would be full loath that my lady the queen should die such a shameful death. But an it be so that ye will counsel me to rescue her, I must do much harm or I rescue her, and peradventure I shall there destroy some of my best friends, and that should much repent me.[20] And peradventure there be some, an they could well bring it about or disobey my lord King Arthur, they would soon come to me, the which[1] I were loath to hurt. And if so be that I may win the queen away, where shall I keep her?'

---

[14] remain loyal to
[15] shameful
[16] through my failure to take up the challenge
[17] matter
[18] captured
[19] honourable

[20] and that I should regret very much
[1] whom; *i.e. those who, like Gareth, would have willingly disobeyed King Arthur and joined Lancelot.*

'Sir, that shall be the least care of us all,' said Sir Bors, 'for how did the most noble knight Sir Tristram? By your good will, kept not he with him La Beale Isode near three year in Joyous Gard, the which was done by your althers advice?[2] And that same place is your own, and in like wise may ye do, an ye list,[3] and take the queen knightly away with you, if so be that the king will judge her to be brent. And in Joyous Gard may ye keep her long enough until the heat[4] be past of the king, and then it may fortune[5] you to bring the queen again to the king with great worship,[6] and peradventure you shall have then thank for your bringing home, whether other may happen to have maugre.'[7]

'That is hard for to do,' said Sir Lancelot, 'for by Sir Tristram I may have a warning: for when by means of treatise[8] Sir Tristram brought again La Beale Isode unto King Mark from Joyous Gard, look ye now what fell[9] on the end, how shamefully that false traitor King Mark slew him as he sat harping afore his lady, La Beale Isode. With a grounden glave[10] he thrust him in behind to the heart, which grieveth sore me,' said Sir Lancelot, 'to speak of his death, for all the world may not find such another knight.'

'All this is truth,' said Sir Bors, 'but there is one thing shall courage[11] you and us all: you know well that King Arthur and King Mark were never like of conditions,[12] for there was never yet man that ever could prove King Arthur untrue of his promise.'

But so, to make short tale, they were all condescended[13] that, for better other for worse, if so were that the queen were brought on that morn to the fire, shortly they all would rescue her. And so by the advice of Sir Lancelot they put them all in a bushment[14] in a wood as nigh Carlisle as they might, and there they abode still to wit what the king would do.

Now turn we again, that when Sir Mordred was escaped from Sir Lancelot he got his horse and mounted upon him, and came to King Arthur sore wounded and all forbled,[15] and there he

[2] the advice of you all
[3] if you so desire
[4] anger
[5] befall
[6] honour
[7] no matter who may happen to be hostile
[8] an agreement
[9] befell
[10] sharpened lance
[11] comfort
[12] alike in character
[13] agreed
[14] ambush
[15] weak from loss of blood

told the king all how it was, and how they were all slain save himself alone.

'Ah, Jesu, mercy! How may this be?' said the king. 'Took ye him in the queen's chamber?'

'Yea, so God me help,' said Sir Mordred, 'there we found him unarmed, and anon he slew Sir Colgrevance and armed him in his armour.'

And so he told the king from the beginning to the ending.

'Jesu mercy!' said the king, 'he is a marvellous knight of prowess. And alas,' said the king, 'me sore repenteth[16] that ever Sir Lancelot should be against me, for now I am sure the noble fellowship of the Round Table is broken for ever, for with him will many a noble knight hold.[17] And now it is fallen so,'[18] said the king, 'that I may not with my worship but[19] my queen must suffer death,' and was sore amoved.[20]

So then there was made great ordinance[1] in this ire,[2] and the queen must needs be judged[3] to the death. And the law was such in those days that whatsoever they were, of what estate or degree, if they were found guilty of treason there should be none other remedy but death, and other the menour[4] other the taking with the deed[5] should be causer of their hasty[6] judgement. And right so was it ordained for Queen Guinevere: because Sir Mordred was escaped sore wounded, and the death of thirteen knights of the Round Table, these proofs and experiences[7] caused King Arthur to command the queen to the fire, and there to be brent.

Then spake Sir Gawain and said,

'My lord Arthur, I would counsel you not to be over-hasty, but that ye would put it in respite,[8] this judgement of my lady the queen, for many causes. One is this, though it were so that Sir Lancelot were found in the queen's chamber, yet it might be so that he came thither for none evil. For you know, my lord,' said Sir Gawain, 'that my lady the queen has oftentimes

---

[16] it grieves me
[17] remain loyal
[18] has happened
[19] my honour demands that *etc.* *In the earlier versions the queen is sentenced to death by the barons, not by the king. Malory tends to see in Arthur a 15th-century monarch rather than a feudal overlord.*
[20] grieved

[1] harsh judgment
[2] wrath
[3] condemned
[4] behaviour, demeanour (*in this case, circumstantial evidence*)
[5] in the act
[6] speedy
[7] evidence
[8] postpone it

been greatly beholden unto Sir Lancelot, more than to any other knight; for oftentimes he hath saved her life and done battle for her when all the court refused the queen. And peradventure she sent for him for goodness and for none evil, to reward him for his good deeds that he had done to her in times past. And peradventure my lady the queen sent for him to that intent that[9] Sir Lancelot should come privily[10] to her, weening[11] that it had be best in eschewing[12] and dreading of slander; for oftentimes we do many things that we ween[11] for the best be, and yet peradventure it turns to the worst. For I dare say,' said Sir Gawain, 'my lady, your queen, is to you both good and true. And as for Sir Lancelot, I dare say he will make it good upon any knight living that will put upon him[13] villainy or shame, and in like wise he will make good for my lady the queen.'

'That I believe well,' said King Arthur, 'but I will not that way work with[14] Sir Lancelot, for he trusteth so much upon his hands and his might that he doubteth[15] no man. And therefore for my queen he shall nevermore fight, for she shall have the law. And if I may get[16] Sir Lancelot, wit you well he shall have as shameful a death.'

'Jesu defend me,' said Sir Gawain, 'that I never see it nor know it!'

'Why say you so?' said King Arthur. 'For, pardy,[17] ye have no cause to love him! For this night last past he slew your brother, Sir Agravain, a full good knight, and almost he had slain your other brother, Sir Mordred, and also there he slew thirteen noble knights. And also remember you, Sir Gawain, he slew two sons of yours, Sir Florence and Sir Lovell.'

'My lord,' said Sir Gawain, 'of all this I have a knowledge, which of their deaths sore repents me.[18] But insomuch as I gave them warning and told my brother and my sons aforehand what would fall on the end,[19] and insomuch as they would not do by my counsel,[20] I will not meddle me thereof, nor revenge me nothing of their deaths; for I told them that there was no boot[1] to strive with Sir Lancelot. Howbeit I am sorry

---

[9] so that
[10] secretly
[11] expect (ing)
[12] avoiding
[13] charge him with
[14] I will not behave that way towards
[15] fears
[16] capture
[17] indeed
[18] and knowing what I do I grieve at their deaths
[19] how it would end
[20] as I advised them
[1] no use

of the death of my brother and of my two sons, but they are the causers of their own death; and oftentimes I warned my brother Sir Agravain, and I told him of the perils the which be now fallen.'[2]

Then said King Arthur unto Sir Gawain,

'Make you ready, I pray you, in your best armour, with your brethren, Sir Gaheris and Sir Gareth, to bring my queen to the fire and there to have her judgement.'

'Nay, my noble king,' said Sir Gawain, 'that will I never do, for wit you well I will never be in that place where so noble a queen as is my lady Dame Guinevere shall take such a shameful end. For wit you well,' said Sir Gawain, 'my heart will not serve me for to see her die, and it shall never be said that ever I was of your counsel[3] for her death.'

'Then,' said the king unto Sir Gawain, 'suffer[4] your brethren Sir Gaheris and Sir Gareth to be there.'

'My lord,' said Sir Gawain, 'wit you well they will be loath to be there present, because of many adventures that is like to fall,[5] but they are young and full unable to say you nay.'

Then spake Sir Gaheris and the good knight Sir Gareth unto King Arthur,

'Sir, you may well command us to be there, but wit you well it shall be sore against our will. But an we be there by your straight commandment, ye shall plainly hold us there excused: we will be there in peaceable wise, and bear none harness of war upon us.'

'In the name of God,' said the king, 'then make you ready, for she shall have soon her judgement.'

'Alas,' said Sir Gawain, 'that ever I should endure to see this woeful day!'

So Sir Gawain turned him and wept heartily, and so he went into his chamber. And so the queen was led forth without Carlisle, and anon she was despoiled into[6] her smock. And then her ghostly[7] father was brought to her to be shriven[8] of her misdeeds. Then was there weeping and wailing and wringing of hands of many lords and ladies; but there were but few in comparison that would bear any armour for to strength[9] the death of the queen.

Then was there one that Sir Lancelot had sent unto that

<hr />

2 which have now occurred
3 I agreed to your plan
4 allow
5 are likely to happen

6 stripped down to
7 spiritual
8 to shrive her
9 to show support for

place, which went to espy what time the queen should go unto her death. And anon as he saw the queen despoiled into[6] her smock and shriven, then he gave Sir Lancelot warning anon. Then was there but spurring and plucking up[10] of horse, and right so they came unto the fire. And who that stood against them, there were they slain; there might none withstand Sir Lancelot.

So all that bore arms and withstood them, there were they slain, full many a noble knight. For there was slain Sir Belias le Orgulous, Sir Segwarides, Sir Griflet, Sir Brandiles, Sir Aglovale, Sir Tor, Sir Gauter, Sir Gillimer, Sir Reynold, three brethren, and Sir Damas, Sir Priamus, Sir Kay l'Estrange, Sir Driant, Sir Lambegus, Sir Herminde, Sir Pertolip, Sir Perimones, two brethren which were called the Green Knight and the Red Knight.

And so in this rushing and hurling,[11] as Sir Lancelot thrang[12] here and there, it misfortuned him[13] to slay Sir Gaheris and Sir Gareth, the noble knight, for they were unarmed and unawares.[14] As the French book saith, Sir Lancelot smote Sir Gareth upon the brain-pans, wherethrough that they were slain in the field. Howbeit in very truth Sir Lancelot saw them not. And so were they found dead among the thickest of the press.[15]

Then Sir Lancelot, when he had thus done, and slain and put to flight all that would withstand him, then he rode straight unto Queen Guinevere and made cast a kirtle and a gown upon her, and then he made her to be set behind him and prayed her to be of good cheer. Now wit you well the queen was glad that she was at that time escaped from the death, and then she thanked God and Sir Lancelot.

And so he rode his way with the queen, as the French book saith, unto Joyous Gard, and there he kept her as a noble knight should. And many great lords and many good knights were sent him, and many full noble knights drew unto him. When they heard that King Arthur and Sir Lancelot were at debate[16] many knights were glad, and many were sorry of their debate.[17]

---

[10] urging forward
[11] pushing, dashing
[12] dashed
[13] he unfortunately happened

[14] unprepared. *'Unaware' in* C.
[15] throng
[16] had quarrelled
[17] strife

II

The Vengeance of Sir Gawain

Now turn we again unto King Arthur, that when it was told him how and in what manner the queen was taken away from the fire, and when he heard of the death of his noble knights, and in especial Sir Gaheris and Sir Gareth, then he swooned for very pure sorrow.[1] And when he awoke of his swough, then he said,

'Alas, that ever I bore crown upon my head! For now have I lost the fairest fellowship of noble knights that ever held Christian king together. Alas, my good knights be slain and gone away from me, that now within this two days I have lost nigh forty knights, and also the noble fellowship of Sir Lancelot and his blood, for now I may nevermore hold them together with my worship.[2] Now, alas, that ever this war began!'

'Now, fair fellows,' said the king, 'I charge you that no man tell Sir Gawain of the death of his two brethren, for I am sure,' said the king, 'when he heareth tell that Sir Gareth is dead, he will go nigh out of his mind. Mercy Jesu,' said the king, 'why slew he Sir Gaheris and Sir Gareth? For I dare say, as for Sir Gareth, he loved Sir Lancelot of[3] all men earthly.'

'That is truth,' said some knights, 'but they were slain in the hurling[4] as Sir Lancelot thrang[5] in the thickest of the press.[6] And as they were unarmed he smote them and wist not whom that he smote, and so unhappily[7] they were slain.'

'Well,' said Arthur, 'the death of them will cause the greatest mortal war that ever was, for I am sure that when Sir Gawain knoweth thereof that Sir Gareth is slain, I shall never have rest[8] of him till I have destroyed Sir Lancelot's kin and himself both, other else he to destroy me. And therefore,' said the king, 'wit you well, my heart was never so heavy as it is now. And much more I am sorrier for my good knights' loss than for the loss of my fair queen; for queens I might have enough, but such a

---

[1] in sheer grief	[5] pressed
[2] honour	[6] throng
[3] above	[7] by an unlucky chance
[4] turmoil	[8] peace

173

fellowship of good knights shall never be together in no company. And now I dare say,' said King Arthur, 'there was never Christian king that ever held such a fellowship together. And alas, that ever Sir Lancelot and I should be at debate![9] Ah, Agravain, Agravain!' said the king, 'Jesu forgive it thy soul, for thine evil will[10] that thou hadst and Sir Mordred, thy brother, unto Sir Lancelot has caused all this sorrow.'

And ever among these complaints the king wept and swooned.

Then came there one to Sir Gawain and told him how the queen was led away with Sir Lancelot, and nigh a four-and-twenty knights slain.

'Ah, Jesu, save me my two brethren!' said Sir Gawain, 'For full well wist I,' said Sir Gawain, 'that Sir Lancelot would rescue her, other else he would die in that field; and to say the truth he were not of worship but if he had rescued the queen,[11] insomuch as she should have been brent for his sake. And as in[12] that,' said Sir Gawain, 'he has done but knightly, and as I would have done myself an I had stood[13] in like case. But where are my brethren?' said Sir Gawain, 'I marvel that I see not of them.'

Then said that man, 'Truly, Sir Gaheris and Sir Gareth be slain.'

'Jesu defend!' said Sir Gawain, 'For all this world I would not that they were slain, and in especial my good brother, Sir Gareth.'

'Sir,' said the man, 'he is slain, and that is great pity.'

'Who slew him?' said Sir Gawain.

'Sir Lancelot,' said the man, 'slew them both.'

'That may I not believe,' said Sir Gawain, 'that ever he slew my good brother, Sir Gareth, for I dare say, my brother loved him better than me and all his brethren, and the king both. Also I dare say, an Sir Lancelot had desired my brother Sir Gareth with him, he would have been with him against the king and us all. And therefore I may never believe that Sir Lancelot slew my brethren.'

'Verily, sir,' said the man, 'it is noised[14] that he slew him.'

'Alas,' said Sir Gawain, 'now is my joy gone!'

---

[9] in strife
[10] malice
[11] he would have been dishonoured if he had not rescued the queen
[12] for
[13] been
[14] 'It is truly reported, sir,' said the man. . . .

And then he fell down and swooned, and long he lay there as he had been dead. And when he arose out of his swough he cried out sorrowfully, and said,

'Alas!'

And forthwith he ran unto the king, crying and weeping, and said,

'Ah, mine uncle King Arthur! My good brother Sir Gareth is slain, and so is my brother Sir Gaheris, which were two noble knights.'

Then the king wept and he both, and so they fell on-swooning. And when they were revived, then spake Sir Gawain and said,

'Sir, I will go and see my brother Sir Gareth.'

'Sir, you may not see him,' said the king, 'for I caused him to be interred and Sir Gaheris both, for I well understood that you would make overmuch sorrow, and the sight of Sir Gareth should have caused your double sorrow.'

'Alas, my lord,' said Sir Gawain, 'how slew he my brother, Sir Gareth? I pray you tell me.'

'Truly,' said the king, 'I shall tell you as it hath been told me: Sir Lancelot slew him and Sir Gaheris both.'

'Alas,' said Sir Gawain, 'they bore none arms against him, neither of them both.'

'I wot not how it was,' said the king, 'but as it is said, Sir Lancelot slew them in the thick press,[15] and knew them not. And therefore let us shape a remedy for to revenge their deaths.'

'My king, my lord, and mine uncle,' said Sir Gawain, 'wit you well, now I shall make you a promise which I shall hold by my knighthood, that from this day forward I shall never fail[16] Sir Lancelot until that one of us have slain that other. And therefore I require you, my lord and king, dress you unto[17] the war, for wit you well, I will be revenged upon Sir Lancelot; and therefore, as ye will have my service and my love, now haste you thereto and assay[18] your friends. For I promise unto God,' said Sir Gawain, 'for the death of my brother, Sir Gareth, I shall seek Sir Lancelot throughout seven kings' realms, but I shall slay him, other else he shall slay me.'

'Sir, you shall not need to seek him so far,' said the king, 'for as I hear say, Sir Lancelot will abide[19] me and us all within the

---

[15] in the thick of battle
[16] abandon the pursuit of
[17] make ready for

[18] appeal to, try to gain over
[19] await

castle of Joyous Gard. And much people draweth unto him as I hear say.'

'That may I right well believe,' said Sir Gawain; 'but, my lord,' he said, 'assay[18] your friends and I will assay mine.'

'It shall be done,' said the king, 'and as I suppose I shall be big enough to drive him out of the biggest tower of his castle.'

So then the king sent letters and writs throughout all England, both the length and the breadth, for to assummon all his knights. And so unto King Arthur drew many knights, dukes, and earls, that he had a great host, and when they were assembled the king informed them how Sir Lancelot had bereft him his queen. Then the king and all his host made them ready to lay siege about Sir Lancelot where he lay within Joyous Gard.

And anon Sir Lancelot heard thereof and purveyed him of[20] many good knights; for with him held many knights, some for his own sake and some for the queen's sake. Thus they were on both parties well furnished and garnished of[1] all manner of things that longed unto[2] the war. But King Arthur's host was so great that Sir Lancelot's host would not abide[3] him in the field. For he was full loath to do battle against the king; but Sir Lancelot drew him unto his strong castle with all manner of victual plenty,[4] and as many noble men as he might suffice[5] within the town and the castle.

Then came King Arthur with Sir Gawain with a great host and laid siege all about Joyous Gard, both the town and the castle. And there they made strong war on both parties, but in no wise Sir Lancelot would ride out, nor go out of the castle, of long time; and neither he would not suffer[6] none of his good knights to issue out, neither of the town neither of the castle, until fifteen weeks were past.

So it fell upon a day in harvest time that Sir Lancelot looked over the walls and spake on height[7] unto King Arthur and to Sir Gawain:

'My lords both, wit you well all this is in vain that ye make at this siege, for here win ye no worship,[8] but maugre[9] and dishonour. For an it list me[10] to come myself out and my very good knights, I should full soon make an end of this war.'

---

[20] provided himself with
[1] well provided with
[2] were required for
[3] meet
[4] plenty of food of all kinds
[5] provide food for

[6] allow (ed)
[7] in a loud voice
[8] honour
[9] enmity
[10] if I should want

'Come forth,' said King Arthur unto Sir Lancelot, 'an thou darest, and I promise thee I shall meet thee in midst of this field.'

'God defend me,' said Sir Lancelot, 'that ever I should encounter with the most noble king that made me knight.'

'Now, fie upon thy fair language!' said the king, 'for wit thou well and trust it, I am thy mortal foe and ever will to my death-day; for thou hast slain my good knights and full noble men of my blood, that shall I never recover again. Also thou hast lain by my queen, and holden her many winters, and sithen, like a traitor, taken her away from me by force.'

'My most noble lord and king,' said Sir Lancelot, 'ye may say what ye will, for ye wot well with yourself I will not strive. But thereas[11] ye say that I have slain your good knights, I wot well that I have done so, and that me sore repenteth;[12] but I was forced to do battle with them in saving of my life, other else I must have suffered[6] them to have slain me. And as for my lady, Queen Guinevere, except your person of your highness and my lord Sir Gawain, there is no knight under heaven that dare make it good upon me[13] that ever I was traitor unto your person. And where[14] it please you to say that I have holden my lady, your queen, years and winters, unto that I shall ever make a large[15] answer, and prove it upon any knight that beareth the life, except your person and Sir Gawain, that my lady, Queen Guinevere, is as true a lady unto your person as is any lady living unto her lord, and that will I make good with my hands. Howbeit it hath liked[16] her good grace to have me in favour and cherish me more than any other knight; and unto my power[17] again[18] I have deserved[19] her love, for oftentimes, my lord, you have consented that she should have be brent and destroyed in your heat,[20] and then it fortuned me[1] to do battle for her; and or I departed from her adversary they confessed their untruth, and she full worshipfully excused.[2] And at such times, my lord Arthur,' said Sir Lancelot, 'you loved me and thanked me when I saved your queen from the fire, and then you promised me for ever to be my good lord. And now methinketh you reward me evil for my good service. And, my

---

[11] when
[12] grieves me
[13] prove by combat with me
[14] if
[15] proper
[16] pleased

[17] as much as it was in my power
[18] in return
[19] endeavoured to merit
[20] anger
[1] fell for me
[2] honourably acquitted

lord, meseemeth I had lost a great part of my worship[3] in my knighthood an I had suffered[4] my lady, your queen, to have been brent, and insomuch as she should have been brent for my sake; for sithen I have done battles for your queen in other quarrels than in mine own quarrel, meseemeth now I had more right to do battle for her in her right quarrel. And therefore, my good and gracious lord,' said Sir Lancelot, 'take your queen unto your good grace,[5] for she is both true and good.'

'Fie on thee, false recreant[6] knight!' said Sir Gawain. 'For I let thee wit: my lord, mine uncle King Arthur shall have his queen and thee both maugre thy visage,[7] and slay you both and save you, whether it please him.'[8]

'It may well be,' said Sir Lancelot, 'but wit thou well, my lord Sir Gawain, an me list[9] to come out of this castle you should win me and the queen more harder than ever you won a strong battle.'

'Now, fie on thy proud words!' said Sir Gawain. 'As for my lady the queen, wit thou well I will never say of her shame. But thou, false and recreant[6] knight,' said Sir Gawain, 'what cause hadst thou to slay my good brother, Sir Gareth, that loved thee more than me and all my kin? And alas, thou madest him knight thine own hands![10] Why slewest thou him that loved thee so well?'

'For to excuse me,' said Sir Lancelot, 'it boteneth[11] me not, but by Jesu, and by the faith that I owe unto the high Order of Knighthood, I would with as good a will have slain my nephew Sir Bors de Ganis at that time. And alas, that ever I was so unhappy,'[12] said Sir Lancelot, 'that I had not seen Sir Gareth and Sir Gaheris!'

'Thou liest, recreant[6] knight,' said Sir Gawain, 'thou slewest them in the despite of me![13] And therefore wit thou well, Sir Lancelot, I shall make war upon thee, and all the while that I may live be thine enemy!'

'That me repents,'[14] said Sir Lancelot, 'for well I understand it boteneth[11] me not to seek none accordment[15] while ye, Sir Gawain, are so mischievously set.[16] And if ye were not, I

[3] honour
[4] allowed
[5] pardon your queen
[6] cowardly
[7] in spite of you
[8] whichever may please him
[9] if I desired
[10] with thy own hands
[11] avails
[12] unfortunate
[13] to injure me
[14] That grieves me
[15] reconciliation
[16] full of evil intent

would not doubt to have the good grace of my lord King Arthur.'

'I lieve[17] well, false recreant[6] knight, for thou hast many long days overlaid[18] me and us all, and destroyed many of our good knights.'

'Sir, you say as it pleaseth you,' said Sir Lancelot, 'yet may it never be said on me and openly proved that ever I by forecast of treason[19] slew no good knight as ye, my lord Sir Gawain, have done; and so did I never but in my defence, that I was driven thereto in saving of my life.'

'Ah, thou false knight,' said Sir Gawain, 'that thou meanest by Sir Lamorak.[20] But wit thou well, I slew him!'

'Sir, you slew him not yourself,' said Sir Lancelot, 'for it had been overmuch for you, for he was one of the best knights christened of his age. And it was great pity of his death!'

'Well, well, Sir Lancelot,' said Sir Gawain, 'sithen thou enbraidest[1] me of Sir Lamorak, wit thou well, I shall never leave thee till I have thee at such avail[2] that thou shalt not escape my hands.'

'I trust you well enough,' said Sir Lancelot, 'an ye may get me,[3] I get but little mercy.'

But the French book saith King Arthur would have taken his queen again and to have been accorded[4] with Sir Lancelot, but Sir Gawain would not suffer[5] him by no manner of mean. And so Sir Gawain made many men to blow upon[6] Sir Lancelot, and so all at once they called him 'false recreant[7] knight.' But when Sir Bors de Ganis, Sir Ector de Maris and Sir Lionel heard this outcry they called unto them Sir Palomides and Sir Lavain and Sir Urry with many more knights of their blood, and all they went unto Sir Lancelot and said thus:

'My lord, wit you well we have great scorn of the great rebukes[8] that we have heard Sir Gawain say unto you; wherefore we pray you, and charge[9] you as you will have our service, keep us no longer within these walls, for we let you wit plainly we will ride into the field and do battle with them. For you fare as a man that were afeard, and for all your fair speech it

---

[17] believe
[18] oppressed
[19] by a deliberate betrayal
[20] you are now speaking of Sir Lamorak
[1] upbraid
[2] disadvantage

[3] if you capture me
[4] reconciled
[5] permit
[6] to defame
[7] cowardly
[8] insults
[9] command(ed)

will not avail you, for wit you well Sir Gawain will never suffer you to accord[10] with King Arthur. And therefore fight for your life and right, an ye dare.'

'Alas,' said Sir Lancelot, 'for to ride out of this castle and to do battle I am full loath.'

Then Sir Lancelot spake on height[11] unto King Arthur and Sir Gawain:

'My lord, I require you and beseech you, sithen that I am thus required and conjured[12] to ride into the field, that neither you, my lord King Arthur, neither you, Sir Gawain, come not into the field.'

'What shall we do then?' said Sir Gawain. 'Is not this the king's quarrel to fight with thee? And also it is my quarrel to fight with thee because of the death of my brother, Sir Gareth.'

'Then must I needs unto battle,' said Sir Lancelot. 'Now wit you well, my lord Arthur and Sir Gawain, ye will repent[13] it whensomever I do battle with you.'

And so then they departed either from other; and then either party made them ready on the morn for to do battle, and great purveyance[14] was made on both sides. And Sir Gawain let purvey[15] many knights for to wait upon Sir Lancelot, for to overset him[16] and to slay him. And on the morn at underne[17] King Arthur was ready in the field with three great hosts.

And then Sir Lancelot's fellowship came out at the three gates in full good array; and Sir Lionel came in the foremost battle,[18] and Sir Lancelot came in the middle, and Sir Bors came out at the third gate. And thus they came in order and rule as full noble knights. And ever Sir Lancelot charged[9] all his knights in any wise to save King Arthur and Sir Gawain.

Then came forth Sir Gawain from the king's host and proffered[19] to joust. And Sir Lionel was a fierce knight, and lightly[20] he encountered with him, and there Sir Gawain smote Sir Lionel throughout the body, that he dashed to the earth like as he had been dead. And then Sir Ector de Maris and other mo[1] bare him into the castle.

And anon there began a great stour,[2] and much people were

[10] allow you to be reconciled
[11] in a loud voice
[12] urged
[13] regret
[14] preparation
[15] chose
[16] to lie in wait so as to set upon him
[17] about nine o'clock
[18] group of warriors
[19] offered
[20] fiercely
[1] many others
[2] battle

slain; and ever Sir Lancelot did what he might to save the people on King Arthur's party. For Sir Bors and Sir Palomides and Sir Saphir overthrew many knights, for they were deadly knights, and Sir Blamour de Ganis and Sir Bleoberis, with Sir Bellengere le Beuse, these six knights did much harm. And ever was King Arthur about Sir Lancelot to have slain him, and ever Sir Lancelot suffered[3] him and would not strike again.[4] So Sir Bors encountered with King Arthur, and Sir Bors smote him; and so he[5] alight[6] and drew his sword, and said to Sir Lancelot,

'Sir, shall I make an end of this war?' (For he meant to have slain him.[7])

'Not so hardy,'[8] said Sir Lancelot, 'upon pain of thy head, that thou touch him no more! For I will never see that most noble king that made me knight neither slain nor shamed.'

And therewithall Sir Lancelot alight[6] of his horse and took up the king and horsed him again, and said thus:

'My lord the king, for God's love, stint[9] this strife, for ye get here no worship[10] an I would do mine utterance.[11] But always I forbear[12] you and ye nor none of yours forbeareth[12] not me. And therefore, my lord, I pray you remember what I have done in many places, and now am I evil rewarded.'

So when King Arthur was on horseback he looked on Sir Lancelot; then the tears brast out of his eyen, thinking of the great courtesy that was in Sir Lancelot more than in any other man. And therewith the king rode his way, and might no longer behold him, saying to himself, 'Alas, alas, that ever yet this war began!'

And then either party of the battles[13] withdrew them to repose them, and buried the dead, and searched[14] the wounded men, and laid to their wounds soft salves; and thus they endured[15] that night till on the morn. And on the morn by underne[16] they made them ready to do battle, and then Sir Bors lead the vaward.[17]

So upon the morn there came Sir Gawain, as brim[18] as any boar, with a great spear in his hand. And when Sir Bors saw

[3] allowed
[4] back
[5] Sir Bors
[6] dismounted
[7] = King Arthur
[8] stay your hand
[9] cease
[10] honour
[11] utmost
[12] have patience with, spare
[13] both hosts
[14] examined
[15] waited
[16] about nine o'clock
[17] vanguard
[18] fierce

him he thought to revenge his brother, Sir Lionel, of the de-spite[19] Sir Gawain gave him the other day.

And so, as they that knew either other,[20] fewtred[1] their spears, and with all their might of their horses and themselves so fiercely they met together and so felonously[2] that either bare other through, and so they fell both to the bare earth.

And then the battle joined, and there was much slaughter on both parties. Then Sir Lancelot rescued Sir Bors and sent him into the castle, but neither Sir Gawain neither Sir Bors died not of their wounds, for they were well holpen.[3]

Then Sir Lavain and Sir Urry prayed Sir Lancelot to do his pain[4] and fight as they do:

'For we see that ye forbear and spare,[5] and that doth us much harm. And therefore we pray you spare not your en-emies no more than they do you.'

'Alas,' said Sir Lancelot, 'I have no heart to fight against my lord Arthur, for ever meseemeth I do not as me ought to do.'

'My lord,' said Sir Palomides, 'though ye spare them, never so much[6] all this day they will never con you thank;[7] and if they may get you at avail[8] ye are but a dead man.'

So then Sir Lancelot understood that they said him truth. Then he strained himself more than he did toforehand, and be-cause of[9] his nephew, Sir Bors, was sore wounded he pained[10] himself the more. And so within a little while, by evensong time,[11] Sir Lancelot's party the better stood; for their horses went in blood past the fetlocks, there were so many people slain.

And then for very[12] pity Sir Lancelot withheld his knights and suffered[13] King Arthur's party to withdraw them inside. And so he withdrew his meiny[14] into the castle, and either par-ties buried the dead and put salve unto the wounded men. So when Sir Gawain was hurt, they on King Arthur's party were not so orgulous[15] as they were toforehand to do battle.

So of this war that was noised[16] through all Christian realms,

19 injury
20 each other
1 fixed
2 violently
3 helped
4 utmost
5 have patience with them and spare them
6 however much you spare them
7 they will never be grateful ('con' = 'know,' 'be able')
8 a disadvantage
9 because
10 exerted
11 about sunset
12 true, sheer
13 allowed
14 retainers
15 eager
16 reported, rumoured

and so it came at the last by relation[17] unto the Pope. And then the Pope took a consideration of the great goodness of King Arthur and of the high prowess of Sir Lancelot, that was called the most noblest knight of the world. Wherefore the Pope called unto him a noble clerk that at that time was there present (the French book saith it was the Bishop of Rochester), and the Pope gave him bulls under lead,[18] and sent them unto the king, charging[19] him upon pain of interdicting[20] of all England that he take his queen again[1] and accord[2] with Sir Lancelot.

So when this Bishop was come unto Carlisle he showed the king his bulls, and when the king understood them he wist not what to do: but full fain he would have been accorded[2] with Sir Lancelot, but Sir Gawain would not suffer[3] him. But to have the queen, he thereto agreed; but in no wise he would suffer[3] the king to accord[2] with Sir Lancelot; but as for the queen, he consented. So the Bishop had of the king his great seal and his assurance, as he was a true and anointed king, that Sir Lancelot should go safe and come safe, and that the queen should not be said unto of[4] the king, neither of none other, for nothing done of time past. And of all these appointments[5] the Bishop brought with him sure writing[6] to show unto Sir Lancelot.

So when the Bishop was come to Joyous Gard, there he showed Sir Lancelot how he came from the Pope with writing unto King Arthur and unto him. And there he told him the perils, if he withheld the queen from the king.

'Sir, it was never in my thought,' said Sir Lancelot, 'to withhold the queen from my lord Arthur, but I keep her for this cause: insomuch as she should have be brent for my sake, me-seemed it was my part to save her life and put her from that danger till better recover[7] might come. And now I thank God,' said Sir Lancelot, 'that the Pope hath made her peace. For God knoweth,' said Sir Lancelot, 'I will be a thousandfold more gladder to bring her again than ever I was of her taking away, with this[8] I may be sure to come safe and go safe, and that the queen shall have her liberty as she had before, and never for nothing that hath be surmised afore this time that she never from this stand in no peril. For else,' said Sir Lancelot, 'I dare

---

[17] by report
[18] edicts sealed with lead
[19] commanding
[20] the excommunication
[1] back
[2] (be) reconciled

[3] allow
[4] be reproached by
[5] agreements
[6] confirmation in writing
[7] release, rescue
[8] on this condition that

adventure me to keep her from an harder shour than[9] ever yet I had.'

'Sir, it shall not need you,' said the Bishop, 'to dread thus much, for wit you well, the Pope must be obeyed, and it were not the Pope's worship[10] neither my poor[11] honesty to know you distressed neither the queen, neither in peril neither shamed.'

And then he showed Sir Lancelot all his writing, both from the Pope and King Arthur.

'This is sure enough,' said Sir Lancelot, 'for full well I dare trust my lord's own writing and his seal, for he was never shamed of[12] his promise. Therefore,' said Sir Lancelot unto the Bishop, 'ye shall ride unto the king afore and recommend me unto his good grace, and let him have knowledging that this same day eight days,[13] by the grace of God, I myself shall bring the queen unto him. And then say ye to my redoubted[14] king that I will say largely for the queen;[15] that I shall none except for dread neither for fear but the king himself and my lord Sir Gawain, and that is for the king's love[16] more than for himself.'[17]

So the Bishop departed and came to the king to Carlisle, and told him all how Sir Lancelot answered him; so that made the tears fall out at the king's eyen. Then Sir Lancelot purveyed him[18] an hundred knights, and all well clothed in green velvet, and their horses trapped in the same to the heels, and every knight held a branch of olive in his hand in tokening of peace. And the queen had four-and-twenty gentlewomen following her in the same wise. And Sir Lancelot had twelve coursers following him, and on every courser sat a young gentleman; and all they were arrayed in white velvet with sarps[19] of gold about their quarters,[20] and the horse trapped in the same wise down to the heels, with many ouches[1] iset[2] with stones and pearls in gold, to the number of a thousand. And in the same wise was the queen arrayed, and Sir Lancelot in the same, of white cloth of gold tissue.

---

[9] I venture to take it upon myself to save her by fighting the hardest battle that
[10] glory
[11] humble
[12] untrue to
[13] eight days from to-day
[14] noble

[15] speak freely in the queen's defense
[16] for the king's sake
[17] = Gawain
[18] chose for himself
[19] girdles, chains
[20] around their thigh⸱
[1] ornaments
[2] set

And right so as you have heard, as the French book maketh mention, he rode with the queen from Joyous Gard to Carlisle. And so Sir Lancelot rode throughout Carlisle, and so into the castle, that all men might behold them. And there was many a weeping eyen. And then Sir Lancelot himself alight and voided[3] his horse, and took adown the queen, and so led her where King Arthur was in his seat; and Sir Gawain sat afore him, and many other great lords.

So when Sir Lancelot saw the king and Sir Gawain, then he led the queen by the arm, and then he kneeled down and the queen both. Wit you well, then was there many a bold knight with King Arthur that wept as tenderly as[4] they had seen all their kin dead afore them! So the king sat still and said no word. And when Sir Lancelot saw his countenance he arose up and pulled up the queen with him, and thus he said full knightly:

'My most redoubted[5] king, ye shall understand, by the Pope's commandment and yours, I have brought to you my lady the queen, as right requireth. And if there be any knight, of what degree that ever he be of, except your person, that will say or dare say but that she is true and clean to you, I here myself, Sir Lancelot du Lake, will make it good upon his body that she is a true lady unto you.

'But, sir, liars ye have listened, and that hath caused great debate betwixt you and me. For time hath been, my lord Arthur, that ye were greatly pleased with me when I did battle for my lady, your queen; and full well you know, my most noble king, that she hath be put to great wrong or this time. And sithen it pleased you at many times that I should fight for her, therefore meseemeth, my good lord, I had more cause to rescue her from the fire when she should have been brent for my sake.

'For they that told you those tales were liars, and so it fell upon them: for by likelihood, had not the might of God been with me, I might never have endured with fourteen knights. And they were armed and afore purposed,[6] and I unarmed and not purposed;[6] for I was sent unto my lady, your queen, I wot not for what cause, but I was not so soon within the chamber door but anon Sir Agravain and Sir Mordred called me traitor and false recreant[7] knight.'

[3] dismounted from   [6] prepared
[4] as if   [7] cowardly
[5] noble

'By my faith, they called thee right!' said Sir Gawain.

'My lord, Sir Gawain,' said Sir Lancelot, 'in their quarrel they proved not themselves the best, neither in the right.'

'Well, well, Sir Lancelot,' said the king, 'I have given you no cause to do to me as ye have done, for I have worshipped[8] you and yours more than any other knights.'

'My lord,' said Sir Lancelot, 'so ye be not displeased, ye shall understand that I and mine have done you oftentimes better service than any other knights have done, in many diverse places; and where ye have been full hard bestad[9] diverse times, I have rescued you from many dangers; and ever unto my power[10] I was glad to please you and my lord Sir Gawain. In jousts and in tournaments and in battles set, both on horseback and on foot, I have often rescued you, and you, my lord Sir Gawain, and many mo[11] of your knights in many diverse places.

'For now I will make avaunt,'[12] said Sir Lancelot: 'I will that ye all wit that as yet I found never no manner of knight but that I was overhard for him an I had done mine utterance,[13] God grant mercy! Howbeit I have been matched with good knights, as Sir Tristram and Sir Lamorak, but ever I had favour unto them and a deeming[14] what they were. And I take God to record, I never was wroth nor greatly heavy with no[15] good knight an I saw him busy and about to win worship;[8] and glad I was ever when I found a good knight that might anything[16] endure me on horseback and on foot. Howbeit Sir Carados of the Dolorous Tower was a full noble knight and a passing strong man, and that wot ye, my lord Sir Gawain; for he might well be called a noble knight when he by fine[17] force pulled you out of your saddle and bound you overthwart[18] afore him to his saddle-bow. And there, my lord Sir Gawain, I rescued you and slew him afore your sight. Also I found your brother, Sir Gaheris, and Sir Tarquin leading him abounden afore him; and there also I rescued your brother and slew Sir Tarquin and delivered three-score-and-four of my lord Arthur's knights out of his prison. And now I dare say,' said Sir Lance-

---

8 honour(ed)
9 pressed
10 as far as I was able
11 more
12 make so bold as to say this
13 as yet I have never found any manner of knight for whom I

should not have been too strong if I had done my utmost
14 suspicion
15 hard upon any
16 at all
17 superior
18 crosswise

lot, 'I met never with so strong a knight nor so well-fighting as was Sir Carados and Sir Tarquin, for they and I fought to the uttermost. And therefore,' said Sir Lancelot unto Sir Gawain, 'meseemeth ye ought of right to remember this; for, an I might have your good will, I would trust to God for to have my lord Arthur's good grace.'

'Sir, the king may do as he will,' said Sir Gawain, 'but wit thou well, Sir Lancelot, thou and I shall never be accorded[19] while we live, for thou hast slain three of my brethren. And two of them thou slew traitorly and piteously, for they bore none harness[20] against thee, neither none would do.'[1]

'Sir, God would they had been armed,' said Sir Lancelot, 'for then had they been on life. And wit ye well, Sir Gawain, as for Gareth, I loved no kinsman I had more than I loved him, and ever while I live,' said Sir Lancelot, 'I will bewail Sir Gareth his[2] death, not all only for the great fear I have of you, but for many causes which causeth me to be sorrowful. One is that I made him knight; another is, I wot well he loved me above all other knights; and the third is, he was passing noble and true, courteous and gentle and well-conditioned.[3] The fourth is, I wist well, anon as I heard that Sir Gareth was dead, I knew well that I should never after have your love, my lord Sir Gawain, but everlasting war betwixt us. And also I wist well that you would cause my noble lord King Arthur for ever to be my mortal foe. And as Jesu be my help, and by my knighthood, I slew never Sir Gareth neither his brother by my willing; but alas that ever they were unarmed that unhappy[4] day!

'But this much I shall offer me to you,' said Sir Lancelot, 'if it may please the king's good grace and you, my lord Sir Gawain: I shall first begin at Sandwich, and there I shall go in my shirt, bare-foot; and at every ten miles' end I shall found and gar make[5] an house of religion, of what order that you will assign me, with an holy convent, to sing and read day and night in especial for Sir Gareth and Sir Gaheris. And this shall I perform from Sandwich until Carlisle; and every house shall have sufficient livelihood.[6] And this shall I perform while that I have any livelihood[6] in Christendom, and there is none of all these religious places but they shall be performed, furnished and

---

[19] reconciled
[20] armour
[1] and did not wish to bear any
[2] = Gareth's

[3] with a happy disposition
[4] disastrous
[5] cause to be built
[6] endowment

garnished[7] with all things as an holy place ought to be. And this were fairer and more holier and more parfit to[8] their souls than ye, my most noble king, and you, Sir Gawain, to war upon me, for thereby shall you get none avail.'[9]

Then all the knights and ladies that were there wept as they were mad, and the tears fell on King Arthur his[10] cheeks.

'Sir Lancelot,' said Sir Gawain, 'I have right well heard thy language and thy great proffers.[11] But wit thou well, let the king do as it pleaseth him, I will never forgive thee my brothers' death, and in especial the death of my brother Sir Gareth. And if mine uncle, King Arthur, will accord[12] with thee, he shall lose my service, for wit thou well,' said Sir Gawain, 'thou art both false to the king and to me.'

'Sir,' said Sir Lancelot, 'he beareth not the life[13] that may make it good! And ye, Sir Gawain, will charge me with so high[14] a thing, ye must pardon me, for then needs must I answer you.'

'Nay, nay,' said Sir Gawain, 'we are past that as at this time, and that causeth the Pope,[15] for he hath charged[16] mine uncle the king that he shall take again his queen and to accord[12] with thee, Sir Lancelot, as for this season, and therefore thou shalt go safe as thou came. But in this land thou shalt not abide past a fifteen-dayes, such summons I give thee,[17] for so the king and we were condescended and accorded[18] ere thou came. And else,' said Gawain, 'wit thou well, thou should not a-comen here but if it were maugre thine head.[19] And if it were not for the Pope's commandment,' said Sir Gawain, 'I should do battle with thee mine own hands, body for body, and prove it upon thee that thou hast been false unto mine uncle, King Arthur, and to me both; and that shall I prove on thy body, when thou art departed from hence, wheresomever that I find thee!'

Then Sir Lancelot sighed, and therewith the tears fell on his cheeks, and then said he thus:

'Most noblest Christian realm, whom I have loved aboven all other realms! And in thee I have gotten a great part of my worship,[20] and now that I shall depart in this wise, truly me re-

[7] completed, prepared and supplied
[8] worthy of
[9] advantage
[10] = Arthur's
[11] offers
[12] be reconciled
[13] he is not alive
[14] grave
[15] is because of the Pope
[16] ordered
[17] these are my terms
[18] consented and agreed
[19] you should not have come here unless it were against your will
[20] honour

pents[1] that ever I came in this realm, that I should be thus shamefully banished, undeserved and causeless. But fortune is so variant, and the wheel[2] so mutable[3] that there is no constant abiding. And that may be proved by many chronicles, as of noble Hector of Troy and Alexander, the mighty conqueror, and many more other: when they were most in their royalty, they alight[4] passing low. And so fareth it by me,' said Sir Lancelot, 'for in this realm I had worship,[5] and by me and mine all the whole Round Table hath been increased more in worship,[5] by me and mine, than ever it was by any of you all.

'And therefore wit thou well, Sir Gawain, I may live upon lands as well as any knight that here is. And if ye, my most redoubted[6] king, will come upon my lands with Sir Gawain to war upon me, I must endure you[7] as well as I may. But as to you, Sir Gawain, if that ye come there, I pray you charge me not with treason neither felony, for an ye do, I must answer you.'

'Do thou thy best,' said Sir Gawain, 'and therefore hie thee fast that thou were gone! And wit thou well we shall soon come after, and break the strongest castle that thou hast, upon[8] thy head!'

'It shall not need that,' said Sir Lancelot, 'for an I were as orgulous set[9] as ye are, wit you well I should meet you in midst of the field.'

'Make thou no more language,'[10] said Sir Gawain, 'but deliver the queen from thee, and pike thee lightly out of this court!'[11]

'Well,' said Sir Lancelot, 'an I had wist of this shortcoming,[12] I would a advised me[13] twice or that I had come here. For an the queen had been so dear unto me as ye noise her,[14] I durst have kept[15] her from the fellowship of the best knights under heaven.'

And then Sir Lancelot said unto Queen Guinevere, in hearing of the king and them all,

'Madam, now I must depart from you and this noble fellowship for ever. And sithen it is so, I beseech you to pray for me,

---

[1] I am grieved
[2] the wheel of Fortune
[3] changeable
[4] come down (on the wheel of Fortune)
[5] honour
[6] noble
[7] be patient with you
[8] I swear by
[9] haughty
[10] talk
[11] quickly leave this court
[12] mishap
[13] have thought
[14] as you say she is
[15] should have dared to keep

and I shall pray for you. And tell ye me, an if ye be hard bestead[16] by any false tongues, but lightly,[17] my good lady, send me word; and if any knight's hands under the heaven may deliver you by battle, I shall deliver you.'

And therewithall Sir Lancelot kissed the queen, and then he said all openly,[18]

'Now let see[19] whatsomever he be in this place that dare say the queen is not true unto my lord Arthur, let see[19] who will speak an he dare speak.'

And therewith he brought the queen to the king, and then Sir Lancelot took his leave and departed. And there was neither king, duke, earl, baron, nor knight, lady nor gentlewoman, but all they wept as people out of mind, except Sir Gawain. And when this noble knight Sir Lancelot took his horse to ride out of Carlisle, there was sobbing and weeping for pure dole of his departing.

And so he took his way to Joyous Gard, and then ever after he called it the 'Dolorous Gard.' And thus departed Sir Lancelot from the court for ever.

And so when he came to Joyous Gard he called his fellowship unto him and asked them what they would do. Then they answered all wholly together with one voice, they would do as he would do.

'Then, my fair fellows,' said Sir Lancelot, 'I must depart out of this most noble realm. And now I shall depart, it grieveth me sore, for I shall depart with no worship;[20] for a fleamed[1] man departeth never[2] out of a realm with no worship. (And that is to me great heaviness, for ever I fear after my days that men shall chronicle upon me that I was fleamed[1] out of this land. And else, my fair lords, be ye sure, an I had not dread shame, my lady Queen Guinevere and I should never have departed.'[3]

Then spake noble knights, as Sir Palomides and Sir Saphir, his brother, and Sir Bellengere le Beuse, and Sir Urry with Sir Lavain, with many other:

'Sir, an ye will so be disposed to abide in this land we will never fail you; and if ye list not[4] abide in this land, there is none of the good knights that here be that will fail you, for many causes. One is, all we that be not of your blood shall

---

[16] pressed, pursued
[17] quickly
[18] in the hearing of all
[19] let us see
[20] honour

[1] banished
[2] ever. *The double negative is used for emphasis.*
[3] parted
[4] you do not wish to

never be welcome unto the court. And sithen it liked[5] us to take a part with you in your distress in this realm, wit you well it shall like[5] us as well to go in other countries with you, and there to to take such part as you do.'[6]

'My fair lords,' said Sir Lancelot, 'I well understand you, and as I can, I thank you. And you shall understand, such livelihood[7] as I am born unto I shall depart[8] with you in this manner of wise: that is for to say, I shall depart all my livelihood[7] and all my lands freely among you, and myself will have as little as any of you; for, have I sufficient that may long unto my person,[9] I will ask none other riches neither array. And I trust to God to maintain you[10] on my lands as well as ever you were maintained.'

Then spake all the knights at once: 'Have he shame that will leave you! For we all understand in this realm will be no quiet, but ever debate[11] and strife now the fellowship of the Round Table is broken. For by the noble fellowship of the Round Table was King Arthur upborne,[12] and by their noblesse[13] the king and all the realm was ever in quiet and rest. And a great part,' they said all, 'was because of your most noblesse,[13] Sir Lancelot.'

'Now, truly I thank you all of your good saying! Howbeit, I wot well that in me was not all the stability of this realm, but in that I might I did my dever.[14] And well I am sure I knew many rebellions in my days that by me and mine were peased;[15] and that I trow[16] we all shall hear of in short space, and that me sore repenteth.[17] For ever I dread me,' said Sir Lancelot, 'that Sir Mordred will make trouble, for he is passing envious, and applyeth him much to trouble.'

And so they were accorded[18] to depart with Sir Lancelot to his lands. And to make short this tale, they trussed,[19] and paid[20] all that would ask them; and wholly an hundred knights departed with Sir Lancelot at once, and made their avows they would never leave him for weal ne[1] for woe.

And so they shipped at Cardiff, and sailed unto Benwick:

[5] please (d)
[6] throw in our lot with yours
[7] possessions
[8] divide
[9] if I have whatever I require for myself
[10] that I shall provide for you
[11] struggle (*'debate' can also mean 'strife'*)
[12] sustained
[13] valour
[14] whenever I could I did my duty
[15] quelled
[16] believe
[17] I am most distressed about
[18] agreed
[19] equipped themselves
[20] engaged
[1] nor

some men call it Bayan[2] and some men call it Beaune, where the wine of Beaune is. But say the sooth, Sir Lancelot and[3] his nephews was lord of all France and of all the lands that longed[4] unto France; he and his kindred rejoiced it,[5] all through Sir Lancelot's noble prowess.

And then he stuffed and furnished and garnished[6] all his noble towns and castles. Then all the people of those lands came unto Sir Lancelot on foot and hands.[7] And so when he had stablished[8] all those countries, he shortly called a parliament; and there he crowned Sir Lionel king of France,[9] and Sir Bors he crowned him king of all King Claudas' lands, and Sir Ector de Maris, Sir Lancelot's younger brother, he crowned him king of Benwick and king of all Guienne, which was Sir Lancelot's own lands. And he made Sir Ector prince of them all.

And thus he departed[10] his lands and advanced all his noble knights. And first he advanced them of his blood, as Sir Blamour, he made him duke of Limousin in Guienne, and Sir Bleoberis, he made him duke of Poitiers. And Sir Gahalantin, he made him duke of Auvergne; and Sir Galyhodin, he made him duke of Saintonge; and Sir Galihud, he made him earl of Périgord; and Sir Menaduke, he made him earl of Rouergue; and Sir Villiers the Valiant, he made him earl of Béarn; and Sir Hebes le Renown, he made him earl of Comminges; and Sir Lavain, he made him earl of Armagnac; and Sir Urry, he made him earl of Astarac; and Sir Neroveous, he made him earl of Pardiac; and Sir Plenorius, he made him earl of Foix; and Sir Selises of the Dolorous Tower, he made him earl of Marsan; and Sir Melias de Lisle, he made him earl of Tursan; and Sir Bellengere le Beuse, he made him earl of the Landes; and Sir Palomides, he made him duke of Provence; and Sir Saphir, he made him duke of Languedoc. And Sir Clegis, he gave him the earldom of Agen; and Sir Sadok, he gave him the earldom of Sarlat; and Sir Dinas le Seneschal, he made him duke of Anjou; and Sir Clarrus, he made him duke of Normandy.

Thus Sir Lancelot rewarded his noble knights, and many more meseemeth it were too long to rehearse.[11]

---

2 *Presumably* Bayonne

3 with. *Cf.* '*he and his kindred*' *in the next sentence.*

4 belonged

5 possessed it

6 provisioned, prepared and supplied

7 offering submission

8 put in order

9 *i.e. the kingdom of France as it was before the reconquest of Aquitaine and Normandy (1453).*

10 divided

11 record

III

The Siege of Benwick

So leave we Sir Lancelot in his lands and his noble knights with him, and return we again unto King Arthur and unto Sir Gawain that made a great host aready to the number of three-score thousand. And all thing was made ready for shipping to pass over the sea, to war upon Sir Lancelot and upon his lands. And so they shipped at Cardiff.

And there King Arthur made Sir Mordred chief ruler of all England, and also he put the queen under his governance: because Sir Mordred was King Arthur's son, he gave him rule of his land and of his wife.

And so the king passed the sea and landed upon Sir Lancelot's lands, and there he brent and wasted, through the vengeance of Sir Gawain, all that they might overrun. So when this word was come unto Sir Lancelot, that King Arthur and Sir Gawain were landed upon his lands and made full great destruction and waste, then spake Sir Bors and said,

'My lord, Sir Lancelot, it is shame that we suffer[1] them thus to ride over our lands. For wit you well, suffer ye them as long as ye will, they will do you no favour an they may handle[2] you.'

Then said Sir Lionel that was ware[3] and wise, 'My lord, Sir Lancelot, I will give you this counsel: let us keep our strong-walled towns until they have hunger and cold and blow on their nails; and then let us freshly[4] set upon them and shred[5] them down as sheep in a fold, that ever after aliaunts[6] may take ensample[7] how they[8] land upon our lands!'

Then spoke King Bagdemagus to Sir Lancelot and said, 'Sir, your courtesy will shend[9] us all, and your courtesy hath waked all this sorrow; for an they thus override our lands, they shall by process[10] bring us all to nought while we thus in holes us hide.'

---

[1] allow
[2] capture
[3] cautious, wary
[4] promptly
[5] cut

[6] foreigners
[7] warning
[8] how they will fare if they
[9] injure
[10] in course of time

Then said Sir Galihud unto Sir Lancelot, 'Sir, here been knights come of king's blood that will not long droop[11] and dare[12] within these walls. Therefore give us leave, like as we been knights,[13] to meet them in the field, and we shall slay them and so deal with them that they shall curse the time that ever they came into this country.'

Then spake seven brethren of North Wales which were seven noble knights; for a man might seek seven kings' lands or he might find such seven knights. And these seven noble knights said all at once,

'Sir Lancelot, for Christ's sake, let us ride out with Sir Galihud, for we were never wont to cower in castles neither in noble towns.'

Then spake Sir Lancelot, that was master and governor of them all, and said,

'My fair lords, wit you well I am full loath to ride out with my knights for shedding of Christian blood; and yet my lands I understand be[14] full bare for to sustain any host awhile for the mighty wars that whilom[15] made King Claudas upon this country and upon my father, King Ban, and on mine uncle, King Bors. Howbeit we will at this time keep our strong walls. And I shall send a messenger unto my lord Arthur a treatise[16] for to take, for better is peace than always war.'

So Sir Lancelot sent forth a damsel with a dwarf with her, requiring King Arthur to leave his warring upon his lands. And so he[17] start upon a palfrey, and a dwarf ran by her side. And when she came to the pavilion of King Arthur, there she alight; and there met her a gentle knight, Sir Lucan the Butler, and said,

'Fair damsel, come you from Sir Lancelot du Lake?'

'Yea, sir,' she said, 'therefore came I hither to speak with my lord the king.'

'Alas,' said Sir Lucan, 'my lord Arthur would accord[18] with Sir Lancelot, but Sir Gawain will not suffer him.' And then he said, 'I pray to God, damsel, that ye may speed well,[19] for all we that been about the king would that Lancelot did best of any knight living.'

---

[11] cower
[12] remain motionless
[13] befits a knight
[14] I believe to be
[15] at times

[16] treaty
[17] = she
[18] be reconciled
[19] succeed

And so with this Sir Lucan led the damsel to the king, where he sat with Sir Gawain, for to hear what she would say. So when she had told her tale the water ran out of the king's eyen. And all the lords were full glad for to advise the king to be accorded[18] with Sir Lancelot, save all only Sir Gawain. And he said,

'My lord, mine uncle, what will ye do? Will ye now turn again,[20] now ye are past this far upon your journey? All the world will speak of you villainy and shame.'

'Now,' said King Arthur, 'wit you well, Sir Gawain, I will do as ye advise me; and yet meseemeth,' said King Arthur, 'his fair proffers were not good to be refused. But sithen I am come so far upon this journey, I will that ye give the damsel her answer, for I may not speak to her for pity: for her proffers been so large.'[1]

Then Sir Gawain said unto the damsel thus: 'Say ye to Sir Lancelot that it is waste labour now to sue[2] to mine uncle. For tell him, an he would have made any labour for peace, he should have made it or this time, for tell him now it is too late. And say to him that I, Sir Gawain, so send him word, that I promise him by the faith that I owe to God and to knighthood, I shall never leave him till he has slain me or I him!'

So the damsel wept and departed, and so there was many a weeping eye. And then Sir Lucan brought the damsel to her palfrey; and so she came to Sir Lancelot, where he was among all his knights, and when Sir Lancelot had heard her answer, then the tears ran down by his cheeks. And then his noble knights came about him and said,

'Sir Lancelot, wherefore make ye such cheer? Now think what ye are, and what men we are, and let us, noble knights, match them in midst of the field.'

'That may be lightly[3] done,' said Sir Lancelot, 'but I was never so loath to do battle. And therefore I pray you, sirs, as ye love me, be ruled at this time as I will have you. For I will always flee that noble king that made me knight; and when I may no further, I must needs defend me. And that will be more worship[4] for me and us all than to compare[5] with that noble king whom we have all served.'

---

[20] back
  [1] offers are so generous
  [2] appeal

[3] easily
[4] honour
[5] contend

Then they held their language,[6] and as that night they took their rest. And upon the morning early, in the dawning of the day, as knights looked out, they saw the city of Benwick besieged round about, and gan[7] fast to set up ladders. And they within kept them out of the town and beat them mightily from the walls. Then came forth Sir Gawain, well armed, upon a stiff[8] steed, and he came before the chief gate with his spear in his hand, crying:

'Where art thou, Sir Lancelot? Is there none of all your proud knights that dare break a spear with me?'

Then Sir Bors made him ready and came forth out of the town. And there Sir Gawain encountered with Sir Bors, and at that time he smote him down from his horse, and almost he had slain him. And so Sir Bors was rescued and borne into the town.

Then came forth Sir Lionel, brother to Sir Bors, and thought to revenge him, and either feutred[9] their spears and so ran together, and there they met spiteously,[10] but Sir Gawain had such a grace[11] that he smote Sir Lionel down and wounded him there passingly sore.[12] And then Sir Lionel was rescued and borne into the town.

And thus Sir Gawain came every day, and failed not but that he smote down one knight or other. So thus they endured half a year, and much slaughter was of people on both parties.

Then it befell upon a day that Sir Gawain came afore the gates, armed at all pieces,[13] on a noble horse, with a great spear in his hand, and then he cried with a loud voice and said,

'Where art thou now, thou false traitor, Sir Lancelot? Why holdest thou thyself within holes and walls like a coward? Look out, thou false traitor knight, and here I shall revenge upon thy body the death of my three brethren!'

And all this language heard Sir Lancelot every deal.[14] Then his kin and his knights drew about him, and all they said at once unto Sir Lancelot,

'Sir, now must you defend you like a knight, either else ye be shamed for ever, for now ye be called upon[15] treason it is time for you to stir! For ye have slept over long and suffered[16] overmuch.'

---

6 were silent
7 the besieging army began
8 stout
9 fixed in its rest
10 violently
11 such good fortune
12 gravely, grievously
13 fully armed
14 from beginning to end
15 now that you are accused of
16 endured

'So God me help,' said Sir Lancelot, 'I am right heavy at Sir Gawain's words, for now he charges me with a great charge.[17] And therefore I wot as well as ye I must needs defend me, either else to be recreant.'[18]

Then Sir Lancelot bade saddle his strongest horse and bade let fetch his arms and bring all to the tower of the gate. And then Sir Lancelot spake on high[19] unto the king and said,

'My lord Arthur and noble king that made me knight! Wit you well I am right heavy for your sake that ye thus sue upon me.[20] And always I forbear you, for an I would be vengeable[1] I might have met you in midst the field or this time, and there to have made your boldest knights full tame. And now I have forborne you and suffered[2] you half a year, and Sir Gawain, to do what you would do. And now I may no longer suffer to endure,[3] but needs I must defend myself, insomuch as Sir Gawain hath becalled me of treason; which is greatly against my will that ever I should fight against any of your blood, but now I may not forsake[4] it: for I am driven thereto as beast till a bay.'[5]

Then Sir Gawain said unto Sir Lancelot,

'An thou darest do battle, leave thy babbling and come off, and let us ease our hearts!'

Then Sir Lancelot armed him and mounted upon his horse, and either of them got great spears in their hands. And so the host without stood still all apart, and the noble knights of the city came a great number, that when King Arthur saw the number of men and knights he marvelled and said to himself,

'Alas, that ever Sir Lancelot was against me! For now I see that he has forborne me.'

And so the covenant was made, there should no man nigh them neither deal with them till the tone[6] were dead other yolden.[7]

Then Sir Lancelot and Sir Gawain departed a great way in sunder,[8] and then they came together with all their horse[9] mights as fast as they might run, and either smote other in midst of their shields. But the knights were so strong and their spears so big that their horses might not endure their buffets,

[17] lays a heavy blame upon me
[18] called cowardly
[19] loudly
[20] pursue me
[1] revengeful
[2] let
[3] allow it to continue

[4] avoid
[5] at bay
[6] one
[7] or yielded
[8] apart
[9] horses'

and so their horses fell to the earth. And then they avoided[10] their horses and dressed their shields afore them; then they came together and gave many sad strokes on diverse places of their bodies, that the blood brast out on many sides.

Then had Sir Gawain such a grace and gift[11] that an holy man had given him, that every day in the year, from undern[12] till high noon, his might increased those three hours as much as thrice his strength. And that caused Sir Gawain to win great honour. And for his sake King Arthur made an ordinance that all manner of battles for any quarrels that should be done afore King Arthur should begin at undern;[12] and all was done for Sir Gawain's love,[13] that by likelihood if Sir Gawain were on the tone[14] party, he should have the better in battle while his strength endured three hours. But there were that time but few knights living that knew this advantage that Sir Gawain had, but King Arthur all only.

So Sir Lancelot fought with Sir Gawain, and when Sir Lancelot felt his[15] might evermore increase, Sir Lancelot wondered and dread him sore to be shamed; for, as the French book saith, he wende,[16] when he felt Sir Gawain's double his strength,[17] that he had been a fiend and none earthly man. Wherefore Sir Lancelot traced and traversed,[18] and covered himself with his shield, and kept his might and his breath during three hours. And that while Sir Gawain gave him many sad brunts[19] and many sad strokes, that all knights that beheld Sir Lancelot marvelled how he might endure him, but full little understood they that travail that Sir Lancelot had to endure him.

And then when it was past noon Sir Gawain's strength was gone and he had no more but his own might. When Sir Lancelot felt him so come down, then he stretched him up and strode near Sir Gawain and said thus:

'Now I feel ye have done your worst! And now, my lord Sir Gawain, I must do my part, for many a great and grievous strokes I have endured you this day with great pain.'

And so Sir Lancelot doubled his strokes and gave Sir Gawain such a stroke upon the helmet that sideling[20] he fell down upon his one side. And Sir Lancelot withdrew him from him.

---

10 dismounted from
11 quality and power
12 about nine o'clock in the morning
13 sake
14 one
15 = Gawain's
16 thought
17 Sir Gawain's double strength
18 dodged
19 sharp blows
20 sideways

'Why withdrawest thou thee?' said Sir Gawain. 'Turn again, false traitor knight, and slay me out! For an thou leave me thus, anon as I am whole I shall do battle with thee again.'

'Sir,' said Sir Lancelot, 'I shall endure you, by God's grace! But wit thou well, Sir Gawain, I will never smite a felled knight.'

And so Sir Lancelot departed and went unto the city. And Sir Gawain was borne unto King Arthur's pavilion, and anon leeches[1] were brought unto him of the best, and searched[2] and salved him with soft ointments. And then Sir Lancelot said,

'Now have good day, my lord and king! For wit you well ye win no worship[3] at these walls, for an I would my knights out-bring, there should many a doughty[4] man die. And therefore, my lord Arthur, remember you of old kindness, and howsoever I fare, Jesu be your guide in all places.'

'Now, alas,' said the king, 'that ever this unhappy[5] war began! For ever Sir Lancelot forbeareth me in all places, and in like wise my kin, and that is seen well this day, what courtesy he showed my nephew, Sir Gawain.'

Then King Arthur fell sick for sorrow of Sir Gawain, that he was so sore hurt, and because of the war betwixt him and Sir Lancelot. So after that they on King Arthur's party kept the siege with little war withoutforth, and they withinforth kept their walls and defended them when need was.

Thus Sir Gawain lay sick and unsound three weeks in his tents with all manner of leechcraft[6] that might be had. And as soon as Sir Gawain might go and ride, he armed him at all points[7] and bestrode a stiff courser[8] and gat a great spear in his hand, and so he came riding afore the chief gate of Benwick. And there he cried on high[9] and said,

'Where art thou, Sir Lancelot? Come forth, thou false traitor knight and recreant,[10] for I am here, Sir Gawain, that will prove this that I say upon thee!'

And all this language Sir Lancelot heard and said thus:

'Sir Gawain, me repents of[11] your foul saying, that ye will not cease your language. For ye wot well, Sir Gawain, I know your might and all that ye may do, and well ye wot, Sir Gawain, ye may not greatly hurt me.'

---

[1] physicians
[2] examined his wounds
[3] honour
[4] valiant
[5] unfortunate
[6] medical care
[7] armed himself completely
[8] stout horse
[9] loudly
[10] coward
[11] I regret

'Come down, traitor knight,' said he, 'and make it good the contrary with thy hands! For it mishapped me[12] the last battle to be hurt of thy hands, therefore, wit thou well, I am come this day to make amends, for I ween this day to lay thee as low as thou laidest me.'

'Jesu defend me,' said Sir Lancelot, 'that ever I be so far in your danger[13] as ye have been in mine, for then my days were done. But, Gawain,' said Lancelot, 'ye shall not think that I shall tarry long, but sithen that ye unknightly call[14] me thus of treason, ye shall have both your hands full of me!'

And then Sir Lancelot armed him at all points[7] and mounted upon his horse and gat a great spear in his hand and rode out at the gate. And both their hosts were assembled, of them without and within, and stood in array full manly, and both parties were charged[15] to hold them still to see and behold the battle of these two noble knights.

And then they laid their spears in their rests and so came together as thunder. And Sir Gawain brake his spear in an hundred pieces to his hand, and Sir Lancelot smote him with a greater might, that Sir Gawain's horse[16] feet raised, and so the horse and he fell to the earth. Then Sir Gawain deliverly[17] devoided[18] his horse and put his shield afore him, and eagerly drew his sword and bade Sir Lancelot, 'Alight, traitor knight!' and said,

'If a mare's son hath failed me, wit thou well a king's son and a queen's son shall not fail thee!'

Then Sir Lancelot devoided[18] his horse and dressed his shield afore him and drew his sword, and so came eagerly together and gave many sad[19] strokes, that all men on both parties had wonder.

But when Sir Lancelot felt Sir Gawain's might so marvellously increase, he then withheld his courage[20] and his wind, and so he kept him under covert of his might and of his shield:[1] he traced and traversed[2] here and there to break Sir Gawain's strokes and his courage.[20] And ever Sir Gawain enforced[3] himself with all his might and power to destroy Sir Lancelot, for,

[12] it was my misfortune in
[13] within your power
[14] accuse
[15] ordered
[16] horse's
[17] quickly
[18] dismounted from
[19] sharp
[20] vigour, strength
[1] he protected himself by holding on to his shield with all his strength
[2] dodged
[3] exerted

as the French book saith, ever as Sir Gawain's might increased, right so increased his wind and his evil will.[4]

And thus he did great pain unto Sir Lancelot three hours, that he had much ado to defend him.[5] And when the three hours were passed, that he felt Sir Gawain was come home to his own proper strength, then Sir Lancelot said,

'Sir, now I have proved you twice that you are a full dangerous knight[6] and a wonderful man of your might! And many wonder[7] deeds have ye done in your days, for by your might increasing ye have deceived many a full noble knight. And now I feel that ye have done your mighty deeds, and now, wit you well, I must do my deeds!'

And then Sir Lancelot strode near Sir Gawain and doubled his strokes, and ever Sir Gawain defended him mightily, but nevertheless Sir Lancelot smote such a stroke upon his helm, and upon the old wound, that Sir Gawain sank down and swooned. And anon as he did awake he waved and foined[8] at Sir Lancelot as he lay, and said,

'Traitor knight, wit thou well I am not yet slain. Therefore come thou near me and perform this battle to the utterance!'[9]

'I will no more do than I have done,' said Sir Lancelot. 'For when I see you on foot I will do battle upon you all the while I see you stand upon your feet; but to strike a wounded man that may not stand, God defend me from such a shame!'

And then he turned him and went his way toward the city, and Sir Gawain evermore calling him 'traitor knight,' and said,

'Traitor knight! Wit thou well, Sir Lancelot, when I am whole I shall do battle with you again, for I shall never leave thee till the tone[10] of us be slain!'

Thus as this siege endured, and as Sir Gawain lay sick near-hand[11] a month, and when he was well recovered and ready within three days to do battle again with Sir Lancelot, right so came tidings unto King Arthur from England that made King Arthur and all his host to remove.

---

[4] malice *or* wrath (Old Fr.: *maltalent*)
[5] himself
[6] I have twice found you to be a formidable knight

[7] wonderful
[8] thrust
[9] finish
[10] until one
[11] nearly

IV
The Day of Destiny

As Sir Mordred was ruler of all England, he let make[1] letters
as though that they had come from beyond the sea, and the
letters specified that King Arthur was slain in battle with Sir
Lancelot. Wherefore Sir Mordred made a parliament, and
called the lords together, and there he made them to choose
him king. And so was he crowned at Canterbury, and held a
feast there fifteen days.

And afterward he drew him unto Winchester, and there he
took Queen Guinevere, and said plainly that he would wed her
(which was his uncle's wife and his father's wife). And so he
made ready for the feast, and a day prefixed that they should
be wedded; wherefore Queen Guinevere was passing heavy,[2]
but spake fair, and agreed to Sir Mordred's will.

And anon she desired of Sir Mordred to go to London to buy
all manner things that longed to[3] the bridal. And because of her
fair speech Sir Mordred trusted her and gave her leave; and so
when she came to London she took the Tower of London and
suddenly in all haste possible she stuffed[4] it with all manner of
victual,[5] and well garnished[6] it with men, and so kept it.

And when Sir Mordred wist this he was passing wroth out of
measure. And short tale to make, he laid a mighty siege about
the Tower and made many assaults, and threw engines[7] unto
them, and shot great guns. But all might not prevail, for Queen
Guinevere would never, for fair speech neither for foul, never
to trust unto Sir Mordred to come in his hands again.

Then came the Bishop of Canterbury, which was a noble
clerk and an holy man, and thus he said unto Sir Mordred:

'Sir, what will ye do? Will you first displease God and sithen
shame yourself and all knighthood? For is not King Arthur
your uncle, and no farther but your mother's brother, and upon
her he himself begat you, upon his own sister? Therefore how

---

[1] ordered to be made
[2] sad
[3] were required for
[4] provisioned
[5] food
[6] garrisoned
[7] war engines

may you wed your own father's wife? And therefore, sir,' said the Bishop, 'leave this opinion,[8] other else I shall curse you with book, bell and candle.'

'Do thou thy worst,' said Sir Mordred, 'and I defy thee!'

'Sir,' said the Bishop, 'and wit you well I shall not fear me to do that me ought to do. And also ye noise[9] that my lord Arthur is slain, and that is not so, and therefore ye will make a foul work[10] in this land!'

'Peace, thou false priest!' said Sir Mordred, 'for an thou chafe[11] me any more, I shall strike off thy head.'

So the Bishop departed, and did the cursing in the most orgulust[12] wise that might be done. And then Sir Mordred sought the Bishop of Canterbury for to have slain him. Then the Bishop fled, and took part of his goods with him, and went nigh unto Glastonbury. And there he was a priest-hermit in a chapel, and lived in poverty and in holy prayers; for well he understood that mischievous[13] war was at hand.

Then Sir Mordred sought upon[14] Queen Guinevere by letters and sonds,[15] and by fair means and foul means, to have her to come out of the Tower of London; but all this availed nought, for she answered him shortly,[16] openly and privily,[17] that she had liefer[18] slay herself than be married with him.

Then came there word unto Sir Mordred that King Arthur had araised the siege from Sir Lancelot and was coming homeward with a great host to be avenged upon Sir Mordred; wherefore Sir Mordred made write writs unto all the barony of this land, and much people drew unto him. For then was the common voice among them that with King Arthur was never other life but war and strife, and with Sir Mordred was great joy and bliss. Thus was King Arthur depraved[19] and evil said of; and many there were that King Arthur had brought up of[20] nought, and given them lands, that might not then say him[1] a good word.

Lo ye Englishmen, see ye not what a mischief[2] here was? For he that was the most king and noblest knight of the world,

[8] scheme
[9] spread the rumour
[10] affliction
[11] anger
[12] determined
[13] a shameful
[14] tempted, besought
[15] messengers
[16] promptly
[17] in private
[18] rather
[19] defamed
[20] from
[1] for him
[2] evil

and most loved the fellowship of noble knights, and by him they all were upholden, and yet might not these Englishmen hold them content with him. Lo thus was the old custom and the usages of this land, and men say that we of this land have not yet lost that custom. Alas! this is a great default[3] of us Englishmen, for there may no thing us please no term.[4]

And so fared the people at that time: they were better pleased with Sir Mordred than they were with the noble King Arthur, and much people drew unto Sir Mordred and said they would abide with him for better and for worse. And so Sir Mordred drew with a great host to Dover, for there he heard say that King Arthur would arrive, and so he thought to beat his own father from his own lands. And the most party of all England held with Sir Mordred, for the people were so newfangle.[5]

And so as Sir Mordred was at Dover with his host, so came King Arthur with a great navy of ships and galleys and carracks, and there was Sir Mordred ready awaiting upon his landing, to let his own father to land[6] upon the land that he was king over.

Then there was launching of great boats and small, and full of noble men of arms; and there was much slaughter of gentle knights, and many a full bold baron was laid full low, on both parties. But King Arthur was so courageous that there might no manner of knight let him to land,[7] and his knights fiercely followed him. And so they landed maugre Sir Mordred's head[8] and all his power, and put Sir Mordred aback, that he fled and all his people.

So when this battle was done King Arthur let search his people[9] that were hurt and dead. And then was noble Sir Gawain found in a great boat, lying more than half dead. When King Arthur knew that he was laid so low he went unto him and so found him. And there the king made great sorrow out of measure, and took Sir Gawain in his arms, and thrice he there swooned. And then when he was waked, King Arthur said,

'Alas! Sir Gawain, my sister[10] son, here now thou liest, the man in the world that I loved most. And now is my joy gone! For now, my nephew, Sir Gawain, I will discover me[11] unto you, that in your person and in Sir Lancelot I most had my

---

[3] fault
[4] space of time
[5] fond of new things
[6] prevent his own father from landing
[7] prevent him from landing
[8] against Sir Mordred's will
[9] had his people searched for
[10] sister's
[11] disclose

joy and my affiance.[12] And now have I lost my joy of you both, wherefore all mine earthly joy is gone from me!'

'Ah, mine uncle,' said Sir Gawain, 'now I will that ye wit that my death-days be come! And all I may wite mine own hastiness and my wilfulness,[13] for through my wilfulness I was causer of mine own death; for I was this day hurt and smitten upon mine old wound that Sir Lancelot gave me, and I feel myself that I must needs be dead by the hour of noon. And through me and my pride ye have all this shame and disease,[14] for had that noble knight, Sir Lancelot, been with you, as he was and would have been, this unhappy[15] war had never been begun; for he, through his noble knighthood and his noble blood, held all your cankered[16] enemies in subjection and danger.[17] And now,' said Sir Gawain, 'ye shall miss Sir Lancelot. But alas that I would not accord[18] with him! And therefore, fair uncle, I pray you that I may have paper, pen and ink, that I may write unto Sir Lancelot a letter written with mine own hand.'

So when paper, pen and ink was brought, then Sir Gawain was set up weakly[19] by King Arthur, for he was shriven a little afore. And then he took his pen and wrote thus, as the French book maketh mention:

'Unto thee, Sir Lancelot, flower of all noble knights that ever I heard of or saw by my days, I, Sir Gawain, King Lot's son of Orkney, and sister's son unto the noble King Arthur, send thee greeting, letting thee to have knowledge that the tenth day of May I was smitten upon the old wound that thou gave me afore the city of Benwick, and through that wound I am come to my death-day. And I will that all the world wit that I, Sir Gawain, knight of the Table Round, sought my death, and not through thy deserving, but mine own seeking. Wherefore I beseech thee, Sir Lancelot, to return again[20] unto this realm and see my tomb and pray some prayer more other less[1] for my soul. And this same day that I wrote the same cedle[2] I was hurt to the death, which wound was first given of thine hand, Sir Lancelot; for of a more nobler man might I not be slain.

'Also, Sir Lancelot, for all the love that ever was betwixt us,

12 trust
13 for all this I have reason to blame (*wite*) my own rashness and stubbornness
14 sorrow
15 unfortunate
16 malignant
17 control
18 be reconciled
19 gently
20 come back
1 long or short
2 this letter

make no tarrying, but come over the sea in all the goodly haste that ye may, with your noble knights, and rescue that noble king that made thee knight, for he is full straitly bestead[3] with a false traitor which is my half-brother, Sir Mordred. For he hath crowned himself king and would have wedded my lady, Queen Guinevere; and so had he done, had she not kept the Tower of London with strong hand. And so the tenth day of May last past my lord King Arthur and we all landed upon them at Dover, and there he put that false traitor, Sir Mordred, to flight. And so it misfortuned me to be smitten upon the stroke that ye gave me of old.

'And the date of this letter was written but two hours and a half before my death, written with mine own hand and subscribed with part of my heart blood. And therefore I require thee, most famous knight of the world, that thou wilt see my tomb.'

And then he wept and King Arthur both, and swooned. And when they were awaked both, the king made Sir Gawain to receive his sacrament, and then Sir Gawain prayed the king for to send for Sir Lancelot and to cherish him above all other knights.

And so at the hour of noon Sir Gawain yielded up the ghost. And then the king let inter him[4] in a chapel within Dover Castle. And there yet all men may see the skull of him, and the same wound is seen that Sir Lancelot gave in battle.

Then was it told the king that Sir Mordred had pight a new field[5] upon Barham Down.[6] And so upon the morn King Arthur rode thither to him, and there was a great battle betwixt them, and much people were slain on both parties. But at the last King Arthur's party stood best, and Sir Mordred and his party fled unto Canterbury.

And there the king let search all the downs[7] for his knights that were slain and interred them; and salved them with soft salves[8] that full sore were wounded. Then much people drew unto King Arthur, and then they said that Sir Mordred warred upon King Arthur with wrong.

And anon King Arthur drew him with his host down by the

---

3 hard pressed
4 ordered him to be buried
5 had arranged a new field of battle
6 '*Bareon Downe*' in Malory.

Now a village six miles southeast of Canterbury.
7 had the downs searched
8 put ointments on their wounds

seaside westward, toward Salisbury. And there was a day[9] assigned betwixt King Arthur and Sir Mordred, that they should meet upon a down beside Salisbury, and not far from the seaside. And this day was assigned on Monday after Trinity Sunday, whereof King Arthur was passing glad that he might be avenged upon Sir Mordred.

Then Sir Mordred araised much people about London, for they of Kent, Sussex and Surrey, Essex, Suffolk and Norfolk held the most party with Sir Mordred. And many a full noble knight drew unto him and also to the king; but they that loved Sir Lancelot drew unto Sir Mordred.

So upon Trinity Sunday at night King Arthur dreamed a wonderful dream, and in his dream him seemed that he saw upon a chafflet[10] a chair, and the chair was fast to a wheel, and thereupon sat King Arthur in the richest cloth of gold that might be made. And the king thought there was under him, far from him, an hideous deep black water, and therein was all manner of serpents and worms[11] and wild beasts, foul and horrible. And suddenly the king thought that the wheel turned up-so-down, and he fell among the serpents, and every beast took him by a limb. And then the king cried as he lay in his bed, 'Help! help!'

And then knights, squires and yeomen awaked the king, and then he was so amazed that he wist not where he was. And then so he awaked[12] until it was nigh day, and then he fell on slumbering again, not sleeping nor thoroughly waking. So the king seemed verily[13] that there came Sir Gawain unto him with a number of fair ladies with him. So when King Arthur saw him he said,

'Welcome, my sister's son, I weened[14] ye had been dead. And now I see thee on live, much am I beholden unto Almighty Jesu. Ah, fair nephew, what been[15] these ladies that hither be come with you?'

'Sir,' said Sir Gawain, 'all these be ladies for whom I have foughten for, when I was man living. And all these are those that I did battle for in righteous quarrels, and God hath given them that grace at their great prayer, because I did battle for them for their right, that they should bring me hither unto you.

---

[9] time
[10] platform
[11] dragons
[12] remained awake

[13] it truly appeared to the king
[14] thought
[15] who are

Thus much hath given me leave God for to warn you of your death: for an ye fight as to-morn with Sir Mordred, as ye both have assigned, doubt ye not ye shall be slain, and the most party of your people on both parties. And for the great grace and goodness that Almighty Jesu hath unto you, and for pity of you and many more other good men there shall be slain, God hath sent me to you of His especial grace to give you warning that in no wise ye do battle as to-morn, but that ye take a treatise[16] for a month-day.[17] And proffer you largely,[18] so that to-morn ye put in a delay. For within a month shall come Sir Lancelot with all his noble knights, and rescue you worshipfully,[19] and slay Sir Mordred and all that ever will hold with[20] him.'

Then Sir Gawain and all the ladies vanished, and anon the king called upon his knights, squires, and yeomen, and charged[1] them mightly to fetch his noble lords and wise bishops unto him. And when they were come the king told them of his avision:[2] that Sir Gawain had told him and warned him that an he fought on the morn he should be slain. Then the king commanded Sir Lucan the Butler and his brother Sir Bedivere the Bold, with two bishops with them, and charged[1] them in any wise to take a treatise[16] for a month-day[17] with Sir Mordred:

'And spare not, proffer him lands and goods as much as you think reasonable.'

So then they departed and came to Sir Mordred where he had a grim[3] host of an hundred thousand. And there they entreated[4] Sir Mordred long time, and at the last Sir Mordred was agreed for to have Cornwall and Kent by King Arthur's days;[5] and after that all England, after the days of King Arthur. Then were they condescended[6] that King Arthur and Sir Mordred should meet betwixt both their hosts, and every each of them should bring fourteen persons. And so they came with this word unto Arthur. Then said he,

'I am glad that this is done,' and so he went into the field.

And when King Arthur should depart he warned all his host that an they see any sword drawn, 'look ye come on fiercely and slay that traitor, Sir Mordred, for I in no wise trust him.' In like wise Sir Mordred warned his host that 'an ye see any

16 make an agreement	2 dream
17 a month from today	3 formidable
18 make generous offers	4 negotiated with
19 honourably	5 during King Arthur's lifetime
20 remain loyal to	6 agreed
1 ordered	

The Battle of Salisbury Plain. *Morte d'Arthur*, edition of Wynkyn de Worde, 1498. *The John Rylands University Library of
Manchester.*

manner of sword drawn look that ye come on fiercely and so slay all that ever before you standeth, for in no wise I will not trust for this treatise.'[7] And in the same wise said Sir Mordred unto his host: 'for I know well my father will be avenged upon me.'

And so they met as their pointment was,[8] and were agreed and accorded thoroughly. And wine was fette,[9] and they drank together. Right so came out an adder of a little heath-bush, and it stang a knight in the foot. And so when the knight felt him so stung, he looked down and saw the adder; and anon he drew his sword to slay the adder, and thought none other harm. And when the host on both parties saw that sword drawn, then they blew beams, trumpets, and horns,[10] and shouted grimly, and so both hosts dressed them together.[11] And King Arthur took his horse and said, 'Alas, this unhappy[12] day!' And so rode to his party, and Sir Mordred in like wise.

And never since was there seen a more dolefuller battle in no Christian land, for there was but rushing and riding, foin-ing[13] and striking, and many a grim word was there spoken of either to other, and many a deadly stroke. But ever King Arthur rode throughout the battle[14] of Sir Mordred many times and did full nobly, as a noble king should do, and at all times he fainted never. And Sir Mordred did his devour[15] that day and put himself in great peril.

And thus they fought all the long day, and never stinted[16] till the noble knights were laid to the cold earth. And ever they fought still till it was near night, and by then was there an hundred thousand laid dead upon the earth. Then was King Arthur wood wroth[17] out of measure, when he saw his people so slain from him.[18]

And so he looked about him and could see no mo[19] of all his host, and good knights left no mo[19] on live but two knights: the tone[20] was Sir Lucan de Butler and his brother, Sir Bedivere; and yet they were full sore wounded.

'Jesu mercy!' said the king, 'where are all my noble knights

[7] despite this arrangement
[8] as was arranged between them
[9] fetched
[10] trumpets, large and small, and horns
[11] arrayed themselves against each other
[12] unfortunate
[13] thrusting
[14] battle formation
[15] utmost
[16] ceased
[17] wild with anger
[18] killed and taken away from him
[19] more
[20] one

become? Alas, that ever I should see this doleful day! For now,' said King Arthur, 'I am come to mine end. But would to God,' said he, 'that I wist now where were that traitor Sir Mordred that hath caused all this mischief.'[1]

Then King Arthur looked about and was ware where stood Sir Mordred leaning upon his sword among a great heap of dead men.

'Now, give me my spear,' said King Arthur unto Sir Lucan, 'for yonder I have espied the traitor that all this woe hath wrought.'

'Sir, let him be,' said Sir Lucan, 'for he is unhappy.[2] And if ye pass this unhappy[3] day ye shall be right well revenged. And, good lord, remember ye of your night's dream and what the spirit of Sir Gawain told you to-night, and yet God of His great goodness hath preserved you hitherto. And for God's sake, my lord, leave off this, for, blessed be God, ye have won the field: for yet we been here three on live, and with Sir Mordred is not one of live.[4] And therefore if ye leave off now, this wicked day of Destiny is past!'

'Now tide[5] me death, tide me life,' said the king, 'now I see him yonder alone, he shall never escape mine hands! For at a better avail[6] shall I never have him.'

'God speed you well!' said Sir Bedivere.

Then the king gat his spear in both his hands, and ran toward Sir Mordred, crying and saying,

'Traitor, now is thy death-day come!'

And when Sir Mordred saw King Arthur he ran until[7] him with his sword drawn in his hand, and there King Arthur smote Sir Mordred under the shield with a foin[8] of his spear throughout the body more than a fathom. And when Sir Mordred felt that he had his death wound he trust himself with the might that he had up to the burr[9] of King Arthur's spear, and right so he smote his father, King Arthur, with his sword holding in both his hands, upon the side of the head, that the sword pierced the helmet and the tay[10] of the brain. And therewith Mordred dashed down stark dead to the earth.

And noble King Arthur fell in a swough to the earth, and

---

[1] wickedness, evil
[2] brings misfortune
[3] unfortunate
[4] living
[5] befall

[6] advantage
[7] towards
[8] thrust
[9] hand guard
[10] outer membrane

there he swooned oftentimes, and Sir Lucan and Sir Bedivere oftentimes hove[11] him up. And so weakly[12] betwixt them they led him to a little chapel not far from the sea, and when the king was there, him thought him reasonably eased.

Then heard they people cry in the field.

'Now go thou, Sir Lucan,' said the king, 'and do me to wit[13] what betokens that noise in the field.'

So Sir Lucan departed, for he was grievously wounded in many places; and so as he rode he saw and harkened by the moonlight how that pillers[14] and robbers were come into the field to pille[14] and to rob many a full noble knight of brooches and bees[15] and of many a good ring and many a rich jewel. And who that were not dead all out, there they slew them for their harness[16] and their riches.

When Sir Lucan understood his work he came to the king as soon as he might, and told him all what he had heard and seen.

'Therefore by my rede,'[17] said Sir Lucan, 'it is best that we bring you to some town.'

'I would it were so,' said the king, 'but I may not stand, my head works[18] so . . . Ah, Sir Lancelot!' said King Arthur, 'this day have I sore missed thee! And alas, that ever I was against thee! For now have I my death, whereof Sir Gawain me warned in my dream.'

Then Sir Lucan took up the king the tone party[19] and Sir Bedivere the other party,[20] and in the lifting up the king swooned, and in the lifting Sir Lucan fell in a swoon, that part of his guts fell out of his body; and therewith the noble knight his[1] heart brast. And when the king awoke he beheld Sir Lucan, how he lay foaming at the mouth and part of his guts lay at his feet.

'Alas,' said the king, 'this is to me a full heavy sight, to see this noble duke so die for my sake, for he would have holpen[2] me that had more need of help than I! Alas, that he would not complain him, for his heart was so set to help me. Now Jesu have mercy upon his soul!'

---

[11] lifted
[12] gently
[13] and find out for me
[14] plunder (ers)
[15] rings
[16] armour

[17] counsel
[18] aches
[19] on one side
[20] on the other side
[1] knight's
[2] helped

Then Sir Bedivere wept for the death of his brother.

'Now leave this mourning and weeping, gentle knight,' said the king, 'for all this will not avail[3] me. For wit thou well an I might live myself, the death of Sir Lucan would grieve me evermore. But my time passeth on fast,' said the king. 'Therefore,' said King Arthur unto Sir Bedivere, 'take thou here Excalibur, my good sword, and go with it to yonder water's side; and when thou comest there, I charge thee throw my sword in that water, and come again and tell me what thou seest there.'

'My lord,' said Sir Bedivere, 'your commandment shall be done, and lightly[4] bring you word again.'

So Sir Bedivere departed. And by the way he beheld that noble sword, and the pomell and the haft[5] was all precious stones. And then he said to himself, 'If I throw this rich sword in the water, thereof shall never come good, but harm and loss.' And then Sir Bedivere hid Excalibur under a tree, and so soon as he might he came again unto the king and said he had been at the water and thrown the sword into the water.

'What saw thou there?' said the king.

'Sir,' he said, 'I saw nothing but waves and winds.'

'That is untruly said of thee,' said the king. 'And therefore go thou lightly[6] again, and do my commandment as thou art to me lief and dear:[7] spare not but throw it in.'

Then Sir Bedivere returned again and took the sword in his hand; and yet him thought sin and shame to throw away that noble sword. And so eft[8] he hid the sword and returned again and told the king that he had been at the water and done his commandment.

'What sawest thou there?' said the king.

'Sir,' he said, 'I saw nothing but waters wap and waves wan.'[9]

'Ah, traitor unto me and untrue,' said King Arthur, 'now hast thou betrayed me twice! Who would ween[10] that thou who has been to me so lief[11] and dear, and also named so noble a knight, that thou would betray me for the riches of this sword? But now go again lightly;[6] for thy long tarrying putteth me in great jeopardy of my life, for I have taken cold. And but if thou do[12] now as I bid thee, if ever I may see thee, I shall

---

[3] aid
[4] I will quickly
[5] handle
[6] quickly
[7] as I love you dearly
[8] again

[9] the lapping of the water and the dark waves
[10] think
[11] beloved
[12] And unless you do

The passing of Arthur. From a late Italian version. Ms. Palatino
556, c171. *Biblioteca Nazionale Centrale, Florence.*

slay thee mine own[13] hands, for thou wouldest for my rich sword see me dead.'

Then Sir Bedivere departed and went to the sword and lightly[6] took it up, and so he went unto the water's side. And there he bound the girdle about the hilt, and threw the sword as far into the water as he might. And there came an arm and an hand above the water, and took it and cleight[14] it, and shook it thrice and brandished, and then vanished with the sword into the water.

So Sir Bedivere came again to the king and told him what he saw.

'Alas!' said the king, 'help me hence, for I dread me I have tarried over long.'

Then Sir Bedivere took the king upon his back and so went with him to the water's side. And when they were there, even fast by the bank hoved[15] a little barge with many fair ladies in it, and among them all was a queen, and all they had black hoods. And all they wept and shrieked[16] when they saw King Arthur.

'Now put me into that barge,' said the king.

And so he did softly, and there received him three ladies with great mourning. And so they set him down, and in one of their laps King Arthur laid his head. And then the queen said,

'Ah, my dear brother! Why have you tarried so long from me? Alas, this wound on your head hath caught overmuch cold!'

And anon they rowed fromward[17] the land, and Sir Bedivere beheld all those ladies go fromward him. Then Sir Bedivere cried and said,

'Ah, my lord Arthur, what shall become of me, now ye go from me and leave me here alone among mine enemies?'

'Comfort thyself,' said the king, 'and do as well as thou mayst, for in me is no trust for to trust in. For I must into the vale of Avalon to heal me of my grievous wound. And if thou hear nevermore of me, pray for my soul!'

But ever the queen and ladies wept and shrieked, that it was pity to hear. And as soon as Sir Bedivere had lost sight of the barge he wept and wailed, and so took the forest and went all that night.

[13] with my own
[14] seized
[15] floated

[16] uttered a cry
[17] away from

And in the morning he was ware, betwixt two holts hoar,[18] of a chapel and an hermitage. Then was Sir Bedivere fain,[19] and thither he went, and when he came into the chapel he saw where lay an hermit grovelling[20] on all fours, fast thereby[1] a tomb was new graven.[2] When the hermit saw Sir Bedivere he knew him well, for he was but little tofore Bishop of Canterbury, that Sir Mordred fleamed.[3]

'Sir,' said Sir Bedivere, 'what man is there here interred[4] that you pray so fast[5] for?'

'Fair son,' said the hermit, 'I wot not verily but by deeming.[6] But this same night, at midnight, here came a number of ladies and brought here a dead corse[7] and prayed me to inter[8] him. And here they offered an hundred tapers, and gave me a thousand besants.'[9]

'Alas,' said Sir Bedivere, 'that was my lord King Arthur, which lieth here graven[4] in this chapel.'

Then Sir Bedivere swooned, and when he awoke he prayed the hermit that he might abide with him still, there to live with fasting and prayers:

'For from hence will I never go,' said Sir Bedivere, 'by my will, but all the days of my life here to pray for my lord Arthur.'

'Sir, ye are welcome to me,' said the hermit, 'for I know you better than ye ween[10] that I do: for ye are Sir Bedivere the Bold, and the full noble duke Sir Lucan de Butler was your brother.'

Then Sir Bedivere told the hermit all as you have heard tofore, and so he beleft[11] with the hermit that was beforehand Bishop of Canterbury. And there Sir Bedivere put upon him poor clothes, and served the hermit full lowly in fasting and in prayers.

Thus of Arthur I find no more written in books that been authorised, neither more of the very certainty of his death heard I never read,[12] but thus was he led away in a ship wherein were three queens; that one was King Arthur's sister, Queen

---

[18] bare woods
[19] glad
[20] face downward
[1] nearby
[2] newly dug
[3] put to flight
[4] buried
[5] intently

[6] guessing
[7] corpse
[8] bury
[9] gold coins
[10] think
[11] remained
[12] I have neither heard nor read

Morgan le Fay, the tother[13] was the Queen of North Galis, and the third was the Queen of the Waste Lands.[14]

Now more of the death of King Arthur could I never find, but that these ladies brought him to his grave, and such one was interred[15] there which the hermit bare witness that sometime[16] Bishop of Canterbury. But yet the hermit knew not in certain that he was verily the body of King Arthur; for this tale Sir Bedivere, a knight of the Table Round, made it to be written.

Yet some men say in many parts of England that King Arthur is not dead, but had[17] by the will of our Lord Jesu into another place; and men say that he shall come again, and he shall win the Holy Cross. Yet I will not say that it shall be so, but rather I would say: here in this world he changed his life.[18] And many men say that there is written upon the tomb this:

HIC IACET ARTHURUS REX QUONDAM REXQUE FUTURUS[19]

And thus leave I here Sir Bedivere with the hermit that dwelled that time in a chapel beside Glastonbury, and there was his hermitage. And so they lived in prayers and fastings and great abstinence.

And when Queen Guinevere understood that King Arthur was dead and all the noble knights, Sir Mordred and all the remnant, then she stole away with five ladies with her, and so she went to Amesbury. And there she let make herself[20] a nun, and weared white clothes and black, and great penance she took upon her, as ever did sinful woman in this land. And never creature could make her merry, but ever she lived in fasting, prayers and alms-deeds, that all manner of people marvelled how virtuously she was changed.

[13] other
[14] *Here Malory inserts the following reference to Ninive and Pelleas:* 'Also there was Dame Ninive, the chief Lady of the Lake, which had wedded Sir Pelleas, the good knight; and this lady had done much for King Arthur. And this dame Ninive would never suffer Sir Pelleas to be in no place where he should be in danger of his life, and so he lived unto the uttermost of his days with her in great rest.' *This is an elaboration of the last sentence of the story of* Pelleas and Ettard, *totally unrelated to the present context.*
[15] buried
[16] who at one time was
[17] had been carried away
[18] he changed his form of life
[19] Here Lies Arthur, Former and Future King.
[20] she had herself made

V

The Dolorous Death and Departing
Out of This World
of Sir Lancelot and Queen Guinevere

Now leave we the queen in Amesbury, a nun in white clothes and black — and there she was abbess and ruler, as reason would[1] — and now turn we from her and speak we of Sir Lancelot du Lake, that when he heard in his country that Sir Mordred was crowned king in England and made war against King Arthur, his own father, and would let him to land[2] in his own land (also it was told him how Sir Mordred had laid a siege about the Tower of London, because the queen would not wed him), then was Sir Lancelot wroth out of measure and said to his kinsmen,

'Alas! that double traitor, Sir Mordred, now me repenteth[3] that ever he escaped my hands, for much shame hath he done unto my lord Arthur. For I feel by this doleful letter that Sir Gawain sent me, on whose soul Jesu have mercy, that my lord Arthur is full hard bestead.[4] Alas,' said Sir Lancelot, 'that ever I should live to hear of that most noble king that made me knight thus to be overset with[5] his subject in his own realm! And this doleful letter that my lord Sir Gawain hath sent me afore his death, praying me to see his tomb, wit you well his doleful words shall never go from my heart. For he was a full noble knight as ever was born! And in an unhappy[6] hour was I born that ever I should have that mishap[7] to slay first Sir Gawain, Sir Gaheris, the good knight, and mine own friend Sir Gareth that was a full noble knight. Now, alas, I may say I am unhappy[6] that ever I should do thus. And yet, alas, might I never have hap[8] to slay that traitor, Sir Mordred!'

'Now leave your complaints,' said Sir Bors, 'and first revenge you of the death of Sir Gawain, on whose soul Jesu have

[1] as was fitting
[2] prevent him from landing
[3] I regret
[4] pressed
[5] defeated by
[6] unfortunate
[7] misfortune
[8] the chance

216

mercy! And it will be well done that ye see his tomb, and secondly that ye revenge my lord Arthur and my lady Queen Guinevere.'

'I thank you,' said Sir Lancelot, 'for ever ye will my worship.'[9]

Then they made them ready in all haste that might be, with ships and galleys, with him and his host to pass into England. And so at the last he came to Dover, and there he landed with seven kings, and the number was hideous to behold.

Then Sir Lancelot spered[10] of men of Dover where was the king become.[11] And anon the people told him how he was slain and Sir Mordred too, with an hundred thousand that died upon a day; and how Sir Mordred gave King Arthur the first battle there at his landing, and there was Sir Gawain slain. 'And upon the morn Sir Mordred fought with the king on Barham Down, and there the king put Sir Mordred to the worse.'[12]

'Alas!' said Sir Lancelot, 'this is the heaviest tidings that ever came to my heart. Now, fair sirs,' said Sir Lancelot, 'show me the tomb of Sir Gawain.'

And anon he was brought into the castle of Dover, and so they showed him the tomb. Then Sir Lancelot kneeled down by the tomb and wept, and prayed heartily for his soul.

And that night he let make a dole,[13] and all that would come of the town or of the country they had as much flesh and fish and wine and ale, and every man and woman he dealt to[14] twelve pence, come whoso would. Thus with his own hand dealt[14] he this money, in a mourning gown; and ever he wept heartily, and prayed the people to pray for the soul of Sir Gawain.

And on the morn all the priests and clerks that might be gotten in the country and in the town were there, and sang masses of Requiem. And there offered first Sir Lancelot, and he offered an hundred pound, and then the seven kings offered, and every of them offered forty pound. Also there was a thousand knights, and every of them offered a pound; and the offering dured[15] from the morn to night.

And there Sir Lancelot lay two nights upon his tomb in prayers and in doleful weeping. Then, on the third day, Sir

9 for always you wish me to act honourably
10 inquired
11 where the king had gone

12 defeated Sir Mordred
13 he held a wake
14 gave
15 lasted

Lancelot called the kings, dukes and earls, with the barons and all his noble knights, and said thus:

'My fair lords, I thank you all of your coming into this country with me. But wit you well all, we are come too late, and that shall repent[16] me while I live, but against death may no man rebel. But sithen it is so,' said Sir Lancelot, 'I will myself ride and seek my lady, Queen Guinevere. For, as I hear say, she hath great pain and much disease,[17] and I hear say that she is fled into the west. And therefore ye all shall abide me[18] here, and but if[19] I come again within these fifteen days, take your ships and your fellowship and depart into your country, for I will do as I say you.'

Then came Sir Bors and said, 'My lord, Sir Lancelot, what think ye for to do, now for to ride in this realm? Wit you well ye shall do find[20] few friends.'

'Be as be may as for that,'[1] said Sir Lancelot, 'keep you still here, for I will further on my journey, and no man nor childe[2] shall go with me.'

So it was no boot to strive,[3] but he departed and rode westerly, and there he sought a seven or eight days. And at last he came to a nunnery; and anon Queen Guinevere was ware of Sir Lancelot as she walked in the cloister. And anon as she saw him there, she swooned thrice, that all ladies and gentlewomen had work enough to hold the queen from the earth. So when she might speak she called her ladies and gentlewomen to her, and then she said thus:

'Ye marvel, fair ladies, why I make this fare.[4] Truly,' she said, 'it is for the sight of yonder knight that yonder standeth. Wherefore I pray you call him hither to me.'

Then Sir Lancelot was brought before her; then the queen said to all those ladies,

'Through this same man and me hath all this war be wrought, and the death of the most noblest knights of the world; for through our love that we have loved together is my most noble lord slain. Therefore, Sir Lancelot, wit thou well I am set in such a plight to get my soul-heal.[5] And yet I trust, through God's grace and through His Passion of His wounds wide, that

---

16 grieve
17 sorrow, anguish
18 wait for me
19 unless
20 you shall find

1 be that as it may
2 knight or squire
3 no use to argue
4 why I am so moved
5 salvation

after my death I may have a sight of the blessed face of Christ Jesu, and on Doomsday to sit on His right side; for as sinful as ever I was now are saints in heaven. And therefore, Sir Lancelot, I require thee and beseech thee heartily, for all the love that ever was betwixt us, that thou never see me no more in the visage.[6] And I command thee, on God's behalf, that thou forsake my company. And to thy kingdom look thou turn again, and keep well thy realm from war and wrack;[7] for as well as I have loved thee heretofore, mine heart will not serve now to see thee; for through thee and me is the flower of kings and knights destroyed. And therefore go thou to thy realm, and there take thee a wife, and live with her with joy and bliss. And I pray thee heartily to pray for me to the Everlasting Lord that I may amend my misliving.'

'Now, my sweet madam,' said Sir Lancelot, 'would ye that I should turn again[8] unto my country, and there to wed a lady? Nay, madam, wit you well that I shall never do, for I shall never be so false unto you of that I have promised. But the self[9] destiny that ye have taken you to, I will take me to, for the pleasure of Jesu, and ever for you I cast me[10] specially to pray.'

'Ah, Sir Lancelot, if ye will do so and hold thy promise! But I may never believe you,' said the queen, 'but that ye will turn to the world again.'

'Well, madam,' said he, 'ye say as it pleaseth you, for yet wist ye me never false of my promise. And God defend but that I should[11] forsake the world as ye have done! For in the quest of the Sankgreal I had that time forsaken the vanities of the world, had not your love been. And if I had done so at that time with my heart, will and thought, I had passed[12] all the knights that ever were in the Sankgreal except Galahad, my son. And therefore, lady, sithen ye have taken you to perfection, I must needs take me to perfection, of right. For I take record of God, in you I have had mine earthly joy; and if I had found you now so disposed, I had cast me to have had you into mine own realm.[13] But sithen I find you thus disposed, I ensure[14] you faithfully, I will ever take me to penance and pray while my life lasts, if that I may find any hermit, either gray or white, that

---

[6] face
[7] destruction
[8] return
[9] same
[10] resolve
[11] God forbid that I should not

[12] surpassed
[13] I had resolved to take you to my own kingdom if I had found that such was your wish
[14] promise

will receive me. Wherefore, madam, I pray you kiss me, and never no more.'

'Nay,' said the queen, 'that I shall never do, but abstain you from such works.'[15]

And they departed; but there was never so hard an hearted man but he would have wept to see the dolour that they made, for there was lamentation as they had be stung with spears, and many times they swooned. And the ladies bare the queen to her chamber.

And Sir Lancelot awoke, and went and took his horse, and rode all that day and all night in a forest, weeping. And at last he was ware of an hermitage and a chapel stood betwixt two cliffs; and then he heard a little bell ring to mass. And thither he rode and alight,[16] and tied his horse to the gate, and heard mass.

And he that sang mass was the Bishop of Canterbury. Both the Bishop and Sir Bedivere knew Sir Lancelot, and they spake together after mass. But when Sir Bedivere had told his tale all whole, Sir Lancelot's heart almost brast for sorrow, and Sir Lancelot threw his arms abroad,[17] and said,

'Alas! Who may trust this world?'

And then he kneeled down on his knee and prayed the Bishop to shrive him and assoil[18] him; and then he besought the Bishop that he might be his brother. Then the Bishop said, 'I will gladly,' and there he put an habit upon Sir Lancelot. And there he served God day and night with prayers and fastings.

Thus the great host abode at Dover. And then Sir Lionel took fifteen lords with him and rode to London to seek Sir Lancelot; and there Sir Lionel was slain and many of his lords. Then Sir Bors de Ganis made[19] the great host for to[20] go home again, and Sir Bors, Sir Ector de Maris, Sir Blamour, Sir Bleoberis, with mo[1] other of Sir Lancelot's kin, took on them to ride all England overthwart and endlong[2] to seek Sir Lancelot.

So Sir Bors by fortune rode so long till he came to the same chapel where Sir Lancelot was. And so Sir Bors heard a little bell knell,[3] that rang to mass; and there he alight[4] and heard mass. And when mass was done the Bishop, Sir Lancelot and Sir Bedivere came to Sir Bors, and when Sir Bors saw Sir Lan-

---

15 behaviour
16 dismounted
17 widely apart
18 absolve
19 prepared

20 in order to
1 more
2 up and down all England
3 toll
4 dismounted

celot in that manner clothing, then he prayed the Bishop that he might be in the same suit. And so there was an habit put upon him, and there he lived in prayers and fasting.

And within half a year there was come Sir Galihud, Sir Galyhodin, Sir Blamour, Sir Bleoberis, Sir Villiars, Sir Clarrus, and Sir Gahalantin. So all these seven noble knights there abode still. And when they saw Sir Lancelot had taken him to such perfection they had no lust[5] to depart, but took such an habit as he had.

Thus they endured in great penance six year. And then Sir Lancelot took the habit of priesthood of the Bishop, and a twelve-month he sang mass. And there was none of these other knights but they read in books and holp for to sing mass, and rang bells, and did lowly all manner of service. And so their horses went where they would, for they took no regard of no worldly riches; for when they saw Sir Lancelot endure such penance in prayers and fastings they took no force[6] what pain they endured, for to see the noblest knight of the world take such abstinance that he waxed full lean.

And thus upon a night there came a vision[7] to Sir Lancelot and charged[8] him, in remission of his sins, to haste him unto Amesbury: 'And by then thou come there, thou shalt find Queen Guinevere dead. And therefore take thy fellows with thee, and purvey them of[9] an horse bier, and fetch thou the corse[10] of her, and bury her by her husband, the noble King Arthur.'

So this avision[7] came to Lancelot thrice in one night. Then Sir Lancelot rose up or day and told the hermit.

'It were well done,' said the hermit, 'that ye made you ready and that ye disobey not the avision.'[7]

Then Sir Lancelot took his seven fellows with him, and on foot they yede[11] from Glastonbury to Amesbury, the which is little more than thirty mile, and thither they came within two days, for they were weak and feeble to go.

And when Sir Lancelot was come to Amesbury within the nunnery, Queen Guinevere died but half an hour before. And the ladies told Sir Lancelot that Queen Guinevere told them all or she passed that Sir Lancelot had been priest near a twelve-

[5] desire
[6] did not care
[7] dream
[8] ordered
[9] arrange for
[10] body
[11] went

month: 'and hither he cometh as fast as he may to fetch my corse,[10] and beside my lord King Arthur he shall bury me.' Wherefore the Queen said in hearing of them all, 'I beseech Almighty God that I may never have power to see Sir Lancelot with my worldly eyen!'

'And thus,' said all the ladies, 'was ever her prayer these two days till she was dead.'

Then Sir Lancelot saw her visage,[12] but he wept not greatly, but sighed. And so he did all the observance of the service himself, both the Dirige, and on the morn he sang mass. And there was ordained[13] an horse-bier, and so with an hundred torches ever brenning about the corse[10] of the queen and ever Sir Lancelot with his eight fellows went about the horse-bier, singing and reading many an holy orison, and frankincense upon the corse[10] incensed.

Thus Sir Lancelot and his eight fellows went on foot from Amesbury unto Glastonbury; and when they were come to the chapel and the hermitage, there she had a Dirige, with great devotion. And on the morn the hermit that sometime[14] was Bishop of Canterbury sang the mass of Requiem with great devotion, and Sir Lancelot was the first that offered, and then all his eight fellows. And then she was wrapped in cered[15] cloth of Rennes,[16] from the top to the toe, in thirtyfold; and after she was put in a web[17] of lead, and then in a coffin of marble.

And when she was put in the earth Sir Lancelot swooned, and lay long still while the hermit came and awaked him, and said,

'Ye be to blame, for ye displease God with such manner of sorrow-making.'

'Truly,' said Sir Lancelot, 'I trust I do not displease God, for He knoweth mine intent: for my sorrow was not, nor is not, for any rejoicing of sin, but my sorrow may never have end. For when I remember of her beauty and of her noblesse,[18] that was both with her king and with her, so when I saw his corpse and her corpse so lie together, truly mine heart would not serve to sustain my careful body.[19] Also when I remember me how by my default, mine orgule[20] and my pride that they were both laid full low that were peerless that ever was living of Christian

---

[12] face
[13] prepared
[14] once
[15] waxed
[16] *Rennes was noted for its waxed linen.*

[17] sheet
[18] noble conduct
[19] my care-filled body
[20] haughtiness

people, wit you well,' said Sir Lancelot, 'this remembered, of
their kindness and mine unkindness, sank so to mine heart that
I might not sustain myself.' So the French book maketh mention.

Then Sir Lancelot never after ate but little meat,[1] nor drank,
till he was dead, for then he sickened more and more and dried
and dwined[2] away. For the Bishop nor none of his fellows
might not make him to eat and little he drank, that he was
waxen by a cubit shorter than he was, that people could not
know him. For evermore, day and night, he prayed, but sometime he slumbered a broken sleep. Ever he was lying grovelling[3] on the tomb of King Arthur and Queen Guinevere, and
there was no comfort that the Bishop nor Sir Bors nor none of
his fellows could make him, it availed not.

So within six weeks after, Sir Lancelot fell sick, and lay in
his bed. And then he sent for the Bishop that there was hermit,
and all his true fellows. Then Sir Lancelot said with dreary
steven,[4]

'Sir Bishop, I pray you give to me all my rites that longeth[5]
to a Christian man.'

'It shall not need you,'[6] said the hermit and all his fellows.
'It is but heaviness of your blood. You shall be well mended by
the grace of God to-morn.'

'My fair lords,' said Sir Lancelot, 'wit you well my careful
body[7] will into the earth, I have warning more than now I will
say. Therefore give me my rites.'

So when he was houseled[8] and anealed[9] and had all that a
Christian man ought to have, he prayed the Bishop that his
fellows might bear his body to Joyous Gard. (Some men say
it was Alnwick, and some men say it was Bamborough.)

'Howbeit,' said Sir Lancelot, 'me repenteth sore,[10] but I made
mine avow sometime[11] that in Joyous Gard I would be buried.
And because of breaking of mine avow,[12] I pray you all, lead
me thither.'

Then there was weeping and wringing of hands among his
fellows.

---

[1] food	[7] my care-filled body
[2] wasted	[8] given the Eucharist
[3] face downward	[9] received extreme unction
[4] voice	[10] I regret
[5] belong	[11] once
[6] you shall not need it	[12] to avoid breaking my vow

So at a season[13] of the night they all went to their beds, for they all lay in one chamber. And so after midnight, against day,[14] the Bishop that was hermit, as he lay in his bed asleep, he fell upon a great laughter.[15] And therewith all the fellowship awoke and came to the Bishop and asked him what he ailed.

'Ah, Jesu mercy!' said the Bishop, 'why did ye awake me? I was never in all my life so merry and so well at ease.'

'Wherefore?' said Sir Bors.

'Truly,' said the Bishop, 'here was Sir Lancelot with me, with mo[16] angels than ever I saw men in one day. And I saw the angels heave up Sir Lancelot unto heaven, and the gates of heaven opened against him.'[17]

'It is but dretching of swevens,'[18] said Sir Bors, 'for I doubt not Sir Lancelot aileth nothing but good.'[19]

'It may well be,' said the Bishop. 'Go ye to his bed, and then shall ye prove the sooth.'[20]

So when Sir Bors and his fellows came to his bed they found him stark dead; and he lay as he had smiled,[1] and the sweetest savour about him that ever they felt.[2] Then was there weeping and wringing of hands, and the greatest dole they made that ever made men.[3]

And on the morn the Bishop did his mass of Requiem, and after the Bishop and all the nine knights put Sir Lancelot in the same horse-bier that Queen Guinevere was laid in tofore[4] that she was buried. And so the Bishop and they all together went with the body of Sir Lancelot daily till they came to Joyous Gard; and ever they had an hundred torches brenning about him.

And so within fifteen days they came to Joyous Gard. And there they laid his corpse in the body of the quire,[5] and sang and read many psalters and prayers over him and about him.[6] And ever his visage[7] was laid open and naked, that all folks might behold him; for such was the custom in those days that all men of worship[8] should so lie with open visage[7] till that they were buried.

---

[13] at the proper time
[14] shortly before daybreak
[15] he began to laugh loudly
[16] more
[17] at his coming
[18] confusion of dreams
[19] feels well
[20] find out the truth

[1] as though he smiled
[2] experienced
[3] that men ever made
[4] before
[5] in the centre of the chancel
[6] standing by him
[7] face
[8] repute

And right thus as they were at their service, there came Sir Ector de Maris, that had seven year sought all England, Scotland, and Wales, seeking his brother, Sir Lancelot. And when Sir Ector heard such noise and light in the quire[5] of Joyous Gard, he alight[9] and put his horse from him and came into the quire.[5] And there he saw men sing and weep, and all they knew Sir Ector, but he knew not them.

Then went Sir Bors unto Sir Ector and told him how there lay his brother, Sir Lancelot, dead. And then Sir Ector threw his shield, sword and helm from him, and when he beheld Sir Lancelot's visage[7] he fell down in a swoon. And when he waked, it were hard[10] any tongue to tell the doleful complaints[11] that he made for his brother.

'Ah, Lancelot!' he said, 'thou were head of all Christian knights! And now I dare say,' said Sir Ector, 'thou Sir Lancelot, there thou liest, that thou were never matched of[12] earthly knight's hand! And thou were the courteoust knight that ever bare shield! And thou were the truest friend to thy lover that ever bestrad horse, and thou were the truest lover of a sinful man[13] that ever loved woman, and thou were the kindest man that ever strake[14] with sword. And thou were the godliest person that ever came among press[15] of knights, and thou was the meekest man and the gentlest that ever ate in hall among ladies, and thou were the sternest knight to thy mortal foe that ever put spear in the rest.'

Then there was weeping and dolour out of measure.

Thus they kept Sir Lancelot's corpse on-loft[16] fifteen days, and then they buried it with great devotion. And then at leisure they went all with the Bishop of Canterbury to his hermitage, and there they were together more than a month.

Then Sir Constantine, that was Sir Cador's son of Cornwall, was chosen king of England. And he was a full noble knight, and worshipfully[17] he ruled this realm. And then this King Constantine sent for the Bishop of Canterbury, for he heard say where he was. And so he was restored unto his Bishopric, and left that hermitage. And Sir Bedivere was there ever still hermit to his life's end.

[9] dismounted
[10] it would be difficult for
[11] lamentations
[12] by
[13] among all sinful men
[14] fought
[15] throng
[16] on display
[17] honourably

Then Sir Bors de Ganis, Sir Ector de Maris, Sir Gahalantine, Sir Galihud, Sir Galihodin, Sir Blamour, Sir Bleoberis, Sir Villiars le Valiant, Sir Clarrus of Clermount, all these knights drew them to their countries. Howbeit King Constantine would have had them with him, but they would not abide in this realm. And there they all lived in their countries as holy men.

And some English books make mention that they went never out of England after the death of Sir Lancelot — but that was but the favour of makers.[18] For the French book maketh mention — and is authorised — that Sir Bors, Sir Ector, Sir Blamour and Sir Bleoberis went into the Holy Land, thereas Jesu Christ was quick[19] and dead, and anon as they had established their lands. For, the book saith, so Sir Lancelot commanded them for to do or ever he passed out of this world. And these four knights did many battles upon the miscreants,[20] or Turks. And there they died upon a Good Friday for God's sake.

HERE IS THE END OF THE WHOLE BOOK OF KING ARTHUR AND OF HIS NOBLE KNIGHTS OF THE ROUND TABLE, THAT WHEN THEY WERE WHOLE TOGETHER THERE WAS EVER AN HUNDRED AND FORTY. AND HERE IS THE END OF *The Death of Arthur.*

I PRAY YOU ALL GENTLEMEN AND GENTLEWOMEN THAT READETH THIS BOOK OF ARTHUR AND HIS KNIGHTS FROM THE BEGINNING TO THE ENDING, PRAY FOR ME WHILE I AM ON LIVE THAT GOD SEND ME GOOD DELIVERANCE.[1] AND WHEN I AM DEAD, I PRAY YOU ALL PRAY FOR MY SOUL.

FOR THIS BOOK WAS ENDED THE NINTH YEAR OF THE REIGN OF KING EDWARD THE FOURTH,[2] BY SIR THOMAS MALORY,[3] KNIGHT, AS JESU HELP HIM FOR HIS GREAT MIGHT, AS HE IS THE SERVANT OF JESU BOTH DAY AND NIGHT.

---

[18] the authors' whim
[19] alive
[20] infidels
[1] release (*from prison*)

[2] *The ninth year of Edward IV's reign began on March 4, 1469.*
[3] *The author spells his name* Maleore (*elsewhere* Mal[l]eorre).

BIBLIOGRAPHICAL NOTE

All the editions of Malory's works produced before 1947 were based directly or indirectly on the folio volume published by William Caxton under the title of *Le Morte Darthur* 'in the abbey of Westminster, the last day of July, the year of Our Lord MCCCCLXXXV.' Two copies of this volume are extant; one, which is complete but for the fly-leaf, in the Pierpont Morgan Library in New York, the other, wanting eleven leaves, in the John Rylands Library in Manchester. The text was reprinted with some alterations by Wynkyn de Worde in 1498. No fewer than three editions, including a reprint of Wynkyn de Worde's (1529), appeared in the sixteenth century and one in the seventeenth (William Stansby's, 1634). Of the numerous modern editions the most important are Southey's (1817), Thomas Wright's (1858 and 1866), Edward Strachey's (1868), H. Oskar Sommer's (in three volumes, 1889–91), and A. W. Pollard's (Macmillan, 1900, 1903, and 1927).

In 1934 a fifteenth-century manuscript of Malory's romances in two different hands was discovered in the Fellows' Library of Winchester College by Mr. W. F. Oakeshott, now Rector of Lincoln College, Oxford. This manuscript and Caxton's *Le Morte Darthur* represent two collateral versions of Malory's text, even though the manuscript is in most respects much closer to it than Caxton, who took considerable liberties with his original. Any critical edition must obviously be based on the Winchester manuscript, occasionally emended with the help of readings which Caxton has preserved in a more authentic form. Hence the method adopted in my three-volume edition of *The Works of Sir Thomas Malory*, first published by the Clarendon Press in 1947. A second, revised edition appeared in 1967.

The discovery of the Winchester manuscript confirmed some of the conclusions previously reached with regard to the author's identity. The first to identify him was G. L. Kittredge in a study entitled *Who Was Sir Thomas Malory?* (Boston, 1897; reprinted from *Studies and Notes in Philology and Literature*, vol. V). Subsequent biographical studies include: E. K. Chambers, *Sir Thomas Malory* (English Association, Pamphlet no. 51), London, 1922 (reprinted in *Sir Thomas Wyatt and Some Collected Studies*, London, 1933); Edward Hicks, *Sir Thomas Malory, His Turbulent Career*, Harvard University Press, 1928; Chapter I of my *Malory*, Oxford, 1929; A. C. Baugh, 'Documenting Sir Thomas Malory,' *Speculum*, vol. VIII(1933); and William Matthews, *The Ill-framed Knight, A Skeptical Inquiry into the Identity of Sir Thomas Malory*, University of California Press, 1966.

Most of the reviews of Professor Matthews' book show as much scepticism for his candidate — a Thomas Malory, of Yorkshire — as he has shown about the 'knight-prisoner' of Warwickshire. The only thing in favour of the Yorkshire Malory is that nothing is known about him and that nothing therefore can be said against him. There is nothing to show that he was either a knight or a prisoner. Two further weak links in Professor Matthews' chain of arguments can be briefly disposed of here. Professor Matthews makes a great deal of the fact that the best existing copy of the source of Malory's *Tale of King Arthur* (to which the first of the tales presented here belongs) was found in Yorkshire. What he seems to have overlooked is that on textual grounds it is impossible to regard this manuscript as Malory's *direct* source. There is a similar error concerning a group of fifteenth-century Arthurian manuscripts which used to belong to the library of Jacques d'Armagnac. Some of them happen to be very close to what must have been Malory's source for the *Tristan* portion of his work. Professor Matthews finds it convenient to infer from this fact a whole theory of how Malory the author was imprisoned, not at Newgate where conditions for writing were far from favourable, but in some French castle, as a result of his possible involvement in the military operations in southwestern France. This incidentally could easily have happened to the Warwickshire Malory, but the theory, for all its attraction, needs more support than it has at present because the manuscripts in question were *not* Malory's sources. The nearest extant representative of the source he used is a century earlier; it was discovered not long ago in the State Library in Leningrad. Sir Thomas Malory of Warwickshire still remains, therefore, the most likely person to have written the book ascribed by Caxton to Sir Thomas Malory, Knight. The identification has recently received strong support from an inquiry by Mr. P. J. C. Field, the result of which he published under the title of *Sir Thomas Malory M.P.* in the *Bulletin of the Institute of Historical Research*, vol. XLVII, May 1974. Mr. Field has successfully disposed of objections concerning the would-be discrepancy between the character of the man and the nature of the work and has established positive links between the two.

Sir Thomas Malory (or Maleoré) is the author of eight Arthurian romances forming what he calls 'the book of King Arthur and his knights of the Round Table' (the title *Le Morte Darthur* is in fact that of his last romance — the *Morte Arthur* — applied by

Caxton, with little justification, to the entire collection). The first to be written was an adaptation of the English alliterative *Morte Arthure*(*The Noble Tale of King Arthur and the Emperor Lucius*). This was followed by five romances based on French models (the 'French books,' as Malory calls them), viz. *The Tale of King Arthur, The Noble Tale of Sir Lancelot, The Book of Sir Gareth, The Book of Sir Tristram, The Quest of the Holy Grail.* For his last two romances — *The Book of Sir Lancelot and Queen Guinevere* and *The Tale of the Death of King Arthur* or *The Morte Arthur Saunz Guerdon* — he used, in addition to a French source, the English stanzaic *Le Morte Arthur*.

The discovery of the 'books' he had at his disposal has been a slow and difficult process. One of his major sources is still unknown — that of *The Book of Sir Gareth;* some are still unpublished, and comparatively few are available in reliable modern editions. But so far as the present selection is concerned, the only work which presents any serious difficulty is *The Knight of the Cart.* The story was originally part of a twelfth-century French poem by Chrétien de Troyes (*Li conte de la charrete*). Malory's immediate source, not adequately represented in any known text, must have been a prose work of the thirteenth century closely related to the French prose romance of Lancelot (*Le Roman en prose de Lancelot: le conte de la charrette,* ed. Gweneth Hutchings, Paris, 1938). The work has no connection with the 'Book' in which it occurs — *The Book of Sir Lancelot and Queen Guinevere* — and it seemed justifiable, therefore, to transfer it to its normal chronological place. The next section — *Lancelot and Elaine* — is based upon a text which is extant, but of which there is no satisfactory edition. Malory seems to have used a manuscript of the prose *Tristan* similar to MS. Bibl. Nat. fr. 99 (ff. 508 verso–547 recto) and somewhat different from the one published by H. O. Sommer in *Modern Philology,* Vol. V (pp. 55–84; 181–200, and 291–341) under the title of *Galahad and Perceval.*

Merlin, Balin, and *Pelleas and Ettard* are adaptations of parts of a thirteenth-century cyclic romance generally known as *La Suite du Merlin* (a branch of the *Roman du Graal*) and preserved in two manuscripts: British Museum Add. 38117 and Cambridge University Library Add. 7071. The latter, discovered in 1945, is still unpublished. The text of the British Museum manuscript was edited by Gaston Paris and Jacob Ulrich in 1886 under the title of *Merlin.* There is also a more recent edition of the portion corresponding to Malory's *Balin* (*Le Roman de Balain* edited by M. D. Legge, Manchester, 1942).

The Holy Grail is an extract from Malory's *Quest of the Holy*

Grail which is substantially an abridged translation of the Grail branch of the French Arthurian Cycle. There are three modern editions of the French text: F. J. Furnivall's (Roxburghe Club, 1864), H. O. Sommer's (*The Vulgate Version of the Arthurian Romances*, Vol. VI, 1913), and Albert Pauphilet's (*La Queste del Saint Graal*, Paris, 1923), by far the most reliable of the three.

The Poisoned Apple and *The Fair Maid of Astolat* belong, like *The Knight of the Cart*, to Malory's *Book of Sir Lancelot and Queen Guinevere*, based mainly upon the final branch of the French Arthurian Cycle (*Mort Artu* or *La Mort le roi Artu*). This branch has been published four times (by J. D. Bruce in 1910, by H. O. Sommer in *The Vulgate Version of the Arthurian Romances* in 1913, and by M. Jean Frappier in 1936 and again in 1954), but the only critical editions are the last two. The portions corresponding to Malory's two stories occur at the beginning of the French text (pp. 5–84 of the 1936 edition), interwoven with each other and interspersed with other material. There is evidence to show that Malory also used the English stanzaic poem known as *Le Morte Arthur*. There are five editions of this text: Thomas Ponton's (Roxburghe Club, 1819), F. J. Furnivall's (1864), J. D. Bruce's (E.E.T.S., 1903), Samuel B. Hemingway's (Riverside Literature Series, 1912) and Lucy Allen Paton's (Everyman's Library, 1912).

For his last and most important work — *The Tale of the Death of King Arthur* — Malory again used these two sources, the French *Mort Artu* and the English *Le Morte Arthur*, but displayed greater originality in the handling of his material than he did in any of his earlier writings. My edition of the text, published as a separate volume in 1955, contains a commentary and a bibliography, both of which now have to be supplemented by reference to the second edition of *The Works of Sir Thomas Malory* (Oxford, 1967).

The following critical studies have a special bearing on the tales included in the present volume:

Bennett, J. A. W. (ed.), *Essays on Malory*, Oxford, 1963, pp. 14–25 and 64–113.

Chambers, E. K., *English Literature at the Close of the Middle Ages*, Oxford, 1945, pp. 185–205.

Ferrier, Janet M., *Forerunners of the French Novel*, Manchester, 1954, pp. 7–21.

Field, P. J. C., *Romance and Chronicle*, *A Study of Malory's Prose Style*, Bloomington and London, 1971.

Hibbard, Laura A., 'Malory's Book of Balin' (in *Medieval Studies in Memory of Gertrude Schoepperle Loomis*, Paris and New York, 1927, pp. 175–195).

Knight, Stephen, *The Structure of Sir Thomas Malory's Arthuriad*, Australian Humanities Research Council Monograph 14, Sydney, 1969.

Lawlor, John, [Introduction to] *Le Morte d'Arthur*, edited by Janet Cowen, London (Penguin Books), 1968, pp. vii–xxxi.

Lumiansky, R. M. (ed.), *Malory's Originality*, Baltimore, 1964, pp. 205–274.

MacNeice, Louis, 'Sir Thomas Malory' (in *The English Novelists: A Survey of the Novel by Twenty Contemporary Novelists*, edited by Derek Verschoyle, London, 1926, pp. 19–28).

Mellizo, Felipe, 'Arturo y *Le Morte*,' *Cuadernos hispanoamericanos*, vol. 77, No. 229 (1969), pp. 78–100.

Mike, Stephen J., 'Malory and the Chivalric Order,' *Medium AEvum*, vol. 35 (1966), pp. 211–30.

Reiss, Edmund, *Sir Thomas Malory*, New York, 1966, pp. 35–54 and 158–192.

Scudder, Vida D., *Le Morte Darthur of Sir Thomas Malory: A Study of the Book and Its Sources*, London and New York, 1921, pp. 195–200 and 259–362.

Starr, Nathan C., 'The Moral Problem in Malory,' *Dalhousie Review*, vol. 47 (1967), pp. 467–74.

Vinaver, Eugène (ed.), *The Works of Sir Thomas Malory* in three volumes, Oxford, 1967 (Second Edition), pp. 1282–87, 1304–23, 1358–61, 1523–31, 1581–84, 1585–1611, and 1615–63.

——, *The Tale of the Death of King Arthur* by Sir Thomas Malory, Oxford, 1955, pp. vii–xxv.

Whitehead, F., 'On Certain Episodes in the Fourth Book of Malory's *Morte Darthur*,' *Medium AEvum*, vol. II (October 1933), pp. 199–216.

York, Ernest C., 'The Duel of Chivalry in Malory's Book XIX,' *Philological Quarterly*, vol. 48 (1969), pp. 186–91.